PRAISE FOR

Her Ladyship's Companion

"Beautifully written, with scorching hot love scenes that push the boundaries of Regency romance in a new and exciting direction."

—Kate Pearce, author of *Simply Sinful*

"Ms. Collins has written a very tender and passionate love story that really tugs at your heartstrings. *Her Ladyship's Companion* is exciting, thrilling, sensual, and pure reading bliss." —*Fresh Fiction*

"Collins's carefully crafted story gives readers a different view of the Regency era. She writes about a man and a woman from vastly unconventional backgrounds, and a love that knows no bounds, in this intensely passionate, sexually charged, and deeply touching romance."

—*Romantic Times*

"Almost elegantly beautiful . . . *Her Ladyship's Companion* should leave many historical readers hopeful that a new author might be stepping up to the auto-buy plate." —*All About Romance*

Berkley Sensation titles by Evangeline Collins

HER LADYSHIP'S COMPANION

SEVEN NIGHTS TO FOREVER

Seven Nights to Forever

EVANGELINE COLLINS

BERKLEY SENSATION, NEW YORK

THE BERKLEY PUBLISHING GROUP
Published by the Penguin Group
Penguin Group (USA) Inc.
375 Hudson Street, New York, New York 10014, USA
Penguin Group (Canada), 90 Eglinton Avenue East, Suite 700, Toronto, Ontario M4P 2Y3, Canada
(a division of Pearson Penguin Canada Inc.)
Penguin Books Ltd., 80 Strand, London WC2R 0RL, England
Penguin Group Ireland, 25 St. Stephen's Green, Dublin 2, Ireland (a division of Penguin Books Ltd.)
Penguin Group (Australia), 250 Camberwell Road, Camberwell, Victoria 3124, Australia
(a division of Pearson Australia Group Pty. Ltd.)
Penguin Books India Pvt. Ltd., 11 Community Centre, Panchsheel Park, New Delhi—110 017, India
Penguin Group (NZ), 67 Apollo Drive, Rosedale, North Shore 0632, New Zealand
(a division of Pearson New Zealand Ltd.)
Penguin Books (South Africa) (Pty.) Ltd., 24 Sturdee Avenue, Rosebank, Johannesburg 2196,
South Africa

Penguin Books Ltd., Registered Offices: 80 Strand, London WC2R 0RL, England

This book is an original publication of The Berkley Publishing Group.

This is a work of fiction. Names, characters, places, and incidents either are the product of the author's imagination or are used fictitiously, and any resemblance to actual persons, living or dead, business establishments, events, or locales is entirely coincidental. The publisher does not have any control over and does not assume any responsibility for author or third-party websites or their content.

PRINTING HISTORY
Berkley Sensation trade paperback edition / November 2010

Library of Congress Cataloging-in-Publication Data

Collins, Evangeline.
    Seven nights to forever / Evangeline Collins.
       p.   cm.
    ISBN 978-0-425-23683-3
    1. Brothers and sisters—Fiction. 2. Single women—Social life and customs—19th century—Fiction. 3. London (England)—19th century—Fiction. I. Title. II. Title: 7 nights to forever.
    PS3603.O45423S48   2010
    813'.6—dc22   2010022759

PRINTED IN THE UNITED STATES OF AMERICA

10   9   8   7   6   5   4   3   2   1

To Diane,
for all of your support,
for all of your love,
and for helping me to become
the woman I am today.
I love you, Mom.

One

❦

MARCH 31, 1819
LONDON, ENGLAND

CLOAKED in the midnight shadows, Mr. James Archer shifted against the darkened streetlamp and watched as two gentlemen went up the stone steps of the large white house across the street. The fifth set of visitors over the past half hour. Deliberately tousled hair, strict black evening attire, the slight swagger in their strides . . . young bucks intent on a night of debauchery. The pair knocked on one of the scarlet double doors. The taller of the two let out a bark of laughter and then pushed the other inside when the door opened.

Had he ever been so young and carefree? So unfettered, so untouched by life's responsibilities? If he had, he certainly couldn't recall it. He was only five and twenty, but the last three years had taken a heavy toll, aging him far beyond his years.

The door closed behind the two men, shutting out the faint hum of voices from within. James rubbed his tired eyes. Well over fifteen hours at his office today, but he would have willingly stayed through to tomorrow if his secretary hadn't practically shoved him out the door.

He looked right, up Curzon Street, in the direction that led to his town house. A wince furrowed his brow, his lips compressing in a straight line, dread jabbing into his gut. Then his gaze swept over the large, white painted brick house with its many windows and neat stone portico, settling on those scarlet double doors.

Heaving a sigh, he pushed from the streetlamp he had been leaning against and crossed the street, heading around to the back of that white house.

The night air was cool and thick, holding little promise of the warm spring days ahead. Not one lamp lit the narrow alley. There could be thieves aplenty lurking in the shadows, but he didn't bother to quicken his pace. He walked most everywhere he went in London and had yet to be accosted, no matter the hour of the day or night. There were some that were not fond of his size—well, one in particular—but it did prove useful at times.

The sound of his double knock echoed in the small courtyard. *Brilliant.* He let out another heavy sigh. He'd been reduced to knocking on the back door of a brothel.

But the loneliness had become too much to bear. It had long since eaten its way into his chest, leaving a hollow ache he knew well. He thought himself well reconciled to his fate. Duty to one's family came before all else, after all. Yet tonight the prospect of returning home to *her* seemed next to impossible. Perhaps it was the thought of the approaching Season and all it would entail. Donning the mask of polite civility while pretending she did not flaunt her infidelities, enduring one tirade after another . . . it was a wonder he had not become a drunkard.

One night. That was all he needed. One night with a woman who did not despise him, or at the very least would keep such thoughts to herself. A woman who wouldn't hate him for where he had come from or for who he was. And at this point, he didn't much care if he had to part with a fold of pound notes to see the task done.

A triangle of light fell into the courtyard as the door opened.

With one dirt-smudged hand on the knob, the maid used her slight form to block the entry into the house.

"Good evening," he said.

She quickly took him in, from his expertly tailored yet plain bottle green coat to the tan trousers to the dust his shoes had picked up on the long walk from the docks. Her blonde head tilted back to meet his gaze. Her eyes narrowed with puzzlement. "Guests are received around front."

He ignored her statement of the obvious. "I wish to speak with the proprietor."

"Madame Rubicon?"

"Yes." He may have never frequented this particular establishment before—his one foray at a brothel had occurred years ago, while on holiday from Cambridge—but most every man in London was aware of the house with the twin scarlet doors on Curzon Street. Madame Rubicon's. Lauded for its beautiful women willing to accede to a man's every whim and renowned for its discretion, a commodity he valued above all. And the reason he currently stood in the back courtyard.

A crease notched the space between her brows. "Why?"

Must he spell it out? That he had asked for the madam should be answer enough. He fought the urge to shift his weight. "To discuss business."

She opened her mouth. He braced for yet another question. If she asked what type of business he wished to discuss, he would leave rather than admit to this servant that he needed to procure the services of a woman, as if he was unable to find a willing female on his own. His pride had taken enough beatings. It certainly did not need one more. He would simply return to his office. Decker, his secretary, would be long gone by now. There was still a sizable pile of paperwork on his desk. Perhaps he could make a dent in it by dawn, before Decker added to the pile. James kept a change of clothes and a shaving kit at his office for a reason. And if sleep pulled too heavily on his eyes, he'd make use of the leather couch. Not the most comfortable, but better than falling asleep at his desk.

To his surprise, she merely opened the door fully and motioned for him to step inside. The space was small and bare and lit by a plain lantern suspended by a chain in the ceiling. Stairs before him, a closed door on the right, the one on the left open, revealing a glimpse of the kitchen. A rotund, older woman stood at the sink, scrubbing a copper pot. He heard the *clink* of glasses, the shuffle of feet, the murmur of voices. A busy kitchen to match the busy house.

"She's in the receiving room. Would ye care to meet with her there or in her office?"

If he had wanted to be seen in the receiving room, he would have used the damn front door. Nerves rubbed raw, he had to push aside the surge of irritation. "Her office, please."

She gave a nod and turned. He followed her up the stairs and along an equally narrow corridor. Obviously the servants' area of the house. The walls and floors clean but bare. They passed through a door. And this must be the general area of house. Delicate crystal sconces, plush rugs, and a soothing pale taupe silk paper lined the walls.

The girl rounded a corner and opened a heavy oak door. She flicked her fingers toward the interior. "Ye can wait here. She'll be along shortly."

With that, she left him standing there in the corridor.

He went into the office to wait, closing the door behind him. Ignoring the two scarlet leather armchairs stationed in front of the desk, he chose to stand. He trailed his fingertips over the edge of the desk. Teakwood. From the Orient, and expertly crafted. Definitely not an inexpensive piece of furniture.

He glanced about the office. White paneled walls, gilt-framed paintings, and furniture similar in quality to the desk. Opulent, but not on a gaudy, grand scale. Enough to make those of the aristocracy feel at home. It matched what little he had seen of the general area of the house. The madam clearly knew her clientele, and if she could afford these surroundings, then she was likely a very adept businesswoman, and one who charged a hefty fee for the use of her employees.

He passed a hand over the back of his neck, his stomach tightening with unease at the blunt reminder of exactly what he planned to do tonight. At least he hoped it was unease and not the first taste of regret, or worst yet, guilt. But now that he was here, inside the house he had walked past many times on his route home, he couldn't help but wonder if knocking on the back door had been the wisest course of action. The ton didn't seem to hold much respect for the sanctity of marriage, but he wasn't one of them. Regardless of the circumstances or of her demands, one-sided though they were, he had entered into his marriage with his eyes open and with every intention of honoring his commitment.

He had endured three years. What was another? And were his own selfish needs worth the risk of discovery? Especially when this year was the most important of them all.

Perhaps he should leave. Take the opportunity before the madam arrived. Return to his office and bury himself in work, as he had done on most every night for the past three years.

That hollow ache flared in his chest, a raw lance that seemed to encompass his entire being.

Gripping the edge of the desk, he hung his head, a harsh wince tightening his features.

One time, and she'll never know, he told himself. In any case, could it truly be classified as infidelity if the other party never had, and still did not, want him?

Heaving a great sigh, he pushed from the desk, straightening. Then he settled in one of the scarlet leather armchairs and waited for the madam to arrive.

※

THE carriage slowed to a stop. Rose Marlowe did not have to look out the window to know she had arrived. The dread that had been building for the past sixteen hours descended like a heavy iron blanket weighing down every inch of her body and every bit of her soul, her shoulders rounding, her head bowing under the force of it. The feeling so familiar, yet no matter how many times she experienced it, she swore it was denser and thicker than the last.

Savoring the last remaining moments of solitude, she closed her eyes. The absence of the rhythmic clop of the horses' hooves and the crunch of gravel beneath the carriage wheels felt odd to her ears. She would have much preferred to instruct the driver to continue on, to return from whence they came, but no matter how much she wished it otherwise, she knew she could not change the inevitable.

Her sigh, laden with resignation, filled the darkness inside the carriage. Slowly turning her head, she looked out the window. The small back courtyard was plain and utilitarian, lacking the elegant grandeur of the front façade. Twilight had come and gone hours ago. The moon hung high in the night sky, shrouded by gray wisps of clouds. Only the golden light streaming from the kitchen's two windows lit the flagstones leading to the black door. Heavy draperies covered the other windows, effectively obscuring the interior from prying eyes and providing the discretion the establishment's clients preferred.

"It's only one week," she said in an effort to bolster her spirits, but her whispered words held little reassurance.

Seven nights. She had done it many times before and could certainly do it again. It had long since stopped being about whether she *could* do it, and it had never been about whether she wanted to do it. It was a matter of necessity. A lesser of evils, a means to an end. And each time the rented carriage slowed to a stop at the back door of Madame Rubicon's brothel, it became a test of will. Her ability to will herself through yet another week before she could return once again to her quiet Bedfordshire country home.

The carriage shifted as the driver moved about on the bench, the springs creaking in protest, recalling her to the task at hand.

Maudlin thoughts never accomplished anything and lingering would not pay the bills her younger brother, Dashell, had most certainly incurred since her last visit to London.

Gathering her resolve, she gave a firm nod and reached for the valise on the floor at her feet.

"Next Wednesday?" the driver asked as she got out of the carriage.

"Yes, Frank." She reached into the pocket of her cloak and, lifting up onto her toes, handed the fold of pound notes to him. A kind, strapping man in his midfifties, Frank Miller had been her driver for four years now and knew the routine well. He showed up at her doorstep at eight o'clock in the morning on the last Wednesday of every month and returned to the courtyard the following week to take her home. The times set to ensure one day of travel, preventing a stay at an inn along the way.

Frank tipped his head and gathered the leather lines in his gloved hands. He did not say another word, did not wish her a good evening. He somehow knew such pleasantries were wholly unnecessary. One of the horses tossed its head, impatient to be off again, but he held the beasts steady. She could feel the weight of his gaze on her as she followed the short path to the back door.

Her knock was answered almost immediately.

The door opened, revealing a girl with frizzy dark blonde hair and a smudged white apron over her plain brown dress. "Yer late."

Rose ignored the hard bite in the maid's tone and stepped inside. "Yesterday's rains wreaked havoc on the roads. Not much to be done about it." She didn't mention how one of the horses had thrown a shoe or trouble they had had procuring a fresh team in Luton. The servant cared not for the trials of Rose's day, only for the opportunity to voice her displeasure to someone who would bear it.

The second before the maid shut the door, Rose heard the snap of leather lines and the jangle of harness as the carriage departed. Frank never left until she was inside, an unasked-for kindness she was most grateful for. Four years, and she still wasn't fully comfortable venturing about London on her own. The urge to glance over her shoulder had receded with time, but had yet to vanish completely even with the madam's reassurances. Odd, to associate the place she dreaded returning to month after month with safety. But she had learned long ago that in her line of work common logic rarely prevailed.

The maid didn't offer to take Rose's valise, nor had Rose expected it. The girl merely locked the door and turned on her heel, grumbling under her breath as she went into the kitchen.

Rose took the narrow back stairs to the second floor. The house seemed to hum about her with the familiar sounds of a busy evening. The barely perceptible drone of voices, the *click* of shoes on floorboards, the occasional bout of drunken laughter. She paused at the door before opening it and took a deep breath, willing the exhale to flow smoothly. Thankfully the corridor was empty. The plush rugs silenced her footsteps as she made her way to the last door on the right. She tried to close her ears to the faint feminine squeal of delight leaching from the room across from hers. The sound grated down her spine, a heavy reminder of what her next seven nights would entail.

But perhaps, if she was fortunate, only six nights. Shifting her valise to her other hand, she pulled the brass key from her pocket. She knew she shouldn't wish for it—she came to London for a specific purpose, after all—but she simply could not stifle the hope. Most greeted news of a travel delay with a harsh scowl of impatience, but as ten hours had grown to sixteen, she had only been grateful for the possibility of a reprieve, even if only temporary.

The *click* of the lock sliding home resounded in the corridor. A mocking taunt that all but killed every trace of hope that had seeped into her veins. It mattered not that it must surely be well past midnight. The pursuit of pleasure knew not day or night. It cared only for itself, for the bliss to be found in release, and it particularly did not care who it had to use to find it.

Letting out a sigh, she slipped through the door and shut it behind her. A fire burned in the marble-manteled fireplace. The three-arm candelabra on the side table next to the cream brocade settee had already been lit. Jane must have recently checked on the room, for the candles had not burned themselves down to stubs and instead appeared fresh.

She made her way through the small sitting room and into the adjoining bedchamber where she found the fire had been lit there as well. There wasn't a single wrinkle in the bronze silk coverlet on the large four-poster bed that dominated the room. The pillows were fluffed and neatly arranged at the mahogany headboard. The dresser and bedside tables held not a trace of dust. Nothing at Rubicon's came without a price. A maid to ready her rooms, never mind the rooms themselves. Her own private suite, small though it might be, and the luxury of leaving it empty for three weeks out of every month did not come cheap, but Rose had deemed it well worth the expense ages ago.

It took only a few moments to unpack the contents of her valise. As her Town and country lives never mixed, she did not have need to bring much with her. A plain cambric day dress, similar to one she currently wore except in a slightly faded navy, to don on her errands about Town. Her favorite brush, its wooden handle smoothed from years of use, and a miniature of Dashell that had been commissioned just months before their father had gone to his grave. A reminder of why she was here, for those instances when her will teetered on the verge of crumbling.

She traced the oval frame with a loving fingertip. Now eighteen and determined to be seen as a man, Dash barely resembled the boy with the mop of unruly black curls and the smooth, round face. He had grown significantly in the past five years, to the point where he towered over her, but he still had the same impish glint in his light blue eyes. One that announced trouble followed in his wake. Before she left London, she would need to have another discussion with him regarding Oxford. Hopefully her advice would not fall on deaf ears again.

And if it did . . . She shrugged. The most she could do was provide him with the opportunities he was meant to have. Whether he availed himself of them was another matter altogether.

The small portrait was tucked in the top drawer of the dresser, behind the neat rows of fine silk stockings. The traveling dress was hung on a peg in the back corner of the closet where she stowed her empty valise. A quick check revealed the buttons on the bodice on the violet gown had been mended in her absence. Impatient clients usually promised a short evening, but they did tend to wreak havoc on her wardrobe. Thankfully Jane was handy with a needle and thread.

Contemplating the gown, she rubbed the silk between her forefinger and thumb, but the rich, vibrant shade far from matched her mood. Instead she selected the mauve. Smokey and subdued with cap sleeves and a low, square neckline designed to draw the eye and hold it. Even though it was unadorned with ribbon or lace trim, it was still very much a gown fit for a whore.

"Which is what you are," she whispered.

A wince crossed her brow. She loathed that word. So base and blunt. But she could not hide what she had become behind a prettier label. She had turned herself into a whore. Had done it deliberately years ago, with her eyes open and fully aware of the consequences. Regretting it now was simply an act in futility.

She laid the gown on the bed, along with stockings, stays, chemise, and slippers. Might as well get on with it. The first night was always the hardest and dwelling on it would only make it harder to do what was needed to see herself through to the dawn.

She was doing up the tiny row of buttons on the front of the gown's bodice when Jane entered the bedchamber. Wisps of the girl's long dark hair had escaped the braid knotted at her nape, the strands framing her flushed face.

"She asked after you. Twice in the past couple of hours," Jane said, as she poured water from the pitcher on the washstand into the porcelain bowl.

That meant Rubicon had already turned down two clients for her. *Lovely.* She would be sure to hear about the incidents tomorrow, from the madam herself.

At the wince flickering across her face, Jane added, "Not to worry. I spotted quite a few wealthy-looking gentlemen in the receiving room. She was heading down there when I came up here. The night won't go to waste."

Not the reassurance Rose was hoping for. It wouldn't take long for the small silver bell to ring in her receiving room, signaling the madam had found her a client. God, how she hated that sound.

"Do you need assistance with anything?" Jane asked.

"No, thank you. I'm almost ready as it is." A few flicks of her fingers, and she removed the pins from her hair. The length unwound from its tight bun, tumbling over her shoulders and unleashing the light scent of roses from the soap she had used that morning to wash her hair. She carefully worked her fingers through the dark waves and then coiled them into a loose knot. Holding it in place with one hand, she rummaged in the dresser drawer, pushing aside pins, ribbons, and silver combs until she found what she was looking for. A twist of her wrist was all it took to secure the knot with the ivory knitting needle.

Jane grabbed her sage green traveling dress and practical white stockings from the closet and folded them over her arm. "All right, then. Have a good evening."

Highly unlikely. But Rose forced herself to smile, to give the maid the expected response. Jane's kindness was born from the pound notes Rose paid her; still, it wouldn't do to be rude.

The moment Jane left the room, Rose's shoulders slumped. Standing there in her elegant little bedchamber and clothed in a rich, silk gown, seven nights suddenly felt like forever. The days would slip quickly by, but the nights . . . each one an eternity.

The despair that had long since killed every one of her girlhood dreams began to wind its way around her heart. She swore every time she smiled at a new gentleman, every time she pressed her lips to his, opened her arms to him, she lost a tiny bit of her soul. But what other choice did she have?

None.

At least none that guaranteed the necessary income. And she would never go back to life in the demimonde. At least at Madame Rubicon's decadent West End brothel, she wasn't dependent on one man's whims for her livelihood. There were no worries over what one slight misstep would cost her. She was here of her own free will. And if one of her clients got out of hand, the brothel's burly guards would come to her aid.

All in all, it could be much worse. She could be destitute and hungry. She could have lost Paxton Manor, Dash's birthright, to creditors. She could be working on her back at some nunnery in the stews for barely enough coin for her and Dash's supper.

Instead she was here. Earning in seven nights what most of the other women like her earned in a month. She should count herself fortunate.

She let out a sardonic huff.

Nor would she be fortunate for much longer if she continued to dally.

Smoothing wrinkles that didn't exist on her gown, she crossed to the bedside table on the right side of the bed, next to the discreet trifold screen with its red roses and lush green leaves painted in watercolors on its semitransparent fabric. Inside the top drawer she found the silver box filled with small wool sponges, each about the size of a walnut and tied with a length of white thread. The copper tin had been refilled as well. Even though most of her clients thought sheaths beneath them, it wouldn't do to have none on hand in the event one was requested.

She dabbed the tiniest bit of perfume between her breasts and went out to the sitting room. She glanced about to ensure all was at the ready. The three crystal decanters on the silver tray on the cabinet behind the settee. Brandy, whisky, and port, with the necessary glassware. The drapes on the window were already closed tight. She prodded the flames in the hearth to full life and then settled on the settee.

Hands folded demurely on her lap and her shoulders back and chin tilted down, she braced for the light, tinkling sound of the small bell suspended on a hook near the ceiling in the corner. She kept her gaze from straying to the section of the barren white paneled wall directly before her and did her best not to think about the type of man—never mind what he would want from her—who would soon stride through the hidden door.

⚜

THERE was a soft, metallic *click*. James quickly stood and turned toward the door. After waiting for what felt like an eternity, though in actuality he was certain ten minutes could not have passed, what could only be the house's proprietor entered the office.

"Good evening, sir. And welcome. It is always a pleasure to make a new acquaintance." Taller than the average woman and dressed in a figure-hugging scarlet silk gown, she appeared to be somewhere in the vicinity of forty years of age. Not so old that the yellow blonde hair piled high on her head was liberally streaked with silver, nor young enough to be free of the fine lines around her rouged mouth.

He took her proffered hand and executed a slight bow over her ringed fingers. "Good evening."

"Please, have a seat." With a little flick of her wrist, she indicated the armchairs. "Would you care for a glass of brandy, or perhaps whisky?"

"No, thank you," he said, sitting back in the armchair he had just vacated.

She swept behind the desk and settled in the chair. The cant of

her shoulders put her ample breasts on full display, the deep V of
the bodice barely containing them. With a hint of a smile playing
on her lips, she folded her hands on the neat surface of the desk.
"What can I do for you this evening?"

No pleasantries. No talk of the weather. No easing into it. She
cut straight to the heart of the matter. Nor did it escape his notice
that she did not ask for his name. Only what he wanted. He lifted
his chin and looked directly into her kohl-rimmed eyes. "I wish to
procure the services of a woman."

"Well then, you have come to the right place. Is there a type of
woman you prefer?"

Someone who doesn't have an aristocratic bone in her body.

He was tempted to answer no—the brothel most certainly
would not have a true lady in its employ—but he caught the word
before it left his mouth. He wouldn't commission a new ship without detailed specifications. If he was going to go through with the
evening and part with a significant sum, then he might as well be
specific. "I prefer a woman with dark hair. Not too thin."

Though what he really wanted was someone kind. Someone who
would demand nothing in return except for his presence. But he
would surely mark himself as a desperate man if he told the madam
that.

For a moment she considered his response. Her gaze traveled
over his body, settling on his hands as he tried not to grip the arms
of the chair, to appear as nonchalant as she.

"Do you have any particular preferences?"

He frowned, taken aback by the question. Hadn't he just told
her what he preferred? But her emphasis on the word *particular*
made him suspect she was asking about something else. "What
type of preferences?"

"This house holds many beautiful women, some more skilled
in . . . certain areas than others. Your preferences will help me to
narrow the selection to those who will best suit you."

Though she couched her words in the politest terms possible, he had the distinct impression she was trying to determine if he was one of those depraved souls who sought the services of whores to perform deviant, illicit acts. No wonder, given the maid had surely told her that he had slunk up the back stairs. "No. I do not have any particular preferences."

She tipped her head. She was so casual with her questions they could very well be discussing a new ship. He couldn't decide if the ease with which she dealt with him was comforting or off-putting. It just all seemed so very . . . impersonal.

"Are there any limitations I should be made aware of?" she asked.

"Pardon?"

"In regards to your pocket."

He shook his head. If the madam's price exceeded the thick fold of pound notes in his coat pocket, then he'd simply write her a bank draft for the difference. The sum mattered not, only the time it would gain with a woman whose lip would not curl in disdain when her eyes landed on him. "No."

Her eyes glinted with a distinct note of greed. A slow smile spread across her face. "I have the perfect woman for you. She possesses the body of a goddess. Lush, voluptuous, made for a man's touch. Beyond beautiful and highly skilled in the art of pleasure. She will take your breath away, in more ways than one. With such beauty and skill, one might expect a slightly . . . spoiled creature, sure of her allure. But not with her. She is all gracious accommodation. Refined of manner and kind of soul. She, quite simply, has no rival."

Beautiful, willing, and *kind?* He highly doubted such a woman existed.

His disbelief must have shown itself, for she added, "She is the prize of my establishment. Lauded above all others. So exquisite she has no need to grace the receiving room with her presence. The moment you lay eyes on her, you will understand why gentlemen

have come to blows over the privilege of her company." She pulled
a square of white paper from a desk drawer. A quick scratch of her
pen, and she pushed the note to him. "And that is all it will take for
her to be yours, and only yours, this evening."

He picked up the paper. A high price he expected, but this? But
it was more than the price that gave him pause—though he wasn't
accustomed to spending such a sum on something for himself, he
could easily afford it—rather the knowledge that there would be no
going back from this point forward.

. . . and kind of soul.

The indecision vanished. Shifting in the chair, he reached into
his coat pocket. If he remembered correctly from his previous visit
to a brothel, the madam would expect payment before services were
rendered. And he had to admit, he was more than a bit curious to
meet this paragon of the female gender.

He set the correct amount and the note on her desk.

Not bothering to verify the sum, she tucked the pile into her
desk drawer. "You have my assurances you will not be disappointed.
Now if you will come with me."

She reached behind her and pulled on a bellpull, then crossed
the room and pressed on a section of the white paneled wall. A door
hidden in the wall swung silently open. The corridor was barely
wide enough to accommodate the width of his shoulders. The candle she had taken from the small console table next to the door
threw patterns of light and shadow on the walls. He followed her up
a flight of stairs. Her silk skirts swooshed with each step, the sound
amplified in the confined space.

She stopped before a door and turned to him. "May I have your
name?" she asked, her voice pitched low.

He hesitated.

"Discretion is this establishment's most coveted possession." The
hint of a smile flitted back on her lips. "Introductions go so much
better when there is a name involved. Don't you agree?"

He swallowed. "James."

"Would you like to see her before your introduction?" She reached up and swung aside a small circle of wood. Stepping aside, she motioned to the thin beam of golden light streaming from the door.

His feet were moving toward the door before he was even aware of it. Anticipation surged within him, his pulse quickening. He pressed his eye to the door and his gaze went immediately to her.

His heart skipped a beat. The madam had not been exaggerating.

She was seated on a cream settee about four paces directly in front of him in a small, well-appointed sitting room. Her thick, silken hair, the color of midnight, was pulled back in a loose knot at her nape, a few stray, wavy strands brushing the graceful lines of her neck. Plump, rose red lips, flawless porcelain skin, lush breasts barely contained within the dangerously low neckline of her bodice . . .

He clenched his hand at his side. The urge to touch was so strong it nearly overwhelmed him.

"Her name is Rose." The whispered words floated past his ear. "Are you pleased?"

He could only nod. With her red lips and fair skin, the name fit her, perfectly, to the point where he wondered if it was indeed her real given name.

Even though she was an exquisitely beautiful young woman, truly possessing the body of a goddess, soft curves in all the right places, she had an unmistakable aura of approachability about her. This was not a harshly elegant creature accustomed to looking down her nose at others.

With a little flick of her wrist, she rearranged the skirt of her mauve gown about her legs. Her attention was fixed off toward the draperies covering the single window, but she didn't seem to be actually looking at anything in particular. Her straight shoulders slumped the tiniest bit, a hint of . . . sadness flickered across her beautiful heart-shaped face. So quickly he wasn't certain if he imagined it or not.

It suddenly felt so very wrong to intrude on an unguarded moment. He took a quick step back.

"If you would do the honor," he said in an undertone, indicating the door.

"It would be my pleasure." The madam moved the wooden cover back in place, closing off the narrow beam of light.

She opened the door and he went inside, stopping at the madam's shoulder.

"Good evening, Rose. I have a gentleman who wishes to make your acquaintance."

In a soft rustle of silk, she stood. If something had saddened her moments ago, there was certainly no trace of it now. A smile curved her lips, her light blue eyes alight with genuine welcome.

"This is James. James, may I introduce you to Rose."

She extended one pale arm, offering him her hand. She wore no gloves. Her delicate hand was soft and warm in his as he made his bow. Though she was midheight for a woman and certainly no slight wisp of a thing he had to fear he'd break if he touched, with his six-foot-two frame, he still felt as though he towered over her. "It is my pleasure to make your acquaintance."

"The pleasure is all mine, James." The rich, feminine timbre of her voice felt so good to his ears. Polished and smooth, without a coy, affected lilt. And she had spoken his name as if she had said it countless times before. Familiar and easy. A sound he was certain he would never forget.

He looked beside him, his thanks for the introduction on the tip of his tongue, but the madam was gone.

Two

THE man glanced about the room, as if suddenly uncertain. Rose waited for him to release her hand. His long fingers were folded around her palm, his thumb resting on the back of her ring finger. His grip was light yet secure; a gentleman well accustomed to introductions to the fairer sex. Yet she could feel the calluses on his palm and on the tips of his fingers.

Soft, olive green eyes met hers and held her captive for a seemingly endless moment. She was vaguely aware her breathing had quickened. Good Lord, he had long lashes. Not only long but thick, a full shade darker than his neatly cropped chestnut brown hair, and so unexpected for such a rugged face. There wasn't a hint of nobility in his features, only strength and a confidence that matched his impressive frame. His gaze dropped, lingering on her mouth before venturing lower. Heat blossomed across her chest, the tips of her breasts tightening into hard buds under the intensity of his regard.

"Come. Have a seat." Was that her voice? It sounded hoarse even to her own ears.

When he didn't immediately respond, she gave his hand a brief, light squeeze. His head snapped up and his arm dropped to his side as he relinquished his hold.

"My apologies." The deep, low murmur was more a rumble from his broad chest than actual words.

"No apologies are necessary, I assure you." She smiled to emphasize her point. "Come, you needn't stand by the door all evening."

Turning, she crossed the room, letting her hips sway the slightest bit with each step. She hadn't missed the single finger Rubicon had held up behind the man's back as she had slipped out the door. James was a new client, at least to Rubicon's. This was his first visit to the house, and it was on Rose's shoulders to make certain he would leave tonight with a strong desire to return. A man wealthy enough to afford her was a valuable commodity, one Rubicon would not want to lose.

Though judging by his hesitation, he likely was not a regular patron of any similar establishment in London. Once he recovered his bearings, he'd either pounce on her, eager to see the deed done, or continue to hold back, uncertain how to proceed. If he held back, she would need to prod him along, hold his hand, so to speak. Reassure him she welcomed his advances. Give him the cues he needed to take the evening to its eventual conclusion.

A conclusion that strangely enough did not inspire the usual stirrings of dread.

"Brandy, whisky, or port?" she asked.

"Pardon?"

She indicated the crystal decanters. "To drink. Would you care for a glass of brandy, whisky, or port?"

"No, thank you."

The man certainly could use one. Spine straight and shoulders stiff, he did not look at all at ease. He at least had moved from his spot by the door, now standing before the settee, but had yet to sit.

"If you'd care for something else, I can ring for a maid."

He shook his head.

She selected a tumbler and poured a healthy splash of whisky. Port was too potent for her tastes, and brandy . . . he didn't look like the brandy sort. If he refused the offer on her account, then she would show him he needn't bother. Turning from the cabinet, she brought the glass to her lips and took a delicate sip, the well-aged whisky flowing down her throat.

The moment after she settled on the settee, he sat as well. His timing took her aback. He hadn't remained standing out of hesitation, but out of respect for her. Well, considering the purpose of the evening, *respect* was too strong a word. More a mere polite gesture. One likely ingrained in him since his youth.

Not just a man who would call himself a gentleman, but a true gentleman. One whose manners did not fall aside the moment the situation no longer demanded them. Yet she doubted he was an aristocrat. There wasn't a hint of arrogance, of superiority about him.

She set the whisky on the spindly-legged side table and turned her shoulders to him. The settee was sized to fit the limited dimensions of the room, and even with his elbow resting on the cream silk arm, her skirt touched his thigh. But it was more than the conveniently sized furniture. James would have dwarfed one of the comfortable leather couches in the receiving room. And it wasn't only his height. She knew without touching that his tailor had not needed to employ a bit of padding to accentuate his frame. There was nothing but solid muscle beneath the bottle green coat and tan trousers. From his impossibly broad shoulders to his strong, capable hands, this was a man who understood the value of an honest day's work and had the body to prove it.

With a small start, she realized she was staring, and quite boldly. Clasping her hands on her lap, she swallowed to moisten her dry mouth and recalled herself to the task at hand. No matter how appealing the view, he would expect her to do far more than stare at him.

"Do you reside in London, James, or are you a guest to the city?" she asked, in an effort to engage him in conversation.

"No, not a guest."

A response that consisted of more than three words. Not much more, but a move in the right direction. "And how do you fill your days?"

He hesitated, his brows drawing together the slightest bit. "I work."

Most men did some sort of work, even if it just involved a short discussion with a secretary who saw to their business affairs. She opened her mouth, about to inquire as to the type of work he did, when he spoke.

"How do you spend your days? When you're not"—he tipped his head to indicate the room—"here, that is."

"Ah, I . . ." *Track down Dash, to make certain he's taking care of himself. Make arrangements with tradesmen to see to the repairs at Paxton Manor. Wish the sun would never set.* "I take walks in the park." The lush expanse of green grass. The gentle murmur of the Serpentine. Quiet, peaceful, a treasured reminder of home.

He passed a hand over his strong jaw. His attention skipped about the room before settling on her. "I can't recall the last time I went to the park during daylight hours. I sometimes take a detour through Hyde Park on my way home, but that's well into the evening. What hour do you prefer for your walks?"

"Late morning. Before the sun is high in the sky." Far before the fashionable hour, and after the gentlemen let their horses stretch their legs along Rotten Row. She shared Hyde Park with the nurses pushing prams and governesses tending their errant charges, not with the elegant ladies of the ton or with gentlemen who were apt to recognize her.

His gaze strayed again to the hidden door. A furrow marred his brow. "Can we be watched?" he asked, voice pitched low.

"Did you grant Madame Rubicon that liberty?"

"No."

"Then no. Guests are not allowed in the servants' areas unless accompanied by Rubicon, and that passageway only leads from this room to her office." She didn't mention how Rubicon herself was apt to check on the room to ensure James was behaving himself, especially considering he was an unknown entity to the brothel. "Though if the thought appeals, you can let her know that you are open to such play. There are guests who gain pleasure from watching another, just as there are guests who gain pleasure from being watched."

She kept the casual, inquiring expression in place, and waited for his response.

"And does the thought appeal to you?"

Did he wish for her to engage in such play with him? On only a small handful of occasions had a gentleman made that request. Tame, really, in comparison to activities that went on elsewhere in the house. Still, the experience had not been comfortable. She had not been able to forget about the eyes upon her, watching her every move. Odd, considering her nights here were always a performance.

But it wouldn't do to stifle James's desires if that was what he truly wanted. She was here to please *him*, and she must never forget that.

Forcing a sly, teasing smile, she lifted one arm and reached across the short distance separating them to trail her fingertips down his forearm, over the soft wool of his coat sleeve. "It appeals to me if it appeals to you."

The moment she reached the warm skin on the back of his hand, he twisted his wrist, easily capturing her fingers.

"I didn't ask about me. I asked about you."

Was he truly interested in her preferences? Some pretended to care, but it was only a guise, a way to ease their conscience, to reassure themselves they were not taking something against her wishes. As if the exchange of money wasn't enough to placate any concerns on that front. But the conviction in James's steady gaze told her loud and clear he was not one of them.

If he wanted an honest answer then she could give it to him, at least in this. "No. It does not appeal," she said, her voice just above a whisper.

His grip loosened, and she slid her fingers free. She shifted, arranging her skirt about her legs, needing to do . . . something. She felt so oddly exposed, as if she sat bare before not only him, but an entire crowd. The word *yes* flowed so smoothly off her tongue that it had been difficult to get that *no* out. She wanted to roll her shoulders, try to throw off the discomposure.

Instead, she gathered herself, pushing that wall to the forefront, distancing herself from her emotions, employing that critical skill she had learned so very long ago. The one that allowed her to get through each and every evening at Rubicon's. In any case, it was time to give James another little nudge.

She reached for the tumbler and took another slow sip. Her gaze dropped from his face, down his chest, lingering on the placket of his trousers before sliding back up to his. Then she offered the glass to him.

"Are you trying to get me foxed?" he asked, a hint of an amused smile playing on his lips.

"Foxed? No. What use is a foxed man to a woman?"

"We can have our uses." His fingers brushed hers as he took the tumbler. Sensation shot up her arm, radiating across her chest. Her breaths stuttered. His coat stretched across the expanse of his back as he leaned down to set the glass on the plush rug by his feet.

When he straightened, she thought for certain he would move closer. Lean in to taste the sheen of whisky she knew lightly coated her lips. But he sat back and merely turned his attention to her.

He seemed more relaxed, those shoulders no longer held so rigidly straight. His long legs casually spread. A man at his ease. Still . . .

She was going to have to be bolder.

"Yes. I wholeheartedly agree. Men can definitely have their uses."
With a calculated lean of her upper body, one designed to display her
assets to their best advantage, she rested her hand on his leg. The powerful thigh trembled beneath her touch. Then his entire body went still.
He was most assuredly not unaffected by her. She tipped her head in
the direction behind him. "My bedchamber is just beyond that door."

He didn't look over his broad shoulder, but instead kept his gaze
locked with hers. "Is it?"

She arched a brow, her lips quirking. "Yes. Would you care to
have a look?"

His gaze swept over her face, studying, considering. Just when
she thought he would not answer, he gave a small shake of his head.
"Unnecessary. This is acceptable."

"It is?"

"Yes."

He did not want to move to her bedchamber? It was an almost
completely foreign notion. She had heard tales from others in the
house of men who only wanted a willing ear, a pretty woman to pay
attention to them. Those who wanted companionship and nothing
more. But she had never encountered such a specimen.

Perhaps he only wanted . . .

She let her hand slowly drift up his leg, her touch light, teasing yet deliberate in its intent. The heat from his body penetrated
the soft wool of his trousers, warming the fabric as if he had been
lazing beneath the hot summer sun for hours. The moment her fingertips coasted over the placket of his trousers, the heavy bulk hidden within jumped. A quick thump that sent a bolt of unexpected
desire straight to her core.

Then those long fingers captured hers again.

He laced his fingers through hers, resting their joined hands on
his thigh. The hoarse scratch as he cleared his throat seemed to fill
the room. "What is your favorite spot in Hyde Park?"

She blinked, her wits scrambled from the abrupt return to their previous topic of conversation. "The Serpentine," she heard herself answer, as if from a great distance.

"I shall have to remember to stop there on my next detour."

The desire that had begun to seep into her veins withered and died under the weight of confusion. He wanted to remain in her sitting room, and nothing more? Did he not understand what he had purchased? Oh, that was surely a ridiculous notion. No man paid for the most expensive whore in the house without a firm understanding of the pleasures that awaited him. Rubicon would have seen to that. Yet he did not seem to want them. She cast her mind about, desperately searching for some sort of explanation for his perplexing behavior. His body reacted to her touch, yet he steadfastly refused to take the openings she gave him.

They should be in her bedchamber by now. She should be finding those places on his body, those spots unique unto each man that would ratchet his lust to the heavens. He should be panting for more and not looking at her with an unnerving hint of compassion on his handsome face.

Was it something she said, or had not said? Something she had done to cause him to reconsider? Or was his hesitation not borne of the situation? Perhaps it was simply *her* he did not want.

Perhaps he had decided he did not wish to follow in so many men's footsteps.

If that were the case, then she certainly could not fault him. Did any man truly want what could so easily be bought?

It made her acutely aware of how many men she had opened her arms to since she had first walked into this house. So many pairs of greedy hands had groped her body, used her, taken their fill of her, only to be followed by yet another. They all blended together, indistinguishable from the next, yet she felt the distinct weight of each individual that made up the whole.

Each one tarnishing her, tainting her, until she had at last been rendered sullied beyond even lust's negligible standards.

"You are beautiful, Rose."

She did not know what caught her off guard more. The sound of her name in his low, rumbling, masculine voice, or the way he had voiced the compliment. Genuine, but as if he believed she needed to hear it. As if she needed the reassurance.

How had he known?

"You are too kind," she demurred, falling back on the expected response. She made to lean back, to put distance between them once again, but his grip on her hand remained light and secure. Holding her to him.

"It's not a kindness, it's the truth. You *are* beautiful."

Countless men had spoken those words to her. They had waxed eloquently and some not-so-eloquently on her fine features and the curves of her body. She had smiled and murmured her thanks, but their empty words had slid over her with no effect.

Never had a man made her *feel* beautiful.

Until now.

She could only answer with a breathless "Thank you." The tingle building in her belly spread out to her fingers and toes in a wave of light, airy sensation. She dipped her chin to her chest, trying but failing to hide the smile she could not keep from her lips.

"I quite like your gown as well."

A little giggle bubbled up from her chest. "Thank you."

"You're very welcome. The color is nice, too."

"Mauve. Is it a favorite of yours, then?" she teased.

"Not in general. I usually prefer blue."

"I have a blue gown. Well, more navy than a true blue. If you'd like, I can change . . . and you can assist me."

His smile transformed his face, erasing the years. With his imposing build and rugged features, she had taken him for a man at least a decade her senior. But she now doubted he was more than a handful of years older than her two and twenty.

"No, that's not necessary," he said with a chuckle that warmed the room.

She read the desire, the need, clear as day, in his eyes. Yet the realization hit her that her body was not the primary commodity he sought. He wanted her time. Regardless of his compliments, she had the distinct impression she could be passably pretty, and he would be equally content with her.

The weight of expectation, of duty, of obligation, lifted from her shoulders. The last lingering bit of tension eased out of her and she shifted, moving closer to him. Drawn to him. With her shoulder pressed against his biceps and her arm draped lightly over his, their hands still entwined, she rested against him. His coat held the cool, crisp scent of the night air and a light, spicy hint of a man. Of James.

"Since you are not a guest, I take it you reside in London. Do you also work in the city?"

"Yes. My office is near the docks."

Not the most pleasant part of town. Surely he could afford to situate himself in a more prosperous area. "By choice?"

"By convenience. My interests are in shipping."

She could well imagine him on the deck of a ship, effortlessly working the rigging. His skin coated in a light sheen of sweat, his muscles bunching and flexing under the hot sun. Though merchants were apt to spend their days behind a desk, his work-roughened hands indicated he was not averse to a bit of hard labor. "You must be experiencing quite the boom since the trade restrictions were lifted and Bonaparte's ships no longer troll the seas."

"I've seen the benefits, yes."

She paused, waiting for him to elaborate, but he remained silent. Modesty. Not a trait often seen in men. Most grabbed any opportunity to try to impress her with their successes, however large or small.

She tried to discover more about him, but all of her questions led to the same answer. He worked. He did not belong to a club, had a decided preference against the theatre, and judging by the frown at the mention of social functions, he did not care for those, either. "Do you spend every waking moment at your office?"

"That is my intention, yes."

"Why?"

"I prefer it there over being at home."

What an odd response. "Do you at least enjoy your time at work?"

He shrugged, the wool sleeve of his coat a soft rub against her bare arm. "Do you enjoy your time here?"

Was that a thinly veiled "no" to her question, or was he merely indifferent? Viewing his work as a nonnegotiable facet of life. Regardless of how luxurious the surroundings, surely he could not believe she would ever go so far as to classify her nights spent on her back as enjoyable. That was the last word she associated with this house.

Well, perhaps that wasn't entirely correct. Her gaze traced his strong profile, from the straight line of his nose to his jaw darkened with a shadow of a day's beard. It wasn't that she had never had a handsome client. A rarity for certain, but not unheard of. It was more . . . him. James. She sensed a quiet kindness in his soul, along with a distinct echo of loneliness that matched her own.

"I enjoy being with you." The truth fell from her lips before she could stop it.

A little smile tugged on his mouth. "Thank you." He rubbed his thumb over the back of her hand. A gentle, almost absent motion that spoke of companionship and nothing more. "Have you tired of the subject of me?"

"Not necessarily."

"Alas, I have. I find you much more interesting. Will you tell me about yourself? Do you have a family?"

"Doesn't everyone? None of us are simply placed on this earth."

He cast her a glance, one eyebrow lifted, at her glib retort. But she found no shade of censure in his expression. Rather, a touch of humor lurked in the depths of his eyes.

And he continued. One question after another. He never pressed too hard, but nor would he be diverted. She parried to the best of her abilities, fortifying each response with just enough truth to keep it from ringing with the hollow note of a lie. For the sum her clients paid Rubicon, they received the use of her body, her expertise in the art of pleasure, and her conversation skills, if so desired. But she never gave them herself. And no matter how enjoyable her time with James, she knew it would not and could not last beyond the dawn. A fact etched in stone.

So she pushed aside the temptation to open even a tiny bit of herself to him, and instead cherished the evening for what it was. The reprieve she had desperately needed when she had entered her sitting room but a handful of hours ago.

Even reprieves, however, must come to an end. She could not say who had allowed their conversation to lull. Perhaps it had been by mutual design. The silence was only broken by the occasional pop and crack of the logs shifting. The fire in the white marble hearth was in sore need of a prodding, yet she made not one move toward the iron poker. She had passed the point of merely resting against him some time ago, and now leaned into him, her cheek pressed against his shoulder, her legs folded beside her on the settee. The solid weight of his body a comfort she did not want to give up.

He glanced about the room and then over his shoulder. "Do you not have a clock?"

"Not in here, no." As clients rarely lingered in the sitting room, she had never bothered to acquire a clock for the room. And more importantly, with only one client an evening, time was of little importance. The only requirement a departure by dawn.

Shifting, he pulled a plain silver pocket watch from his waistcoat pocket and glanced at the face. "It's quite late," he said, tucking the watch back in his pocket. "I don't want to keep you from your rest, so I will be on my way."

She took the cue for what it was and reluctantly swung her feet to the floor. He stood and, with her hand still in his, helped her to stand. Her skirt was a wrinkled mess, but it was the least of her concerns as she led him the short distance to the door.

He stopped and turned to face her. "Thank you."

"You are most welcome." *Please, ask for me tomorrow night.* She tamped down the words, kept the request hidden within. James would never return. She felt it in her bones. He was not a man who made a habit of spending his evenings with a woman like her.

His gaze dropped down to his shoes and then back up to meet hers. "You must think me quite odd."

He could not be further from the truth. She thought him wonderful, and she would ever be grateful for whatever had prompted him to enter this house.

"Why must I think you odd?"

"Because I spent an evening with a beautiful woman and didn't once attempt to steal so much as a kiss."

She took a half step toward him. "That can be remedied," she whispered.

His grip on her hand tightened, and she swore she felt the tremor race through his body. His eyes darkened. No longer a soft, olive green but banked with an undeniable need. He slowly, ever so slowly, lowered his head. Her free hand coasted up his sleeve to his biceps, the muscles hard as iron beneath her touch. She tipped her chin up, her spine lengthening, reaching for him. Her pulse pounded through her veins. She felt his arm wrap around her waist. Just before her lips brushed his, he ducked his head. Then warm lips pressed against her neck. The lightest of touches. The lightest of kisses.

The short, rapid puffs of his breaths singed her skin, the hint of beard the gentlest of scrapes. The soft strands of his hair tickled her ear. A flush of heat washed over her. Gooseflesh pricked her skin. Breath catching, she rocked on her feet, swaying into him, her eyes drifting closed. A small part of her mind marveled at the intensity of her response to him. Just his lips gliding over the delicate skin of her neck made every nerve in her body hum with a need for more.

A sigh of longing fluttered past her lips. She arched her neck, granting him greater access. His lips slowly whispered up over her jaw, across her cheek. And finally found hers.

His kiss was light, reverent, a soft slow meld of skin against skin that she never wanted to end. At the flick of his tongue against the seam of her lips, she eagerly opened to him, needing more. His hot tongue found hers, twined decadently with hers, and she lost herself in him. Gave herself over to the pure need and longing in his kiss.

She somehow kept the moan of protest from shaking her throat when his lips left hers. He pulled her that last remaining distance toward him, until she was pressed full against him, until she could feel his heart slamming against his chest.

For she didn't know how long, he simply held her. Her cheek resting against his chest, his powerful body folded around her, their hands still entwined.

Then he pressed his lips to the top of her head and took a step back, his arm unwinding from around her waist. His lashes swept down, a harsh wince flickering across his face, tightening his lips into a straight line. But when he opened his eyes an instant later, that desperation was gone. The need was still there, lurking in the olive green depths, but the stark, painful desperation had vanished.

And it struck her. He had needed this evening as badly as she.

His grip on her hand loosened. It took all of her willpower to relinquish her hold on him as his long fingers slipped from hers.

Without another word, he tipped his head to her. In a daze, she reached out to press against the wall. The well-oiled latch made nary a sound as it released, the hidden door swinging open. And he turned on his heel and disappeared down the darkened corridor, leaving her standing there in her elegant little sitting room, her hand, still warmed from his grasp, clenched at her side.

Three

JAMES tied his cravat in a simple knot and went into his dressing room. After donning a cream waistcoat, he grabbed his nut brown coat and slipped his arms into the sleeves. Most gentlemen employed the services of a valet, but he was of the firm belief that dressing oneself was not all that difficult of a task. He had managed it as a lad and could continue to do so as an adult. The size of his bank account had thankfully not stripped that knowledge from him.

Doing up the buttons of his coat, he went back to his bedchamber. He tugged on the edge of his sleeve, righting it beneath his coat, and looked to the window beside the bed he had recently vacated. The navy drapes were drawn back, revealing a never-ending swath of gray that hung low in the sky. The weak, hazy daylight gave little indication of the time of day. But that the sun even showed itself reminded him he had risen far past his usual hour.

He had never had need of a servant or a valet to wake him. Even his sleeping mind wished to limit the hours in his bed. But he had slept better last night than he had . . . ever. With that kiss playing itself in his mind, he had laid his head on his pillow, not to stir again for hours.

He had spent countless nights in his bed with only his hand for companionship. Long, lonely, sleepless nights. The only light from the smoldering embers in the fireplace, the massive town house quiet as a grave about him. He certainly would not have refused an offer from a woman during any of them. Yet the one night when he had actually received an offer, and not just one, what had he done?

Refused them.

He gave his head a self-deprecating shake, the beginnings of a chuckle rumbling in his chest. "James, you most definitely have become an old man."

But the offer had not truly been an offer, and that he had not been able to forget. Rose had been beyond beautiful. An image conjured straight from his fantasies. But once he had stood face-to-face with her, the thought of using her to sate his own selfish desires had posed too formidable an obstacle.

His body had been more than willing. His damn prick jumping to life, eager and needy, at every one of her smiles, never mind when she actually touched him. He could still feel the path her delicate fingertips had taken as they had coasted up his thigh, branding the arch of his arousal with her touch. No doubt in his dreams that touch would shift, his trousers slip away. Her grip would turn sure, gliding up and down his length slicked from the lush pleasures of her beautiful mouth, her eyes glinting with a need that matched his own as she urged him to completion.

He let out a short grunt and reached down to adjust himself. That thought alone would fuel his fantasies for many nights to come.

But above all, it had felt so good to hold her, to have the soft, light weight of her body pressed against his. To have her small hand held tight in his. To have the sweet, subtle feminine scent of her fill his every breath. It had been much too long since he had simply held a woman. Before his marriage, he would never have considered such a simple act a luxury. But after three years of famine, he had soaked up Rose's presence as if she were a precious drop of rain in the desert.

He would have much preferred to stay with Rose, to extend their chaste evening through the dawn, to not have to return here. Even though days upon days could pass without him even laying eyes on *her*, just being in this house was difficult. That damn stark desolation settling about him like a cloak whenever he walked through the front door.

But there was nothing he could do to change his fate. The best he could do was bear it, and try not to allow the loneliness to get the better of him again.

Frowning at the clouds, he turned on his heel and left his bedchamber. Hopefully the rain would hold off. He didn't relish the thought of arriving at his office soaked to the bone.

A bit of coffee and he could be on his way. Decker was likely fretting over his absence about now. James was usually seated behind his desk before eight, and it was already half past ten.

He tipped his head to the maid bustling toward the room at the other end of the corridor. The pale pink cambric morning dress in her arms did not escape his notice. He quickened his pace as he went down the stairs. He found the formal dining room empty save for an ivory pot and a matching cup and saucer at the head of the long mahogany table. The sideboard along the wall was bare except for the two silver candelabras stationed on each end. He never bothered the kitchen with breakfast. Just because he was eager to vacate the house did not mean Cook had to be sentenced to drag herself out of bed well before dawn to prepare a meal for him. It took little to see to a pot of coffee. Any servant could handle the task, and one need not even be fully awake.

He sat down and reached for the pot of coffee.

"I've alerted the kitchen to bring a fresh pot, Mr. Archer."

Somehow he kept from giving a start. Damnation, his staff could move about without making a sound. He had thought himself alone.

A footman clad in dark green livery had materialized at his elbow. Hands clasped behind his back, the servant shifted his weight, worry etched in his features, as if bracing for a reprimand.

James couldn't help but feel sympathy for the poor souls who labored under his roof. "There's no need for such concern, Hiller. You are not to blame for my tardy appearance this morning. The fault lies with myself, therefore I am willing to bear the consequences."

The worry eased a bit from the servant's features, but it didn't disappear completely. "The morning post has arrived. Would you care to take it now, or would you prefer to have it delivered to your office?"

"Might as well take it now and save you the ride to the docks."

Hiller practically scurried from the room. The man reappeared a moment later bearing a silver tray.

James murmured his thanks and flicked through the stack, ignoring those addressed to Mr. and Mrs. James Archer. Judging by the crisp, white parchment, they were all invitations of some sort. Mixed in with the unwelcome reminders of the upcoming Season that was only two weeks away were a couple of obvious bills and a letter for him.

Miss Rebecca Archer was written in precise script in the upper left-hand corner above the address of his father's Somerset country estate. He tucked the bills in his coat pocket and opened the letter.

My dearest brother James—I do hope this letter finds you well. The weather has been horribly gloomy in Somerset of late. I do not believe I have seen the sun in over a week. Father is unfortunately standing strong on his stance that I not come up to London until the sixth of April, but that is days and days away. And lest you believe the lure of balls filled with handsome, eligible lords is the

sole source of my impatience, I must have you know that I miss
you terribly. Therefore, I will not relent in my effort to depart the
countryside ahead of schedule. I would also not be adverse if you
wrote Father yourself, informing him that my imminent arrival in
London is of the utmost importance.

                                        —Your loving sister, Rebecca

A smile curved his mouth. He might be dreading the Season,
but Rebecca certainly was not. Her excitement leapt from the page.
If she showed up on his doorstep before the sixth, he would not be
surprised. His father had spent years planning his only daughter's
debut into Society, but James did not doubt that his sweet, biddable
sister could convince the old man that a slight alteration to his plan
would be for the best. Nor did he doubt that her trunks, filled with
the wardrobe she had commissioned two months ago when she had
last been to Town, were already packed, just waiting to be loaded
into the traveling carriage.

A young lady with her sights set on her first Season in London
would be a force impossible to resist. A letter from him would be
entirely unnecessary, but he would pen it all the same.

Hiller appeared once again at his elbow. "Your coffee, Mr. Archer." Little wisps of steam rose from the rich, dark liquid as he
poured a cup from the freshly brewed pot of coffee.

"Thank you, Hiller." James took a sip. Hot, but not so hot as to
render it undrinkable. *Perfect.* "And please alert the household that
Miss Archer may be joining us before Tuesday."

"Yes, sir. Is there anything else I can do for you?"

"No," he replied, tucking Rebecca's letter in with the bills in his
coat pocket.

With a short bow, Hiller left the dining room. James took a
couple of moments to finish his coffee and then pushed from the
table. Giving his coat a sharp tug to straighten it, he made his way
to the front door.

He enjoyed spending time with his only sibling. He adored her and would do anything to see her happy. To place in her small hands the opportunity she longed to have. Even the sacrifice of his own happiness had not been too great a price. But having her as a guest meant he would need to maintain the façade of domestic tranquility not only at various ton functions, but in his own home as well. The thought wiped all semblance of a smile from his face.

His aging butler, Markus, shut the front door and set a vase of flowers on the narrow console table just inside the door. A beautiful riot of reds, yellows, and pinks that livened the austere entrance hall.

Markus gave him a nod and turned from the table, his footsteps a faint *click* on the pristine white marble floors. James couldn't stop himself from reaching for the card nestled in with the blooms. It was addressed not to Mrs. James Archer but to Amelia Archer. An obvious gift from her latest lover.

His shoulders slumped. He was well aware the majority of aristocratic marriages involved infidelity. He and Amelia were two completely different people, forced together by the machinations of their fathers. Well, more accurately, his father's machinations and her father's need for funds to settle his massive debts. She certainly had not chosen him. He could not, in good conscience, begrudge her wish to find a spot of happiness, but hell, did she have to flaunt it so? It felt as though every lover was some sort of new victory over him. Yet another reminder he was completely at her whims.

Letting out a sigh, he tucked the card back into the flowers.

A soft rustle of fabric caught his attention. He looked over his shoulder to see his wife descending the grand staircase. Her gaze was on her lace fichu as she adjusted it above her bodice. The pale pink must not have met with her satisfaction, for she wore a green and white striped morning dress. The daughter of a viscount, her aristocratic blood was stamped in every feature from her narrow nose to her high cheekbones to the fine arch of her brows. Petite and slight of frame with guinea gold hair and large, light blue eyes, her beauty and breeding were to have garnered her a husband with a title and blood as pure as hers flowing through his veins. Instead, she had been forced to accept him. And she never passed up an opportunity to remind him of that unfortunate fact.

A delicate-slippered foot touched the marble floor when she looked up and stopped in her tracks. "You haven't left yet?"

He ignored the hard bite in her tone, ignored her question. He pasted a pleasant expression on his face, the one he would soon be wearing to cover the truth of his marriage, and took a step back from the flowers. "Good morning, Amelia."

She lifted a haughty brow and swept across the entrance hall.

She reached out an arm, her fingertips brushing a pink bloom. A smile of pure joy lit her face. Chin tipping down, her other hand fluttered up to cover the expanse of bare skin above the bodice of her dress. A slight flush warmed her pale cheeks. In that brief moment, she actually looked like the young woman of one and twenty that she was. Carefree. Happy. Without a single concern in her pretty little head.

Guilt stabbed into him. He could not change who he was or where he had come from, but he did wish matters had been different between them. Not for the first time, he wondered if he should have tried harder with her to breach the damn chasm between them. He had not gone into this marriage with high hopes, but he at least had wanted some sort of amiable relationship. Surely that had not been asking for too much. Someone to spend an evening with in pleasant conversation. Someone to share his life with. Someone to give him a child he could call his own.

Those hopes had been dashed on his wedding night. Well, at their wedding breakfast, more accurately. With a polite smile on her face for all the guests to see, she had hissed at him under her breath, *You are not welcome in my bed.*

"Langholm is such a dear fellow," she said on a wistful sigh.

"Lord Albert Langholm, a son of the Marquis of Hallbrook." As if she would invite a man into her bed who wasn't like her. "So very generous with his affections." She looked up to James, her features hardening, etched with the harsh, cruel edge of disdain. Her eyes were the exact same shade as Rose's, a clear, pure light blue, but so very different. "You could take a lesson from him."

He could not keep his brows from rising in shock. She now wanted flowers from him? He had tried that years ago, when they were first wed. Flowers, pretty baubles, jewelry. The flowers had promptly gone into the waste bin, the baubles chucked across the room and broken, the jewelry . . . that she had kept. If anything, the gifts had only made her loathe him all the more. And he was certainly more than generous with her—the woman didn't have need of pin money like many other married women. She had full access to two of his bank accounts.

Refusing to be drawn into an argument, he tipped his head to the flowers. "Best have them put in the drawing room so your afternoon callers can be sufficiently impressed. Good day, Amelia." He turned on his heel.

But the door did not close fast enough.

"Why won't you die?"

Her vile words smacked his back. He couldn't help but flinch. One would think he would be immune by now. The sting didn't linger as it once had, but the initial smack still hurt. Radiating across his back and seeping into his chest. And after last night, the smack hurt much more than usual.

Those few hours with Rose had been a treasured respite. He would not trade them for anything. And he had not realized at the time just how much he had needed them. But they were also a blunt reminder he had indeed willingly condemned himself to a loveless marriage.

If not for Rebecca, he would never have agreed. Duty to one's family held a certain responsibility, but simply his father's ambitions to have a title in the family would not have been enough to convince him to tie himself to a woman who would never look upon him with anything but pure and unadulterated loathing.

It had been so difficult to relinquish that last bit of hope. To fully accept that no matter what he did, no matter how hard he tried or the kindness he showed her, she would never change her opinion of him. He was a commoner. Not a drop of aristocratic blood flowed in his veins. His wealth and his family's wealth not born from the land but from trade.

A fact she would not and could not ever overlook.

He scrubbed a hand over his face and started up the street, doing his best to ignore the tug on his chest that begged him for something more.

✳

ROSE set the plate of raspberry tarts on the side table and settled on the settee. Bringing the ivory cup to her lips, she blew lightly over the surface and then took a sip. Rich and smooth, the hot chocolate flowed like velvet down her throat. Tarts and chocolate for breakfast. An indulgence indeed. But if she had to be here for a week, then she might as well avail herself of the amenities.

Rubicon certainly did not force her employees to reside in squalor. Far from it. The house belonged in the West End with its neat rows of stately town homes dotted with the occasional mansion. But the luxurious surroundings just made her feel like a pet in a gilded cage, waiting to perform for the evening's guest.

But last night's guest had not wanted a performance. A smile stole across her lips. She took a moment, just a moment, to savor the memory. Of James, so solid and strong, yet so . . . achingly lonely. And the way he had held her . . . never before had a man made her feel so safe and so needed. Not needed for the pleasure she could offer him, but simply needed for herself.

To have such a man, to be able to call him her own . . .

An ache pulsed to life, one she had thought dead and buried long ago. Sharp and acute, it flared across her chest. Startled by the intensity, she squeezed her eyes shut, a wince crossing her brow.

With a firm shake of her head, she pushed the thought from her mind. It would not do to dwell on him. In ten hours or so another man would walk through her door. The most she could hope for would be a young buck with more money in his pockets than he knew what to do with, and without a pretty young wife waiting for him at home. With them, there were no ulterior motives. They wanted the pleasures she offered and nothing more. They were the easiest to manage because there was no need to play the delicate game of guessing their desires. There was no lingering in the sitting room, pretending as though they had not paid for the use of her body. They went straight to her bedchamber where she could focus on them and forget about herself.

Last night was best forgotten. James roused old needs within her that must remain buried.

A distinctive double knock sounded on her sitting room door. Thankful for the interruption, Rose set her cup on its saucer. Tugging on the end of the fabric belt of her pale green silk dressing gown, tightening it about her waist, she crossed the room and opened the door.

"Thank goodness. You had me worried."

"It is good to see you as well." She stepped aside, allowing her one true friend to enter. "And what did I do to cause such worry?"

"You were late. I thought perhaps . . ." Timothy Ashton dragged a hand through his antique blond hair, further disheveling the untidy layers that were the current height of fashion, and then he shook his head. "But you're here."

"Yes, I am. My apologies if I caused you to worry. It was not my intention." She settled back in her spot on the settee. "Would you care for a tart?"

He waved aside the offer. "I already stopped by the kitchen for a bite to eat."

Clad in only a white shirt and dark brown trousers, his state of casual undress matched her own. Few clients visited the house in the midmorning hours, giving the servants the opportunity to right the house, polishing the floors and removing all signs of the prior night's revelry. And employees like herself and Timothy were afforded a few hours to themselves. The strict rules of decorum lifted, the "wait" for the next client temporarily suspended. Lax and informal, without anyone to please but herself, it was the favorite part of her days at Rubicon's.

Timothy flopped down next to her. The instant his back touched the settee, a grimace flickered across his face, pulling his full lips into a straight line. Concern tightening her brows, she opened her mouth, but he answered her question before she could give it voice.

"Winthrop's a damn brute," he grumbled.

"Why didn't you refuse him?"

"He paid for my time and can therefore do as he pleases with me. In any case, I prefer the likes of him. The ladies can be downright cruel, and I never know what to expect from them."

Even though she had asked, she knew he would not have been allowed to refuse. That was a kindness Rubicon only bestowed on her female employees. The handful of men in the madam's employ who resided in the house understood their wishes were of no importance to her. It was the price they paid for the opportunity to work here, and not at some molly house in the stews.

"Do you want me to take a look at it for you? You should inform Rubicon. She'll have Winthrop's head if he left permanent marks." Guests could do as they pleased . . . as long as they didn't damage the merchandise. That roused Rubicon's anger like nothing else.

"It's nothing. I checked in the mirror and it's not as if he left welts or anything. Just a bit sore, that's all."

That wince had said it was more than "a bit sore." Where Rose had a luxurious little suite, Timothy resided in a tiny room in the attic with the maids and footmen, and worked in a room tucked far below, known only to those guests who had a need for it. She never understood why he subjected himself to that room. Why he chose it over one of the many bedchambers lining the corridor outside her room. She had asked him once and received a puzzling response— he preferred it. How one could prefer to submit so completely to another, to willingly allow oneself to be restrained and abused, never mind how one could derive any pleasure from it . . . Not that she held any illusion Timothy took any pleasure from his time in that room. Far from it.

"You should cry off tonight."

He shook his head. "I worked the last three nights. Likely no one will ask for me tonight anyway. Most of the guests prefer a beautiful woman like you." He gave her a playful wink, but it couldn't hide that sense of stark vulnerability lurking in his deep brown eyes.

She patted her lap. With an ease borne of their years of friendship, he lay down on his side, resting his head on her thigh and draping his long, elegant frame over the settee, knees hooked over the other arm and calves dangling over the edge.

She combed his forelock off his brow, drawing her fingers lightly through his hair, the strands soft as silk. His long lashes drifted closed to rest on the perfect contours of his cheekbones. He had a sort of male beauty that drew the eye of both men and women alike. His features were distinctly masculine yet one could not deny the innate elegance in the sweep of his light brown lashes or the sensual curve of his lower lip. But she had long since stopped being dazzled by his beauty. When she looked on him, she simply saw Timothy. Her dear friend and the only person she had ever confided in.

He let out a little sigh of contentment. "How was your evening?"

"Better than yours."

"Usually is."

With her other hand, she reached for her cup and brought it to her lips. "He kissed me." Her whisper floated over the rich, dark surface of the hot chocolate.

He turned his head to look up at her. "That was all?"

She nodded and tried to hide her smile behind her cup. A little tingle invaded her belly, her cheeks heating with a slight flush.

"Guilt can do strange things to a man," he said pragmatically.

She stared at him for a long moment, and then her stomach dropped.

Why hadn't it occurred to her before?

She wanted to shake her head at her own blindness. And she knew in her gut Timothy had it spot-on. James's hesitation, his reluctance to move into her bedchamber, to ask anything of her . . . it had all been borne from guilt.

Too off balanced by his odd behavior, she had not been able to identify it at the time. But now she knew. He'd had the air of a married man about him, an unhappily married man. One who did not treat infidelity lightly. A rarity, for certain. Most men did not have such a conscience.

Most who frequented the house gave little indication they thought at all of their wives, yet she could never forget the women waiting for them. Those fortunate souls who had a man to call their own. Who had what she had given up so very long ago.

It was why she had left her first protector, after all. She was well aware a fair number of married men kept mistresses, but she refused to ever be one of them. She had made it a rule of sorts when she first came to London all those years ago. She would sell her body but never presume to usurp another's place in a man's heart.

Handsome, intelligent, polite, and obviously wealthy, if he could afford an evening with her, James was the type of man a woman would cherish as a husband. The type that filled the dreams of young girls. There was a lucky woman out there who knew what it felt like to be held by him. Who had been given the gift of his kiss many times over, and then some. But . . . then why was he so lonely, so painfully unhappy?

The answer mattered not. He was married. And it truly was for the best that he never walk through her door again.

"Is something amiss, Rose?"

"No," she replied, forcing her lips into a little smile she hoped would appear nonchalant. It had only been one night. It had not equated with taking something that did not belong to her.

His gaze swept over her face, consideration heavy in his eyes. She braced for him to question her response, but dear friend that he was, he somehow knew not to press the subject.

"Any plans for the day?" he asked.

With a little click, she set the cup down. "I need to make a few stops on St. James Street. The tailor, the boot maker, White's, and I should check at Tattersalls. Dash had mentioned acquiring a team, though I'm hoping he didn't actually purchase one." That would mean he planned to stay in Town and not return to university for the next term.

Timothy frowned. "It's absolutely dreary outside. Surely the errands can wait another day."

"It's best I take care of them today." She would rather find out sooner than later the extent of the damages.

"But what if it rains?"

"When has a bit of rain caused you harm? We'll hire a hackney anyway. Come along." She nudged his shoulder. "I need to get dressed, and you need to get your coat."

"All right," Timothy said on a resigned sigh. He got to his feet and then held out a hand, helping her to stand.

"I'll meet you outside Rubicon's office." She would need funds, after all, to settle Dash's latest bills, and the madam had not yet stopped by her room to deliver the envelope from the prior night's work.

Though last night had been the furthest thing from work.

His parting kiss floated through her mind. Pressing her tingling lips together, trying to vanquish the lingering sensation of his lips upon hers, she went into her bedchamber to change into a practical day dress, suddenly eager to leave the sitting room and escape the memories of James.

Four

"Mr. Archer, it's almost nine o'clock."

James looked up from the paperwork on his desk. The slim form of his secretary, Decker, stood in the open doorway to his office. His plain brown coat held a few wrinkles, his cravat was rumpled as if he had tugged on it a time or two, and his once neatly combed brown hair was a bit untidy. He looked like a man who had spent the better part of his day behind a desk. If James looked in a mirror, he was certain he'd appear just as ragged about the edges as his young secretary.

"Then why are you still here?" James asked.

"Because you are."

At least he was honest about it. Decker had been with him for almost a year. Eager to please and eager to prove himself, he had yet to take James at his word when he told him his hours at the office did not need to match James's. Surely an unmarried man of two-and-twenty had better things to do with his evenings than tend to his employer.

"Have you finished reviewing the manifest for the *Wilmington?*" Decker asked, approaching his desk.

"Yes. Just finished it." James flipped through the pile of documents at his elbow, locating the one in question.

Decker reached out, but James pulled back, keeping the papers out of reach of his ink-stained fingertips. "You needn't see to them tonight. Tomorrow will suffice."

"It will only take a moment—"

"Tomorrow," he said firmly.

Decker stared at the manifest. He opened his mouth and then shut it, his arm dropping to his side, clearly thinking better of pursuing the matter. The candlelight illuminated the dark smudges under his eyes, the exhaustion even more evident in the slump of his usually straight shoulders.

Ah hell. The man wouldn't walk out the door unless James followed close on his heels. Not something James was looking forward to. Just the thought of returning home made him recoil. Perhaps he would merely make a pretense of leaving and then return to his spot behind his desk. He'd receive a heavy scowl from Decker in the morning. Even though he was usually at the office before Decker arrived, the man somehow knew when he spent the night on the leather couch.

The scowl was much preferable to the prospect of coming face-to-face with Amelia. Once a day was more than enough.

"And speaking of tomorrow, we should both head home." He slipped his pen into its holder next to the inkwell and stood, suppressing the wince as his muscles protested the movement. He rolled his shoulders, his joints popping and cracking, reminding him he had not spent the entire day with a pen in hand but a nice portion of the early afternoon in the warehouse.

As he rounded the desk, Decker busied himself extinguishing the candles stationed about the room. The office wasn't impressive by any means. Hell, his dressing room was larger. Just enough space to hold a couple of chairs for visitors, a squat cabinet with more than a handful of scratches marring its surface, a tall book-shelf, his desk, and the brown leather couch, its cushions just on the comfortable side of lumpy. Everything in the room spoke of function over aesthetics. It was a place of business, not a showplace to impress, and James felt more at home here than he did at his town house.

He heard Decker's footsteps behind him as he went out into the main room. A shelf filled with books, ledgers, and rolled-up maps took up one wall. File cabinets, each drawer bearing a little label identifying its contents, lined another wall with Decker's desk just outside the door to James's office, the surface neat and tidy, just like the efficient man.

After grabbing his dark coat and hat, Decker followed him out into the cool night, the scent of the Thames heavy in the damp air, and then James locked the main door and pocketed the key. What had once been a small shipping company was now a thriving enterprise, though one would not know it from the sight of it. His offices were housed in a large, plain, utilitarian warehouse. He had never bothered to relocate to a more fashionable part of town. He preferred to be closer to his business. He could not very well run it properly when he wasn't apprised of the details. All it took was a few steps beyond his office door to verify the quality of the lace from Spain or to inspect the timbers from the Far East. In any case, he would rather do it himself than rely on another. It was the way he had learned to run the business when he had received it as a gift from his father, a reward of sorts, on the event of his marriage.

He bade Decker good evening and watched the young man's retreating back turn the street corner, then James stopped in his tracks. Heaving a sigh, he turned on his heel and retraced his steps. His footsteps echoed on the bare floorboards as he passed through the main room. Weak moonlight seeped through the windows, pro-viding little light. But he didn't need it to reach his destination. He could close his eyes and find his way to his desk without grazing a chair or bumping his thigh on the edge of Decker's desk.

He lit the candle in the plain pewter holder on the corner of his desk. The pool of golden light barely penetrated the darkness beyond his desk, but he didn't bother lighting any of the other candles in the room. The leather chair creaked as he sat down. He rubbed his tired eyes, trying to trick them into believing he hadn't already spent too many hours reading. A useless effort if ever there was one. Giving it up as a lost cause, he took the document off the top of the stack on his left—the "need to do" pile, the "done" being the shorter one on his right—and picked up his pen.

It was so quiet he swore he could hear his pocket watch ticking in his waistcoat pocket. Decker could be working at his desk, the door to James's office closed, and those little noises like a shuffle of feet or the flip of papers would not register in James's mind. He didn't know if it was the darkness backing the windows or the lateness of the hour or the fact that he knew Decker had gone home, but now even the smallest sound seemed amplified. Each little *creak* or *flick* announcing he was all alone.

Three completed pages had been added to the stack on the right when he realized he could not remember a word he had read. With a curse, he went back to the first page and tried to will himself to focus.

Unbidden, plump rose red lips, the edges turned up, materialized in his mind's eye. Damnation, that smile had made him feel good. Just one had been enough to temporarily vanquish the emptiness. He curled his left hand into a fist, savoring the memory of her small, warm hand in his.

His mind began to wander down a path it should not take when the clop of hooves and the rattle of carriage wheels passing the warehouse broke the silence.

No, he should not go to Rubicon's again.

One time. That had been the bargain he had made with himself. And one time it would remain, regardless of how tempting the lure.

He focused again on the document before him, but it refused to hold his attention. Maybe another would do the trick. He shuffled through the stack, pausing on each document as he did so, debating the interestingness of its contents before moving on to the next.

Why had he never realized just how . . . boring his work was? Manifests and contracts, bills of sale and reports on foreign ports, ship repair lists and captains' logs from recent voyages. The epitome of dull.

Letting out a disgusted huff, he pushed back from his desk and grabbed a ledger from the shelf. Perhaps the accounts would hold his attention. The tally at the bottom of the latest entry would hold most any man's attention and certainly garner a decent amount of jealousy. It was the only good thing to come thus far from his marriage. The only success he could claim.

He considered himself a driven fellow, one who strove for success and who took his responsibilities seriously. His father spent his days working, tending to his various business interests and continuing to fill the family's ridiculously large coffers, so naturally as a boy James had envisioned himself following in his father's footsteps. But James doubted even his father could have produced this result over such a short number of years. It took an iron will to be anywhere but at home, and with no place else to go, to be able to produce these staggering results. Hell, if he kept up this pace, he would likely surpass the King's bank account soon enough.

Did he want to keep up this pace? Did he truly need more money? His sigh filled the room, the sound backed with a weariness that could not be disguised. He had more money than he could ever reasonably spend in three lifetimes, so no, he didn't need any more. His office . . . He took pride in what he'd built, but he wasn't so fond of it that he would choose it to the exclusion of all else. If given the choice, he'd much rather not be here at ten in the evening, when all the other souls who labored in his warehouse and in the surrounding buildings had long since gone home to relax and unwind, to enjoy themselves, and for the lucky ones, to spend a few precious hours with someone whose eyes would light with joy at the mere sight of them and would not wish them to an early grave.

He'd much rather be . . .

He glanced over his shoulder to the squat cabinet behind him. It held a pair of trousers, a shirt, cravat, his shaving kit, and the door to the safe hidden in the wall. A safe that contained a couple thousand pounds, more than enough for—

Giving his head a sharp shake, he turned back to the ledger. But before he knew it, he was glancing over his shoulder again. One more visit to see Rose wouldn't cause any harm, would it? Amelia had had scores of lovers, whereas he had never taken one. Had not, until last night, pressed his lips to a woman's since he had said his vows three years ago. But it was more than Amelia's dictates and the unfortunate fact that he was a married man that were responsible for his celibacy. If he only wanted a quick tryst, it could be accomplished easily enough and word of it would never reach Amelia's ears. He passed many taverns on the route home, had occasionally stopped at The Black Dog for a bite to eat, and, on most every visit, the pretty young barmaid had let him know in no uncertain terms that she was more than willing to spread her legs for him.

But quick, meaningless trysts simply weren't in his nature. Twenty-five years of age, and he could count the number of women he had been with on one hand. Hell, he could add Rose to that number and still only need one hand.

Though he would definitely put both hands to good use if given the opportunity again. Those firm, full breasts, the lush flare of her hips, the trim indent of her waist . . . she had a body made for a man's touch. A body that begged to be touched, kissed, thoroughly explored, and thoroughly pleasured.

Her lips had certainly tasted as sweet as she looked. Would the rest of her taste as sweet?

Shifting in his chair, he reached down to reposition his cock in his trousers. Damnation, just thinking of her got him hard. It had been much too long since he'd been with a woman, and at the moment, he felt every one of those long, lonely hours. Each one pressing heavily on him. Each one pleading with him to open that safe. To seize the opportunity he had refused last night.

Letting out a low curse, he dragged both hands through his hair. For God's sake, he was a man. Surely he could not be expected to live the life of a monk forever. Even if Amelia discovered the truth, as long as he was discreet, as long as word never reached her vaunted acquaintances' ears that he wanted anyone other than her, then she could not reasonably refuse to sponsor Rebecca.

Purposefully ignoring the little nudge that Amelia had never shown herself to be reasonable about anything, he pushed from the desk and turned to the squat cabinet. For once in his life he was going to do something simply because he wanted to, and he refused to feel a drop of guilt over it.

⚜

MINDFUL of the madam watching him from the doorway along the white paneled wall in her office, James did his best to keep to a sedate pace as he went up the narrow stairs. The anticipation that had been building for the past hour, during the walk from the docks, pounded through his veins. It felt as though an invisible tether was pulling him toward that darkened door, toward *her*.

He reached for the brass knob and turned it. The last bit of that deadened feeling in his chest slipped away the moment he laid eyes on her.

Clad in a deep amber gown and with her dark hair loosely knotted at her nape, Rose was even more exquisite than he remembered. She rose from her place on the settee and walked to him, unable to mask the slight surprise upon seeing him. Hopefully it was the good kind of surprise.

"Good evening, James."

He held out his hand and she placed hers in his. A jolt shot up his arm. "Good evening, Rose." Bowing, he pressed a light kiss on the back of her hand, just grazing her warm skin. He wanted more. Wanted to pull her close and kiss those beautiful red lips. To have her in his arms once again. But something about the way she looked at him made him hold back.

"Come. Have a seat."

He allowed her to lead him to the settee and took up a spot next to her.

"Would you care for a drink this evening?" she asked, indicating the three glass bottles on the table behind the settee.

He shook his head. He had never been one for spirits. One would think given his size, he could consume an entire bottle of brandy with no ill effects. But since he rarely partook, anything more than one glass dulled his wits. And he had yet to find a spirit that didn't make him grimace at the taste. He had enough reasons to grimace on a daily basis. No need to invite another.

Her gaze went from him to her offering and back to him again. "What do you usually prefer?"

"Coffee. Black."

"Always?"

"When given the option, yes."

Her hand slid free from his as she got to her feet. Crossing the room, she tugged on a bellpull by the bedchamber door. Within a minute she answered the light scratch, opening the sitting room door partway. He heard the soft murmur of her voice but couldn't make out her words.

When she returned to his side, he reached for her hand once again. Silly really, but he couldn't explain why he received so much comfort from simply holding her hand.

Her gaze traveled over his face once again, studying him. The barest hint of a frown pulled her fine brows.

"Is something the matter?" he asked.

"No."

"Well, something's on your mind." That much was obvious.

"I . . ." She lifted one shoulder, dropping her gaze to their joined hands. "I did not expect you to walk through the door tonight." The tone of her voice revealed nothing about her thoughts on the matter.

"To be honest, I didn't anticipate returning, either. It's not something I had planned yesterday. But here I am. Is it a problem that I returned?"

"No."

That "no" had come much too easily, as though automatically. A required response, one not her own. "Would you have preferred it if I had not returned? I'll leave now if you'd like. It is not my wish to impose."

With her free hand, she gave her amber skirt a slight tug, adjusting it. Her silence hung between them. As good as a yes.

At least she did not try to fool him with a lie. He couldn't stomach the thought of her acquiescing because of the pound notes he had paid the madam. The truth, while painful, was much preferable.

She had not wanted to see him again.

Doing his best to keep the stark, sinking disappointment from revealing itself, he made to get to his feet.

Her grip tightened on his hand. "Don't leave."

Breath held, he looked at her askance.

"My apologies. I didn't mean to imply . . ." She shook her head, clearly struggling to explain herself. With a little shrug, she ducked her chin. "You threw me off balance. I thought for certain you would never return."

"Why?"

"You do not seem the type of man to frequent such establishments."

"I don't. This is the only one that contains you."

She glanced up at him through her lashes and captured the edge of her plump bottom lip between her teeth, a question lurking in her light blue eyes.

"Yes?" he queried.

"You are tense tonight."

He highly doubted that was what had been on her mind a second ago. "Versus last night?"

"That was different. And you weren't so tense the entire night." She arched a delicate brow. "But . . . you're holding yourself differently."

"I spent the greater part of the early afternoon sorting a new load of timber in the warehouse." And he had the sore muscles to prove it. Not that he made a habit of lazing about. If he wasn't behind his desk, Decker knew to look for him in the warehouse. But he'd challenge even the strongest of men not to feel the aftereffects of the work he'd done that afternoon. In hindsight, he had likely pushed harder than he should have, but mind-numbing physical labor pushed thoughts of Amelia out of his head like nothing else could.

A knock sounded on the door. She crossed the room, returning with a silver tray bearing a stout white porcelain pot and two cups. The cups clinked lightly on their saucers as she set the tray on the side table. "Couldn't you hire someone to do the work for you?" All traces of her earlier discomposure were gone. Her movements were efficient yet graceful as she poured him a cup of coffee.

She was bent at the waist, displaying her luscious breasts to their best advantage. He dug his fingers into the cushion at his hip, resisting the urge to trace the valley between them, to cup the lush, ivory swells spilling from her bodice, to have the weight of them in his palm.

He felt her gaze on him and looked up, dragging his attention from her chest and back to her question. "I am better able to negotiate the sale if I am familiar with the goods. The choicest timbers fetch the best prices. Though I probably should have asked for more help. I doubt the two who assisted me will be standing tomorrow."

"For you," she murmured, handing him the cup. She walked around behind the settee as he took a sip. He felt her presence behind him the instant before small hands rested on his shoulders and began to knead. "Well then, I shouldn't want you to join their ranks."

Blindly reaching to his right, he set the cup on the side table.

His head lolled forward, chin dropping to his chest. All the pent-up stress whooshed out of him. With unerring accuracy, she found all the right places, carefully working the taut tendons and muscles, massaging out to the apples of his shoulders and then back toward his spine. He couldn't suppress the low grunt as she found a particularly sore spot at the base of his neck and pressed harder, staying just on the pleasurable side of pain.

His eyes drifted shut as slow, sensuous desire washed over him at the feel of her fingers combing through his hair and massaging his scalp. Slow and unhurried, she made her way to his temples, rubbing in soothing circles for a long moment, before traveling back to the nape of his neck. Then those fingers drifted down, over his cravat, pausing to give more attention to his shoulders before working the sore muscles of his biceps.

He felt her warm breath fan his ear a second before she spoke.

"Lie on the floor." Small hands pushed lightly against his shoulder blades.

So utterly relaxed, it took a moment to wrap his mind around her request. He blinked open his eyes. "The floor?"

"Unless you'd prefer my bed." Her whispered words were both a taunt and an open invitation.

"The floor is acceptable." Regardless of his decision to seize the opportunity tonight, he just could not get over the reluctance to walk through the door so many men had gone through. It was as if by remaining here, he could convince himself he was not using her to slake his own selfish desires.

"Come along." She pushed again, though she barely budged him. "Unless you want me to stop?"

Hell, no. He shook his head.

"And remove your coat and waistcoat. All that fabric gets in the way."

Standing, he did as he was bidden, stripping down to his shirt-sleeves, though it wasn't an easy feat since his attention was fixed on her as she swept around from behind the settee. He wouldn't be surprised if he had lost a button or two in the process. Not that he cared. His tailor could see to it tomorrow.

He lowered himself to his knees, then lay on his stomach on the plush rug, resting his head on his folded arms. Her skirts brushed his sides. Silk rustled. And then her weight settled on his lower back. He felt the heat from her core even through the linen of his shirt.

She was bare beneath that dress.

He couldn't keep the deep, low groan inside.

"Am I too heavy for you?" she asked, misinterpreting the source of his groan.

"Oh God, no. Not at all. You're perfect."

She chuckled, light and airy. "I'm glad you think so."

Her hands were pure magic as she worked down the length of his back, her thumbs bracketing his spine and coaxing his muscles to relax. When she reached the waistband of his trousers, she scooted back, and her hands continued down over his buttocks, the tips of her fingers just grazing the crease, and down his legs. He twitched, an involuntary start of a laugh tickling his throat, when she rubbed the backs of his knees.

"Ticklish?" she asked in a soft, playful whisper.

"Apparently."

"I'll have to remember that."

Then she slowly worked her way back up, adept hands coasting over his back in long, slow, generous sweeps, the motion lulling his senses, tempting him to drift off to sleep. She could rub his back all night long and he wouldn't say a word in protest.

Never in his life had he been the object of such undivided attention from a woman. It was a heady feeling, one he could easily grow accustomed to if given the opportunity.

"Turn over." The soft command swept past his ear.

Her weight left his lower back as she moved to kneel beside him. It took more effort than should be required to organize his limbs enough to roll over. Gathering her skirt, she straddled his waist, the amber silk pooling about them. She was positioned perfectly. If only she had asked him to remove his trousers, in addition to the coat and waistcoat . . .

Dragging his attention from the spot where they could have been joined, he looked up at her through his heavily lidded eyes. A lock of her dark hair had escaped the loose knot, and with every move she made, it swayed, the end tickling the valley between her breasts. She rubbed his upper arms, his chest, and down lower. Her fingers lightly brushed his semi-erect cock, making it jump beneath the placket, eager for more attention. Blood pooled in his groin, his length hardening, pushing against the soft wool fabric. But she seemed not to notice, so intent was her concentration as she focused on his thighs.

Just as slowly and thoroughly, she crawled up his body, retracing her path. He was absolutely relaxed yet highly aroused, his body strumming with a unique mixture of bone-melting lethargy and urgent need.

When she reached his shoulders once again, he captured her face and brought her mouth down to meet his.

The first press of her lips placated the frantic lust that had seized his senses. As though he had all the time in the world, he kissed her, relearning the feel of her lips beneath his. Slowly brought his tongue into play, slipping into her mouth, stroking hers. Gently nipped her lower lip, kissed the spot, soothing any lingering sting before diving once again into her kiss and losing himself in the scent of her, the taste of her.

He broke the kiss long before he had taken his fill, somehow knowing he could never get enough of kissing her. It took barely a tug to free her breasts from the confines of her bodice. He wasted no time at all, cupping one firm globe and bringing his mouth to the hardened tip. Sucking at first lightly and then increasing the pressure. He glanced up to see her eyes flutter closed. A slight flush stained her cheekbones. Her lips, glistening wet from their kisses, were parted on quick breaths.

Gathering her in his arms, he reversed their positions, bringing her under him and settling between her thighs, her legs bracketing his hips in undeniable welcome. Shifting his attention to her other breast, flicking his tongue over the sweet tip, he coasted his other hand down her side to delve beneath her skirt, needing to further fuel her passions. Her fingers tangled in his hair. She arched into his touch. To have her pliant in his arms and eager beneath him . . .

He fought back the urge to claim her, to tear at the placket of his trousers and sink into her hot, welcoming body. Instead he let her responses guide him, his fingertips sliding over her slick flesh, pausing every now and then to tease the spot that made her gasp for more. The urge to taste her, to drink up her pleasure, built until he could no longer deny it.

After delivering one last playful nip, he pulled free of her breast and crawled down her body. With hands that shook slightly, he pushed her skirt higher up her waist, revealing the triangle of neatly trimmed dark hair. He caught her gaze, caught her eyes wide with surprise, and then he dropped down and let his ragged breath fan her most intimate flesh.

"James?" His name was caught on a gasp, her body tightening.

"Please, let me," he whispered, needing more than anything to pleasure her.

Her answer came out on a moan of purest need, and it was the most beautiful sound he had ever heard.

A lightning bolt of unadulterated pleasure shot through Rose's body. His mouth was so hot. His tongue slick and agile, with a hint of hesitation behind each hot stroke.

"Oh, James," she sighed.

Then the hesitation slipped away. He explored every fold, every bit of her sex. Light licks, soft flicks, and decadent kisses that threatened to rob her of all sense.

Still, a part of her braced for him to pull away, to quickly crawl up her body and plunge into her. To take what he wanted. She had certainly been the recipient of such pleasures before, but it had been more as a prelude for what they wanted. A small gift thrown to her, and only long enough to tease.

But she had never had a man *ask* to pleasure her. And certainly not as though he wanted it above all. Her skirts were crumpled at her waist, his strong, callused hands on her thighs, holding her open. Persistent, determined, focused solely on her pleasure, he gave no indication of having his sights set on anything more.

She levered up onto her elbows and feasted on James's powerful form laid out before her. His head bowed, tousled hair tickling her sensitive inner thighs, the muscles of his shoulders and biceps rippling beneath the white linen shirt with every movement.

She gasped at the intrusion as one finger was eased inside her. And the next second, before her mind could even fully process the extra layer he had added to his delicious torture, her back arched as he took her clit into his mouth. He sucked, his tongue dancing on the apex of her pleasure. The sensations built within her, coiling ever tighter, winding unbelievably taut. Until they threw her over the edge, the climax rushing through her, her head thrown back in rapture, his name on her lips.

Then her arms gave out and she collapsed back onto the rug. Staring at the white ceiling, she panted for breath, her pulse pounding, shocked over what he had done for her.

He crawled up her body, his eyes heavily lidded and banked with unmistakable triumph. With a quick swipe of his forearm, he wiped his wet mouth.

A firm nudge prodded the back of her hazy mind, reminding her that she needed to get to work. He hadn't paid Rubicon simply to pleasure her. He would expect something in return. She cupped his jaw. "Allow me to repay the favor."

He gave his head a small shake. "Unnecessary." With the lightest of touches, he brushed the loose strands of hair behind her ear.

She thought for certain he was going to kiss her again, but then he dropped his forehead to her chest, his breaths puffing across her bare skin.

She smoothed her hand over his hair, giving him the moment he clearly needed. His body was tensed almost to the point of trembling, the need within him was so strong it was palpable, but he wasn't acting on it. The hard arch pressing into her upper thigh could not be anything but a raging erection. For a reason known only to him, he seemed content to remain in discomfort.

Then she remembered. He was not a man who treated infidelity lightly.

She closed her eyes on a wince as that old ache flared in her chest. Why hadn't she let him leave earlier? She should have. But she hadn't been able to let him walk away, the hurt reflected so clearly on his face at the belief that she did not want him. Because that was the furthest thing from the truth.

A shuddering sigh shook his chest and then he rocked back on his haunches. His hands trembling slightly, a bit of a scowl pulling his brow, he tugged her bodice back in place and then got to his feet, holding out his hand. After helping her up, he turned to retrieve his coat and waistcoat from the floor.

"Do you need assistance?" she asked, as he slipped his arms into his waistcoat.

He shook his head.

Unsure of what to do, she sat on the settee and busied herself trying to smooth the wrinkles in her skirt. The usual course of events apparently did not apply to James. She couldn't offer him a drink—the coffee had surely gone cold by now. And her mind was strangely blank of any topic of conversation, even light, meaningless banter. One would think she was a mere novice and had not watched a man pull on his coat a hundred times before.

"May I see you again tomorrow night?" he asked, as he did up the last button.

An outright refusal was out of the question, of course. A suitable reason would need to be given, and she would not have Rubicon believe James was anything but kind. An evasive answer was her best option. She should definitely not encourage him. Nothing could come from continuing down this path with him. But as she looked into his eyes, as she saw the hurt begin to cloud the soft, olive green depths, she heard the words fall from her mouth.

"I would like that."

Five

ROSE tugged on the cuff of her plain, black leather glove, straightening it. "I shouldn't be long."

Timothy stretched out his long legs as best he could in the confines of the hackney and picked up the newspaper from beside him on the bench, clearly settling in for a wait. "No need to hurry on my account. It's not as if I have anywhere else I need to be at the moment."

A little smile tipped her lips, breaking the determined expression. He accompanied her whenever she left the brothel, even if it was only to remain in a rented hackney while she visited various shops and tradesmen. Just knowing he was nearby was a welcome reassurance, one she could never thank him enough for. But that didn't mean she shouldn't try.

"Thank you."

"For what? For not having any plans for the afternoon?"

"No," she said, with an indulgent shake of her head. "For . . . well, graciously allowing me to drag you with me about town. I truly appreciate it." She didn't know what she would do without him.

"Think nothing of it, my dear." So casually spoken, but his warm smile indicated he understood. He leaned forward and gave her knee a little pat. "Best get on with it. I would ask you to give Dash my regards, but seeing as he doesn't know I exist . . ." He trailed off on a half shrug. "I'll simply wish you a pleasant visit."

"One can hope." After flicking the hood of her cloak up over her head, she reached for the brass lever and exited the hackney. The sun hung high in the clear, blue sky, glinting off the windows of the large, white stucco building. It was a beautiful, warm day. A rarity for early April. She shut the door and went up the stone steps leading to the exclusive bachelor residence. Fortunately she found the corridors empty as she made her way up to the third floor.

The low rumble of a male voice seeped through the first door she passed. Stopping at the second door, she flipped back her hood and knocked once. She had written Dash over a week ago that she planned to be in Town and would visit today, so he should be expecting her.

She had just about given up hope when the door opened, revealing her brother, his black hair disheveled and a pair of wrinkled trousers hanging from his lean hips. Had he gotten taller in the past two months? It seemed like it. He must be over six feet now with another stone's worth of muscle filling out his once lanky frame. New muscles that were on display for all to see, courtesy of the fact that he had neglected to pull on a shirt.

He scrubbed a hand over his face, squinting down at her through eyes heavy with sleep. "Must you stop by so early?"

"It's two in the afternoon," she said, stepping inside. Given Dash had developed a preference for late nights, she had purposely waited until early afternoon to visit.

After giving her cloak to him, she passed through the small entrance hall and into the parlor. Shafts of glittering sunlight cut through the breaks in the partially closed drapes covering the windows, providing enough light to illuminate the room in all its untidy glory. At least a half dozen empty glasses were strewn about, on the cabinet, the side table, and one on its side next to the couch. A black coat, one of its sleeves turned out, covered the back of the wingback chair next to the gray marble fireplace. The dining room beyond the parlor was in an equal state of disarray. Discarded playing cards and a couple of empty bottles littered the mahogany dining table, the chairs pulled out, clearly left exactly as they were when their occupants got up from the table. His bedroom was just off the parlor, the door open, revealing a glimpse of his untidy bed, the dark green damask coverlet bunched at the footboard. Thankfully the bed appeared empty. She would be absolutely mortified if she saw a pair of bare feminine feet sticking out from beneath that coverlet. Dash may be eighteen years of age, but he was still her younger brother.

"I thought you had a maid." She paid the bill for one, in addition to all his other bills.

"I do. She doesn't come by until later." He tugged open the curtains on one of the two windows and then draped her cloak over the back of a nearby armchair. "You can sit down if you'd like," he said, indicating the couch.

Careful to avoid the empty glass on the floor, she settled on the couch. "Do you think you could put a shirt on?"

"Why bother? I'm going back to bed as soon as you leave." He sat down on the arm of the chair that held her cloak. At her disapproving frown, he added, his light blue eyes alight with mischief, "Just be thankful I pulled on a pair of trousers before answering the door."

"Dashell Robert Marlowe," she muttered with a roll of her eyes. "One does not answer the door in the nude."

"It's not like you haven't seen me in all my glory."

"You were three." And he had been running through the house, adeptly avoiding his nanny. The poor woman had definitely had her hands full with him. She stared at him, waiting for his sense of proper decorum to kick in and for him to get off that chair to retrieve a shirt.

He didn't move. He simply met her stare, a chunk of his wavy hair hanging over his brow.

"What brings you to Town?" he asked.

"You. I haven't seen you in a couple months. I just want to make certain you are getting along all right."

"Thanks, Rosie," he said, with that sweet bashful smile that never failed to make her want to envelop him in a great big hug. "But your concern is unnecessary. I'm getting along just fine."

"I can see." She passed an eye over the room.

"The maid will set it all back to rights."

"So you can untidy it again tonight?"

He gave a little confident tip of his head. "Exactly."

She chuckled. She shouldn't encourage him, but she couldn't help it.

"And how have you been? Any news from Bedfordshire? Has any gentleman caught your eye yet?"

"I am fine, as always. No news, and no, no gentlemen have caught my eye." That last part was a lie, but she knew what Dash was asking, and her line of work notwithstanding, James could never be a candidate to fill that particular role.

He passed a hand over the back of his neck, the devil-may-care confidence giving way to concern. "I worry about you, Rose. All alone at that house. Don't you want a husband?"

Why did he have to ask that question? *Of course I do*, she wanted to scream, gripping her clasped hands tightly. But no decent man would ever take a whore to wife. She had reconciled herself to that ugly fact ages ago, but still, the reminder hurt.

Squaring her shoulders, she did her best to appear nonchalant. "I am perfectly content on my own." Yet another lie. "And I am not alone at the house. I have Mrs. Thompson to keep me company," she said, referring to her housekeeper, the only household servant she could afford to employ. "Though if you're so worried, you could visit from time to time."

A scowl flickered over his face.

He hadn't been to Paxton Manor in years, preferring to spend holidays with his friends, and now that he wasn't in school, he spent his time in London. She wished he would at least visit occasionally, if for nothing else than to show some interest in the property that was his birthright, but on the other hand, his complete lack of visits meant he was blissfully unaware she was not at the house one week out of every month.

"Have you given any thought to returning to Oxford for Easter term?"

That scowl deepened. "You came by to pester me about university again, didn't you?"

"Dash," she used her most patient voice, "it's important that you finish school."

"And I will, in my own time."

The same determined and vague answer he had given the last time she had asked. She had learned yesterday on her visit to Tattersalls that he had not planned to return for the next term, but she had to bring up the subject. One didn't purchase a team of two and a curricle unless one planned to stay in Town to show it off. Horses. One more bill to add to Dash's ever-growing pile. A pile that had been much larger than anticipated when she had made her rounds yesterday afternoon with Timothy.

"So you intend to stay in Town for the interim?"

"I like London. It suits me, and it has none of the monotony of the country. It's so frighteningly dull in Oxford."

"It's not supposed to be exciting. You're supposed to be focused on your studies."

His pursed lips said that was the last thing he wanted to be

focused on. To some extent, she could understand. He was a young
gentleman from a good family who believed he had a significant
inheritance at his disposal. London surely posed a strong lure.

"I stopped at the bank today and put some more money into
your account." An account he had bled dry. Again.

"Must you keep me on an allowance?"

"Yes. I daresay most of your acquaintances live on an allowance
from their fathers, so you cannot claim it is unheard of." The allowance kept him from discovering the truth of his inheritance. Not
that it limited his spending one bit. He simply purchased on credit,
leaving her to see to it. She knew that if he was aware his bills were
paid from her own pocket, then he would not be so frivolous. But
she couldn't very well disclose that fact—he would then ask how
she had come about the money. That was the last thing she ever
wanted him to discover. Still, even though the situation was partly
of her own making, she needed to somehow rein him in. If he kept
spending at this rate, he would soon surpass her means and then
she would never succeed in replacing what their father had gambled
away from the family's coffers. "I've also taken care of the bills at
your tailor, the boot maker, your club, and Tattersalls. Are there
any others that I'm not aware of?"

"Thank you, Rose," he mumbled. His gaze skipped about the
room before dropping to his bare feet.

"Dash." Suspicion began to tighten her stomach at the way he
was avoiding her gaze. She looked to the dining room, to the cards
strewn across the table. His bank account had been empty and his
bills much larger than usual, indicating he had not paid for anything with his own funds for some time. Were those cards the reason? Gambling was a common pastime for gentlemen, but Dash
was an impetuous sort. "Are there any other bills?"

"I have an *allowance*." He practically spat the word. His demeanor changed in a blink of an eye. From a defensive boy to a man

fairly bristling with affront. "I'm capable of taking care of *some* of my own affairs."

Oh no. *Please, don't let him be in debt.* She could not watch him become their father. "Dash, have you been gambling?"

He stood, his back ramrod straight and his eyes hard. "Is there anything else you wish to pester me about? If not, thank you for the visit. It was good to see you." With that, he held out her cloak.

So much for a pleasant visit, she thought with a heavy heart as she settled the cloak about her shoulders. She wanted to say something to help him understand how very concerned she was for him, how she only had his best interests at heart, how everything she did was for him, but feared any attempt would push him further away. At the moment, she felt the loss of their father acutely. The man had his vices, but he had been the only person Dash respected. *Adored* was the more apt term. Dash would not have practically shoved him out the door, but listened and given weight to his concerns. Her own? Chalked up to pestering. So without merit that an eighteen-year-old adolescent refused to even consider them.

"I do love you," she whispered.

He let out a heavy breath that broke some of the tension in his spine. "And I you." Then he turned on his heel. "I trust you can see yourself to the door," he called in a flat voice, as he disappeared into his bedchamber.

She made her way back down to the hackney and found Timothy in the same spot she had left him, sprawled on the bench and with the newspaper in his lap.

He glanced up when she opened the door. As soon as she took a place opposite him, he rapped once on the roof and the carriage lurched forward. She looked out to the third floor of the white stucco building, to the window with the open drapes, the one beside it closed. Dash had gotten so defensive, so quickly. Did that mean he was already heavily in debt? What would happen when he could not make good on his vows? She hadn't a clue who he was currently associating with in London. From what little she knew, his old friends were still at university. Why hadn't she thought to ask? She either had met at some point or knew by reputation most of the male population of London. Perhaps that was exaggerating. At least most of the male population who had any sort of social standing. There was a good probability she would have recognized any name he threw out, and then she would have an idea if he was rubbing elbows with the wrong sort, who would not react well if Dash couldn't repay his debts.

The carriage turned a corner and she lost sight of the building. He had given her no real information. Hadn't confirmed or denied her questions. Still, her mind couldn't help but jump to the worst possible outcome.

"Young Mr. Marlowe was not receptive to a discussion about the bills he had left about town?"

"No." She turned to Timothy. "I fear he's gotten himself into debt." At his raised brow, she clarified, "Gambling. Oh, Timothy. What am I going to do? What if something happens to him?"

He flicked his paper to the bench and moved to sit beside her. "Is it that bad?" he asked, taking her hand in his, concern reflected all over his face.

"I don't know. He wouldn't discuss it other than to practically shove me out the door when I asked if he had been gambling. One would think if he wasn't, he would have denied it."

"He shoved you out the door?" His incredulous tone left no doubt to his feelings on the subject.

"No, not physically. More told me to leave in no uncertain terms."

"That brother of yours needs to be reminded of how one behaves around a lady."

"Timothy, the sentiment is appreciated, but Dash's manners are the least of my worries." Nor was she in the mood to deal with another bristly male at the moment.

"Yes, of course." He patted her hand. "Forgive me. We can stop by a few hells, and I can inquire with the croupiers and cashiers. We can start there. He hasn't been in town all that long. Surely it can't be so bad."

. . . yet. But Timothy's suggestion was a good one. She should not allow the worry to overwhelm her until she had something more concrete to base it on. Vague, whisper-thin assumptions did more harm than good.

"Shall we start now?" He made to raise his knuckles toward the ceiling, to alert the driver of a new destination.

"No," she said, suddenly too weary to deal with more unpleasant news today. "There isn't enough time, and I can't be late again. Best we return to the house—I need to start getting ready for work."

A bath, wash her hair, have a bite to eat, select a gown, and then the dreaded wait for the door to open. *May I see you again tomorrow night?* James's voice drifted through her head. An evening where she wouldn't have to spread her legs for a selfish stranger, but where she could spend a few precious hours with *him.* Last night, alone in her bed, she had finally decided to stop trying to make sense of his perplexing behavior. He'd had his own reasons for walking through her doorway and leaving without availing himself of her offer. Unhappily married or not, it was highly unlikely she'd ever learn the truth.

But he had not actually said he would return tonight. Merely asked if the possibility existed. One would have thought he'd be more definitive if he truly wished to see her again. And Rubicon had made no mention earlier today that James had secured her for the coming evening.

No use at all getting her hopes up. He wouldn't return. It would be too much to ask. And in her experience, needing something was a sure way to have it ripped from her grasp.

❧

JAMES set down his pen and pulled out his pocket watch. Only a quarter till eight? It felt like significantly more than ten minutes had passed since he had last checked his watch. He glanced to the stacks of papers on his desk. Everything that absolutely needed to be completed today had been finished and passed off to Decker before noon, leaving the afternoon to oversee the sale of the timber and visit Canning Dock to check how the repairs were progressing on the *Prosperous*.

The stacks remaining on his desk would not take care of themselves but . . .

The hell with it.

He flicked the cover closed on his watch, tucked it back in his waistcoat pocket, and pushed from his desk. Less than a minute later he was closing his office door behind him, his coat pocket no longer empty and his step considerably lighter.

"Is there something you need, sir?" Decker asked, his pen poised above the open ledger on his desk.

"Yes. For you to head home."

"But . . ." Decker glanced to the brass clock on the wall. "Are you leaving?"

James couldn't help but chuckle. The young man could not look any more perplexed. "Yes. I do believe you've seen enough of me for one day. Come along and put the pen down. Whatever you're working on can wait until tomorrow."

He made quick work of extinguishing the candles as Decker grabbed his hat and coat. Key in hand, he left the office, his secretary hurrying after him, and locked the door.

"Have a good evening, Mr. Archer," Decker said as he pulled on his coat.

"Thank you. I shall." Though he planned to have more than merely a "good" evening. "And a good evening to you as well."

They parted ways, Decker heading north toward his apartments in Cheapside and James heading west, to Curzon Street. To Rose.

The anticipation that had been strumming his nerves, pushing him to continually check his watch and pulling his attention from his work, began to course through his veins. Since he had awoken that morning, thoughts of her had been ever present. How many times had he wanted to smack himself for not letting her put those amazing hands to good use? Instead, what had he done? Put his own hand to use the moment he had laid his head on his pillow last night. The sweet taste of her lingering on his tongue, the image of her sprawled decadently on the floor of her sitting room fixed in his mind, her skirt at her waist and bared to his view . . . It hadn't taken but a minute before his hand had been coated in his seed. He had promptly fallen to sleep, only to be awoken before the sun had risen, the dream so fresh in his mind he had frankly been amazed he hadn't found a wet spot on the sheet.

He shook his head at himself, a laugh rumbling in his chest. The woman had the power to make him feel like an adolescent. Hell, he hadn't woken up to a wet sheet since he was fourteen.

But that dream . . . His stride faltered as a jolt of lust shot through him. He fully intended to realize it tonight. The only thing he had not yet sorted out was where.

He looked up. The beautiful day had carried into the night, the air like warmed velvet whisking across his face, the stars bright in the clear sky. On rare nights like this he usually took a short detour into Hyde Park where he would sit on one of the benches and enjoy the tranquility before heading to his town house. The park was the closest thing to the country that could be found in the city. Sitting on that bench, surrounded by green grass and with the oak trees behind him, he could imagine himself in the back garden at Honey House, the country property he had purchased shortly after his marriage.

Pausing at a street corner, he waited for a hackney to pass and then crossed the street. Hadn't Rose mentioned that she enjoyed walks in the park? Her favorite spot was the Serpentine.

A smile spread across James's mouth. He quickened his pace, suddenly more than eager to reach Curzon Street.

Six

JAMES tugged the drapes open. His tall, broad-shouldered form blocked the view beyond her sitting room, but Rose knew there wasn't much to see in the dark back courtyard below. Instead she contented herself admiring the way his navy coat stretched across his muscular back, tapering to his hard waist.

"It's a beautiful night," he said.

Well, that explained why he had wanted to open the drapes she usually kept shut. Though she thought it an odd request from him, she had indulged him all the same.

He turned from the window. "Though it cannot compare to you."

"Of course not. What could?" she teased.

Rich and full-bodied like a fine Bordeaux, James's laugh filled the room as he returned to the settee, settling beside her once again, her hand instinctively finding his. "Indeed."

His mood was remarkably light and completely infectious, a smile lurking on his mouth since he had walked through her door.

The same smile that had curved her lips the moment she had laid eyes on him tonight.

He had returned.

She chuckled, unable to keep it inside. Having convinced herself he would not return, his appearance had been so unexpected it felt like a gift. On some level she was aware she should not want him to be here. It was a dangerous thing to be presented with her heart's deepest desire night after night yet knowing nothing but the most painful disappointment could ultimately come from it. But it was becoming so very difficult to think beyond the moment when she was with him. Each moment precious, each one demanding she savor it to its fullest.

They sat side by side on the settee, so close she was pressed against him, one long line from her shoulder to her knee. The coffee service was on the side table, the lone cup now half full. She should have asked him to prod the fire in the hearth when he had gotten up to open the drapes, but the fire could burn down to embers for all she cared. Just being with James warmed her from the inside out.

He brought their joined hands up, pressing a light kiss to the back of her hand. "Will you take a walk with me in the park? It is a beautiful night, and I want to share it with you."

She stiffened. "The park?"

"Yes. Hyde Park. You said you enjoyed walks about the park. You could show me your favorite spot by the Serpentine."

"Tonight?" That light, airy feeling in her chest drained away.

A crease formed between his brows. "Yes. Or is this a request I should not be asking of you?"

"You may ask," she murmured. Though no man had asked before. The same request from any other would have been answered with a coy refusal. No consideration at all. Within these walls, her safety was assured. One shout or one tug on a bellpull would right any situation. But by leaving, she would give up that security.

James had certainly given her no cause at all to distrust him. Still, she couldn't stifle the tension that wound its way into her belly at the mere thought of leaving the house.

His gaze swept over her face. "Is there a reason why you don't want to accompany me on a walk?"

"It's late. London's not safe at night." She threw the excuse out there, though it was a very valid excuse. Even the streets in Mayfair were not safe at night for a young woman on her own.

"I won't allow any harm to come to you." He spoke so casually, like one who didn't need to back his words with conviction. His mere word was enough. Turning his shoulders toward her, he cupped her cheek with his free hand. He brushed the pad of his thumb over her bottom lip. "Please. Share the night with me."

The pleading look in his eyes, as though he needed it more than anything . . .

Capturing her bottom lip between her teeth, she nodded.

"Yes?"

"Yes," she confirmed.

A grin split his face. He pressed a quick kiss to her lips then shot to his feet, moving remarkably fast for such a large man. "Shall we depart?" he asked, helping her to stand.

She pushed the hesitation aside. "If you would like. Let me get my cloak. I'll be but a moment."

When she returned to the sitting room, the cloak about her shoulders, she found him standing exactly where she had left him. He held out his hand and she placed hers in his. She made to lead him out the main door of her sitting room, but this time it was he who hesitated.

He glanced to the narrow door.

"That door only leads to Rubicon's office. We have to go out this way. But I prefer to avoid the receiving room whenever possible, so we won't use the front door." They would have to pass through the receiving room to reach the front door, and Rubicon would likely be presiding over the evening as the other women in the house did their best to tempt the guests to part with a fold of pound notes. Though Rubicon had never specifically forbidden her from leaving the brothel with a client, she doubted it was something the madam would encourage and she would rather avoid any questions, if at all possible. "We'll take the servants' stairs to the back door, if that is acceptable with you."

The smile returned. "Quite acceptable, thank you."

Was it her imagination, or was that relief in his voice? Whatever the cause, she was grateful for it. She led him out the main door of her sitting room, along the corridor that was thankfully empty, and down the stairs, where she paused to flip up her hood before going out to the back courtyard.

A light breeze ruffled the hem of her cloak. She stayed so close to him that her shoulder brushed his biceps with each step she took. He seemed completely at his ease in the darkened alley behind the brothel, his strides loose yet obviously slowed to match hers. His tall, powerful presence provided a welcome reassurance, and by the time they reached the street, she had stopped glancing into the shadows.

The Season hadn't yet started so the streets were relatively empty so late at night. Just the occasional carriage passed as they wound their way to Park Lane and then around to the entrance of the park. The moment they stepped through the gates the sounds of the city seemed to fade to nothingness.

They passed Rotten Row, heading toward the Serpentine. Trees bordered the lane, the leaves rustling softly in the breeze. The moon hung high in the sky, gilding the surrounds in silver light. It was the same park she had visited countless times, yet it looked so much more beautiful at night. Like a veil of tranquility had fallen over it.

"I've never been to the park at night." She spoke in a low voice. The quiet around them amplified every sound, making even the crunch of dirt beneath her slippers seem loud to her ears.

"I have. Many times. I usually sit on that bench over there." He indicated a wooden bench tucked beneath the high branches of an oak tree. Then he stopped in his tracks, pulling her to a stop as well. "It's difficult to talk to you when you're hiding in that hood. I can't see your beautiful face." He reached up, his hand hovering at the edge of her hood. "May I?" he asked in an undertone.

It was only the two of them. She hadn't seen another soul since they had stepped into the park. Looking up at him, she nodded. Warm air brushed over her head as he lowered the hood.

"Better," he declared. "But . . ."

He reached up again. She felt a light tug on the back of her head and then her hair tumbled down her back.

"That's much better." He tucked the ivory knitting needle she had used to secure her hair in a knot into his coat pocket. "Now where is this favorite spot of yours?"

"Up ahead a bit. Right before the lane curves toward The Ring."

They picked up their ambling pace and had continued on for a bit in companionable silence when he spoke again.

"Did you spend your morning at the park today?"

"No. A couple errands took up most of my day." *Dash*, she thought with a frown, recalling her visit. But she refused to allow the worries to spoil her evening with James. "How about yourself? I assume you spent your day at your desk and not with a load of timber."

"And why is that?"

"You aren't stiff like you were last night."

"I split my day between my desk and the docks, checking on a ship. I also took care of the sale of the timber. And thank you, by the way, for last night. My apologies for not giving it at the time, but in my defense I was rendered quite senseless by the experience. I've never before been the recipient of such attentions. You are truly a woman of exceptional talents."

She hadn't done much of anything except give him a massage,

blatantly using the opportunity to run her hands over every inch of his body. "You're welcome, but I believe I am the one who should be thanking you." A flush heated her cheeks, a tingle sweeping through her body at the memory of his mouth on her most intimate flesh.

His grip briefly tightened. She swore she heard his breath catch.

"Your thanks, while appreciated, are unnecessary." He leaned closer, his voice dropping to a low rumble that brushed her ear. "I enjoyed myself far too much."

The once easy, companionable air between them was engulfed by a sharp spark of attraction. She was suddenly intensely aware of him. Of the way his coat brushed her arm. The way the clean, masculine scent of him filled her every breath. Of the strength and the power of the man beside her. She wanted to touch him, run her hands over those strong muscles she had lavished with attention last night. Press her lips to his and experience his kiss once again.

Her pulse quickened, liquid warmth pooling between her thighs. In a daze of desire, she led him off the path and toward her favorite spot along the Serpentine. He pulled his hand free from hers and removed his coat. Ignoring the nearby bench, he laid his coat out on the grassy, downward-sloping bank.

"For you," he said with a little bow, his cream waistcoat and white shirtsleeves so very bright against the darkness of the trees behind him.

With a murmur of thanks, she sat down on his coat, adjusting her skirt about her legs folded neatly beside her. He settled next to her, one leg stretched out before him, the other casually pulled up, his elbow resting on his knee and his other hand braced behind him. It seemed so natural for him to be there, as if he belonged at her side. The night was quiet around them, the reflection of the stars above glittering like diamonds in the water. But the sight did not hold her attention for long. She looked to him, soaking up the way the moonlight caressed his profile, highlighting the strong line of his jaw, the curve of his cheekbones, and the fan of his lashes.

As if he had felt her regard, he turned his shoulders to her, catching her gaze. It was too dark for her to make out the color of his eyes, but she swore they had turned darker, to the deep passion-soaked green she had glimpsed last night when he had been crouched above her, his hot mouth on her breast.

Her nipples hardened, the sensitive tips pressing against her chemise, eager to be tormented anew. Her lashes fluttering, it was all she could do to keep the moan of longing inside.

He slowly reached out to cup her cheek, his long fingers curving around the side of her neck, and ever so slowly leaned closer. She felt herself swaying toward him, her lips parting, wanting his kiss more than anything. But when his mouth met hers, it wasn't with the harsh bite of tightly leashed lust that crackled between them. Rather his lips glided over hers in a sweetly passionate kiss that went on and on.

His kisses made her feel so young, as though each one were her first, wiping away every other that had come before him. How she wished this man could have been her first. Her only.

They had snuck out into the night, escaping like young lovers. It made this night so very different. There were no obligations. No press of responsibility to see to his desires. Only a shared wish for pleasure. She did not *have* to be here with him. Yet she wanted more than anything to be right here, where she was. Next to him.

It seemed like forever and yet no time at all when the kiss shifted, the innocence falling away. With a groan that rumbled in his chest, he slanted his lips over hers, his tongue slipping into her mouth to stroke hers, fueling the flames of desire.

Then he leaned into her until she was on her back, he half on his side, his weight braced on an elbow, their kiss still unbroken. As their tongues tangled together, warm fingers drifted from her neck to brush her collarbone. She felt the clasp release, and the soft wool of her cloak was pushed aside.

She arched into him as he palmed one breast, thumb teasing the tip, sending a jolt of need straight to her core. Unwilling to lose his kiss, she blindly reached out until her fingertips located the small fabric-covered buttons on his waistcoat. A moment later she had the buttons undone and was tugging on the placket of his trousers. A quick tug and his shirt was pulled from his trousers. She delved eagerly beneath the hem, encountering bare skin so hot it almost scorched her palm. Her hands glided over the hard ridges of his abdomen, his muscles jumping beneath her touch.

So absorbed by his kiss, by the harsh breaths puffing against her cheek, by the masculine scent of him mixed with the spicy hint of sweat, and by the luxury of being able to finally touch his bare skin, she wasn't aware he had inched up her skirt until a work-roughened hand began coasting up from her knee, leaving a path of tingling skin in its wake. At the whisper-light touch on her inner thigh, she couldn't stifle the moan. She pressed against him, needing more, her legs falling open. One fingertip slipped over her most delicate flesh, slicked from her arousal. Gasping into his mouth, she slid a hand down to reach into the open placket of his trousers.

He dropped his head to her neck, breaking the kiss. "Oh God, Rose. *Yes.* Touch me."

Raw and stripped bare, the heavy need in his plea turned into a ragged groan as she curled her hand around hot silken skin, carefully pulling him free of the confines of his trousers. A shudder racked his body. His mouth on her pulse, his day's beard tickling her neck, he thrust his hips into her touch as she learned every inch of his impressive length. Her insides fluttered at the thought of his thick cock sliding into her. Taking her. Possessing her. Making her his own.

The passion built between them to almost unbearable levels; his hand between her thighs, adept fingers sweeping over her clit, coaxing the orgasm ever nearer. Then with a low growl, he shifted, moving until he was crouched above her, his white-shirted arms on either side of her shoulders. With her skirt bunched up to her waist, her legs came up to bracket his hips, welcoming his weight. Relinquishing her hold on his erection, she curved around to the sleek sweep of his lower back, sliding down beyond his loosened waistband to grip the firm globes of his arse.

He captured her mouth again, the kiss pulling her even further under his spell. The only thought in her head was giving herself over to him completely, becoming his, until the blunt head of his cock pressed against her core, jolting her harshly to her senses.

Twisting her head, she broke the kiss and pushed abruptly on his shoulders. Crouched above her, he immediately stopped.

She panted, struggling to catch her breath. The harsh bite of need rode over every inch of her skin. A part of her wanted him so desperately . . . regardless. Wanted to be with him here and now, with the moon high in the velvet sky and soft sounds of the Serpentine surrounding them. But practicality reared its ugly head. The risk was much too great.

"I'm sorry, James, but we can't."

"Pardon?"

Even in the darkness, she could make out the confusion on his face. "Not here, at least. I want you." She cupped his jaw, willed him to believe her. "I do. Desperately. But before we left the house, I neglected to . . ." Her cheeks heated with more than desire. With the stinging flush of embarrassment. Why was it so hard to explain it to him? "I'm sorry. I should have known you would want . . ."

Why hadn't it occurred to her? It certainly should have. He clearly did not want to be in her bedchamber, and after last night, this was the next logical step. She should have known he would find some way to be with her, on his own terms. But she had been too preoccupied with his request to leave the brothel to discreetly excuse herself for a moment and slip behind the silk screen to see to a sponge before walking out the door. And she highly doubted he had a sheath in one of his pockets. If he had, then he would have put it to use and she would not be in this horribly uncomfortable position right now.

"We can return to the house, if you'd like. Or I could . . ." She drifted her hand down from his shoulder.

He gave his head a sharp shake, halting her hand before she reached the open placket of his trousers. "You speak of protection against conception?"

"Yes," she admitted, mortified it was even a requirement. A man like James should be with a woman who loved him, who welcomed the opportunity to bear his sons. Not someone like her.

"I don't want to return to that house. I want to be with you here, far away from there." He paused. "Do you trust me?"

She opened her mouth, but could not get the word out. It should not be so difficult to say yes. But she held back. The years had taught her that trust was not something to be given lightly.

"I will not spill myself inside of you. You have my word." His still-labored breaths fanned her cheek. "You trusted me enough to come here with me. Trust me in this. Please."

It was a risk she had never been willing to take. Never even been given a reason to contemplate. But . . . it wasn't a risk with him. Her gaze swept over his face. Stark, raw need coupled with conviction. He did not demand. He asked. She knew in her gut that he would not take anything she did not want to give. If she refused him, he would not vent his frustrations on her, but simply abide by her wishes. A gentleman to his core. And her trust in him was all-complete.

Her lashes swept down and she nodded.

"Thank you." The words rumbled around her, more breath than sound. The relief clear as the night's sky.

His mouth found hers and passion ignited, seizing hold of her once again. She arched into him, needing him, wishing she could bare every inch of her body to him. To press skin against skin.

Slowly, ever so slowly, he pushed inside, stretching her to her limits in the most delicious, scandalous way. Buried to the hilt, he paused. A tremor shook his powerful body.

"Rose, you're so . . . *perfect*." The reverent awe in his voice stole the breath from her chest. Then he eased back and glided in deep.

His mouth was on hers, on her cheek, on her neck, the most beautiful words whispered against her skin, as he plied her with slow, purposeful strokes, lavishing her body with the utmost attention. Never in her life had she felt more cherished. Yet she could sense the effort he expended to hold back. It was in the rock-hard biceps beneath her hands, in the hoarse grunts echoing from his broad chest.

She clung to him, lost in the lush tide of sensations, never wanting it to end. The waistband of his trousers rubbed against her inner thighs, the linen shirt grew damp beneath her touch, his pace quickening, matching the need building sharply within her. Shifting up a bit, he changed the angle of his thrusts. Each downward stroke grazing her clit before hitting the most sublime spot inside of her. Again and again. Until the orgasm overtook her, bringing waves of mind-numbing pleasure chasing down on her, her high cry of completion lost in the hot recesses of his mouth.

The climax still rocking her senses, he abruptly pulled back, pulling free of her body, and reached down. An unprecedented urge to hold him close, to keep him with her, seized hold. But she fought it down and instead drank in his groan of completion as a shudder racked his body.

He flopped down on his back on the grass next to her. His panting breaths were sharp and hard in the night air. His hand found hers and he tugged. "Come here."

She eagerly rolled over and moved to lie on top of him. Her legs on either side of his, her cheek pressed to his chest. Strong arms wrapped around her, held her close. A languid, lazy haze fell over her.

The rhythm of his chest gradually slowed until it approached normal levels. She felt his lips brush the top of her head.

"I should see you back home. Can't very well keep you here."

"All right," she said, not wanting to move from the warmth of his body, but knowing he was right. She couldn't remain with him forever. Only for the night.

She reluctantly moved off to kneel beside him and smoothed her fingers through her hair, doing her best to tame the tousled mess. He stood and quickly righted his clothes, tucking in his shirt, doing up his trousers, and buttoning his waistcoat. She handed him his coat and he slipped it on. He helped her to her feet and then reached down for her cloak, gave it a snap, shaking the grass free, and settled it about her shoulders. She smiled as his large hands fumbled a bit with the clasp before it snapped together.

"Turn around." At his furrowed brow, she clarified, "Your coat. I doubt you want to bring blades of grass home with you."

She took her time smoothing her hands down his back, whisking the proof of their night from the navy wool, pausing to briefly knead his shoulders and receiving a soft rumble, almost a purr, in response. Then hand in hand, they went up the bank and followed the path to the entrance of the park in companionable silence.

They reached the back courtyard far quicker than she would have liked. She stopped outside one of the pools of golden light streaming from the kitchen windows.

"Will I see you again?" She wished she could take the words back as soon as they left her lips. Why had she opened herself up to a "no"? Bracing for the inevitable rejection or vague, noncommittal response, her gaze flittered to the door.

"Yes, if you would like that."

Her eyes snapped back to him. "Really?"

"Would you like me to return?"

"Yes. Please." Oh dear Lord, and now she sounded like a desperate, lovesick girl.

"Then I will. Tomorrow." It was all she could do not to lean into his touch as he tucked her loose hair behind one ear. "I promise."

"I would not object if you left your desk a bit earlier than usual."

He tipped his head. "An easy enough request. Consider it done. Good night, Rose." He bowed, pressing a kiss to the back of her hand. "Until tomorrow night."

Seven

DUCKING to fit through the narrow door, James stepped into his town carriage and settled on the black leather bench, careful to keep his legs from brushing the skirt of Amelia's pristine ivory silk gown. Frankly he was surprised she had chosen to sit across from him—she usually made certain to keep as much distance from him as possible, as if mere proximity would somehow taint her. But then again, they had an audience tonight.

The door snapped shut. The carriage shifted slightly as the footman took his place next to the driver. With a jangle of harness, the carriage lurched forward, leaving behind the hustle and bustle of the people and carriages lining the front of Drury Lane.

"The performance was lovely, don't you agree, James?"

"Yes, quite lovely," he replied with a tip of his head.

Adjusting the light blue shawl about her shoulders, Rebecca turned to Amelia, who sat beside her, and launched into a discussion about the evening. The honest and uninhibited joy on her face was a sharp contrast to Amelia's haughty, cool elegance. The light from the small brass lantern hanging on the wall picked up the golden strands in Rebecca's chestnut brown hair coiled in a demure knot at her nape. The two women could not be more different, yet his younger sister seemed to admire Amelia. He could only hope her foray into the ton would not turn her into a replica of his wife.

Apparently Rebecca's efforts to sway their father had been met with complete success. An outcome he hadn't doubted. It had simply been a matter of time before she showed up on his doorstep, her trunks in tow, containing the wardrobe for her first Season. Though he had been a bit surprised when he'd received her note, announcing her arrival, that afternoon. His mind had been firmly on Rose, their night together filling his head and providing a decadent distraction from the papers on his desk. While he had looked forward to his sister's visit, the reminder that the Season was fast approaching was not a welcome one, jolting him harshly back to the reality of his life. Any hope he had held that he'd still have a few evenings of freedom left before him were dashed with the last line of Rebecca's note.

. . . and Amelia's promised an evening at the theatre to celebrate my arrival in Town.

An evening in which he had been certain his presence was included. He kept a box at Drury Lane. It was more Amelia's than his, but he had taken Rebecca a few times in the past. He knew she enjoyed it—she was actually one of the few who watched the proceedings on the stage and did not spend the entire performance socializing and gawking at those in the neighboring boxes. A part of him had been shocked by Amelia's generosity. That she had remembered Rebecca's love of the theatre showed she *was* capable of considering someone other than herself.

Split between a desire to see his sister and dreading the thought of the coming hours with Amelia, he had left his office long before the sun had set. Not that he hadn't planned to leave early, just not quite that early. He had given Rose his word after all. A word he could still loosely hold true to, as it wasn't yet eight in the evening. He'd see his sister and Amelia home, pick up the fold of pound notes he had left in his bedside table drawer, and then head straight to Curzon Street. To Rose.

Turning to look out the carriage window, he reached into his coat pocket, sliding his fingertips over the smooth ivory knitting needle. The night sky backed the buildings that slipped by, one by one, as he moved closer to her. The buildings eventually gave way to neat rows of town houses and neatly manicured squares as they entered Mayfair. They passed Hanover Square and then turned right on Davies Street.

Right?

His head snapped to Amelia. "This isn't the route home."

The straight line of her shoulders stiffened. She pulled her attention from Rebecca. She kept her face schooled in a pleasant expression, the same one she wore whenever they had an audience, the same one that fooled even his sister, but her light blue eyes were completely devoid of warmth. "Of course not. We accepted an invitation to dine with Lord and Lady Markson."

She spoke as though he had reason to have knowledge of their social calendar. Where they went on a given night usually held little importance to him. He had no say in which invitations she chose to accept, nor would he know which ones should be accepted. He had never cared to give the matter much attention. Strict black evening attire fit most every function, so knowledge of the destination was not necessary to dress appropriately.

"But Rebecca just arrived today. The theatre I can understand, but surely she will wish to retire early tonight." Somerset wasn't an easy distance from London. Depending on the condition of the roads and the time of her departure, Rebecca had been traveling since at least Thursday in order for her to arrive by carriage on Saturday afternoon. Hell, she must have convinced their father to allow her to depart early for London before James had even received her letter asking for his assistance in swaying their father.

"I have no wish to retire early, James. The journey was an easy one. All I did was sit for days with only Beth for company," Rebecca said, referring to her staunch and rather intimidating maid. Between Beth and the two burly footmen who accompanied her whenever she traveled, her safety along the roads and at various coaching inns was more than secured. "And it's only a late supper party. No more than a couple dozen guests."

Of course his sister would know more about Amelia's plans for the evening than he did. They had probably discussed it at length that afternoon and likely had been discussing the party for the past half hour, while he had been preoccupied with thoughts of his own plans for the night ahead; the soft drone of their feminine voices simply unable to compete with Rose.

"Lord and Lady Markson's supper party is an ideal event for Rebecca's first introduction into Society." He had to give Amelia credit. She managed to speak to him without her lip curling in disdain. The woman was fit for the stage. "An intimate affair before the start of the Season. And there will be a few eligible and quite suitable gentlemen in attendance, Lord Brackley being one of them."

Brackley? The man was almost double Rebecca's age. A fact James only knew because the man had visited their box during one of the intermissions. James hadn't paid him much notice except to ensure he behaved appropriately toward Rebecca, which he had. But regardless of his age, Brackley was an unmarried earl, and therefore fit his father's requirement that Rebecca marry a titled lord.

This was why he had tied himself to Amelia, after all. She possessed all the right connections and an intimate knowledge of the inner workings of the ton. She knew who would be suitable and who would not, and could provide the all-critical introductions to the former. With Amelia as her sponsor and as her sister by marriage, all

Rebecca would need was the massive dowry from their father to wipe away the stigma of trade and assure her acceptance into Society.

The girl was all sweet kindness, a replica of their beautiful mother they had lost as children. Any man should count himself fortunate to have the opportunity to take her to wife. She shouldn't need anything other than herself, but that was the way of the aristocracy. One's own personal merits mattered little, when compared to blood, connections, and bank accounts.

Rebecca leaned forward, her hands clasped on her lap. "Please, James. I do so want to attend."

How could he deny her, when her excitement was so clear on her face? She had been looking forward to this for years, and he couldn't very well refuse her first supper party simply because he had his own plans for the evening. Not that his opinion truly mattered. He could feel Amelia's gaze on him, feel her annoyance over the fact that he dared to question their destination. She set their social calendar. That he would serve as a mute escort was a foregone conclusion. Well, the Season had not officially started yet, but . . .

The expectant smile lit up Rebecca's face. He adored her, honestly he did. The only thing that had made the theatre even begin to approach enjoyable had been her presence. But he would much rather spend time with her outside of the ton.

He kept the sigh of resignation from filling his chest. "Of course we'll go to the Marksons', Rebecca, if that is what you wish."

One more delay, but as he closed his hand around the ivory in his pocket, he took solace in the knowledge that he could still look forward to seeing Rose afterward.

⚜

CLAD in stockings, chemise, and stays, Rose contemplated the gowns in her closet. Her hair, almost dry from her bath, hung loose about her shoulders. Servants had already taken away the porcelain tub, but the humid air was still thick with the scent of roses.

An early evening bath in her bedchamber. A decadent luxury for certain, but she had not been able to resist. The fire in the grate warming the room as she had lazed in the hot water, savoring the anticipation of the coming night. Of being with James once again.

Dressing for the evening had always been a chore. But not tonight.

She grabbed the skirt of the mauve gown and pulled it from the others. No. He'd already seen her in that one. The violet? Her lips twisted in a grimace. Her fingertips skimmed over gauzy amber muslin, soft gray velvet, settling on the navy silk.

I usually prefer blue. James's voice drifted through her head.

A smile curved her lips. She took the dress off the peg and held it up. Simple and unadorned, designed to draw the attention to the swells of her breasts and not the gown itself.

Perfect. But she would need Jane's help. The gown was the only one in her wardrobe with buttons down the back. Without a regular lady's maid, it was a necessity to have gowns designed so she could easily dress herself, not to mention get out of them herself. Not all gentlemen relished the role of lady's maid. But the modiste had protested that buttons would ruin the simplicity of the plunging, heart-shaped bodice. Rose had not been able to help but agree.

She pulled the bellpull located beside the bedchamber door, not the one within arm's reach of her bed. That one would cause a burly footman to burst into her rooms. A safety precaution, for use in the event of clients who decided not to be on their best behavior.

Too impatient to wait for Jane, she slipped on the gown. Reaching behind, she held the back closed with one hand and studied her reflection in the oval mirror above the dresser. The dark fabric coupled with her dark hair made her skin appear as fair as palest ivory. She avoided black fabric—it washed her of all color. But the rich navy contrasted perfectly with her skin.

A knock soon sounded on her sitting room door. With the gown hanging off her shoulders, she opened the door. It didn't take Jane but a few moments to do up the back, her nimble fingers making quick work of the small, fabric-covered buttons.

"Anything else?" Jane asked.

"No, not at the moment, but I'll ring later for a pot of coffee. No need to bring sugar or cream."

She locked the door behind Jane and hurried back into her bed-chamber. Which slippers to wear tonight? The navy, of course, to match the gown. Lifting the hem, she slipped her feet into them, and then paused. Perhaps white stockings were not the best choice. The hem pulled to her knee, she lifted a leg and contemplated the stockings. Black would not do. It would seem like she was trying but failing to match the navy. She should have thought to purchase a navy pair when she commissioned the gown. Perhaps tomorrow she would drag Timothy to Bond Street. If James liked the gown as much as she anticipated, then he may want her to wear it again for him.

The white would just have to do. In any case, the silk was so fine and sheer it rather blended with her skin.

After brushing her hair that had finally dried from her bath, she pulled open the top dresser drawer and poked around in the copper tin of pins and ribbons, looking for . . .

She closed her eyes. The memory of her hair tumbling down her back and of James's pleased smile materialized in her mind. Had he merely forgotten to return the ivory knitting needle, or had he intended to keep it?

Her feminine vanity wanted to believe the latter. That he had wanted to keep some token of her. Silly notion. Practical, grown men did not do such things. Still . . .

Smiling, she found a few silver pins and pulled up her hair into a loose knot at her nape. Using the mirror, she freed a few select strands and wound them around her finger, encouraging the natural wave of her hair.

She didn't bother with perfume—her skin still held the light scent of the rosewater she had used in her bath. Nor did she bother to glance about her bedchamber to ensure all was at the ready, but she did douse the candles before going out to check the sitting room. The fire in the hearth was still strong, but she moved aside the screen and prodded it all the same.

Then she settled on the settee and folded her hands on her lap, for once not dreading the sound of that silver bell.

⚜

IRRITATION and impatience rubbed hard and harsh against every one of his nerves. By God, how James hated supper parties. Stuck at the table. Unable to hide himself off in the card room. Surrounded by people he would never choose to acquaint himself with if he had the option. Only Rebecca's blissfully happy presence across the table from him kept the scowl from his mouth.

Two dozen? It was more like three dozen guests around the long mahogany table inside the massive dining room of the Marksons' stately mansion. The light from the many silver candelabras glinted off the delicate glassware at each place setting. Stark white linens, heavy silver flatware, fine bone china. The trappings of an elaborate and carefully planned supper party.

His position at the table had been chosen for him by the hostess. An elderly matron on his left who was thankfully more interested in her fish than her supper companions, and Brackley, of all individuals, at his right. The man had tried to engage him in conversation during the first course, but his efforts had been for naught. On the other side of the table, a few places from Rebecca and closer to the vaunted host at the head of the table sat Amelia. If one of those candelabras had been set just half a foot to the left, then it would obstruct his view of her. As it was, the frustration built in tandem with the coarse rub of annoyance every time Amelia batted her eyes at Lord Albert Langholm. At every one of her false, high, tinkling laughs.

At least he now knew the true reason for the acceptance of the

Marksons' invitation. It had had nothing at all to do with a desire to introduce Rebecca to the handful of eligible bachelors in attendance, and everything to do with a need to yet again throw her latest lover in his face.

He leaned back in his chair as a liveried footman took his barely touched plate and deposited yet another. This one contained two neatly arranged slices of roast beef. Who the hell had decided a proper meal needed to include eight courses? Completely unnecessary. It was more food than an army could consume.

Looking over his shoulder, he glanced yet again to the tall clock in the corner of the room. As each minute passed, each minute that felt like an eternity, the worry built, growing from a small nudge of concern until it filled his gut. It took all his self-control not to shift in the chair. If they left now, and if the streets were not crowded, then he could deposit Amelia and Rebecca at home and take a hackney to Rubicon's and still arrive before midnight. He had given Rose his word that he would arrive early. It had taken a lot to earn her trust, and damn Amelia to hell if she caused him to lose it.

✢

Rose stared hard at the little silver bell suspended from the hook in the ceiling.

"Ring. *Please*," she whispered, desperation heavy in the low tone.

Her plea was met with silence.

Anticipation was indeed a cruel mistress. Her stomach in knots, misery hung about her head like a threatening thundercloud. She tried to push it away, but to no avail. It had simply continued to build as the minutes had slipped away.

Unable to remain seated a second longer, she stood to prod the fire again. Smoothing her hand over the front of her gown, she went into her bedchamber. It took a couple of attempts, but she was finally able to light a candle and check the small porcelain clock on the dresser.

Midnight.

Far later than she had imagined.

Her heart sank.

Why was it that when one anticipated every coming moment, time seemed to zip by at a frighteningly quick pace?

In a daze, she returned to the settee. She hung her head and clasped her hands tight to will the tremble from her arms.

He wasn't coming.

She bit the edge of her bottom lip, her eyes closed tight. Excuses could no longer fill the void. She could deny it no longer. James had had his fill of her, taken what he wanted, his palate now quenched of her. There was no real reason for him to return tonight. His promise had been filled with empty words, just like all the rest.

Rosie, you have my word I will never lay a hand on you again. Lord Wheatly's voice, thick with false contrition, drifted through her head.

Oh no, my dear, I do not have a wife. How easy it had been for Lord Biltmore to deny the very existence of the pretty, young Lady Biltmore.

And her father's vow that Dash would never want for anything had been worse than empty. It had been filled with debts that had taken her years on her back to settle.

She was a fool. A fool to believe James. That he could be different than all the others. That he had actually cared about *her.*

Good, decent men did not give a damn about whores.

Why had she allowed their liaison to continue? She should have put a stop to it, whatever the cost. It had been destined to end exactly like this, with her alone, as she always was. Yet still, her heart hadn't been able to resist the lure of him. Of a precious glimpse of what she had given up all those years ago.

He was probably at his office right now, all thoughts of her purged from his mind the moment he had spilled his seed on the dewy grass. Or worse yet, he could be with his wife, the lucky woman who carried his name and had the right to call him her own.

Something Rose could never and would never have.

Her shuddering breaths echoed in the painfully quiet room, the longing, the need so strong it nearly clogged her throat. Then muted voices seeped through her sitting room door. The rumble of a masculine voice, an answering feminine laugh.

Her head snapped up, her gaze settling on the bell once again. That it had not yet rung caused time to press in on her.

It *was* late. Rubicon would be in the receiving room by now, extolling her virtues, or more aptly her skills and her beauty. Clients who arrived at the brothel with the distinct intention of purchasing her for the night knew not to dally. To do so would leave the door open for another gentleman to take their place. But for nights when no man sought out Rubicon by midnight, the madam went in search of one.

That bell would soon ring. A small part of her lonely heart ached at the hope that it could be *him*. Wanted so badly to believe he was a man of his word, even to those who did not deserve that respect. But the hardened, practical side knew he would not walk through that door again.

She shot to her feet and pulled the bellpull. Acutely aware of how her gown brushed her calves as she impatiently shifted her weight, she waited by the sitting room door.

She had the door unlocked and open before the rap of the double knock faded.

The sight of the silver tray with two cups and a pot that was no doubt filled with coffee caused a lance to pierce her chest. Swallowing hard, she shook her head as Jane lifted the tray. "Please inform Rubicon that I am ill tonight," she said, doing her best to sound her usual self.

The moment the door was safely closed again, she reached behind her back and tugged, but her fingers were shaking too hard to manage the small fabric-covered buttons. Beyond desperate to get the gown off, she yanked. Hard.

Buttons popped free, skidding across the floorboards. She wrestled her arms free of the sleeves and pushed the gown to her feet. Gathering it in her arms, she darted into her bedchamber and shoved it into the waste bin. The heap of navy silk completely covered the small bin, pooling onto the floor around it.

Clad in her chemise and stockings, she crumpled to her knees. Shoulders hunched, she buried her face in her hands, pressing the heels of her palms hard against her closed eyes, and tried to push back the tears. But to no avail.

⚜

"She is unavailable this evening. Perhaps I can interest you—"

"Pardon? What do you mean she's unavailable?"

"Just that. Rose is unavailable this evening," the madam responded. Her hands were folded on the neat surface of her desk, her shoulders straight. So calm and composed while a riot of shock and confusion built within him, layered with a distinct note of disappointment.

"Why not?" he demanded.

"It is quite late, sir. Beautiful women never want for companionship. Did you truly expect other gentlemen to allow a woman like her to spend an evening alone?"

She was with another man? At this very moment? Hot and swift, jealousy grabbed hold of his stomach, held it in a viselike grip. It was completely irrational of him to be jealous of another man. Rose's nights were defined by the various men who inhabited her bed. He knew that. Hell, he was having a discussion with a goddamn madam. But logic seemed to have left him. He despised the thought of another man's hands on her body. Of another kissing those lush, full lips. Of another man taking from her what she had given him last night. And he couldn't ignore the rancid taste of betrayal seeping in with the jealousy.

If it wasn't foolish to feel that she had betrayed him, he didn't know what was.

Rose was a prostitute. He should not at all feel like she had somehow been unfaithful to him by simply doing her job. If anything, he should feel this way every time Amelia took a lover, but he never had. Not even a glance of this gruesome monster screaming through his veins, demanding he yank that man off Rose and pummel him for daring to touch her.

Hands clenched in tight fists, he eyed the expanse of white paneled wall that held the hidden door. He was vaguely aware his breathing had quickened. Betrayal jabbed anew into his gut, and it was all he could do not to flinch.

"When will she be available again?" He heard himself speak as if from a great distance.

"Rose only takes one client an evening. She won't be available until tomorrow night." The madam paused. "Do I need to ring for one of the footmen?"

He snapped his head around. "Why?"

She arched one eyebrow.

He stared hard at her for a moment, and then her meaning sank in. By God, he must look a fool. Poised to come to blows over a whore. "The footman is unnecessary." Taking a deep breath, he forced his hands to unclench from the arms of the scarlet leather chair and did his best to calm himself. It did nothing to stem the brutal riot that filled his entire being, but at least he hoped he no longer resembled a crazed lunatic.

Even when Amelia had boasted of her first lover, he had not felt even a drop of jealousy, only resignation and a smart smack to his pride. But something about Rose brought out a possessive streak he had not even known he was capable of.

Goddamn Amelia! This was her fault. She just had to accept that supper invitation. And as if she did not see her lover enough, she had to linger for over two hours in the drawing room after supper, practically hanging off his arm. He should have dragged her from the mansion the moment supper had been completed, used Rebecca as his excuse. But the girl had appeared far from overtired from her long day, chatting animatedly with a circle of young ladies with Brackley hovering at the perimeter and clearly relishing her first night among the ton. Instead, he'd been forced to wait until Amelia had seen fit to depart.

Must she take everything from him? His pride, his self-respect, his hopes, and his dreams weren't enough. She had to yank his evening with Rose from his grasp as well and crush it beneath her small feet.

And to think he had actually awoken this morning looking forward to the evening ahead of him.

"There are many other beautiful women in the house," the madam said, jarring him back to the present. "Perhaps you would care to choose another . . . or two."

He shook his head, a slight sneer pulling his upper lip. How easily she interchanged one for another, as if Rose herself held no value.

"I do so hate for my clients to be disappointed. Successful gentlemen such as yourself have pressing responsibilities that can often cause unforeseen delays in their schedules and wreak havoc on their plans for the evening. If you so desire, you may secure Rose now for tomorrow evening."

"I wish to secure Rose for the next week." And now he must surely look an even bigger fool.

He waited impatiently for her answer while she reached for the short, plain glass near her elbow and took a slow sip. With a little *click*, she set the glass back down and folded her hands once again on the surface of her desk. "I unfortunately must inform you the limit is three. It's best to keep such arrangements shorter in duration. I am sure you can understand. The pursuit of pleasure can be a fickle beast. If you still feel so inclined toward Rose three nights from now, then we can have this discussion again."

He was the furthest thing from fickle, but he resisted the urge to argue the point and instead stood to pull the fold of pound notes from his pocket. It contained only a third of the required amount. "You will understand if the sum is short. I will deliver the remainder tomorrow."

She tipped her head, a pleased smile flittering across her rouged lips. "Whether you choose to visit this house or not, Rose is yours for the next three nights. Not days. Nights. I will expect you no earlier than eight in the evening."

Eight

JAMES pulled out his pocket watch, flipped open the silver cover, and scowled at the small black hands. Five minutes after eight. At least the madam could not claim he had violated the terms of their agreement.

Tucking his watch back into his pocket, he resumed his pacing. From the teakwood desk, between the scarlet leather armchairs, past the mahogany liquor cabinet, to the door and back again. Where was Rubicon? And why the hell was he in her office already? Rose was his for the evening. There was no worry another would usurp his place. Yet still, he had left his office well before his usual hour.

Pivoting on his heel at the door, he let out a huff of self-disgust. It wasn't as if his continued presence behind his desk would have been productive. He hadn't been able to focus on anything all day. He only vaguely recalled signing his name to various documents. What those documents contained, he hadn't the slightest recollection. The mental image of Rose arching in pleasure beneath another, her legs wrapped around a man's waist, her small hands gripping another's shoulders had tormented him to no end. The jealousy building in his gut to near intolerable levels had turned him into a different man, one who could not hold on to even the barest thread of patience. Hell, Decker had barely spoken to him after James had taken issue with the temperature of his coffee that morning.

He scrubbed a hand over his eyes. And bloody hell, he was tired. Damn near exhausted. He hadn't gotten a wink of sleep last night. It wasn't as if he was a stranger to sleepless nights. He'd had more of them over the past three years than he cared to count. But last night under the cover of darkness, the thick, churning mass of jealousy had turned into pure, biting pain. Leaving him wrung out, his nerves frayed to the point of breaking.

Perhaps that was why he felt out of sorts. So at odds with himself. A stranger in his own skin. Never before had he been so consumed with thoughts of a woman. Instead of tending to his business affairs or spending a quiet evening at home with his sister, he had chosen to visit a brothel. By God, if nothing else, he was a married man. Yet he felt not one drop of guilt over the fact that he intended to spend an evening with a woman who was not his wife.

What had become of him?

A growl of purest frustration rumbled in his chest.

At the snap of a door closing, he stopped in his tracks and whirled about to see Rubicon glide into the room.

"Good evening, sir," she said with a smile.

He glared at her, hating the fact that he had been reduced to this. He should not have come back tonight, but he had not been able to stop himself.

Her gaze flickered to the pound notes he had put on her desk the moment he'd entered her office. His impatience must have shown, for she made no attempt at pleasantries, no offer of a drink from the well-stocked liquor cabinet. She went behind her desk to tug on the bellpull then pressed on the wall. The hidden door swung open. "You know the way," she murmured, stepping aside to allow him to pass.

He stalked up the stairs. The light from Rubicon's office seeped up the narrow passageway, leaving the small landing at the top in almost complete darkness. Just one more evening, and then he would put an end to this. The hell with the pound notes. The madam could keep them for all he cared. And he'd take solace in the knowledge that two nights would pass before another touched Rose again. Maybe by then the thought wouldn't make his hands clench into tight fists or that knife jab into his gut, twisting deep.

A small part of his mind tried to remind him that he had absolutely no right to be angry with her. She had done nothing wrong except do her job. It wasn't her fault that Amelia had accepted an invitation to a supper party. If anything, he was to blame for the situation he now found himself in. If he had expended the effort to keep abreast of his wife's social schedule, he would have known an early visit to Rubicon's last night would have been out of the question.

He stopped before the door. Another man had stood in this very place not twenty-four hours ago, and she had welcomed him. Had she made him feel as though he was the only man in her world? The only one who could make her smile?

Reaching out, he grabbed hold of the knob and turned it.

⚜

THE door opened. Her breath caught in her chest. She blinked. Yes, that was James walking through her doorway, his shoulders so broad they barely fit through the narrow opening. Doing her best to mask her surprise, Rose stood from the settee.

"James." She quietly cleared her throat and tried again to speak without a waver in her voice. "What a pleasure to see you."

He flicked the door shut. "Good evening, Rose."

She soaked up the sight of him. So solid and strong, his presence seeming to fill the small sitting room. A thrill sang through her veins at the notion that he had not forgotten about her after all. She wanted to rush to his side, throw her arms around his neck, verify that he had, in fact, done what she had thought unthinkable and actually returned to her. But the absolute lack of the usual warmth in his olive green eyes took her aback and kept her rooted to the spot.

She passed a hand over the front of her gown, smoothing the violet silk. Why had she worn this gown tonight? The soft gray velvet would have been the better choice. "Shall I ring for a pot of coffee?"

He shook his head. He hadn't moved from his position just inside the door. His arms stiff at his sides, his gaze pinned on her.

Apprehension fluttered in her stomach. "Would you care to have a seat?" She indicated the settee behind her.

"No."

"Is . . . is something amiss, James?"

"No."

Something obviously had put him in a foul mood, but if he did not want to discuss it, then she would not press him. Men visited her as an escape from the usual routine of their lives, not to be pestered by a woman.

Struggling to think of something to say to this new, distant version of James, she glanced about the room. He had already refused her offer to make himself comfortable on the settee. There was no point in offering him a glass of brandy or whisky. "Would you like me to show you my bedchamber?"

A pause. "Yes."

She swore her heart stopped for a moment. Pain sliced into her chest, and it was all she could do not to flinch. It was the last answer she had expected from him. The question tossed out to fill a void and for nothing more.

It was only through sheer ingrained habit borne of countless repetition that she managed to paste a welcoming smile on her lips.

Slipping into the routine she knew so well, she tipped her head. "It would be my pleasure."

A muscle ticked along his strong jaw. On weak knees, she turned and crossed to her bedchamber, flexing her empty hand by her side, feeling the loss of his acutely.

His footsteps sounded behind her. Pausing before pushing open the door, she took a deep breath in a failed effort to settle herself. A fire burned in the hearth in the bedchamber. A couple of candles were stationed about the room, enough to cast a veil of soft golden light, but not too many to border on bright. The perfect amount to encourage intimacy, and two too many than if she had anticipated James's visit, yet alone his response to the question she asked most every night.

The door snapped shut, the sound cracking through the room, causing her stride to falter. She stopped at the side of the bed and turned to face him. He leaned a shoulder against the door and crossed his arms over his chest.

His gaze flickered about, pausing on the large bed with its bronze coverlet and neatly arranged pillows at the headboard, before settling once again on her.

Silence hung thick and heavy. Neither of them moved. It was almost as if he were waiting for something . . .

But of course.

With hands that shook the barest bit, she started releasing the buttons on the front of her bodice. Perhaps if she did not look at his handsome face, she could pretend he was just one of the many who had walked into this room. Just another man who wanted only her body and the pleasures she offered. That he had never been someone who had made her feel safe and cherished.

She pushed the gown from her shoulders and it fell to the floor in a soft *whoosh* of silk. The stays were somehow easier to see to, the chemise . . . letting it slip down her body had never been more difficult.

"The stockings as well?" she asked.

He gave a curt nod.

Propping first one and then the other foot on the edge of the mattress, she undid the ribbons holding up her stockings, pushing the sheer white silk down her calves.

Rose stood bare before him, her arms forced to her sides to keep from covering herself. A chill swept over her, gooseflesh pricking her skin. She had never felt so naked in all her life. So much an object and nothing more. So much like a whore. And she despised him for making her feel this way.

How dare he show her kindness only to snatch it away?

And why had he returned tonight, and not last night? She had shed tears over this man. Had crumpled on this very spot, her heart breaking, sobs racking her body. How dare he behave as though he had done nothing wrong? He had given her his word and promptly broken it, without even a token explanation or apology. But given his abrupt demeanor, one would think he thought her in the wrong.

She had done nothing wrong except believe in him.

If she needed another reminder of why men should not be trusted, it stood directly before her, his arms still crossed over his broad chest and his cold eyes still pinned on her.

He was just another client, she reminded herself firmly. If he wanted her body and nothing more, then he could have it.

Anger and determination surged through her veins, effectively masking the stifling vulnerability and painful despair.

He had paid for the most expensive whore in the house. Well then, he would get a demonstration of just what his money had bought him.

Lifting her chin, she arched her back, smoothly rolling back her shoulders. His gaze went directly to her breasts, his grip tightening on his arms. She kept the smirk from her mouth. Let him pretend he was unaffected by her. She knew otherwise. And within minutes, he would not stand a chance at hiding it.

Reaching up, she pulled the pins from her hair, letting them drop to the plush rug beneath her bare feet. The dark length tumbled about her shoulders, the ends tickling her breasts. She gave him a moment to soak up the view and then, letting her hips sway, she walked slowly to him.

The crisp scent of the chill night air and the spicy hint of a man, of James, filled her senses. Pushing aside the ache that threatened to build anew, she peered up at him from under the fan of her lashes. "One of us has too many clothes on." She infused her voice with a soft, teasing lilt to match the smile on her lips.

His response was to drop his arms to his sides.

She was quite proud of the fact that her hands did not shake as she slowly slipped the buttons free on his nut brown coat. Lifting up onto her toes, she pushed the coat from his shoulders, his muscles hard as iron beneath her hands. Fortunately he was not one of those fashionable gentlemen who preferred the cut of their coat to be so strict they were next to impossible to remove without considerable effort. She caught the coat as the sleeves slipped from his wrists. A neat fold, and she placed it on the nearby dresser.

"Did you have a pleasant day at the office?" she asked, as casual as could be, as she set to work on the small fabric-covered buttons running the length of his pale yellow waistcoat. Her day had been spent cloistered in her bedchamber, willing herself to forget James and the feel of his hands on her body and the taste of his kiss. An effort in futility if ever there was one.

Her question was met with silence. She looked up and lifted a brow.

"No," he said, more grunt than a word.

"Well then, perhaps I can make up for it."

The waistcoat joined the coat on the dresser. The room was so quiet she could hear the soft *swoosh* of linen sliding against linen as she untied the simple knot on his cravat. The backs of her fingers brushed his jaw, his day's beard a gentle scrape. A slow tug, and she pulled the long length of white linen from his neck, exposing his throat.

He did the courtesy of whisking the shirt over his head. Her initial assessment of him had been unerringly accurate. There was not an ounce of fat on his frame. She followed the thin line of dark hair to where it disappeared behind the waistband of his trousers, and then her gaze drifted lower.

What could only be a substantial erection tented the placket of his trousers. He was most definitely not unaffected by her. She curled one hand at her side, wanting to reach out, to feather her fingertips over the arched length, to feel it jump in a silent plea for more. To have the weight of him again in her palm.

Her insides fluttered, her body clenching at the memory of that thick length slowly filling her until he possessed her completely. Her head went light, a heavy wave of arousal washing over her.

The sound of a throat clearing recalled her to her senses. She blinked then snatched the shirt from his outstretched hand. She didn't bother folding it, but simply tossed it onto the pile on the dresser.

She trailed her fingertips lightly over his abdomen, just above his waistband. His skin was as soft and smooth as she remembered, but this time she was able to watch as his muscles quivered under her touch.

Refusing to look at his face, she tugged on the buttons on the placket. With his brown trousers hanging on his hips, she undid the string on his drawers. Then she pushed them down, dropping to her knees to slip off his shoes and remove the last of his clothes.

Still on her knees, she looked up. Somehow she kept the purr of appreciation inside. By God, the man was magnificent in the nude. His cock jutted proudly from between his legs, the heavy weight of his ballocks drawn up tight. Raw, brute strength radiated from every line of his body, from his powerful thighs to his impossibly broad chest to his strong, corded forearms. She wanted to touch every inch of him, to feel what she had previously been denied. To finally press her bare skin against his.

Instead, she arched up under his erection, tipping her face up to let her breath fan his ballocks. His breath hitched. His cock twitched. A drop of fluid beaded at the flushed crown. Careful to avoid the one place where she knew he wanted her touch most of all, she got to her feet, coasting her hands up the outsides of his thighs.

She turned her back to him and crawled onto her bed and up the mattress to the headboard. The heat of his gaze scorched her skin, made her derrière tingle with awareness. Her shoulders and back propped up on the pillows, she positioned herself on the bed, spreading her legs just enough to tempt with one knee slightly bent up and the other casually straight. After taking a moment to arrange her hair so the dark waves framed rather than obscured his view of her breasts, she arched a brow at him. "Do you plan to join me?"

Again silence.

"Or perhaps . . . you would prefer to watch."

With a light touch, she traced one nipple, brushed across the hardened tip, briefly captured it between forefinger and thumb. Then she cupped her breast, gently kneaded the weight, and then drifted her fingers down her chest, pausing to circle her navel before grazing the dark triangle of hair between her thighs.

She swore his cock hardened even further, seeming to strain toward her, the tip glistening wet, the head flushed plum red. His breaths had turned heavy, his chest visibly working under the effort. Hands clenched so tightly at his sides his knuckles had gone white. Yet he made not one move to join her on the bed.

He was the one who had wanted to move into her bedchamber. She hadn't dragged him here. But if he wanted to prop up the door all evening, then he was more than welcome to.

A perverse need to torment him grabbed hold. To make him pay, in however small a fashion, for the pain he had caused her last night. For the horrid, yet necessary reminder that she was nothing but a whore to him.

No matter how unpleasant, the reminder had indeed been necessary. Kindness and compassion were dangerous commodities, ones she could not afford to trade in. Desire and lust . . . those she knew well. Just as she knew her place was in this bed, and not his own.

Blocking out the ache for more, she focused solely on him and let her bent leg fall open. Wanton and shameless, she drifted one fingertip lower to slide between the folds of her sex.

⚜

SWEAT pricked between his shoulder blades. A bead slid down his back, tickling his heated skin. James couldn't take his eyes off her. Sprawled on the bed, the dark waves of her hair draping her shoulders, her beautiful lush body on display, she was temptation incarnate. A vision straight from his most decadent fantasies.

With a smile that screamed sinful pleasure, Rose lightly circled her clit before dropping down to her core, gathering the moisture there. So slick and wet. So ready for him.

He ground the inside of his cheek between his teeth. Lust roared through his veins, demanding he take her. *Now.* His damn cock was so hard it hurt. Yet he was locked to the spot, as if an invisible wall stood before that bed. A part of him wasn't so certain he liked this side of her—bold and confident and completely at her ease playing the seductress. He couldn't ignore the nagging sensation that she was performing, simply going through the motions. But the baser side of him panted for more.

Arching her lower back, she continued to torture him. Swirling, playing at her entrance. Her head tilting back slightly, her hips lifting the barest bit into her touch. A slow, sensuous rhythm his body knew only too well, the memory from the night before last forever branded on his senses.

Need rocked through him, so strong it nearly brought him to

his knees. His muscles tightened, coiled to lurch forward. To claim her. Mark her as his own. To take everything she offered and give her more. So much more she would never want another man again.

As if she somehow knew he was teetering on the edge, she brought that teasing finger up to her mouth. Heavily lidded gaze locked with his, she traced her bottom lip.

"Are you certain you don't want a taste?"

And with that, she shoved him over the edge.

He leapt forward, landing on the bed. The next moment he was on top of her, crouched between her spread legs, his face mere inches from hers.

"Yes, I want a taste," he growled. Chest heaving, he leaned down, breaching the remaining distance, to take exactly what she offered. He drew her bottom lip into his mouth, gently sucked on it, savoring the taste of her. Sweet as honey, it lit up his tongue.

Releasing that plump lip, he pulled back just enough to hold her gaze. The brazen, teasing glint was gone, replaced with a need that fueled his even higher. She moved not a muscle, and neither did he. Tension shimmered in the air between them. Crackling and sparking. Drawing tighter and tighter.

"*Kiss me.*" Threadbare and breathless, the plea trembled past her lips.

His mouth came down to claim hers. Her lips opened eagerly beneath his. He swept his tongue inside, explored the hot depths of her delicious mouth. Tangling her fingers in his hair, she arched, meeting the pure passion of his kiss. She writhed beneath him, bare skin sliding against his. Every move she made caressed his erection, trapped between their bodies, ratcheting the need for more until he couldn't hold back another moment.

Panting, he broke the kiss, dragged his lips across her cheek to her ear. "I want you. *Please.*"

"Yes," she said on a moan that matched the raw need in his hoarse plea.

He reached down, positioned himself at her core, and pushed inside. Hot, silken heat surrounded his length. Gripped him so tightly he had to stop for a moment lest the reins of control slip completely through his fingers. The orgasm was right there, teasing the base of his spine. Dragging in a ragged breath, he forced it back.

And then he slid in that last remaining distance, burying himself to the hilt.

"Oh, James."

Her lashes fluttered, her light blue eyes glittering with desire. Her parted lips plumped from their kisses. Her cheeks stained with a pink flush of passion. The sight held him in awe. Something lurched up inside him, a force that tightened his chest. Three years of celibacy could have been a decade for all he cared. All that mattered was that he was with Rose now.

A small hand tugged on the back of his sweat-slicked neck. A thin whimper slid past her lips. Capturing those perfect red lips, he eased back, savoring the lush friction, the hot tug of her most intimate flesh along every inch of his length. And then he glided home.

Her legs came up to wrap around his waist, holding him to her. Skin against skin, they moved together. The firm mounds of her breasts pressed against his chest, the soft curves of her body fit perfectly against the hard bulk of his own. It was an unbelievable feeling to be with a woman who wanted *him*. Who welcomed him with open arms. Who derived pleasure from his touch. Her gasps for more, her sweet sighs, the scent of her aroused body mixed with the hint of roses. The sensations swamped his senses, had him desperate for more.

But first, he needed to give her more. Needed to be with her when the pleasure claimed her. Shifting his weight to one arm, his rhythm unbroken, he worked one hand between their bodies. With his thumb, he found her clit. Circled the hard bud. Not in a soft, light tease but in a determined caress designed to wring the climax from her.

Her legs tightened around his waist, her hips bumping against his. Matching her pace, he sped up his thrusts. Driving deep and hard. Her kisses turned desperate. Stark and needy. Devouring his mouth. Her hands clutched his shoulders, nails digging into his skin. He felt the tension building within her. And then she went taut in his arms, her sleek heat clamping around him, milking his length. He drank up her cries of pleasure, his own body demanding he follow her over the edge. The orgasm he had somehow kept at bay suddenly gripped his ballocks. Tearing his lips from hers, he reared back onto his knees and grabbed his cock, the length slicked with the proof of her pleasure. Two strokes and the climax rushed through him. He let out a hoarse grunt as pearly white seed shot from his cock, landing on her abdomen, her chest, a drop reaching one hard nipple.

He dropped down onto his arms. Hanging his head, he struggled to catch his breath. It felt as though that climax had ripped all the energy from him, leaving him ten times more exhausted than an hour ago when he had knocked on the back door of the brothel. The soft, lulling drag of the arch of her bare foot over his calf tempted him to just collapse beside her and let the heavy haze of lethargy overtake him.

With effort, he resisted the temptation and lifted his head. Only a heartless cad left his seed to dry on a woman's belly.

"Do you have a . . ." He glanced about, his gaze landing on the washstand. "I'll be right back."

A quick kiss and he dragged himself out of her bed. He grabbed the small towel next to the white stone washbasin, dunked half the length in the water, and wrung it out. Strides slow and heavy, he returned to the bed and then sat on the edge.

Lying half on her side, one arm was slung over her head. The most beautiful sated smile curved her lips. With his free hand, he brushed the tousled strands of her hair behind her ear.

"This will be a bit cold." She sucked in a short breath, eyes flaring, her belly tensing when the cloth met her skin. "I tried to warn you," he murmured, as he carefully wiped away the remnants of his climax. Just as carefully, he used the other end of the towel to dry her flawless ivory skin. Unable to resist, he leaned down, flicked his tongue over one nipple, briefly pulled it inside his mouth, and then blew lightly across the tip.

"James." His name came out on a little giggle.

"Yes?"

"That tickled."

He shrugged, unabashed, and let the cloth drop to the floor. "That's what it was supposed to do."

She rolled her eyes at him, but the smile said she wasn't the least bit put out. His hand found hers, fingers sliding together as if they weren't meant to be anywhere else. He should leave now, let her rest. He could certainly use some rest. But . . .

He didn't want to leave her. Not just yet.

She levered up onto an elbow and cupped his jaw. The levity now completely gone. "I missed you last night," she said quietly.

Like an ugly snake, jealousy reared its head, lashing into his gut. "As I you. Hopefully I have removed the memory of him from your bed." At her questioning look, he raised his eyebrows. "You were unavailable last night."

"How—? You . . . you were here last night? When?"

"Around one in the morning. A delay, one completely beyond my control, kept me from arriving earlier." Closing his eyes, he took a deep breath. "My apologies for breaking my word to you." He opened his eyes, held her gaze. Willed her to believe him. "It was not my intention."

It seemed like forever as her light blue eyes searched his, but she finally nodded. "I understand. And . . . there is no memory to remove. I was unavailable, but I wasn't with another. When you didn't arrive by midnight, I cried off sick."

"You did?" And here he had acted an arse for no reason at all.

At least he needn't worry about a repeat performance in the near future. For the next two nights, she was his.

Lifting one shoulder, she made to duck her chin, but a gentle hand on her cheek refused to allow her to hide.

"Yes," she whispered shyly.

"Thank you." He gave her hand a squeeze, and smiled, infinitely pleased. They sat in silence for a few moments, and then a yawn expanded his chest, his eyelids drooping a bit. "My apologies," he murmured.

Her gaze grew concerned, a little furrow marring her brow. She pushed his hair from his forehead and then her fingers drifted down to brush beneath his eyes. "You look as though you haven't slept for days."

"Just one day."

"Why?"

"I was thinking of you," he confessed.

"You should rest for a bit."

He gave his head a little shake. "I can't stay."

"But it's early yet. Rest. I'll wake you later." Before he could voice his refusal, she asked, "When do you want me to wake you? It's"—she glanced over her shoulder to the porcelain clock on the dresser—"half past nine. Is two o'clock all right?"

His town house would be quiet by then. Everyone abed. No risk of coming face-to-face with someone he did not want to see. He could either sleep alone all night, or stay with Rose a while longer. The decision wasn't all that difficult. "Two is perfect."

"Consider it done. Now come here."

At the tug on his hand, he lay out on the bed, gathering her in his arms, the light weight of her body so perfect against his. Soft lips pressed against his chest, directly over his heart.

"Sleep, James. I won't neglect to wake you."

And with her soft voice drifting through his head, he gave up the fight and let the exhaustion overtake him.

Nine

THE late-morning sun heated his shoulders as he escorted Rebecca through the main gates of Hyde Park. Her gloved hand rested on his arm, his strides slowed to match hers. The pale blue bonnet shielded her cheeks from the sun's rays, keeping away the freckles that had graced the bridge of her straight nose as a young girl. She had grown up much too fast. It seemed like just yesterday when she had been eight years old and tugging on his sleeve, asking him to play dolls with her.

As was his habit when she was visiting, he had delayed his departure to his office that morning, spending a couple of hours in his study before joining her for breakfast. A creature of London, Amelia kept Town hours, not rising until late in the morning, whereas Rebecca's upbringing in Somerset had her firmly on country hours. Late nights at balls and soirées would soon push her onto a schedule that more closely mirrored Amelia's. Until that time, he took full advantage of the hours he could spend with his sister without his wife's presence.

The morning's topic of conversation had revolved firmly around the various eligible lords of the ton. Rebecca had spoken with a competence that had frankly shocked him, rattling off names and titles, discounting this one for only being a baron and waxing on about another who was an heir to a marquisate.

As he had mutely listened, the plate of eggs and sausage before him untouched, his concern had started to mount. Yes, he knew she was excited at the prospect of her first Season and focused on garnering a marriage proposal, as were all young girls of her age from good families. But he did not want her focused on a title to the exclusion of all else, simply to fulfill their father's ambitions. The last thing he wanted was for her to learn firsthand just how unpleasant a marriage formed solely on an exchange of social standing and pound notes could be.

So when breakfast had been completed, he had asked her to accompany him for a walk. He hadn't been to the park during daylight hours since the last time Rebecca had visited. Then the air had been crisp and cold with February's wet chill, the frostbitten grass crushing beneath their feet and the trees barren of leaves. Now the grass was lush and green, the trees full and casting fat shadows along the path. The air held the slightest hint of warmth, but was still crisp enough to warrant a pelisse for Rebecca though not enough to push him to don his greatcoat.

"And Amelia has accepted an invitation for Lady Morton's ball," Rebecca said. He nodded, employing the same noncommittal tip of the head he had been using since they left the house. "It's to be *the* event to start the Season. Tomorrow we're to pay her an afternoon call. Oh, I do so hope I don't disappoint and say something I shouldn't. Though today we *must* visit the modiste."

"Must?" he asked, lifting a skeptical brow.

She tilted her face up to his. She had the good sense to look at least a bit abashed. "Well, yes. Yesterday, Amelia and I went through my wardrobe, and I'm in need of a few more gowns. I can't very well wear any more than once."

"Of course not," he said in mock seriousness. "Whatever was I thinking? You must promptly chuck them in the rag bin after they are worn."

"James, please don't think me a silly girl. But . . ." She pulled her gaze from his, her hand tightening on his arm. "I do so want to be a success."

Her worried whisper held a wealth of longing and made him feel like a cad for teasing her. "And you shall be." He gave her gloved hand a reassuring pat. "You are a wonderful young woman, Rebecca. Anyone would be a fool not to see you are even more beautiful on the inside than you are on the outside."

She leaned into him, briefly pressing her cheek to his upper arm. If they hadn't been walking in the park, he was certain she would have enveloped him in a hug. "Thank you. You are the dearest of brothers."

"I am your only brother."

"And I couldn't hope for any better."

He may have a wife who despised him and a father who had sold him off like a load of timber, but he counted himself fortunate to have a sister who loved him. And he had Rose . . . for two more nights. Definitely not nearly long enough.

"I . . ." Rebecca let out a little sigh. "I just don't want to give cause for someone to snub me. Father is counting on my success."

The very reason he had asked her to accompany him to the park. He stopped and turned to face her, needing her full attention.

"Rebecca, I well understand how demanding Father can be." The man didn't sit one down and dictate his wishes with an iron hand. He was subtle, shrewd, just as he was in his business dealings. A line dropped here and there into most every conversation until doing anything but what he wished was simply inconceivable. Even at a young age, James had felt the weight of his father's expectations, the same weight he worried now rested on Rebecca's slim shoulders. "But I must ask you if it is honestly what you want. Father will be disappointed if you don't marry a titled lord." That was an understatement, but if it came down to it, the man would just have to learn to live with disappointment. "Though he will not cut you off." All right. That bit wasn't so certain. But if necessary, James would replace her dowry so she wasn't left penniless. "And I will always be your brother. Your happiness is what matters to me."

"I am happy, James," she said, her large green eyes pleading with him to believe her. "Have I given you any reason to believe otherwise?"

"You are happy now, but marriage is a big step. You will be tied to your future spouse for the rest of your life." A fact he knew quite well. "I want you to feel free to choose who you wish, and not feel forced to choose a man because of his name."

"But you married Amelia to give me this opportunity. I do not want to squander it."

He paused, alarm tightening his spine. He had been very careful to never say a word against Amelia to anyone. It was clear it wasn't a love match, but Rebecca surely could not be aware of the true state of his marriage. She was aware their father had chosen Amelia for him so she could one day have an entrée into the ton. That was all she was referring to and nothing more.

The concern dismissed, he said, grave and solemn, "The opportunity is there to do with as you see fit. Do not feel obligated to take it."

"Thank you." She lifted up onto her toes and pressed a light kiss to his cheek. "You truly are the dearest of brothers. But you needn't worry on my account. While I'd like nothing more than for you to call me Lady one day, I will not marry for that reason alone. The man must suit after all."

"And he must adore you."

She giggled, her chin tipping down. "Of course. That goes without saying."

They continued down the path, passing an older woman in a practical brown pelisse who was overseeing her two young charges. Brandishing sticks, the boys were clearly engaging in a game of pirate. Parrying and retreating, the *smack* as their "swords" connected cracked through the air.

A pang of longing tugged at his chest. Pushing it aside with well-practiced effort, he glanced up to the sky. The sun was nearly overhead. He would need to return Rebecca to the house soon. Preparing for an afternoon call took more than a handful of minutes.

He was just about to stop and retrace his steps when a cloaked figure caught his attention. A woman stood in the shade of a large oak tree next to a wooden bench just off the bank of the Serpentine. The hood of her dark cloak draped her shoulders, exposing a neat knot of midnight black hair. He stopped in his tracks, well aware he was staring and not caring in the slightest. She turned her head toward a blond gentleman sprawled casually on the bench, revealing a profile he knew well. Familiar red lips moved, the same lips he had kissed not twelve hours ago. The rich, feminine timbre of her voice just reached his ears, but he was too far away to make out the words.

His attention snapped to the blond gentleman on the wooden bench. A vicious lash of jealousy bit at his gut, threatening to curl his hands into tight fists. With effort, he tamped it down, determined not to make an arse out of himself once again. In any case, she was his for two more nights, not another's.

"James?"

Ignoring Rebecca, he quickly looked about. His feet had automatically taken him on the same route he had last traveled. And Rose was standing not five paces from the spot where he had made love to her three nights ago.

There, along the bank, she had been his. The grass cool under his hands, her body hot and inviting and arching in pleasure beneath him.

His muscles coiled, poised to turn off the lane, to seize the unexpected opportunity to be near her once again. But his young sister's presence at his side stopped him just in time.

Not here. Not now.

Steeling himself against the disappointment, he gave himself one more moment to soak up the sight of her, and then he'd return Rebecca to the town house.

❧

"WOULD you mind ever so much if we visited a few hells this afternoon?"

Timothy reached into the brown paper sack at his hip and chucked a bit of stale bread into the river. The ducks gliding across the water lunged toward the offering. "Not at all."

Yesterday Rose had been in no condition to leave her suite of rooms, never mind traipse about town. Her mind fixed on trying to forget James, not on her brother's evasive and rude behavior. Today though . . . she should not let the day pass without making an effort to discover if Dash was hiding a gambling habit.

"We should leave soon, then. I need to stop briefly at the house and then we can be on our way. How many hells do you think we can visit? I need to return before five." She wanted to have plenty of time to prepare for the coming evening. *May I see you again tomorrow night?* James's parting words drifted through her head. He had even promised to leave his desk early, and there was not a bit of doubt in her mind that he would do just that.

Timothy threw another chunk of bread to the ducks. "Three or four should be manageable. Is there a reason why you don't wish to be late tonight?"

"Perhaps," she said, fighting to keep the smile from her lips.

"I take it last night went better than expected? You certainly look better today than you did yesterday."

"Yes, much better. On both accounts."

Avoiding Timothy's probing stare, she took a step forward, turning her attention to the ducks. James had been her only client since she had returned to town this month. Something she had a feeling Timothy would not approve of. He would question her, wonder at the wisdom of seeing the same man night after night. It would all be borne from concern for her, but at the moment, she'd rather not be faced with questions she did not want to answer.

Awareness pricked the nape of her neck, the sensation raising the fine hairs.

She whirled around, her gaze immediately catching James's, as if some part of her knew he was there. Clad in a bottle green coat and dark trousers, he stood along the lane. The sun bathed his strong features, making him appear somehow even more handsome.

A smile curved her lips at the unexpected gift. It would never have crossed her mind that she would see him here. On their first night together, he had told her he could not recall the last time he had visited the park during the day. And this wasn't just any time of day—it was late morning. A time chosen deliberately to avoid the gentlemen who rode along Rotten Row at dawn and far before the five o'clock fashionable hour. Her hood even draped her shoulders, so confident was she that she would not happen upon anyone who would recognize her.

A furrow flickered across his brow. He broke eye contact, turning his head to his right. And then he turned toward her, stepping off the lane and into the grass, and revealing the young woman at his side. An ivory kidskin-gloved hand rested on his forearm. A pale blue bonnet framed her pretty face. A morning dress in the same shade peeked from the hem of a light brown pelisse that was clearly the work of an expert modiste, one who would charge far more than Rose could afford.

Rose went stiff. Her pulse quickened, a rapid staccato that filled her ears, at the thought of just who this young woman could be. Muscles poised to turn, to walk away, to escape the agonizing truth she had tried so hard to brush aside as a mere possibility. But she couldn't resist one last look at the woman who had the privilege of calling James her own. Chestnut brown hair peeking from beneath the bonnet. Soft olive green eyes. Where James radiated pure, honest masculinity, she radiated sweet, wholesome femininity. Yet the resemblance was clear.

Relief poured over her. The tingle that started in her belly whenever she laid eyes on him sparked to life anew, bringing the smile back to her lips. "Good morning, James."

Stopping before her, he tipped his head, his gaze flickering to Timothy, who had gotten to his feet to stand at her shoulder. That muscle didn't tick along James's strong jaw, but the question in his eyes could not be more obvious.

"I hope the day finds you well. Please allow me to introduce my friend, Mr. Timothy Ashton."

The two men exchanged greetings, all brief politeness. A half bow from Timothy, a nod from James.

There was a pause, and then he turned to the young woman on his arm. "Rebecca, this is Miss Rose . . ."

Rose caught the leading look from him. Ingrained habit had her holding back, declining the silent request for her family name. Instead she tipped her head in greeting.

"Miss Rose, this is my dearest sister, Miss Rebecca Archer."

His name was James *Archer*. It fit him. Solid, strong, just like the man himself. Unlike the conventions of polite society, first names held no intimacy with her, but family names . . . a tangible symbol of trust.

"Are there other sisters who are not quite so dear?" she asked.

A short chuckle rumbled in his chest. "No, I've only the one."

"So what brings you out to the park at such an early hour? The sun is still shining."

"Alas, Rebecca does not share my nocturnal tendencies."

"And she has my thanks for that."

Standing in the shade of the tree with her, he looked somehow . . . different. It took a moment for her to identify the cause. The slightly wrinkled air about him was gone. His chestnut brown hair neatly combed, not a trace of a day's beard on his jaw. The crisp white cravat tied in a tidy knot. Not a hint of lingering tension in the broad line of his shoulders. It was the morning version of James.

Seeing him like this, before the hours behind his desk had a chance to take their toll, drove home just how very hard he worked. He had mentioned his long hours, but so casually, almost waving them aside, that it hadn't fully sunk in until now. And it made her determined to make his evenings with her as enjoyable as possible.

"James, the ducks have come out today," Rebecca said, glancing around Timothy's shoulder. "I should have thought to bring something for them."

"Not to worry." Timothy reached for the brown sack on the bench. "Two-day-old bread. They seem to like it best. It is yours if you will have it."

"Oh . . ." The girl captured the edge of her bottom lip between her teeth, looking far more torn than the offer should warrant. "I shouldn't."

"There's no use in my returning home with stale bread. I don't much fancy it. But I'm certain the ducks will enjoy it. Shall we?" With a benign smile that nevertheless had an impact on James's sister, at least judging by the slight blush that rose on her cheeks, Timothy gestured toward the river.

Rebecca tipped her face up to her brother, clearly seeking his approval. He didn't look to Timothy, assessing his worthiness to be granted such a duty as to escort his sister a few paces, but to Rose.

Holding his intent gaze, she gave him a small nod.

"The ducks await, Rebecca."

James watched as the girl eagerly joined Timothy on the downward-sloping bank of the river. Then she found herself caught by his gaze once again.

"And who exactly is Mr. Ashton?"

There wasn't a trace of suspicion in his low tone, but it understandably held a definitive need for an answer. "A friend of mine."

"A friend?"

The slight scowl should not please her so. "Yes, a friend. A very good friend." The scowl deepened. Somehow she kept from smiling as she took a step closer to him. Pitching her voice low, she said in an effort to clarify the situation and assure him his jealousy was unfounded, "He works at Rubicon's."

"He's one of the footmen?"

"No." Timothy as a footman? She held back the chuckle of disbelief that tickled her throat. "In addition to the women that fill the receiving room nightly, she has a few men in her employ."

His upper lip curled. "He's a—"

She held up a hand, stopping the word *sodomite* before it could leave his mouth. "Please don't say that word. He's my friend and doesn't deserve to be called such."

His attention flickered over her shoulder, the green depths of his eyes uncertain.

She reached out to touch his arm. If only she wasn't wearing gloves, perhaps she could feel the heat from his body seeping through the bottle green wool. "Your sister is perfectly safe with him. You have my word. He would never act improperly toward a young lady." While she understood the need, it hurt to even have to reassure James. It was an ugly reminder that a person's worth was so readily judged by their lot in life.

The happiness she'd felt upon seeing him drained away.

Her arm dropped to her side.

"He is your friend?"

"Yes. The dearest of friends." Her only friend. But *oh*, how she would like to be able to add James to the short list. To be able to call him *friend*.

A notched *V* pulling his brows, he considered her. A slight breeze ruffled the neat layers of his hair. The leaves overhead rustled as a bird took flight. Whatever he was looking for must have met with his satisfaction, for he nodded.

He held her gaze for a long moment, his expression inscrutable. "It is good to see you, Rose."

"As I you." She flexed her hand by her side. She wanted to reach out, to take hold of his, but proper decorum held her back. It was so very different being at the park with him. Accustomed to the privacy of her bedchamber, without a prying eye to be found, she was suddenly at a loss for what to say, how to behave around him.

There was a splash of water and then a light tickling laugh drifted over her shoulder.

The edges of his mouth quirked. "I should collect Rebecca. She has afternoon calls to ready for."

"Of course. I shall not keep you."

He reached out, took hold of her hand, long fingers wrapping around her palm, his grip so familiar, and bowed. Bent at the waist, he looked up at her from his prone position. His olive green eyes were banked with an undeniable promise of more.

Her breath caught. Passion flared to full life, so quick and so fast she nearly swayed on her feet.

"Until this evening." The low words brushed across the back of her gloved hands, sending a tingling rush through her.

All she could do was nod mutely as her fingers slipped from his. He stood tall, gave his coat a little tug to straighten it, and headed off toward the Serpentine.

⚜

SHIFTING on the leather bench, Rose kept her attention trained out the window of the hackney. Buildings lined the street, but only one in particular—the one with the black door with the plain silver knocker—held any interest to her.

The fourth hell they had visited that day. She hadn't stepped outside the hackney since they had departed from Rubicon's a few hours ago, preferring to remain cloaked in the shadows of the interior while Timothy inquired at each establishment. How exactly he acquired the necessary information, she hadn't a clue, nor had she asked. She had merely handed over all of the pound notes that she had been tucking into her valise after each of Rubicon's morning visits, with instructions to Timothy to use them as he saw fit. The flare of lust and desire James had left in his wake at the park had been doused shortly after Timothy had exited that first hell. His report from the second had been the same as the first. The third a blessed relief. The fourth . . .

She could only hope his instincts about this one were wrong. She had had enough dreadful news for one day. She certainly did not need any more.

A group of men passed the hackney, briefly blocking her view. She leaned right, hands clasped tightly in her lap, trying but failing to see around them. Strides slow and ambling, the group continued to make their way along the walkway, eventually passing that door.

She had only recognized the names of the first three hells. But this one she more than recognized. Bennett's, with its lavish yet comfortable interior designed to mimic one of the many gentlemen's clubs on St. James Street. Five years ago, she had walked through that black door many times, as an ornament hanging from Lord Wheatly's arm. Clad in beautiful gowns and with jewels draping her neck, she had stood at his shoulder whispering a mixture of encouragement and congratulations as he played the various tables, roulette being his game of choice. She had known her role well and performed to the best of her ability. The smile on her lips effectively masking the sharp jolt of apprehension every time the wheel slowed and the *clicketty-clack* of the small white marble came to a halt. When he did well, her nights passed without incident. His mood pleased, bordering on happy, so much so that it wouldn't take much to correctly anticipate his desires in the bedchamber. And when the wheel had not favored him . . .

A shudder gripped her spine.

By God, how she had come to dread even the sight of a roulette wheel. As if the man had needed another reason to be an unpleasant, domineering bastard, the gambling tables contained the heavy threat of one more.

The black door swung open and the tall, elegant form of Timothy emerged. The grim expression on his face spoke for itself. She winced.

He entered the hackney, sat on the bench across from her, and shut the door. At his sharp rap on the roof, the carriage lurched forward and the driver began to take them back to Curzon Street.

He tugged on the edge of his sleeve, a furrow marring his brow.

"Just tell me. There is no use trying to ease into it."

"Well, his total is now at five hundred and fifty-seven pounds, less what I've already used to pacify the hells." He spoke in a flat voice, as if relaying facts and nothing more. "I just parted with the last of the sum you had given me. This one was particularly unpleased at Mr. Marlowe's lack of interest in making good on his vows. I got the distinct impression the situation was not a recent occurrence. I'd hazard to guess he started racking up the total the moment he stepped foot in London."

That meant he had been well over six hundred pounds in debt as of this morning. He had left Oxford after Michaelmas term. A little over three months in London.

All young gentlemen gambled. It was the way of things, and almost expected of a gentleman of good standing. But that much debt in so short a time? It went far beyond keeping up appearances and trod dangerously into the realm of a true problem.

The years on her back had finally repaid her father's debts not that long ago. Definitely not long enough for her to have built any sort of savings or make a dent in repairing the family's coffers. And since his move to London, Dash was proving very expensive to keep. Not to mention the repairs Paxton Manor always seemed to need. The safe hidden in her father's study held a rather pathetically paltry sum, one she had hoped to be able to add to, not deplete.

"Would you mind ever so much returning with me on Wednesday, before I leave for home? Two more nights of work won't nearly be enough to settle the debts, but it will at least be something." A few pounds here and there showed intent to repay, a sign creditors preferred over silence or avoidance.

"Of course I'll return with you. You needn't even ask."

That James's hard-earned money was being put to such a use . . . She let out a sigh. And just the thought of more debts made her want to cover her face with her hands and crumple. She had believed the dreaded beasts finally behind her when she'd paid off the last of her father's creditors. At the end of her week at Rubicon's, she would return to Bedfordshire with not even ten pounds to put in the safe. It would take almost two more weeks of work to pay off Dash's debts. And that was assuming he didn't accrue more in her absence.

Her shoulders sagged, as a bone-deep weariness settled over her. She felt so very alone. Felt it acutely. And she was so very tired of being alone. She had Timothy, and frankly wouldn't know what she would do without him, but it wasn't the same as having someone to help shoulder her burdens. To hold her close and tell her it would be all right.

"You do realize he could also have personal debts?" Timothy asked. "Vowels given during a card game at his club or during an evening of revelry with his friends. There is really no way for us to discover the extent of any of those unless he chooses to reveal them to you."

"Yes, I know." Unless she received a visitor at Paxton Manor. She knew well what those calls would be like. The gentlemen she wasn't concerned about. Dash hadn't gone to his grave, so they would deal directly with him, using the threat of the loss of his honor as leverage against him. The unsavory ones, however, would have no qualms seeking out a relation if Dash's pockets proved empty. And she would be able to give them nothing but her word that she would do her best to remedy the situation.

Timothy dragged a hand through his antique blond hair, pushing it off his brow, and speared her with a solemn stare. "Dash is now eighteen years of age."

"And?" she queried, more than a tad defensive, as she had a fair idea of where this conversation was headed.

"He's a man and should be held responsible for his own actions. You can't coddle him forever."

"I'm not coddling him. I'm merely giving him the opportunities he was meant to have," she said, repeating the words she had used time and again, and refusing to examine how they were starting to ring with the hollow note of an excuse.

Timothy let out a heavy sigh. "I know you love him, Rose." Of course she did. He was her younger brother and the only family she had left. "But you aren't doing him any favors by solving his problems for him. And he will discover the debts have been paid. What will you tell him when he questions you about it?"

"He won't question it. He'll simply be relieved they were taken care of for him." Regardless of Dash's attempt to play the bristly adult male, he had to know deep down that the only way the debts would be cleared would be if she took care of them. He had no income other than his allowance, after all. If their father was alive, if he hadn't beggared the estate, he would see to such matters. As it was, it was left to her. "But he *is* only eighteen. Why would anyone lend such sums to one so young?"

"It's not as if he is penniless. He's from a good family, frequents the best tailors, and runs with others of his ilk. He wouldn't look like much of a risk. And if it comes down to it, he has his bachelor apartments. That place cost you a tidy sum. It could go a decent way toward repayment."

She definitely did not want to think about it coming to that. The irony that all her efforts had led her to this point was not lost on her. She couldn't very well change her course now. One decision five years ago had set it in stone. But however much she wished to delay it, soon she would need to have another discussion with Dash. She could not afford to return to London and find his vowels had multiplied in her absence. In her experience, one rarely succeeded in gambling their way out of a hole, but that didn't mean Dash wouldn't try.

The hackney slowed to a stop in the back courtyard. But rather than bring yet more dread chasing down on her, the sight of the back door raised her spirits for the first time . . . ever. That door would lead her to James. In just a handful of hours, she would see him again. Just the thought of being with him had her reaching for the brass lever on the carriage door, a smile flittering on her lips. And she had no doubt he would make good on his unspoken promise of more.

Ten

GOOSEFLESH rose across her belly, flaring up to tighten her nipples, as James used a damp towel to carefully wipe away the physical proof of his climax. He was not only handsome and kind, but thoughtful and considerate, as well. The man was near perfect.

"Come here and kiss me," Rose murmured, coasting her hand up his arm.

"I thought you'd never ask," he said, his mouth quirking.

As if he had not already spent the evening indulging the pleas tumbling past her lips, she wanted more. More of his kisses, his touch, more of him.

Eyes heavily lidded and hair tousled from her greedy fingers, he dropped the length of towel to the floor and shifted from his seated position on the edge of the bed to move into her open arms.

Sweat-dampened skin met hers as he settled between her legs, his weight braced on his elbows. The light smattering of hair on his chest teased her breasts made sensitive from the attentions of his decadent mouth. No one would guess by looking at him that he could not only do such scandalous things with his mouth, but also took great pleasure in bestowing them on her. The conservative façade hid a sensual side that effortlessly wrapped her in a veil of sublime decadence. His hot tongue adeptly finding the most sensitive spots on her body, his soft yet firm lips made to be on hers.

Slow and lazy, he kissed her, pausing every now and then to rub his nose against hers or to nip lightly at her bottom lip. She adored this new playful side of him. It had made its first real appearance last night, after that dreadful afternoon visiting the hells, and she was quite grateful it had not been a singular event.

The man who had once balked at just the mention of her bedchamber was long gone. The last two evenings had been spent right here in her bed. The bronze coverlet bunched at the foot, the white sheets rumpled and twisted. The fire in the hearth warming the room, the drapes closed tight against the dark sky. Under the soft glow of the candles, he lavished her body with affection, consuming her senses, enveloping her in a world she never wanted to leave. Never before had she so looked forward to the night, and this was her favorite part of all.

Bodies sated, impatient lust appeased, when they could touch and kiss at their leisure, and enjoy simply being together.

She dragged her lips down his neck, mouthed at his pulse. A low growl rumbled in his throat. Then she pushed on his shoulder. That was all that was needed. Just a light nudge and he rolled onto his back, taking her with him.

Her hair tumbled over her shoulders, a dark curtain on either side of her face. One more kiss, and then she pushed up to straddle his waist. Starting at his right shoulder, she worked her way down his arm, gently kneading the hard muscles. Over the bulk of his biceps, his skin smooth as satin, and down to his strong corded forearm, the fine hairs tickling her fingertips. She had vowed to make his evenings as enjoyable as possible, and judging by the raspy grunts of content pleasure, she was succeeding.

His lashes drifted closed. A grateful smile stole across his mouth. Focusing all of her attention on him, she captured his large hand in both of hers, brought it up and massaged his callused palm. Worked the space between his forefinger and thumb. Let his finger slide through her grip, giving it a little tug before moving on to the next.

The big body beneath her was completely lax as she set his arm at his side. His left arm received just as much attention as his right. And then she moved to his chest, sweeping her hands in long slow drags over the broad expanse.

"Come here and kiss me." His eyes were still closed, but the once lazy curve of his mouth had taken on a sinful twist.

"I thought you'd never ask," she replied, throwing his words back at him.

His chest rumbled with the beginnings of a chuckle as she leaned down to press her lips to his. Hands gripped her hips, and then he rolled them so he was on top of her once again. Time and tomorrow had no place in her head when he kissed her. His adept tongue caressing hers, the stubble from his day's beard tickling her cheek.

He gave her chin a little nip and then pulled back. "I should let you get some rest," he said, brushing her temple with his thumb in a gentle, lulling caress.

Cool air hit her skin as he shifted off to get out of bed. With her cheek resting in her palm, she stretched out on her side and watched as he grabbed his trousers and drawers from the floor at the foot of the bed. He was definitely physically perfect, well-defined muscles rippling beneath pale golden skin and with shoulders that seemed to go on forever. The hours he spent in his warehouse had given him a body more suited to manual labor than pushing papers about a desk, and she was quite thankful for it.

The white shirt he found at the side of the bed, where he had thrown it in his haste to remove it. He leaned down to give her a quick kiss before pulling the shirt over his head. As he moved about the room, finding his clothes and putting them on, he continued to gift her with kisses. A press of his lips to the tip of her nose, to her forehead, to her cheek. A faint flush stained his cheekbones, his hair practically standing on end. The soft green depths of his eyes sparkled with happiness.

His good mood should have been infectious, but with each sweet kiss, her spirits dimmed another notch. With each kiss she wondered if it would be her last from him. The last time she felt the warm press of his lips. The last time she could take a deep, full breath of him.

The seventh night. It always defined the end. Never before had she been tempted to remain at Rubicon's longer than one week. But where relief usually resided was now an aching void that grew larger by the second, threatening to encompass her entire chest.

"Why so glum?" he asked, slipping his arms into his tan waistcoat.

"I'm not glum."

"But there's no smile. And no, that one won't do," he added at her failed attempt.

He cupped the back of her head. A whisper-light kiss, then his lips drifted down her neck to her breast. Hot and wet, his tongue trailed over her nipple as a large hand drifted up her inner thigh, a light, ticklish touch.

Giggling, she swatted his hand away.

"Much better," he declared with a satisfied nod before turning his attention to the buttons on his waistcoat.

As he stopped by the bed to grab his cravat from the floor, he stole another kiss. "May I see you tomorrow?"

There wasn't a bit of doubt in his question. He spoke as though he was confident in her answer, but he had asked nonetheless. She adored that about him—he never demanded or assumed. He actually cared about her wishes.

He placed the long length of white linen about his neck, adjusting it under his collar, his full attention on her.

She wanted to remain here forever with him, but knew she could not. He had a life beyond these walls that did not include her. She was well aware of it, even if she had chosen to ignore it these past few nights. After years of being with men who cared only for themselves, who only saw her as a beautiful object of pleasure, was it so wrong to savor these precious moments with James? To have the sun set without dread falling over her. To indulge in a glimpse of the happiness she could never have.

But it was a glimpse and nothing more. Nor could it be more. Their time needed to come to an end, and now was its natural conclusion.

She pushed up to a seated position. That aching void now filling her chest, she shook her head. "No."

Her refusal echoed in the room, hanging in the air between them.

Confusion and shock flickered across on his handsome face before comprehension settled over his features. His fingers stilled. All traces of happiness drained away, and the sight made her want to snatch back the refusal. To leap off the bed, throw her arms around his neck, press her lips to his, and reassure him that she had not meant it at all. Yet she moved not a muscle.

He nodded once, stiff and remote. He turned to the mirror above her dresser and went back to tying his cravat. A sharp tug on the ends, flipping one over the other, forming the knot. But the quick efficient ease he had displayed just last night, of a man seeing to a long-accustomed task, was gone. Lips set in a grim line, he jerked the knot loose and started anew.

She should remain quiet. Should just let him leave silent and clearly hurt. But she did not want their time together to end like this—with him believing she did not want him. For that was what he believed; the rejection reflected in the oval mirror. And it was the furthest thing from the truth.

"James, it's not that I don't want to be with you."

He held up a hand, not meeting her gaze in the mirror. "There is no need to humor me. I understand."

"No. You don't. I won't be here tomorrow. I work one week a month, and tonight is my last night."

He went still once again. Finally met her gaze in the mirror. A crease marred his brow. "You aren't here every night?"

"Only every night of the first week of the month."

"And you're leaving tomorrow?"

She nodded.

That crease turned into a scowl. "Three-night limit my arse," he grumbled under his breath.

"Pardon?"

"When I arrived late to find you unavailable, I attempted to secure you for the next few days, but Rubicon informed me the limit was three. Gave some paltry excuse, but this is the real reason. She knew you would be leaving tomorrow."

Slack-jawed, she blinked in disbelief. He had secured her for tonight and the prior two, which meant he had paid Rubicon in advance. Yet he had still asked to see her again at the end of each night. And she knew in her bones that if she would have refused, he would have acceded to her wishes. Not returned the next night, even though he had already purchased that right.

Reeling, all she could do was stare at him. He was such a noble man. So good and so kind. And after he walked out her door, she would never lay eyes on him again.

"Where will you go?"

"Home," she heard herself say, blinking back the tears that threatened to prick the corners of her eyes. "To the country. Until next month." When she would return to this room and he would not. Time and distance would dull his memories, though certainly not her own. The conscience that had gripped him on their first night together would have weeks to reassert itself, keeping him far from this house, as well it should.

He turned from the dresser. "Come to the country with me." The words popped out of his mouth so quickly, it appeared he startled himself.

He had certainly startled her. "Pardon?"

"I—I . . ." He took a moment, clearly gathering himself. She braced for him to rescind the offer. "I have a house in the country. I would be honored if you would be my guest for the next week."

The fragile hope in his eyes pulled at her heart. Ducking her chin, she twisted the rumpled sheet at her hip. The urge to accept rose within her. To grab hold of that week with both hands and never let go. But she held back. "I can't."

"Why not? I'll compensate you for your time, of course."

That hurt. She tugged the sheet over her lap, covering herself. "James . . ."

"Seven nights, and days. Would a thousand pounds be enough?"

She shook her head, as her pulse began to skitter through her veins.

"No? Fifteen hundred?"

A wince tightened her brow. *Please, make him stop.*

"I'll have to return in the morning with the money anyway, so whatever the sum, simply name it."

If he had tried to hand her a fold of pound notes, she would have refused on the spot. Would have shrunk back, not even touching a fingertip to the notes. The concept of selling herself was easier to swallow when the situation wasn't so blatant. When it didn't make her feel like a pretty pet purchased at a shop.

"The expense matters not to me. Whatever the price, I'll pay it." He let out a frustrated breath. "Two thousand pounds."

Her heart stilled as the sum echoed in her head. A thousand for Rubicon, a thousand to pay off Dash's gambling debts, and then some. More money than she had ever had at any one point in time.

"You'd be my guest at my house in Alton. It's nothing extravagant, but I have a small staff and the grounds are quite nice. You would be free to do as you please, and to leave whenever you please. You have my word, Rose, if you wish to return to London at any time, I'll see you back myself." Then he added in a pleading tone, "I just want to spend more time with you."

"But I don't have appropriate attire for a holiday in the country." *Lovely.* Now she was grasping for excuses.

"Not to worry. I'll see to everything. All you need to bring is yourself." The mattress shifted as he sat on the edge of the bed. "Come away with me," he said softly.

He twined his fingers through hers, and suddenly there wasn't a decision to make.

Peering up at him through her lashes, she nodded.

"Really?"

"Yes."

Capturing her face, he slanted his mouth over hers, the joy and relief clear in his kiss. Pulling back enough to break the kiss, he brushed his nose against hers, the smile back on his lips. "Thank you."

He stood and tugged on the cravat hanging from his neck, realigning the ends.

Crooking a finger, she beckoned him. "I can see to that for you." She moved onto her knees and scooted to the edge of the mattress.

He lifted his chin. "I have a few errands to see to in the morning, and I'll need to make arrangements for my absence," he said. The backs of her fingers brushed his bristly jaw as she looped one end of the white linen over the other, forming the knot. An intimate ritual, one she really should not get accustomed to performing for him. Still, it felt so very right. "Do you think you could be ready to depart by three in the afternoon?"

A little tug to define the creases, and she produced a neat Mathematical knot. "Of course." That would give her time to stop by the hells and also to call on Dash.

"Brilliant," he said, slipping on his brown coat. He tipped his head and made to leave the room.

"Wait," she called.

He turned from the door.

"Come here."

He didn't question, but did as she asked, stopping beside the bed.

"Your hair," she murmured, as she smoothed the tousled strands. Not quite as neat as when she saw him that morning at the park, but the best she could manage without a comb.

He gave a little chuckle. "Thank you, my dear." Capturing her other hand, he brought it up to grace the back with a light kiss. "Until tomorrow, then."

"Yes." *Tomorrow.* She would see him tomorrow, and the day after and the day after. Seven more nights with him.

Eleven

FINGERTIPS brushed lightly against her side, gathering fabric into a neat dart. Rose braced for the prick of the needle, but it never came. The woman was clearly an expert. With quick, efficient, and deft movements, the modiste focused on her task, which was rather monumental. Three young assistants were scattered about the sitting room. Two on the settee and one on a chair Rose had borrowed from another room in the house. Baskets of sewing accoutrements were at their feet, their heads bowed over the garments in their laps.

Rose had not known what to expect when James said he would see to everything, but she certainly hadn't expected this. His generosity knew no bounds.

The modiste and her assistants had arrived at a little after ten in the morning, approximately an hour and a half ago, bearing partially sewn day dresses, traveling dresses, a couple of simple gowns for evenings, a riding habit, and a pelisse. There was no way the women could have started the garments today. They had to have been intended for another, likely a wealthy woman, given the fine fabrics, and James had commandeered them for her. Certainly a considerable sum had been needed to accomplish the deed.

The modiste even did a decent job of masking her scorn for having to dress a whore at a brothel. It had to have been more than a considerable sum. The assistants weren't gawking at her, either.

The money was definitely not something to wave aside as insignificant, but that James had gone out of his way that very morning to arrange a wardrobe for her . . .

The smile that had been hovering on her lips broadened into a grin as warmth filled her chest. She could imagine him, his imposing, masculine presence in stark contrast to the modiste's feminine shop, as he relayed his request and the way the woman's initial refusal had quickly turned into complete acquiescence. She could almost hear his deep, baritone voice—*The expense matters not to me. Whatever the price, I'll pay it.*

A distinctive double knock sounded on her sitting room door. "Come in," she called.

The door swung open. As one, the assistants paused, hands suspended above the garments in their laps, as Timothy entered the room dressed in a white shirt and brown trousers, his usual morning attire. He didn't spare them more than a curious glance as he took up a place near the fireplace, resting a shoulder casually against the wall.

The modiste cleared her throat, the abrupt sound jolting the assistants back to the tasks before them. Though Rose noticed how the one with the mousy brown hair kept sneaking not-so-covert glances at him. She was tempted to tell the girl the effort was futile. To her knowledge, Timothy never dallied with anyone, female or male, unless he was working.

"The pins are in," the modiste said, as she unbuttoned the neat row down the back of the simple evening gown. "Off with this one." She paused, her hands on Rose's shoulders, poised to drag the short cap sleeves down her arms. "Perhaps you would prefer to make use of a screen?"

Rose shook her head. It wasn't as if she was bare beneath the garment, and it was only Timothy. He regularly saw women in a considerably greater state of undress. "Here is fine."

"I heard you had guests." Timothy motioned to the room, the gesture encompassing the modiste and the assistants. "Care to explain?"

She chuckled as the modiste exchanged the dress for another. A lovely muted green lightweight cashmere. A day dress perfect for walks on a brisk spring day. She had never had a small army's worth of tradespeople all focused on her. It was quite the experience, one that fluffed her feminine vanity and made her feel rather like a princess. "I'm in need of a new wardrobe."

He arched a light brown brow in a silent request for more.

"The gentleman you met at the park has extended an invitation for a short holiday in the country."

"And you accepted?" The disbelief was clear on his face.

"Actually, I refused. This lovely modiste showed up on her own, bearing the makings of a necessary wardrobe for such a holiday." She let out an exasperated sigh, but the effect was surely dampened by the smile on her lips. "Of course I accepted. We depart this afternoon."

"You agreed because of Dash's situation, didn't you?"

His suspicious tone prodded her protective instincts, yet she stayed silent. If she agreed, he'd pin the blame on Dash when the full blame should not be laid at his feet. But a denial contained an admission she didn't want to examine.

The modiste bustled about her as Timothy slouched against the wall, arms crossed over his chest and lips pursed.

"Are you certain about this?"

"Yes. It's only for a week."

He raised both eyebrows. She knew he was concerned for her, and she adored him for it, but he needn't be. It wasn't as if James was setting her up in a neat little town house on the edge of Mayfair. The arrangement didn't hold even a shade of permanence. It was only for a week. That was all. A week to see to his pleasure and nothing more. She knew better than to allow softer sentiment to enter the arrangement, to read something into his offer that wasn't there.

As long as she kept their holiday in perspective, she would be just fine. And for all she knew, perhaps he wasn't married. Perhaps he was a recent widower. A rather unlikely notion, but surely not outside the realm of possibilities.

If she was being honest with herself, she would admit she was merely trying to move aside immovable objects. To fool herself into believing her original objections no longer held merit. But . . .

It was only for a week. No true harm could come from it, and she'd be able to spend another seven days with James.

"Do you know where you are headed?" Timothy asked.

"To Alton. He has a house there."

He furrowed his brow, doing a very good imitation of a stern, suspicious father. "What sort of house?"

"A country house. And he has a staff, so it's not as if I'll be there alone with him."

"When are you leaving, and when are you returning?"

"We leave later this afternoon and return next Wednesday. The fourteenth. He will see me back to London himself, and if I wish to leave before then, I am free to do so."

He looked down to his shoes and then back up at her. "Are you certain you can trust him?"

His dark eyes were filled with unmistakable worry. He was the only person she had ever confided in. The only soul who knew exactly why she preferred the brothel over life as a mistress. She had not divulged the full truth to Rubicon when she had first presented herself in the woman's office four years ago. Even after she had struck her deal with the madam, she had only revealed enough to gain Rubicon's assurance that Lord Wheatly would no longer be a concern.

But James had nothing at all in common with his lordship. James never demanded, never expected perfection, never raised his voice nor his hand to her. He wouldn't turn into a different man once he had her under his thumb. He asked and allowed her the courtesy of refusing, though she had yet to actually outright refuse him anything. He was her client, after all. But the opportunity was there if she ever wished to exercise it.

Their conversation had attracted the attention of all three assistants and the modiste, judging by the sudden lack of movement at the hem of her dress where the woman had been pinning. Even though she could feel the expectant stares, she kept her attention trained on Timothy, willing him to read the sincerity in her eyes. "Yes, I trust him. Absolutely."

He studied her for a long moment. Just when she thought he would question her further, he shrugged. "You could certainly use a holiday," he said pragmatically. "I hope you enjoy yourself."

Anticipation bubbled within, light and airy, a wonderful effervescent sensation. She hadn't genuinely looked forward to anything in years, since her father's death. "It won't be a true holiday. I will be working, after all. But I do believe it will turn out to be a pleasant week."

He peppered her with a few more questions, all of them mundane, which she answered to the best of her limited knowledge as the modiste finished pinning the day dress and started on a traveling dress. Why Timothy believed she'd be aware of such details as the number of servants at James's country house or its exact proximity to the village of Alton, she didn't know. He was on the verge of testing her patience when another knock sounded on her door. This one brief, a mere tap of knuckles in prelude to the door swinging open.

Rubicon swept into the room clad in a lace-edged pink silk wrapper. Her hair was pulled up in an elaborate knot, her face painted with the usual rouge and kohl: a madam in deliberately arranged dishabille. Rose's attention snapped to the bundle in the madam's hand. A sheet of paper wrapped around what could only be a thick fold of pound notes. That bundle meant James had been here, at the house, sometime this morning. He had been a floor below her, yet he hadn't asked to see her to even stop in for a quick good morning. She tamped down the little surge of disappointment. James was a busy man. Surely he had many responsibilities to tend to before leaving town.

"Good morning, Rose," Rubicon said, not acknowledging Timothy's presence. The smile curving her rouged lips took Rose aback as she murmured a greeting. She never looked this happy when not in view of clients. No doubt she was pleased at the unexpected income Rose had brought to the house.

Over the years, Rose had found the madam to be stern and shrewd but fair, at least to her. Not someone she would ever call friend, but a tolerable employer. She made no qualms about her expectations of her employees. The house was renowned for the quality of its merchandise. Heaven help anyone who caused even the slightest of smudges to that reputation. But as long as Rose's clients left with a smile on their faces and a will to return, then she'd remain in the madam's good graces. And herself, well . . . she would ever be grateful to the madam for acceding to her unique schedule and assuring her safety while under this roof.

"My dear Rose, you have outdone yourself. You have quite the admirer. So very generous. How ever did you manage it?"

Rose didn't need to ask to know Rubicon was referring to half of the outrageous sum James had delivered that morning. She kept the truth to herself and merely gave a little shrug, as if the task hadn't been any effort at all. Which it hadn't. James had upped the sum until the sheer number had posed too heavy a lure. And the madam certainly did not need to know that James would have continued raising the number until she had agreed. Though it would be nice if someday she could spend time with a gentleman without the need for money to change hands.

Fanciful thinking. That day would never come, even after she left this house never to return. No decent man would want to sully himself with used goods.

"I'm assuming he spoke the truth and you have agreed to be his companion for the next week?" At Rose's nod, she continued, "If I had known you were open to such arrangements, I would have seen to them for you long ago."

"I don't believe it will be something to make a habit of. I'm quite content with our current arrangement." Unwilling to explain herself further, Rose flicked her fingers toward her bedchamber door. The modiste was on her knees, auburn head bowed as she adjusted the hem of the soft blue traveling dress. If she told Rubicon she had agreed only because of the money, then the madam would surely do her best in the future to lure gentlemen to match the sum, thus forcing Rose into the uncomfortable position of having to refuse an identical offer. If she gave James himself as the reason, then she would reveal herself as a fool. A whore knew better than to even allow herself to grow fond of a client, and Rose feared she had crossed that line nights ago. "Could I ask you to please put the package on the dresser? I'm a bit indisposed at the moment."

"Of course, my dear." Rubicon disappeared briefly into the bed-chamber and then reappeared to wish her a pleasant holiday before leaving to tend to other matters within the house. The overall visit was not more than a handful of minutes and exactly the way Rose preferred it.

"Done," the modiste declared. "This is the last one of the bunch. A few hours and the alterations will be complete."

"Do you have plans for the afternoon?" Rose asked Timothy as she took off the dress.

"None," Timothy replied.

"Brilliant. While I get dressed, could you go grab your coat? I need your help with some errands before I leave Town." First the hells, and then Dash. Not a conversation she was looking forward to, but a necessity. James may have provided the means to quickly solve this round of problems, but he would not be there to solve the next, nor should he. Dash was not his responsibility, but hers. And she could not leave town without at least attempting to convince him to curb his gambling.

⚜

REBECCA knocked on the door to her brother's study and turned the knob, not waiting for a response. James was expecting her. A servant had relayed his message that he wished to speak to her. A message she had been surprised to receive. Not because of the request itself, but because of the time. It was early afternoon, and he was still at the house. She had assumed he'd left for his office directly after breakfast. The man worked himself to the bone, just like their father.

The thick Aubusson rug silenced her footsteps as she crossed the study. The rich mahogany paneling lining the walls and the deep saturated color of the green leather wingback chairs lent the room a distinctly masculine feel, marking it in contrast to every other room in the house. Even the furniture was larger, more substantial, so much so that it muted the effect of James's tall frame as he bustled about behind his oak desk, gathering papers and files and stuffing them into a leather bag.

"Good morning," he said, briefly glancing up. "I wanted to inform you that I will be leaving town for a week. A short visit to the country." He pulled open a drawer and grabbed a sheaf of papers. "I doubt you'll even notice my absence, what with the excitement of the upcoming Season. But in the event you remembered you had a brother, I thought it wise to inform you now that you will not find me in the house over the next seven days."

"James," she admonished playfully. "You will have me taking offense. I could never forget you."

"Of course not. I am your dearest brother, after all." He chuckled as he shut the drawer. "Do you have any plans for the day?"

"Amelia mentioned a visit to Bond Street."

"If anything catches your eye, simply—"

". . . send the bill to you. Yes, I know."

Goodness, he seemed . . . happy. Truly happy. She hadn't seen him smile like this, so carefree and without a worry, in ages. It wasn't that James was a melancholy fellow. But he was a rather serious sort, fully focused on his responsibilities, and had grown more so since his marriage. She tilted her head a bit to one side, studying him as he checked the contents of his leather bag. There was a bit of color to his cheeks, and it wasn't due to exertion from his frantic movements. He appeared distracted, as though his mind was elsewhere. And that "elsewhere" was responsible for the smile fixed on his mouth.

She *had* seen that smile recently. The other day at the park, when he had introduced her to that beautiful woman. The one with the black hair and the stunning light blue eyes that hadn't left her brother.

"Will Miss Rose be leaving town as well?" she asked, as casual as could be, just as he reached across his desk toward the silver inkwell and pen.

The pen clattered to the wooden floor.

She stooped down, picked up the pen, and held it out to him. "You're taking her to Honey House, are you not?"

Eyes wide, he stared at her. One would think he was twelve and she had caught him stealing tarts from the kitchen. He snatched the pen from her hand, stuffing it into an inside pocket of his bag. "It is none of your concern, Rebecca."

So she had guessed correctly. Honey House meant a lot to James. She had spent a few short summer holidays there with him. Idyllic sunny days filled with long walks about the countryside. At Honey House, it was almost as if he was once again the carefree adolescent boy who had wanted nothing more than to spend the day with his younger sister. Miss Rose must be very important to him if he was taking her there. "She seemed very pleasant."

His lips thinned. "It is best you forget her."

"Is she your—"

"Rebecca," he said firmly, cutting her off before she could say the word *mistress*. "I am not going to discuss her with you." He went back to gathering his things.

As if she would be intimidated by his stern frown . . . She wanted to give him a kiss on the cheek and tell him she was nothing but happy for him. He needn't feel obligated to shelter her about such topics. It wasn't as if she was an empty-headed miss with no knowledge of the way of things. This wasn't her first visit to London. James and Amelia's marriage was a typical one of the aristocracy, formed more as an alliance than out of any sort of fondness for one another. Though James bore it as best as any man could, it had been clear from the day of their wedding that he and Amelia did not suit. The fault did not lie with either of them; it was just their personalities. Amelia belonged at beautiful, glittering ton balls, whereas James was more at his ease in the country.

It hadn't taken much to notice that Amelia had lovers. She was certain she had been introduced to the current one at the Marksons' supper party. Amelia's entire demeanor had changed when she had spoken to Lord Albert. A certain softness had lit up her face. And now James had found someone who made him smile. She would be ever grateful to Miss Rose for that.

"She is very pretty."

He grunted, his mouth twitching at the corners. "She's beyond beautiful."

"Are you leaving now?"

A flip of the buckle and he closed his bag. "I need to stop by the office first, make arrangements for my absence, and see to one last errand. I've left a note for Amelia informing her I will be gone as well." Something behind her caught his attention, his gaze snapping over her shoulder. "Hiller," he called.

She glanced over her shoulder. Out in the corridor, one of the footmen was passing the study. The man halted and backed up a step to stand in the open door, his hands clasped behind his back.

"Yes, Mr. Archer?"

"Is the traveling carriage ready?"

"Yes, Mr. Archer," the man said with a deferential tip of the head. "All is at the ready. Your valise has already been taken down to the carriage."

"Thank you." James grabbed his leather bag and rounded his desk, stopping at her side. "You will be all right if I leave for a week?" Concern touched his eyes.

"Of course." She gave him a reassuring smile. She would miss him at the breakfast table, but the next week would be filled with shopping excursions, afternoon calls, and discussions over the merits of various invitations. The height of excitement for her, but nothing that would even pique James's interest or require him to serve as escort.

"If you have need of anything, send a note. I'll return posthaste if necessary."

He dropped a kiss on her forehead and left the study, practically running out the door in his haste to leave.

⚜

Rose closed the trunk and flipped the latches. All was set. She had returned to the house to find the dresses completed and laid out for her inspection, along with all of the necessary accoutrements: stockings, chemises, slippers, a pair of sturdy leather half boots, a couple of bonnets, and even a few pairs of kidskin leather gloves. Everything she could possibly need for the coming week. The only item not in the wardrobe—a nightgown. Was that by James's instruction, or had the modiste merely not had the time to complete one? Though the modiste had managed to complete the navy wrapper, the silk so fine it flowed over her fingers like cool water.

As she had changed into something more appropriate for the journey, the modiste's assistants had packed the new trunk, which also had been waiting in her sitting room when she had returned. It truly was a marvel what a considerable sum could accomplish.

Standing, she passed a hand over the front of her new soft blue traveling dress. It was practical yet elegantly tailored with small fabric-covered buttons running from her navel all the way up to the demure neckline at her collarbone. A man had purchased her a dress that did not prominently feature her breasts. Now that was a true marvel.

"Is there anything else you need?" Timothy asked as he emerged from her bedchamber, her dark cloak draped over his arm.

"No." She had already added her brush, the miniature of Dash, and the tin of hairpins to the trunk.

"I'll be sure to inquire at the hells while you are gone."

"Thank you." They had decided that was the best course of action, the only way to determine if or when Dash made use of his newly repaired credit. Her knock on the door of his apartments had been met with silence. In a way, she was rather glad of it. She was certainly not of a mind to begin her holiday with an argument.

Timothy settled the cloak about her shoulders, taking much longer than necessary to see to the clasp. "I will miss you."

The heavy note behind his low words gave her pause. He had been getting progressively quieter as three o'clock drew nearer. "As I you. But it's not as if you won't see me in a week. James will return me here before I set off for Bedfordshire, and then I'll be back next month."

His brows knit together. His lashes were lowered, as he hadn't taken his attention from the clasp on her cloak. "I must have you know how very much I value our friendship."

"Timothy—?"

He pressed his lips to her cheek. The lightest of kisses. A mere whisper of a butterfly's wing. When he straightened, a smile curved his mouth. That worry, that hint of pain that had crossed his features was gone as if it had never been there. But perhaps it had been concern and nothing more.

"I hope you enjoy the country. And let Mr. Archer know that if he takes a step out of line, he'll be answering to me."

"While I appreciate the sentiment, perhaps that's not the wisest choice of threats. James has a few stones' worth of muscle on you."

He scoffed, doing a very good imitation of an indignant aristocrat. "A little thing like size has never intimidated me."

A startled laugh burst from her throat. "Timothy," she admonished.

He shrugged, completely unrepentant, and leaned down to pick up her trunk. "The hour has arrived." He tipped his head toward the door. "Mr. Archer awaits."

A burst of anticipation, so thick and heavy it caused her breaths to stutter, shot through her. One week with James. A week that did not involve this room or this house.

She quickly grabbed the black leather gloves from the side table and opened the main door of her sitting room, allowing Timothy to pass, and then went out to meet James.

Twelve

ROSE'S soft, hitching breaths filled the twilight-dark confines of the traveling carriage. She shifted, her luscious backside rubbing against his painfully hard cock. She was sprawled decadently on his lap with her back to his chest, her knees hooked over his spread thighs, her skirts bunched at her waist, her bodice unbuttoned down to her navel. James drifted his hand up from her hip, to caress one breast, the firm weight heavy in his palm, as he continued to play with her with the other. Gliding over the soft, silken flesh slick from her arousal. Playing at the entrance to her body, then sweeping up to brush her clit.

"There?" he whispered in her ear, though the question wasn't necessary. The way she arched into his touch was answer enough. But he needed to hear her response. Needed to hear how he pleased her.

"Yes, yes," she said, in a heated rush.

She grabbed his hand when he made to move from that highly sensitive spot, demanding his attention where she wanted it. He wanted to wait. To keep her suspended on the knife's edge of bliss, pliant in his arms and begging for more. Needing him and only him. But he let her do as she pleased, taking what she needed from him. Her small hand clutched tightly over his, guiding his movements to match her desires. Later, once they reached the inn and they were alone in their bed, he'd make love to her for hours and wake up with her in his arms. Now, though, wasn't the place to indulge his desires.

A quick tug on the stays freed her breasts. Through the thin fabric of her silk chemise, he captured one nipple between his forefinger and thumb and gently squeezed.

Her breath hitched on a moan of purest pleasure. *"Yes."*

He increased the pressure, pinching to the point of pain, receiving another moan for his efforts. The scent of her arousal hung heavy in the air, teasing his tongue with his every panting breath. He wanted to taste her, to ply her with his mouth instead of his fingers. To capture the sensitive bud between his lips and coax the climax from her body.

The carriage hit a rut in the road, jostling her on his lap, pressing his erection between the rounded halves of her derrière. His ballocks tightened, the orgasm he'd been trying to keep at bay now teasing the base of his spine. All he needed to do was rock his hips against the motion of the carriage. Less than a minute and he would be spilling his seed in his trousers like a green lad, the proof of their traveling activities marking the placket for all at the inn to see.

Gritting his teeth, he fought back the orgasm and focused on driving her over the edge. Her body went taut, her thighs gripping his with surprising force, her fingernails digging into the skin on the back of his hand. He whispered his lips over her ear, nipped at the lobe, and then pressed a kiss over her rapidly beating pulse.

On a soft, high-pitched cry, she shattered in his arms. He felt the release rack her body and then she went lax, slumping against him.

After a moment, she moved off him and snuggled close to his

side. "Now where have my manners gone?" she asked with a teasing twist.

"It's all right." He laid a hand over hers, stopping its progress up his thigh before those wonderfully adept fingers could reach their destination. It was much easier to stick to his plan for the evening when she wasn't touching him.

She tipped her head back to meet his gaze. A few wisps of hair had escaped the neat knot at her nape, framing her face. It was so dark in the carriage he could barely make out her features, let alone her expression. But he didn't need the light to read her confusion.

"Later." He gave her hand a pat and wrapped his arm around her shoulders. "Why don't you rest? I'll wake you when we arrive."

He felt the force of her gaze and then she gave a little shrug. "If that's what you wish," she said, tugging her stays up to cover her breasts. "And I certainly won't protest a bit of rest. I've been in a carriage for most of the day yet I find myself oddly tired. I wonder why?"

He chuckled, not even attempting to mask the smug pride. She saw to the buttons on her bodice and then adjusted her skirt over her legs folded beside her. Shifting slightly on the bench, he did his best to reposition himself without reaching down and tried not to think about the coming night as Rose drifted off to sleep.

Some time later the carriage slowed to a stop, pulling James from that lazy place somewhere between sleep and full consciousness. Rose was nestled up against his side, her cheek pressed to his chest, his arm still draped around her shoulders. The steady rhythm of her sleeping breaths went undisturbed. He was loath to wake her, but they couldn't very well remain in the carriage all night.

He caught the faint scent of cooked meat and his stomach grumbled, reminding him it had been hours since they had last stopped for a bite to eat. A room, then supper, and then to bed with Rose, in that order.

A smile tipped his lips, his prick twitching to life once again.

Rose definitely made the journey to Alton more enjoyable. The hours had slipped by. He had only once opened his leather bag, which currently occupied the opposite bench, and even then it had been out of habit and not from a pressing desire to get any work done. The bag hadn't remained open long. Just knowing Rose was but a touch away had pushed thoughts of his office, and its various concerns, far from his mind.

Not that she had spent the entire day with her skirt bunched at her waist. On the contrary. She had spent most of the day sitting beside him, her small hand in his. They had talked of the weather, of London, and the sights they had passed along the road. Trivial matters. But the subjects didn't concern him so much as simply having her with him. Every now and then he had leaned in to steal a kiss, but other than that, he had resisted the urge to indulge until the sun had started to set. With the inside of the carriage veiled by shadows, those stolen kisses had quickly turned into more.

The sounds of footsteps on gravel outside the carriage jolted him to the present. He heard a boy's voice, likely a groom, and his driver's answering response.

"Rose," he whispered, nuzzling the top of her head. "Wake up, dear."

She let out a little grumpy noise in protest and shifted against him. He reluctantly relinquished his hold, allowing her to push away from him and sit up. She rubbed her eyes and blinked at him. "Where are we?"

"A coaching inn. Up with you now, I need to secure us a room."

She leaned forward, peering around his shoulder and out the window above the door. "We are staying here for the night?"

"Yes. We didn't depart until midafternoon, and Alton is a good day's ride from London." A triangle of golden light from the lamps outside the inn cut across her profile. Her once drowsy eyes were now wide with trepidation. "I often stop here to change horses, and

I've stayed the night a time or two when the weather was not coop-
erating. The inn is quite safe, I assure you."

She didn't look convinced. "Can't we simply change horses and
continue on? There's nary a cloud in the sky."

"No, it's much too late. In any case, my housekeeper isn't expecting us until tomorrow." He held up a hand to the footman
approaching the door, bidding him to wait, and lowered his voice.
"Do you wish me to secure a separate room for you, or do you wish
to stay with me?"

"With you," she said, easing his worry that her concern was
borne from a desire not to share a room with him. But her hands
were clasped tight in her lap, her attention still trained on the inn,
and her slim shoulders held a distinctly defensive hunch.

"Is something the matter?"

"No." Her deep breath filled the carriage. She grabbed her cloak
from the opposite bench, slipped it about her, and then pulled up
the hood. "All right."

He opened his mouth, about to question her further, but stopped.
Maybe she was simply caught off guard. Perhaps he should have
informed her they would need to stay at an inn for the night, but
he was so accustomed to traveling by himself, he hadn't thought to
mention it. Given the time of their departure, the inn was a foregone conclusion.

Nothing to be done about it now. As he got out of the carriage
and held out a hand to help her to exit, he tried to give her a reassuring glance, but her beautiful face was cloaked by the shadows
created by her hood. Side by side, they approached the door. He
made to place his hand on the small of her back, but before his
palm could fully settle on her woolen cloak, she sidestepped just
enough to be out of reach.

He opened the door and followed her inside. Grady's was the
type of posting inn that dotted the roads all along England. Noth-

ing extravagant or luxurious, but the proprietor was pleasant and the rooms clean. A couple of patrons mingled about the small entrance hall. Muted voices and the *clink* of glassware drifted from the dining room down the corridor. He glanced to the parlor on the right, its double doors open, and saw a few more patrons lounging in the armchairs before the hearth, drinks in hand.

Rose remained close to his side and a half step behind him, her head bowed beneath the hood of her cloak, as he made arrangements for the night. Given the fair weather, the inn wasn't bursting at the seams, and he was able to secure the room he usually stayed in without any problem. Tucked in the rear of the inn on the second floor, few other guests would have cause to traipse past the door. And it also had a bed large enough to accommodate his frame. He hated those narrow things that populated most inns.

As he pulled the necessary coins from his pocket, it occurred to him that it was the first night they would share a bed. He suddenly wished they could have made it to Honey House tonight. He would rather not have their first full night in a rented bed. If he hadn't been so fixated on the prospect of having her to himself for a week, he might have planned better and left earlier. But she had needed a wardrobe for their short holiday, and he hadn't wanted to make use of the modiste in Alton. Not much occurred in the country, so gossip had a tendency to spread quickly. He would be able to keep it confined to his house as long as they didn't venture too far from his property or stop for a visit in the village.

A slightly built young man with unruly blond hair arrived, James's bags and her trunk in tow, and showed them to their room. As the servant bustled about, lighting the candles and seeing to the fire, Rose lingered near the window, her head bowed, still hidden beneath her cloak. After giving the man a coin for his troubles, James locked the door behind him and crossed to Rose.

"May I take your cloak?"

She whirled from the window, the dark fabric fluttering about her ankles. "Oh, yes. Thank you," she murmured, undoing the clasp and slipping the garment from her shoulders. She passed a hand over her hair to smooth the stray strands.

He studied her from the corner of his eye as he folded the cloak over the back of a nearby chair. Her back was ramrod straight, quite the feat, as she was now crouched before her trunk, undoing the latch. Getting to her feet, she held up a forest green cambric day dress and shook it out.

"Shall I call for a servant to have it pressed?" he asked.

"No, you needn't bother. It just needs to hang. The wrinkles will be gone come morning."

"Are you hungry?"

"A bit." Her back to him, she hung the dress on a peg on the wall near the washstand.

He frowned. Her unease was palpable, practically radiating from her. "When you're ready, we can go down for supper. The fare is simple, but quite palatable."

She turned from the dress. Her gaze skittered about the room, avoiding his. "Would you mind ever so much if we dined here? The table," she flicked her fingers toward the small, round table in the corner of the room, "could be suitable for dining."

"If you wish," he said, with a tip of his head.

He called for a servant and requested a meal for two. As they waited for the fare to arrive, she busied herself: setting a brush and a small copper tin on the dresser, fiddling with the wrinkles on the skirt of the dress she had hung up, and closing her trunk. The silence was only broken by the soft sounds of her footsteps as she moved about. The bedchamber wasn't large by any means, but every foot separating them felt like a furlong. The distance so vast he hadn't a clue how to breach it.

The reserved quiet continued throughout supper. Her manners were all politeness, but the slight, barely there smiles were distinctly brittle and forced. Hell, it felt like they were mere acquaintances, forced to share a room for the night. It made him remember how he had to really coax her to convince her to come along with him to the country. She had not jumped at the opportunity. Her reluctance had been a tangible force. Only an outrageous sum had garnered her assent. The thought that she was only with him for the thick fold of pound notes he'd given the madam sat like an iron brick in his belly.

The decision to take this holiday was coming back to haunt him. He never did anything impulsive. Every decision carefully thought through, considered, and weighed. And the one time he'd reached out, grabbed what he wanted with both hands without thought to anything but his own selfish desires . . .

He drained the last of the coffee in his cup, the roasted beef on his plate not even half eaten. Worries over the week ahead had killed his appetite. Was this but a taste of what the days would hold for him? Closeted away in her suite of rooms at the brothel, they had never spent any time together that did not involve sex or the prospect of sex. He knew every inch of her beautiful body, had pressed his lips to those luscious curves, been intimately joined with her, but he actually knew so little about *her*. In a way, they were rather like strangers.

"Are you finished?" As if he needed to bother asking. Her appetite had not even approached his. Her wineglass was empty, but he doubted she'd brought more than a couple of the neatly cut squares of beef on her plate to her lips.

"Yes," she said, and he had to fight to keep from wincing when she gave him another of those brittle, forced little smiles.

Even though a servant would readily see to it, he took the tray laden with the remnants of their supper downstairs, giving her the opportunity to prepare for bed without his hovering presence. Should he inquire with the innkeeper about another room? Did she not truly wish to stay with him tonight? Or was it more than just tonight? Did she regret agreeing to come with him to the country?

All thoughts of a blissful night vanished, replaced with a knotted mass of worry. Another lonely night loomed ahead of him, infinitely long, the dawn so patient he'd be left wondering if it would ever rise. It was something he should be more than accustomed to by now, but . . . Rose was supposed to keep those lonely nights away.

But likely not tonight.

He left the tray at the front desk and went outside. The night air brushed his cheeks, the cold nipping his skin. The inn was quiet, the gravel drive empty of carriages as most travelers had already stopped to procure rooms hours ago. Shoving his hands into his pockets, he headed toward the cluster of trees on the side lawn, leaving the golden pools of light from the lanterns behind him. Should he offer to take her back to London in the morning? Christ, he didn't want it to come to that. Didn't want to give up their holiday. His thoughts had been focused on nothing else since she'd given him that nod. One week of shared pleasure and comfortable companionship. Of being with a woman who welcomed his presence, who made him feel . . . wanted. A luxury if ever there was, and one that was fast slipping through his grasp.

Stopping, he looked up to the sky, as if the stars above somehow held the answer. A light breeze rustled the leaves on the nearby trees, masking his shoulder-slumping sigh. Come morning, he'd put the question to her and whatever her answer, he would accept.

Turning on his heel, he went back to the inn. The ride here had been enjoyable, at least. He could be content with that, couldn't he? It was so much more than he'd had eight days ago.

But perhaps . . . His gaze settled on the front door as he approached it. Perhaps it wasn't *him*, per se. The carriage ride *had* been more than enjoyable. Her smiles warm and her kisses sweet. But if she, for a reason known only to her, objected to spending a night with him at an inn, wouldn't it follow that she would have the same concerns at Honey House? Putting him in the same position he was currently in. Confused and adrift and not knowing what the hell to think.

He stopped at the front desk for a quick word with the proprietor. With one brass key clutched tight in his fist and a new one in his pocket, he trudged up the stairs. If she wanted him, she would wait up for him. If not, if she was in bed and more importantly, asleep, then regardless of his own wishes, he would make use of the key in his pocket.

The *click* of the lock echoed in the empty corridor. Breath held, he turned the knob and slipped inside. Only the fire in the hearth lit the room, the flickering golden rays illuminating her outline under the dark woolen coverlet on the large bed.

His stomach dropped, disappointment crashing over him in a suffocating wave. A wince crossed his face. Stepping carefully in an effort to minimize any squeaks of the floorboards, he went to grab his valise and leather bag, which were still propped next to the dresser.

There was a rustle of fabric, accompanied by the faint creak of the ropes under a mattress.

"James, where are you going?" Her soft voice drifted from the shadows.

Bags in hand, he turned to the bed. Her dark hair spilled over her shoulders in loose, untamed waves. The coverlet was clutched over her breasts but the pale ivory expanse of skin above the dark brown wool was completely bare.

She wasn't wearing a nightgown or chemise. She was naked beneath that blanket.

In a quick rush of raw need, lust flared beneath his skin. He swallowed hard, fighting back the almost unstoppable impulse to bolt under the covers, to have her bare body pressed against his, to hold her close. "I've secured another room. You can rest undisturbed for the night."

"But . . ." She twisted the sheet at her hip.

"What?" he asked, going still. A tendril of hope sparked within him.

"I thought you wished to share a room." She released the coverlet. It slipped down her chest, pooling at her waist. "Earlier in the carriage, you said 'Later.'"

With a thud, his bags fell to the floor.

"Do you need assistance undressing?"

"No, I can manage it," he said, wrestling his arms free of his coat.

His waistcoat, cravat, shirt, and trousers quickly joined the coat on the floor, and then he was slipping under the blankets and into her open arms, the undeniable welcome in her kiss vanquishing the last of the hollow ache in his chest.

Thirteen

ROSE looked from the house outside the open carriage door to James's proffered hand. Strong, capable, and bare. He was not a man who wore gloves as a matter of course.

Her gaze went back to the house beyond his broad shoulder. With its honey gold stone exterior, Honey House was an apt name. Neatly tended, low bushes underscored the three sets of windows on the ground floor. Four chimneys jutted from the roofline that kissed the tops of the windows on the first floor. Quaint, charming, and elegant with crisp, clean lines, it was nowhere near as grand as Paxton Manor. Rather it was the perfect residence for a country gentleman, or a London gentleman like James who wished to occasionally rusticate in the country.

She liked it immensely, but that fact did not ease the trepidation that had seeped into her stomach the moment the carriage had slowed to a stop outside the front door.

"Rose?"

Taking a deep breath, she laid her gloved hand in his and exited the carriage. The front door swung open as they approached.

"Mr. Archer. Welcome home." A rotund, older woman with a mop of gray curls closed the door behind them.

"Rose, this is my housekeeper, Mrs. Webb. Mrs. Webb, this is Miss Rose. She will be our guest for the next week."

Rose murmured a welcome, bracing for the friendly smile to slip off the woman's face. That feeling she'd had at the inn returned in full force. Last night, she hadn't been able to push aside the uncomfortable sensation that every pair of eyes in the inn had been fixed on her cloaked figure and well aware she and James had not been a husband and wife stopping along their travels. As if the word *whore* had been emblazoned on her back for all to see. For the first time, she felt self-conscious about holding James's hand. She didn't want to let go—she needed his strength—but she couldn't ignore the impression that Mrs. Webb was doing her best to look everywhere but at their joined hands.

It made her feel as if he was declaring his intentions, telling the housekeeper without words that Rose was more than a mere guest. Even when her primary purpose had been little more than a pretty ornament to hang off her protector's arm, she had not liked being on display, being flaunted for what she was.

"Welcome to Honey House, Miss Rose. Mr. Webb will have your bags inside—" A bump sounded on the door, cutting off the older woman. She flashed Rose a bright smile and reached behind for the doorknob. "And there he is now."

Slim and wiry, the opposite of his wife, Mr. Webb shuffled over the threshold and into the small foyer, Rose's trunk held before him with James's bags looped over each wrist. He barely paused to tip his head to her with a gruff "Welcome, miss" before trudging up the stairs, the bags bumping his thighs with each step.

"If you would like, I can unpack for you." Hands clasped before her, Mrs. Webb looked expectantly at Rose.

She opened her mouth, the polite refusal on her tongue, when James spoke.

"Not at the moment, but perhaps later Miss Rose would welcome your assistance."

Mrs. Webb's gaze flickered briefly to their joined hands. "Of course, you both must be tired from the journey. When you need my assistance, simply call. I'll be there in a trice. Oh, and there was a delivery for you this morning, Mr. Archer. It's on your desk."

"I see Decker is prompt as always." Turning his broad shoulders to her, James motioned toward the stairs with his free hand. "Shall we?"

It was all she could do to keep the smile in place. Not even five minutes in the house, and he wanted her in his bed. Was taking her there right now, under the watchful gaze of his housekeeper. *It's James's holiday, not yours*, she reminded herself as they made their way to the first floor. He had paid for the right to indulge with her whenever he pleased, and her role was one of gracious accommodation.

James turned right at the top of the stairs, leading her down a short corridor. The interior of the home matched the exterior. Neat and tidy, nothing ostentatious or overly elaborate. A couple of small landscapes hung on the walls, and a serviceable brown-patterned rug muffled their footsteps. One would never know that its owner possessed such wealth as to be able to part with two thousand pounds on a whim.

Mr. Webb emerged from a room on the left, his arms empty of their burdens. "Supper at the usual hour, Mr. Archer?"

"Yes, Webb," he replied, opening a door across from the room the servant had just vacated.

She followed James into the room and stopped short. The bedchamber was decorated in sunny yellows and bright whites. The furnishings all held a distinctly comfortable and quite feminine air about them. The delicately carved legs on the small desk next to the white marble fireplace, the neat posts on the four-poster bed, the floral upholstery on the small chair in the corner. Her trunk, the silver banding so new it didn't hold one scratch, was on the floor beside the cherrywood dresser. The gauzy drapes on the group of three tall, narrow windows were drawn back, revealing a glimpse of the front lawn and letting in the afternoon sun.

She looked askance at James. Surely this could not be *his* bedchamber.

"Do you like the room? It's yours for the duration of your stay, if it meets with your approval."

"My room?" She hadn't expected such a courtesy. "You don't want me to stay with you?"

"Of course, but I thought you'd prefer a room of your own. Space for all of your things," he flicked his fingers toward her trunk, "and what have you. Would you rather stay with me?"

"But what about the staff? Wouldn't they think it . . ."—*indecent, shocking, scandalous*—"odd if your guest shared your room?"

"You needn't worry about the Webbs. What would you prefer?"

She glanced about, uncertain what she should choose. She'd much rather not have the option. What if what she wanted wasn't what he wanted? And she couldn't help but wonder at the way his staff had accepted her appearance at James's side. As if it was commonplace for him to bring a woman to his country house. Last night he hadn't batted an eye at securing a room for them. He had spoken to the innkeeper in his usual deep baritone voice. Not one fidget, while she'd had to fight against the feel of those eyes upon her.

Had she misjudged him? She had thought for certain he did not make a habit of spending time with women like herself. But maybe he was simply discreet, limiting his dalliances to the country, far from London.

"Is something the matter, Rose?"

"No. It is a lovely room, as I'm sure your past guests have assured you."

"My past guests? Rose, the only guest I've ever entertained at Honey House is my sister."

"Rebecca?"

"Yes." A frown creased his brow, chasing away her brief surge of relief at learning she was not one of many. "Rose, what's wrong?"

Her spine stiffened. "Nothing."

He let out a breath, that frown deepening, but displeasure thankfully didn't harden his eyes to cold chips of ice. "Please, don't do this again. What's wrong? And do not think to fool me with a claim to the contrary. Your unease is obvious."

How could she explain it to him? She couldn't. It was a combination of so many things it was impossible to isolate one from the many. Her thoughts focused on the opportunity to spend more time with him; she hadn't anticipated how very different it would be to be with him outside of the brothel. Rubicon's provided a level of shelter she had not fully appreciated. Here the full weight of expectation and of the rigid standards of proper decorum rubbed in a harsh coarse mixture against her skin.

Perhaps, though, she could placate him with part of the truth. "I've never traveled with a . . . gentleman," she said, shying away from the word *client*. "It's a new experience."

"You do trust me, don't you, Rose?" he asked, his thumb caressing the back of her hand still held in his.

"Yes." The answer fell from her lips without thought, without a need to even consider it for an instant.

"It is my fondest wish for you to feel comfortable here. To treat my home as your own. But if you find you wish to leave before our week is up, simply say so and I will see you safely back to Town. That offer is always open."

"Thank you," she murmured, taken aback by his generosity. There was no doubt he would hold true to his word. If ever a man embodied trust, it was James.

"And I owe you an apology. It was inconsiderate of me not to inform you of the need to stop at the inn last night. In the future, I will keep you abreast of any plans, travel or otherwise."

Rendered speechless by the sincerity in his voice, she merely nodded.

He considered her for a moment. "Do you feel more at ease about your stay now?"

She made to nod, but could tell he needed more of a definitive answer. "Yes."

"Good." All traces of the frown finally left his mouth. "Now, the room. Here or with me?"

She glanced about the bedchamber again. It would be nice to be able to call it her own, if only for the space of a week. "Here. Thank you, James."

"Think nothing of it, my dear. In any case, my room's not far. It's just across the corridor. I'll leave you to unpack and rest up a bit. Would you like me to call Mrs. Webb?"

"No, I prefer to see to unpacking myself."

"All right, then. I'll be in the study if you need me. Decker's first delivery has already arrived. I can escape London but never the office. But you have my assurance that I will not spend the next week tucked behind my desk. A couple of hours in the morning after the post arrives, but that is all. I'm here to spend time with you."

He brushed his lips to hers in a light, fleeting kiss.

A true smile curving her mouth for the first time since she stepped into the house, her lips still tingling, she watched his broad back disappear out the door.

⚓

TWILIGHT veiled the grounds beyond the windows. Comfortable and informal with its ivory cambric drapes bracketing the windows, the dining room fit the home. The table was only large enough to seat six, so with only her and James, it didn't feel as though they were perched on the edge of a forest's worth of mahogany.

"Sugar or lemon?"

"No, thank you," she murmured to Mrs. Webb, as the woman poured her a cup of tea.

Rose hadn't lingered long in her bedchamber after unpacking and changing into one of her new day dresses before venturing out to find James. With a smile and another offer to lend her assistance if ever the need arose, Mrs. Webb had directed Rose to the study, which was situated toward the back of the house. James had indeed been tucked behind his desk, neat piles of papers covering the oak surface.

Knowing he was a busy man, she kept the interruption to a minimum, only checking in to gauge his mood and determine if he wanted her company for more than a pleasant conversation. He had seemed happy to see her, his eyes alight with welcome, but she could tell his mind hadn't been fully on her. The pen had remained in his grasp, poised over the paper before him. After another request from him that she should treat his home as her own, she had ventured outside. The thought of taking up residence in a drawing room felt . . . not quite right, as if by doing so she would be presuming to be someone she wasn't, yet returning to her bedchamber didn't hold much appeal, either. So she had settled on a wrought iron bench on the back terrace to enjoy the late afternoon sun and the unseasonable warmth, the sun so strong she hadn't needed to make use of her cloak or a shawl.

Not that she had remained on the bench long. James clearly kept country hours, complete with supper before five, which explained why darkness had not fully fallen yet even though Mrs. Webb had cleared the table of their dishes a few minutes ago.

Supper had been simple, yet exceptionally prepared. The bread still warm from the oven, the chicken moist and tender. The atmosphere informal enough so her simple sage green evening gown was the perfect match for the occasion. Clad in a navy evening coat, his freshly shaven jaw grazing his white cravat, James seemed perfectly at his ease at the head of the table. He hadn't prattled on—not that he had ever shown himself to have that tendency—nor had silence reigned. The conversation had effortlessly drifted from the village, to the weather, to Honey House, which she learned he had purchased three years ago.

She hadn't shared a meal with someone like this, complete with a dining table and a servant to tend to her, in so very long. At Paxton Manor, she dined with her housekeeper in the kitchen. At Rubicon's, in her sitting room, though sometimes Timothy joined her. If she wasn't careful, she could quickly grow accustomed to dining with James.

Rose brought her teacup to her lips and took a sip, as James refilled his cup from the ivory pot that Mrs. Webb had left on the table. He caught her gaze and gave her a smile before taking a sip of his coffee. It wasn't as if he had never been relaxed around her. But it was different tonight. Not a hint of tension inhabited his powerful frame. Not a trace of lingering stress in his expression. He was a man fully at his ease. Relaxed and comfortable in his home.

With a little *clink*, James set his cup onto its saucer. "It's been a long day, with the travel and what not. Would you mind if we retired early?"

"Not at all." She didn't believe his excuse for an instant. There wasn't a bit of fatigue in his features. On the contrary. Where a moment ago his green eyes had been soft and warm, banked with the pleased contentment of a satisfying meal, now they held the distinct spark of anticipation.

She took her linen napkin from her lap and placed it beside her teacup as James stood, the legs of his chair scraping lightly against the floorboards. He pulled out her chair and held a hand out to help her to her feet. Hand in hand, they left the room, leaving Mrs. Webb to bustle about the table, clearing the cups and saucers.

As they made their way upstairs, a new concern threaded its way into her mind. She tried to fall back onto the years of experience, searching for something to guide her, but found nothing. Playing the part of a guest was an entirely new situation. Would he expect her to prepare for the night in her own room or in his? When she had been in the demimonde, her protectors had installed her in a house. As she had not entertained any other visitors, only one bedchamber had been used. No need for another, since the men only stayed the night if they wanted to share a bed with her. That was her primary purpose, after all.

She knew James wanted to share a bed with her. His intentions were clear. Did he want her to be discreet and keep up the guise of a guest, slipping into his bedchamber without his servants' notice? But he had earlier told her not to worry about the Webbs. In that case, would he simply take her directly to his room? Was he so comfortable in his home that he had no qualms whatsoever about flaunting the true purpose of their holiday?

A tendril of discomfort leached into her gut. One of the many questions lingering in her mind was answered as he led her to her bedchamber door and stopped before it.

"My bedchamber is right across the corridor." His voice was pitched low, intimate and for her ears only.

"Is it?" she asked, infusing a teasing tone.

"Yes," he replied, his lips quirking.

She arched a brow. "Very good to know."

His lashes lowered, his gaze dropping. A flush of heat spread across her chest. Bringing her hand up, he graced the back with a light kiss.

"And now we part . . ." He took a step closer, so close his warm breath brushed her ear. "But hopefully not for long."

The low rumble of his voice melted into her bones, making her knees weak. An involuntary shiver of anticipation gripped her. Her limp hand slipped from his as he turned on his heel.

The sound of his bedchamber door shutting echoed in the corridor, snapping her to her senses.

With a little shake of her head, she entered her own room. By the glow of the fire in the hearth, she lit the candles on the dresser. As she crossed to the closet, her hands went up to her bodice and then stopped, hovering over the plain expanse of sage green silk. This was not one of *her* evening gowns, but one James had purchased for her. It buttoned down the back.

Her shoulders slumped. A quick try proved she would not be able to tend to them herself. Her gaze went to the bedchamber door. Perhaps she would be presenting herself at James's door significantly sooner than anticipated.

She started, as a sharp knock echoed in her room.

James? No, he had wanted her to go to his room. Hadn't he?

Wary, she opened the door to reveal Mrs. Webb.

"My apologies, Miss Rose. I should have asked before you left the dining room. Do you need the assistance of a maid?"

"Thank you. Just the buttons on my gown, please. I can see to the rest."

It only took a moment for the woman to manage the task. She left with instructions to Rose to leave out whatever she wanted cleaned and pressed, and she would see to it on the morrow.

Without giving herself time to think on it, she went through the ritual she had once known well—removing her slippers, stays, chemise, and stockings, pulling the pins from her hair, dabbing on a bit of perfume, and slipping on a wrapper. The silk was cool against her skin, the hem tickling her bare ankles. She tightened the fabric belt around her waist and adjusted the deep *V* neckline to expose the upper swells of her breasts.

A quick glance in the mirror confirmed she was ready. The waves of her dark hair loose about her shoulders, the silk wrapper so thin it simultaneously draped and molded to the contours of her body. James should certainly like what he saw.

But instead of walking out her door, hesitation kept her rooted to the spot. She knew what he wanted. He could not have been clearer in his wishes. Yet . . .

Letting out a sigh, she sat down on the edge of the bed and shook her head at herself. She was being foolish. She wanted him. Her body yearned for his touch, her lips needed his kiss. Yet it was that sense of . . . requirement that held her back.

She should just be able to do it. To ignore herself and just follow the subtle, and sometimes not-so-subtle, cues that would lead her to a man's utmost desire. But the ability usually right at her fingertips was gone.

A determined frown tightening her lips, she tried to will herself off the bed but . . .

Her shoulders slumped, her head falling so her chin almost grazed her chest. If only she had not accepted his money. Those pound notes hung over their holiday. *Damn Dash.* If only she could have waved aside James's offer and gone away with him. Simply left her life behind for the space of seven days. Savored the unprecedented opportunity to be with a man who only wanted her presence. No obligations of any kind, only a shared desire to enjoy their time together.

Instead she had accepted his offer, and now she could not ignore the sense of obligation that came with those pound notes, spoiling what should have been nothing but pure, giddy anticipation to run straight into his arms. Regardless of his assurances to the contrary, she was here for him and not herself.

It wasn't that she did not adore being with James. She did. And if she was being honest with herself, her feelings for him had grown beyond adoration. But his desires came first, and hers . . . only if they happened to align with his.

And his desire at the moment was for her to make an appearance in his bedchamber.

She got up from the bed, checked the screen to ensure it would fully cover the hearth in her absence, and doused the candles. Breath held, she opened her door, quickly checked the corridor to ensure it was clear, and darted across.

And then paused, knuckles poised to knock, to glance down the corridor again. Thinking better of knocking, she reached for the knob.

The door swung open soundlessly on well-oiled hinges. She slowly released the knob, damping the effect of the *click* of the door shutting, and glanced about.

This was most definitely James's room. A navy coverlet on the large bed, matching curtains covering the windows. The mahogany furniture more substantial than that in her own room. She took a deep breath, catching the faint clean, masculine scent of him on the air. The rapid beat of her pulse slowed to something that approached normal levels as the knot in her stomach began to ease.

He stood before the washstand on the other side of the room. His upper body was bared, his trousers hugging the muscular curves of his arse. The muscles in his back bunched and flexed as he dragged a length of towel over his face. Then green eyes met hers in the mirror. He smiled, slow and sinful. "Good evening."

"Good evening, James."

Turning from the washstand, he dropped the towel next to the ceramic basin. His chestnut brown hair was damp around his face, clinging to his temples. On bare feet, he walked toward her, stopping beside the bed.

She watched as what had been the beginnings of an erection swelled, tenting the placket of his trousers.

"Do you plan to join me, or do you plan to linger by the door all evening? I hope you aren't expecting an offer from me to watch," he said, all playful indignation.

A laugh burst from her throat at the unexpected comment. Her back almost propping up the door, she must look just as he had nights ago, when he had hesitated to take more than a step into her bedchamber. "Not expecting, but if the offer's there . . ." she trailed off, arching a suggestive brow.

His eyes flared slightly, his expression momentarily blanking. Goodness, was that a blush staining his cheeks?

All traces of hesitation gone, she finally moved from the door, walking toward him. "My apologies. I couldn't resist. I was only teasing." Though the thought of watching as he took himself in hand . . . Arousal spiked her senses, lust pooling low between her thighs.

Stopping before him, she tipped her head back to meet his gaze. A little smile curved his mouth, prompting an answering one from her. For a long moment, neither of them moved.

"That's my bed." He inclined his head toward it as if it wasn't already obvious.

"Is it?" She gave him her best politely interested expression.

His lips quirked. "Yes."

Large hands gripped her about the waist and before she knew it, her feet left the floor. She knew a second of being suspended in the air and then she landed on her back in the middle of the bed. The mattress was soft enough to cushion almost any landing, but he had thrown her so gently, so carefully, that the extra padding hadn't been necessary.

She brushed the stray hairs from her face and watched as he settled beside her, stretching out on his side, his jaw propped up in his palm on a bent elbow.

With the lightest of touches, he traced the deep V neckline of her wrapper. Her pulse skipped a beat as his fingertip just grazed the swells of her breasts.

"You're beyond beautiful."

She swallowed, found her voice. "Is there such a thing?" she asked, near breathless from the heat of his stare.

"Yes. And you define it."

The reverent awe, the absolute conviction in his voice, in his eyes, in his touch . . .

"Kiss me." The plea whispered past her lips. The need for him, so strong it suddenly filled her entire being, sent a tremble rocking through her.

His lips met hers in a soft press of skin against skin. Wrapping her arms about his neck, she arched into him, needing more. A low growl shook his chest, reverberating through her, as he shifted fully on top of her, her legs eagerly opening for him. His lips slanted over hers, his hot tongue found hers, and she lost herself in his kiss.

Fourteen

WITH the languid, drowsy haze of sleep clinging to her senses, Rose shifted closer, nuzzling James's broad chest, seeking his warmth. The coverlet had nothing on the heat pouring off his powerful body. The drapes were not fully closed, but the breaks in the navy damask offered little by way of light. Shadows cloaked the bedchamber, the air chilly and damp. Rain lashed the windows, a sharp staccato interspersed with strong gusts of wind that rattled the panes.

James stirred, his arms coming around to loop about her waist. Bare skin slid luxuriously against bare skin, her legs falling open to bracket his, as he pulled her fully on top of him. The hard brand of his erection nudged her upper thigh. Desire curled down her spine, rousing her sleep-fogged senses. She pushed up enough to look into his face. His eyes were still closed, his features relaxed, the notched V between his brows completely absent. The man was so handsome, so ruggedly masculine. The strong body beneath her possessed such great strength, yet he touched her so tenderly, with such great care, that her heart couldn't help but want to throw all caution to the wind. A dangerous temptation indeed.

She should let him rest but . . . she couldn't resist brushing a kiss along the line of his jaw, his morning beard a gentle scrape against her lips.

The edges of his mouth tipped up, his lashes sweeping up just enough to reveal a glimpse of soft, olive green eyes. "Good morning," he said in a scratchy rumble that made her toes curl.

"Good morning to you as well."

Another brush of her lips, this time against his. The strong arms around her waist tightened. A hint of a low, content growl vibrated his chest. The light flick of his tongue against the seam of her lips had her opening eagerly to him. Their tongues twined decadently together. There was nothing hurried or rushed about his kiss. No heated push toward something more. Nothing but a desire to savor their kiss.

His hands roamed her body, coasting along her back, pausing to palm her derrière, the tips of his fingers tickling the crease, as he continued to kiss her. His skin warmed from sleep, his movements slow and lazy, yet backed with intent. Waking with him was such a wonderful experience. An experience she could easily become much too fond of.

A nudge prodded the back of her mind. She pulled back, breaking the kiss. A glance to the brass clock on the mahogany dresser identified the source of the nudge. Yesterday he had been clear about his plans for their holiday. She well understood a busy man like James could never fully escape his responsibilities, even if only for a few days.

"I hadn't realized it was so late. I shouldn't keep you. Surely the morning post has arrived."

"Damn the morning post," he said, in a gravelly growl. He gave her backside a firm squeeze, hitching her higher up so that her sex slid along the hot arch of his arousal. A thoroughly wicked smile curved his lips. "I want to stay in bed with you all day."

"All day?" She chanced a quick glance over her shoulder to the closed door. "But what about the Webbs?"

"What about them?"

"They'll know I'm with you."

"And? You are here as my guest. I do believe the Webbs have deduced we intend to do more than share meals." He passed a soothing palm down her back. "Not that their opinions should matter, but I highly doubt they care either way."

She knew he was right, but still . . . At night, under the cover of darkness when the rest of the house was abed was an entirely different situation than staying closeted with James in his bedchamber in the light of day. If she belonged here with him it would be different. Yes, she had arrived with him, but as an unmarried young woman without a chaperone. There could be no doubt she was not a proper young lady. The right to label herself as such had been thrown aside long ago, but she did not like being so blatant about it. The thought of coming face-to-face with Mrs. Webb again, seeing the censure the woman would not be able to hide . . .

"Don't you wish to stay in bed with me?" With a light touch, he tucked her hair, which had fallen over her shoulder, behind her ear.

The genuine hurt on his handsome face tugged at her heart. It was the height of selfishness to allow her worries to dictate his holiday. And it wasn't as if she didn't want to spend the day with him, right here, in his arms, but . . .

Enough.

No reason to fight with herself, at least not over this.

She pressed her lips to his. "Of course I do."

❧

THE hours fell away with Rose in his arms. Few words were spoken between them, for none were needed. Her soft smiles, beguiling kisses, and tantalizing touches spoke for themselves. Just having her close roused his desires, but James hadn't yet fully given in to his baser instincts. Rather they had simply lazed the hours away, enjoying being together. Never had he done something so hedonistic as to spend a day with a woman in his bed. Closeted away from all responsibility. The only requirements bare skin and indulgence. Not a thing he should make a habit of, but definitely the perfect way to spend a rainy day.

And most definitely not a habit Rose had ever acquired, at least judging by the way her gaze had darted to the door when he'd first given voice to his plan for the day. He hadn't expected her reticence, but he was fast realizing he should have. She possessed an odd mix of traits—a complete lack of inhibition coupled with the manners of a lady. Regardless of her occupation, she was not one to throw propriety to the wind.

He wasn't one to throw propriety to the wind either, but they were at Honey House. The Webbs had been with him since he purchased the house and had shown themselves to be discreet. He had never known them to gossip about even the most mundane of details. Quite simply, he trusted them. If he couldn't indulge here, at the only place that felt like home, then he couldn't indulge anywhere.

He glanced to the silver tray on his dresser that held the plates and cups from their breakfast. While he had been more than fond of the idea of remaining with her, luxuriating in the feel of her warm, naked body and not leaving his bed until the sun rose tomorrow morning, his stomach had had different thoughts on the matter. Mindful of Rose, he had pulled on a pair of trousers and a shirt before stepping out to the corridor to relay his instructions to Mrs. Webb, meeting her again in the corridor, the closed door at his back, when she had returned. Breakfast in bed with a beautiful naked woman—now that had been the height of indulgence.

Rose shifted slightly, her calf rubbing against his. She was nestled beside him beneath the coverlet, her arm slung over his waist. She fit so perfectly beside him, as if she had been made for him. The rain had died down to a faint rhythmic patter against the windows some time ago. The fire in the hearth needed to be prodded again, but . . .

It could wait, just as everything else today could wait until later. Well, everything beyond his bed.

"Come here. I need a kiss."

She arched, stretching her back, her firm breasts pressing against his side, and then pushed up onto an elbow. The coverlet slid down, revealing the delicate curve of a slim, ivory shoulder. "Just one?"

"Definitely more than one."

The kiss quickly turned heated. The arousal that had been simmering right beneath his skin, staying just far enough from the surface to keep him from tackling her, flared to full life. With a little tug, he pulled her fully on top of him.

She gave his bottom lip a nip and pushed up to sit astride his waist. His grip tightened on her hips, fingers pressing into her soft skin, wanting, needing. If he moved her back just a few inches, she'd be perfectly positioned, and then he could lift her hips and slide into the slick, welcoming heat of her body.

She trailed her fingertips from his wrists, over his forearms, her touch so light it sent a ripple of sensation through him, raising the hairs on his arms. Bending slightly at the waist, putting those luscious breasts closer but not quite close enough to his mouth, she reached higher, hands splaying when she reached his upper arms.

"There is so much of you," she murmured, caressing his biceps.

"Yes, well, sorry about that." If he levered up, he could capture one of those perfect nipples in his mouth. Suck on the hard tip until she was writhing for more.

"Why should you apologize? I adore your muscles." A quick kiss and she dragged her lips down over his jaw. "And other parts of you, as well."

Leaving a trail of kisses in her wake, she scooted down his chest, taking the coverlet with her. The cool air in the room did nothing to chill his heated skin. Anticipation built within, his breaths shortening, catching in his throat. Lust shot through him. He knew exactly where she was headed. Her intent could not be any clearer. How many times had she sucked him off in his dreams? Too damn many to count. He had never asked, never so much as nudged her in that direction, wanting her to gift him that particular pleasure of her own accord. And now it was actually going to happen.

A tremor shook his body. He curled his hands into fists at his sides to resist the need to cup the back of her head, to urge her to her target. Her tongue darted out to swirl around his navel, a tantalizing preview of what was to come. With openmouthed kisses, she followed the thin line of hair down to his impatient erection.

Her small hand wrapped securely around the base. The dark fan of her lashes drifted closed. Anticipation roaring through his veins, he watched as those full red lips parted as she leaned down. And then hot, wet heat surrounded the head of his prick. It was all he could do to stifle the soul-deep groan of gratitude. Crouched between his spread legs, bowed over his groin, she bobbed along his length. Her lips were heavenly soft, her mouth a hot haven that defined indulgence. The tousled dark length of her silken hair tickled his inner thighs.

Cheeks hollowing, she sucked hard on the upstroke, almost pulling the orgasm from him, before gliding back down to do it again. Teeth gritted, he fought back the primitive need to spill down her throat, determined to savor the experience.

She paused to swipe her tongue over the crown, lapping up the drop of fluid beading from the tip. Her sheer skill left him breathless, his cock not left untended for even one instant.

By God, it had been years since he had been sucked off. The sole incidence on that long ago visit to a brothel during a holiday from Cambridge. But on that instance, it had only been the unprecedented experience of a woman's mouth on his prick that had brought the orgasm rushing down on him.

With a quick swipe, her rhythm unbroken, Rose tucked her hair behind one ear. The movement caused that old memory to prod his mind. Her lashes swept up. Red lips sliding up his length, she caught his gaze. He half expected to meet hardened, jaded hazel eyes.

The silken dance of her tongue across the head of his prick caused his ballocks to lurch up tighter, as if an invisible thread connected one part of his body to the other. He groaned, every muscle drawn tight, practically trembling under the onslaught. As if reading his thoughts, that secure hand fell away from the base to cup his ballocks. Her grip perfect—light and soft yet firm enough to satisfy that itch for attention.

She pulled free with a pop, the crude sound somehow rousing his lust even higher. Up and down, following the thick vein on the underside, she slowly dragged her lips along his length. Her tongue flicking out to tickle, tease. Then capturing his gaze once again as she wrapped her lips around the needy crown, taking him back inside her mouth.

But this time the determined strokes didn't further fray the taut ropes of his control. When he was on top of her, kissing her senseless and deep inside her, he didn't give her a chance to think. Like this, though . . .

She was clearly focused on his pleasure. But too focused. Those tickling fingertips too adept. Her every move too . . . practiced. His hands unclenched. He made to lift his arms from his sides, to reach toward her, but then she sucked hard and pressed right behind his ballocks, on that smooth expanse of skin, hitting a spot he didn't know he had and triggering an orgasm he could not have stopped if he had tried.

The climax barreled through him, racking his muscles, a powerful quake that kept him from pulling her free.

Her lips softened, the suction easing until she was lapping gently on the head, the caress so gentle it soothed rather than abraded his overly sensitive skin. Releasing him, she swiped a delicate fingertip at the corner of her mouth. What could only be triumph shone in her light blue eyes.

He abruptly swung his legs over the side of the bed and stood. Off balance and oddly irritated, he stalked to the washstand and dropped a cloth in the white ceramic basin of water.

He would never be her first anything. It shouldn't bother him so much, but it did. And he certainly did not like the thought of exactly how she had come by her expertise. It rubbed against his skin, harsh and sharp like jagged rocks.

"James, did I do something wrong?"

He wrung out the cloth and swiped between his legs. "Of course not. The old adage that practice makes perfect is most assuredly true."

Dropping the cloth, he turned from the washstand to face Rose, who was kneeling on the center of the bed. Chin tipping down, shoulders hunching, she tugged the coverlet up to cover her bare breasts.

Silence hung, thick and heavy, as he quickly got dressed. Pulled on his trousers and a shirt. Tied his cravat in the most basic of knots. Slipped on a waistcoat and coat. All the while, he could feel her eyes upon him. Those questioning, hurt, beautiful eyes. But he couldn't bring himself to apologize for his rudeness.

"Where are you going?" she asked, hesitation weighing down her words. Her lips were plumped, even redder than usual. Her dark hair tousled and covering her thin shoulders. The very image of a woman well and truly debauched—a siren who could tempt the will of even the strongest of men to come back for more. "I thought you wanted to stay in bed today."

The buttons on his coat seen to, he paused by the mirror above the dresser to drag a comb through his hair. "I need to see to the morning post."

"But it's afternoon?"

His jaw was darkened with stubble, but the shave would have to wait until later. He needed to get out of this room now. "And therefore the post will be waiting on my desk."

With a sharp snap that echoed in the corridor, he shut the door behind him.

A good couple of hours later and the piles of papers on his desk still hadn't done their duty. He should be blissfully numb inside, fully focused on all the pressing concerns before him. But irritation and frustration still had his lips compressed in a tight line and his fist gripping his pen almost hard enough to break it in two.

At the light rap on his door, he called, "Yes?" Then he took a deep breath, forced the snap out of his tone, and tried again. "Come in."

Bearing a pot of coffee, Mrs. Webb entered the study. "Good afternoon, Mr. Archer." She refilled his cup, set the fresh pot down on his desk, and took the empty one. "I've just delivered tea to Miss Rose's room." A frown flickered across her mouth as she glanced out the window. Droplets of rain clung to the glass, blurring the view of the side grounds. The rain that had eased late that morning had picked back up, tapping against the house in an easy rhythm that would have been soothing under any other circumstance. "This weather is just dreadful. Makes one wish to never leave their bed."

He had left his bed, and so had Rose, if Mrs. Webb had delivered tea to her room. When had she left? Directly after him, or had she waited in vain, hoping he would return?

Mrs. Webb turned back to him. "Is there anything I can bring you? I've some scones in the pantry."

The cold knot forming in his gut killed any trace of an appetite. "No, thank you."

"Would you like supper at the usual time?"

Without any other response at the ready, he nodded.

"It is a nice change to set the table for two. Company does make a meal so much more pleasant." She smiled, as if nothing made her happier than the thought of him having company for supper.

"Indeed," he replied in a flat voice. He shifted in his chair, the leather creaking with his movement. Though he had a strong feeling he would be dining alone this evening. Something he was long accustomed to, yet he already felt the loss of Rose's presence acutely. A situation entirely of his own making.

"I shall leave you to your work," Mrs. Webb said, tipping her head toward his desk. With that, she left the room.

The door clicked shut.

Thick and oppressive, shame fell over him. He called himself a gentleman. Had asked for her trust. And what had he done?

Never before had he been roused to the point of cruelty. To sling such words at another. If anyone deserved such treatment, it was Amelia. But he had stayed ever silent, bitten his tongue, able to hold back the need to lash out, to hurt her as she hurt him. Yet with Rose, with the one woman he adored, who made him feel like a man again, who accepted him as he was, what had he done?

He'd cut her down. Lanced her to the quick. Flayed her with a few choice words. Struck at the core of who she was, using it against her as a ready means to vent his anger.

The pen clattered to his desk as he dropped his head in his hands. How could he have done that to her? He well knew what it felt like to be on the receiving end, to have his knees kicked out from under him. Knew that instinctive need to crawl into himself. Yet unable to do anything but stand tall and keep the pain inside.

It wasn't right of him to get upset with her. It wasn't as if he was not aware of her profession. He had met her at a brothel, after all. Of course she would have been with other men, and would be with men after him.

That thought did not sit well at all.

There was nothing he could do about it now but accept it. If he wasn't able to accept it, to accept her as she was, then there was no point in continuing their holiday. And he wanted more than anything to spend these days with her. To spend afternoons touring the grounds . . . when the weather would cooperate, that was. To look to his right and find her next to him at the dining table. To fall asleep with her in his arms. To have the first thing he saw in the morning when he opened his eyes be her beautiful face.

With a few words, had he ruined it all? Hell, one would think he had learned his lesson by now. When it came to Rose, the hot sting of jealousy was not a foreign beast. Yet on that occasion, the eventual knowledge that it had been for naught had placated it. Soothed it into a peaceful slumber.

There was no way to placate it today. One did not come by such skill without considerable practice. She had knowledge of carnal pleasures he could not even begin to grasp. But deep down he wanted to be her first, her only. A desire he had never before possessed. Christ, he hadn't been his wife's first, not that he'd held any expectations to the contrary. As if she would give such a gift to him. But his heart pleaded for that precious gift from Rose, a gift that could never be his.

So he could either let it destroy his holiday with Rose, or he could embrace this one opportunity to temporarily escape the hard reality of his life. And in order to do that he needed to fully reconcile himself to what ultimately had brought him to her.

A harsh wince tightened his brow.

But what was more important? How she had spent her nights before he had first walked through the door of her sitting room, or being with her now?

The answer required no thought at all.

⚓

ROSE set her empty teacup on its saucer on her bedside table and lay back down, pulling the sunny yellow coverlet up to cover her shoulders. A freshly prodded fire in the hearth warmed the room, yet still she was chilled. Even the hot tea hadn't warded off the cold that seemed to have seeped into her bones.

What would she have done if James hadn't offered her this room? She certainly would not have been able to remain in his. The large bed, which had still held the warmth from his body, had felt so empty. And she had felt . . . dirty.

Used. Like the whore she was.

The disgust, the revulsion he had not been able to hide . . . It was a wonder she had kept the tears from falling.

Wearing only her thin silk wrapper, she had scurried across the corridor to her bedchamber and hadn't left since. Her only visitor? Not James, but Mrs. Webb, who had come to check on her. The elderly woman had to have known she had not spent the night in her own bed. The simple sage green gown she had worn to supper hadn't been in a wrinkled heap on the chair, but returned to the closet, cleaned and pressed. But there had been not one hint of censure on the woman's face. Nothing but kindness as she had bustled about the room tending the fire, freshening the water in the washstand, and trying to tempt Rose with everything the kitchen could offer.

Now that she was alone again, she couldn't help feeling like an unwelcome guest who refused to leave. Surely if James wanted her to leave, he would tell her. Or would he expect her to show some tact and leave on her own? While she knew she should, the thought of leaving him made tears threaten to prick anew.

In any case, the sun was starting to set. The gray daylight gently fading, giving way to the shadows that were beginning to shroud the room. It was much too late to call for a carriage. Tomorrow, if James still looked on her with hard eyes, then she would leave.

But that would mean seeing him, and she was certain she could not bear the disgust again. Just the possibility of it made her flinch.

He hadn't been cruel. Hadn't physically hurt her. He hadn't made a promise he had not kept. He had merely pointed out a fact. And with it had reminded her, lest she ever forget, of just what she had allowed herself to become.

She tugged the coverlet tighter around her shoulders. The worst of it, though? Timothy's concern had not been misplaced. Not his concern about her safety with James, but his concern for her. The disgust wouldn't hurt so much if she had kept that step back from him. Left the distance there and her heart well hidden. Looked on him like she had all the others—as a necessary means to an end and nothing more.

Instead she'd fooled herself into believing she could keep their holiday in perspective. Hell, she'd even conjured up excuses, laying enough doubt to explain his initial reticence, until it had become palatable enough for her to blithely brush aside.

From the start, he had been different. So different from all the rest that the defenses built over the years had been completely worthless. As solid as a thin wisp of air.

Damning herself for a fool wouldn't right the situation, though. Nothing would short of leaving tomorrow. But . . .

An ache flared swiftly across her chest, stealing the breath from her lungs. She squeezed her eyes closed tight, fought with all her might. The effort sapped the last of her strength, and before she knew it, the gentle tap of the rain on the windows coaxed her to give in and just let sleep overtake her.

A whisper-light touch roused her. Before she opened her eyes, she knew it was James smoothing her hair from her face. No one touched her as he did, tender and light, asking rather than taking. She took a moment to savor his touch, to soak it up, her heart pounding in her chest, begging for more. Then she reluctantly opened her eyes.

The room was near dark. Only the firelight cut through the deep twilight shadows, illuminating James's silhouette perched on the side of the bed. "Will you dine with me tonight?"

Uncertain yet unable to refuse, she nodded.

Cool air hit her, instantly seeping through the thin silk, as he drew back the coverlet. Strong arms wrapped around her, gathering her close, to effortlessly lift her. Arms draped about his neck, she rested her cheek against his shoulder and snuggled closer to him, seeking his warmth. He was toeing open the door he'd left cracked when it occurred to her.

Stiffening in his arms, she lifted her head. "Wait, I need to dress."

"It's not necessary."

The door swung open and she squinted against the light in the corridor. "One doesn't sit at a dining table clad only in a silk wrapper."

"Relax," he murmured. "We're not going downstairs."

True to his word, he only traveled the short distance across the corridor, kicking his bedroom door shut behind him.

A two-arm candelabrum was centered on a small round table draped with a white tablecloth before the fireplace. Silver covers were over the dishes of the two place settings, one with a wineglass and the other with an ivory cup and saucer. The curtains were drawn tight, keeping the warmth from the fire within. Mrs. Webb must have been in to tidy the room, for the navy coverlet on the bed held not one wrinkle.

He set her gently on her feet and pulled out one of the armchairs that earlier today had been stationed about the room. Gesturing to the chair, he tipped his head. "For you, my dear."

At the endearment, she glanced up to his face, searching for a clue. But his expression was shuttered, unreadable.

She took a moment to adjust the fabric belt about her waist and right the neckline of her wrapper. Then with a demure "Thank you" she sat down.

He took the covers off the dishes, revealing pork tenderloin with broiled potatoes, and placed them on the mantel beside a bottle of wine, and then grabbed the bottle. His hand shook the slightest bit, just enough so the stream of rich Bordeaux wavered as he filled her glass. After seeing to his own cup from the pot he had also taken off the mantel, he took his place across from her.

"I hope the fare is to your liking." Shoulders and back stiff, he didn't at all resemble the man she had dined with last night.

"It smells delicious, and I'm certain it is. Mrs. Webb has shown herself to be a wonderful cook."

"She doesn't cook," he said, as he placed the linen napkin on his lap. "Mr. Webb tends to the kitchen. She tends to the rest of the house."

That might explain why Rose hadn't seen the man since her arrival yesterday. Had that been only a day ago? It seemed much longer.

Following James's cue, she started to eat. She had only taken two bites when he set down his knife and fork and speared her with a solemn stare that caused tension to grip her spine.

"I should not have spoken to you thus this afternoon, after . . ." His gaze dropped to his plate, his chest visibly expanding on a deep breath. Then olive green eyes met hers again. "It was unconscionable to have said such a thing. It was cruel and you have every reason to think poorly of me. I certainly do."

Was he apologizing for speaking the truth? Her jaw dropped. The absolute last thing she had expected from him tonight. But she should have. James was the most honorable man she had ever met. Good and kind to the core.

"Please, I beg your forgiveness, Rose. Will you accept my apology?"

Her heart slamming against her ribs, she could only nod.

"I . . ." A furrow tightened his brow, his voice dropping to a grave rumble. "It's hard sometimes knowing I won't ever be your first anything. But I won't let it come between us anymore. You have my word."

How she wished he could have been her first everything. The first man who touched her, kissed her, made love to her. Her first and only. But none of the others mattered. None had even come close to leaving their mark on her heart. "You're the first man I have ever wanted to be with," she confessed.

The tight line of his mouth softened. The gravity left his eyes, the green depths warming with an emotion she should not dare to give name to. "Thank you," he whispered, almost awed, as though she had presented him with the rarest of treasures.

Beyond words, the most she could manage was a half smile. She reached across the small table, covered his hand with hers, needing his touch. He turned his wrist, captured her fingers, and held on to her. The moment stretched on, the silence absolute and perfect.

Then the logs in the hearth shifted, breaking the spell.

"Shall we finish dinner before it gets cold?" he asked.

She nodded, relinquishing her hold on him, for now at least. And when dinner was completed, he was there at her shoulder. He didn't even let her get to her feet, but gathered her in his strong arms and carried her to his bed.

Fifteen

CRISP and bright, the late-morning sun streamed through the windows of the dining room, a welcome change from gray skies and rain. A powerful lure James decided not to resist. He'd spent enough hours behind his desk yesterday. No need to repeat the task, especially when he was on holiday and had Rose with whom to share the day.

He looked to the beautiful woman who sat on his right. Clad in a sprigged day dress and with her hair coiled demurely at her nape, she set down her fork and reached for her teacup. As she took a sip, she met his gaze over the ivory rim of the cup, the soft smile clear in her eyes.

Yesterday, with his unconscionable behavior, was behind them. To his eternal gratitude Rose had found it in her heart to forgive him. And he had done his best last night to show her just how thankful he was. Kissed every inch of her body, lavishing the most enticing parts with the utmost attention, left her flushed and panting, eyes so heavily lidded they were mere slits, and then did it again.

He hadn't been the least surprised when she had remained fast asleep in his arms until after ten that morning, and he hadn't minded in the slightest. He also wouldn't mind going back upstairs, where he could continue to express his gratitude, but . . . he'd rather spend the day outside with her.

With a soft *click*, she set her cup on its saucer.

"Do you know how to ride?" he asked.

Her lips twitched at the edges. "I'm assuming you're referring to a horse." A quick glance behind her, to the closed door leading to the kitchen, and then she lowered her voice to a teasing whisper. "If not, then you received your answer last night."

"Indeed I did," he acknowledged with a tip of his head. She had been crouched so low over him he had been able to reach her luscious breasts with his mouth. Sucked on the sensitive tips as he gripped her hips, holding her steady as he thrust up deep and hard . . . His cock jumped, bumping against the placket of his trousers, eager to confirm the lush memory. Before it could fully rise to the occasion, he dragged his thoughts back to the original purpose of his question. "But you assumed correctly. I was referring to a horse."

"In that case, I can stay on a horse but I'm no expert."

"No cause for concern. I have a quiet mare I keep for Rebecca when she visits. Docile thing. She won't give you a bit of trouble. If you'd like, we can take a ride to the pond. Not quite the same as the Serpentine, but it does have some nice geese."

"You're luring me with the prospect of geese?" she asked, one eyebrow delicately raised.

"If it will get you to spend the day with me, then yes. Geese."

She chuckled, the soft sound floating on the air. "Such lures, while appreciated, are wholly unnecessary. If you wish my company for a ride about the countryside, you need only to say so."

His amusement dimmed. He thought he had been quite clear on this point when he had asked her to accompany him to Honey

House, but given the past couple of days, perhaps he had not been. "And you need only to refuse, if you do not wish it. You do understand that, don't you, Rose? You are free to do as you please." He hated the thought that she was bending herself to his will. That she would acquiesce only to suit him, regardless of her own opinions on the matter.

Her charming smile faltered for the briefest of seconds, so quickly he would have missed it if his gaze wasn't fixed on her beautiful face.

"Of course I understand, James."

He reached out to cover her hand with his. "I did not invite you here for you to blindly cater to my every whim. It is perfectly acceptable for you to refuse, to speak your mind, to tell me to go to hell if the situation demands it." Christ, she should have told him to go to hell yesterday afternoon. If ever a situation demanded it, it had been that one. He gave her hand a squeeze. "Please, grant me your honesty. I wish it above all else. Don't burden me with the worry that your acceptance is solely for my benefit and not for your own as well."

"But it's only a ride—"

"Rose," he said, cutting her off. "That's not what I'm asking and you know it." His pleading stare had no effect as she had dropped her attention, nudging her unused spoon with her free hand, straightening it next to her plate. The charming smile was now completely gone. "Why is it so difficult for you to be honest with me?"

She lifted one slim shoulder. She hadn't pulled her hand free, but he knew she would snatch it back to her side the moment he released her. Her fingers were stiff with tension beneath his palm.

"The only excuse I can offer is that I am unaccustomed to such liberties."

The threadbare quality of her voice made his heart clench. "Then accustom yourself to them," he said gently. "When you are with me, you are free to do and say as you please." *With me.* Somehow he kept from cringing. The qualifier shouldn't even be necessary. No woman should ever feel obligated to submit completely to another.

"Thank you," she whispered, her eyes flickering up to briefly meet his.

"Your thanks, while appreciated, are wholly unnecessary."

A hint of a smile flittered across her mouth. "Wholly?"

"Yes. In its entirety. Now then"—he laced his fingers with hers—"that ride. Yes or no?"

She looked to the window, to the beautiful sunny morning. A genuine smile curved her lips. If he did not know her better, he would not be able to tell the difference. But as it was, he could—it was in the way her eyes crinkled at the edges.

"I would like that."

"Brilliant. Are you finished with breakfast?" At her nod, he stood and helped her to her feet. "Your lovely dress, however, won't do you any favors on the back of a horse. Shall we change?"

He caught Mr. Webb in the entrance hall and relayed instructions to have the horses saddled. Webb didn't look twice at their joined hands, merely nodding and disappearing out the front door. Neither did Rose's strides falter the slightest bit at the sight of the servant. Hopefully that meant she was growing more comfortable being here with him.

They went upstairs and parted ways at her bedchamber. It didn't take him long to don a pair of breeches and to pull on his boots. He waited patiently for her in the corridor. She emerged a good ten minutes later, dressed in a brilliant blue riding habit trimmed in ivory. The strict cut of the coat highlighted her trim waist, the skirt skimming the lush flare of her hips. It was a wonder what a fold of pound notes could accomplish. To think the modiste had claimed the task impossible. Elegant and refined, the clothes more than fit her body to perfection; they fit *her*.

She placed her gloved hand in his, and they made their way to the small stable situated around the side of the house. The mare, standing in the aisle, turned her gray head toward them as they entered the stable. The sidesaddle was already on her back, the reins looped around the iron bars of her stall. He looked over the horse's haunches to see Webb saddling his burly bay hunter. James grabbed the mare's reins and led her outside and into the late-morning sun.

"Her name's Pansy. Rebecca named her," he added in explanation, as he stopped in the small yard.

"It's a lovely name," she said, passing a gentle hand over the mare's nose.

"It's her favorite flower." He motioned to Rose. "I'll help you up." Hands spanning her waist, he lifted her onto the mare. Once she had finished adjusting her skirt, he placed the reins in her hands. "She truly is a docile thing, and she listens quite well. A little tug is all you need to get her to stop."

Webb handed the bay over to James, and he swung up into the saddle. They set off out of the yard. When the dirt lane turned right, they continued heading straight, to the grassy field that led to the pond. With one eye on Rose, he kept the pace to an easy canter, forcing the stallion's naturally longer strides to match the mare's. His concern was for naught. Never once did she even begin to lose her balance, something he should have foreseen. If he hadn't been able to unseat her last night, the mare's gentle rocking strides certainly would not.

Once they had traveled a good distance from the stables, they slowed to a walk.

Rose gave the mare's neck a little pat. "She truly is lovely."

"But you are more so."

Chin tipping down, she murmured a demure thank-you. He would never trade his nights with her for anything, but it occurred to him that he had never before seen her under the sun. Outdoors, yes. In cloudy daylight and in the cool shadow of a tree, but not like this. And by God, she was even more exquisite. A slight flush brought color to her cheeks. Long lashes framed eyes glittering like flawless aquamarines. The sun's golden rays picked up the rich chocolate tone of the few strands of hair that had worked free of the sleek knot at her nape. And here he had thought her hair deepest midnight. Now, though, in the full force of the sun, he could see it was so rich and dark it approached black, but didn't quite reach it.

Pulling his attention from Rose, he looked out across the field, the grass lush and green from the recent rains. He could just make out a glimpse of the pond in the distance beyond the small group of trees. It would be much too cold for it today, but on hot summer days, he often made his way there for a swim. The water cool and clear, offering the ultimate in relaxation.

Honey House was his haven. His escape from London and everything that city held. Whenever he could manage it, he visited, even if only for a handful of days. Quiet and peaceful, a treasured respite. But sometimes too quiet. No matter where he went, whether here or in London, he could never fully escape the loneliness.

Actually . . . he could, and he had Rose to thank for it. Her presence alone, just knowing she was near, vanquished that sense of isolation like nothing else ever could.

Turning his attention back to her, he was about to ask if she wanted to pick up the pace again, but the question stopped in his throat. Her attention was fixed straight ahead, yet she didn't seem to be actually looking at anything. The content happiness was gone from her face, replaced with the slightest of frowns.

"Something on your mind, my dear?"

"James, are you married?"

His grip tightened on the reins. "Yes."

She nodded. "I assumed as much." There was no accusation in her tone, no displeasure or jealousy. Only resignation backed with acceptance.

"Why?" He couldn't resist asking. He had never once mentioned Amelia or made reference to her.

"You have the air of an unhappily married man about you."

That was putting it mildly, he thought with a grimace. "Do you live separately?"

"If only I could be so fortunate. Perhaps once Rebecca is wed, I can have that luxury. For now . . ." He looked out to the expanse of grass before them. He wasn't even certain he would ever have that opportunity. It all depended on who Rebecca chose to marry. He wouldn't put it past Amelia to take her ire out on Rebecca if he demanded a separation. If his sister married a powerful lord, she would be safe from Amelia's spite. If not, his wife could very well ruin his beloved sister's reputation. A bit of gossip here, a rumor there, and the damage would be done and Rebecca would be shunned by the ton.

"Why does it hinge on Rebecca's marriage?"

"Because Amelia . . ." he paused, unable to bring himself to say "my wife," "is the daughter of a viscount. An aristocrat. You see, my father has amassed a fortune, but the one thing he cannot buy is a title. He wants one in the family. Desperately. Being a man, I can't obtain one through marriage. I am simply the means he has used to achieve that end. But I only agreed because of Rebecca. She longs for an entrée into Society that only an advantageous match can bring. So I married Amelia, knowing full well it would not be a blissful union, in the hopes she'd honor her word to sponsor Rebecca once her time came to make her debut."

"How long have you been married?" she asked, her tone all gentleness.

"Three years," he said on a sigh. Three very, very long years.

"I take it she doesn't much care for you."

He let out a snort of derision. "She loathes me. Can't stand the sight of me, though she insists I accompany her to social functions. Must keep up appearances, after all. God forbid her vaunted acquaintances suspect the marriage was something she was forced into. To wed a common merchant's son was enough of an embarrassment, to have been commanded by her father to marry me so my father would pay off his debts . . ." He shook his head. "So I do my best not to earn her displeasure. I live by her rules, keep my opinions to myself regarding her many lovers, and every year I paste a smile on my face and escort her around town for the Season."

He glanced back to Rose and was surprised, not by the compassion, but by the longing he found in her steady light blue gaze.

"Your wife is a fool not to cherish having such a man as you for a husband."

He squeezed his eyes closed tight.

"I am sorry." Her soft words, laden with remorse, were barely audible over the sounds of the horses' hooves swooshing through the grass.

Eyes still closed, he pulled the bay to a stop. Pressing his hands on the pommel of the saddle, he struggled to gather his composure.

A gentle hand touched his knee. "She must be horrid to you."

"You cannot comprehend." He swallowed, trying to push back the threat of tears clogging his throat. *You're goddamn pathetic.* So his wife didn't care for him? Many men tolerated unhappy marriages. Yet even from the beginning, Amelia had somehow known just how to strike at him. Her barbs finding the mark with uncanny precision. Each one sinking deep into his chest, striking at how he defined himself as a man, chipping away at his very soul, until there was near to nothing left. "If she knew about you . . . at the very least, she would refuse to sponsor Rebecca."

"But you said she had many lovers. Why would she object to me?"

"Because she does not permit me that liberty. It would be considered an embarrassment. I should want her and no one else. I should feel fortunate to have her for a wife. Do you know, I had to beg her?" The words tumbled out of his mouth before he could stop them. "I was so desperate I begged my own wife to allow me into her bed. And when she at last relented . . . the disgust in her eyes cut right through me. I could not even finish." The most humiliating night of his life. *And you call yourself a man?* A shudder gripped his spine at the memory of Amelia's mocking taunt. He had not been able to get out of her bedchamber fast enough. "That incident provided ample fodder for her for months."

Dropping his arm to his side, he blindly captured her hand in his, needing her touch, her strength. He had never revealed the truth of his marriage to anyone. Had hid it from all, too ashamed to admit his wife had long ago ripped off his ballocks and fed them to him. Hell, how she did it at every opportunity, even seemed to take pleasure in it. And how there wasn't a thing he could do but endure it.

Yet deep inside he knew he could trust Rose with the truth. It was a solid, indisputable fact. She would not judge him or think less of him.

Rose said not a word. Merely held on tight to his hand for many long moments, until he at last regained his composure.

His horse shifted his weight, reminding James they were still stopped. He gave Rose's hand a light squeeze then pulled free. "We should try to make it to the pond before nightfall."

At her nod, they continued across the field and through a small cluster of trees before reaching the pond where a few geese were gliding across the surface. He dropped to his feet, lifted Rose from the mare, and tied both horses to a nearby tree.

He removed his coat, draped it over the old fallen log on the grassy bank, and gestured for her to sit.

"Since I answered all of your questions, will you answer one of mine?" he asked, taking a place beside her.

The line of her shoulders stiffened, as if she knew what he was going to ask. He waited for her to deny his request, to make use of the refusal he had pleaded for earlier, or evade his questions as she had once been fond of doing. Ten days together and he still knew so very little about her. She granted him free access to her beautiful body—he was more than familiar with every inch of her flawless skin. But that wasn't the commodity she kept under lock and key. What he truly wanted was to know *her*, the woman.

"Yes, you may ask."

"Why do you work at Madame Rubicon's?"

"For the money. Why else?" She reached down and snapped off a blade of grass, twisting it around her finger. Just when he thought she wouldn't offer up anything else, she spoke, her tone casual, with a shrug behind it. "A woman has few options in life. Marriage wasn't one of them, as I was not acquainted with any man who was wealthy enough to suit my needs. My mother passed away when I was a child, and when my father followed her to his grave five years ago, he left debts that needed immediate attention, not to mention my brother, Dash. He's now eighteen, but at the time he was expecting to attend Eton. I couldn't very well tell him our father had gambled away the family fortune and then some."

"Why ever not?"

Her head snapped up from the blade of grass. She looked at him, aghast. "Dash adored our father. I couldn't tell him that he had been so irresponsible as to beggar the estate. It was hard enough to tell a thirteen-year-old boy his father had passed away. I could not tarnish his image of him. That would have been cruel."

She spoke as if she was virtually alone in the world. All of the burden resting on her slim shoulders. And had she actually been the one to inform her brother about their father's death? "Did you have no one to help you? No other family?"

"No. It's just Dash and me."

If her father had an estate, that meant she was from a respectable family. "But if Dash was only thirteen at the time of your father's death, then wasn't a guardian appointed to care for him and oversee the estate until he reached his majority?"

"Our uncle is technically his guardian, and he was mine until I reached one and twenty, but he resides in America. I never much cared for him anyway." She wrinkled her nose. "He would have wrung the estate dry if it had not already been beyond dry."

"So how long have you been working at Rubicon's?"

She plucked a new blade of grass and went back to twisting it around her gloved finger. "Four years," she said, not meeting his gaze.

Given he'd parted with the sum seven times, he knew how much she earned for a night. Even only working a week a month, she should have amassed a fortune by now. "You still need to work there?"

She nodded. "I've taken care of the debts. They are at least settled. I'm working on replacing the money my father gambled away, but the country house . . ." She let out a sigh. "Father had sold all the property capable of producing any sort of income, so the estate can't support itself. And Dash is not without expenses, but I hold out hope he will return to university for the coming term."

James raised a brow. "He left university? Was he sent down?"

"No, he wasn't sent down. He simply decided he wished to reside in Town for the time being."

"And you allowed that?"

"I'm not his mother or his father. He does as he wishes. And he's young. Surely you can understand the lure London can pose for a young gentleman. Though I do wish he had not purchased the racing curricle . . ." She trailed off with a resigned shrug. "Not much to be done for it now. The deed is done."

His jaw dropped. "You spoil him," he stated.

Bristling with affront, she drew herself up straight. "I do not."

"Yes, you do."

"No. I am merely providing him with the opportunities he was meant to have. It is not right that he should have to pay for my father's misdeeds."

"But it is all right for you to shoulder that burden?"

"I am his sister. The only family he has. It's my responsibility to care for him."

"There is caring for one, and there is allowing one to indulge in frivolous expenses, such as a racing curricle." If the boy at all bore a family resemblance to Rose, he'd be a handsome devil. James had seen the sort at countless balls. Young and idle and backed by their families' wealth, they spent their nights gallivanting about Town without a single responsibility to force them to behave like the men they were. "I'm assuming you've left him unaware of your place of employment."

"Of course," she scoffed, as if anything else was unthinkable. "Once he went to school, he rarely returned home. In fact, he hasn't been back in years. Hopefully by the time he is old enough to take over management of the estate, I'll have shored up the coffers and he will be none the wiser."

"Why continue to hide it from him? He's eighteen. Old enough to bear the responsibility, and from what you have told me, he could well use something to be responsible for."

She shook her head, one quick motion, apprehension filling her eyes. The indignant bravado vanished, as if it had never been there. "Then he will surely ask how we have gotten along since Father's death." Avoiding his gaze, she ducked her head, her shoulders rounding, almost folding into herself. "And . . . and I don't want him to ever know."

The shame in her voice cut right through him. By God, he was an arse to berate her so. She certainly had not told him he should have taken Amelia in hand long ago. He had received nothing but quiet understanding because she knew what it felt like to sacrifice all for another.

Turning, he wrapped his arms around her and pressed a kiss on the top of her head. A tremble racked her body. "I understand. Sometimes one must forsake one's own wishes for another."

He held her close until the tension eased from her body, until she leaned into him, her cheek pressed against his chest.

How desperate she must have been to seek out Rubicon's. A young woman from a good family pushed to sell herself. No woman should ever be put in that situation, and he had been a party to it. Laid those pound notes on the madam's desk, just like all the others before him. And he certainly did not even want to think about the fact that she had likely been untouched by a man before she had first walked through those scarlet double doors.

Or had she?

He furrowed his brow, the numbers catching in his mind.

Five minus four was not zero.

"Rose, if you've only been at Rubicon's for four years, how did you get the funds for Dash to attend Eton that first year?"

The tension returned, stiffening the body pressed against his. She pushed free from his hold and made quite the little project of adjusting her skirt about her knees.

He let the question hang between them. After a long moment, she dropped her hands to her lap on a sigh that held a distinct note of resignation.

"I didn't always work at Rubicon's," she said, clearly grudgingly. "When I first came to London, I did so intending to find a protector."

"And did you?"

"You are intent on your questions today, aren't you?" She didn't wait for a response. "Yes, I did find a protector. Two, in fact. The first did not last long. He neglected to inform me he had a wife. The second . . . he was what prompted me to seek out Rubicon's." Staring down at her hands, she traced the leather-covered button on the back of one of her gloves. A slight frown tugged the edges of her lips. "I should not have been so hasty in my selection. But I wasn't with Lord Biltmore but a handful of weeks, and since I chose to part ways with him, I couldn't very well ask him for more than the few baubles he had given me. But the headmaster at Eton demanded payment, and then more letters arrived. Gentlemen claiming my father owed them vast sums. And the creditors. A couple of them knocked on my door. I did not have the luxury of time. He seemed a gentleman, and I blindly believed a title meant a man was one. But . . ."

She did not need to fill in the void. Her entire body went rigid. A wince creased her brow. The visible shudder racked her frame.

"You were with him for a year?"

She nodded once.

"He is why you don't like to leave Rubicon's?" Her reluctance on both occasions when he'd asked her to leave her suite of rooms. This had been the source.

Teeth digging into her plump bottom lip, she nodded again, worry written all over her beautiful face. "He said he would never let me leave," she admitted in a thin whisper. "I slipped away in the dead of night, with nothing but the clothes on my back, and struck a deal with Rubicon. She gained a new employee. I gained the security of her house and the ability to refuse a client, if need be."

"His name, please," he bit out, the demand short and clipped.

"Why?"

"So I can show him how it feels to be on the receiving end of a man's fists."

Rose shook her head. "No. He has likely forgotten about me by now. I do not want him reminded."

It took every ounce of self-control to keep the rage building within out of sight. The last thing he wanted was to give her a reason to be frightened of him. To look on him with those panic-stricken eyes. "He never has to know why he is receiving the lesson. The important thing is that he does get it."

"Please don't, James," she implored, clutching his arm, her fingers digging into the muscle with surprising force. "I appreciate the gesture, but it is over and done with. No good can come of you seeking him out now."

"It's not a goddamn gesture. He *hurt* you."

"And he won't do it again. Rubicon has seen to it. She's assured me she had him managed. I am safe there."

Pulling free of her grasp, he shot to his feet, impotent frustration surging within. "You should not need the protection of a brothel's madam. Hell, you shouldn't even be there, Rose." Fists clenched at his sides, his breaths coming hard and fast, he stared down at her.

Head bowed in submission, she wrapped her arms around her stomach, hugging herself tight.

The sight of her frightened and scared killed every trace of anger pounding through his veins. Obliterated it, as if it had never been there.

By God, he had practically been screaming at her. What the hell had come over him?

He dropped to his knees. That she drew up tighter, almost flinching when he touched her, nearly shattered his heart. "You deserve better," he whispered, his voice breaking at the end. "You cannot understand how much it pains me to know there is a man out there who hurt you. Who took advantage of you." He took a deep breath, gathered himself, and tried to will his hands to stop shaking. *Please, don't let me have lost her trust.* "I'm sorry, Rose. I should not have yelled at you. You did nothing wrong." Shifting to sit beside her, he murmured, "Come here."

With her head still bowed, she turned in to him, burrowing against his chest, her arms wrapping around his waist.

Relief poured over him. He had not lost her trust after all.

Many, many long moments later, when the geese had abandoned the water for the bank on the opposite side of the pond and the nearby trees' shadows had begun to lengthen to stretch across the grass, he pressed a kiss to the top of her head.

"We are an odd pair, you and I, are we not?"

He swore he could feel her smile against his chest. "Indeed we are."

"Shall we head back home? Webb will have supper on the table soon."

"All right," she said, tipping her face up to his.

One sweet kiss. Just one, else two would become more and then they wouldn't reach Honey House until dusk. Lifting free from those tempting red lips, he stood to help her to her feet. With her gloved hand in his and his coat in the other, they made their way back to the horses.

Sixteen

GATHERING her shawl about her shoulders, Rose got up from the wrought iron bench on the back terrace. Clearly the clouds had not heard her wish that they hold off for a bit. Not even a handful of minutes after she had sat down, the gray sky had given way to a light, misty rain. Yesterday's sun had only lasted a day. Something that should be expected from an English spring. Still, it would have been nice to be able to spend the afternoon with James touring the countryside. Now they would be confined to the house, likely for the duration of the day . . . though that was not necessarily a hardship. She could think of a few ways, and one way in particular, for them to entertain themselves.

She pulled open the back door and went into the house, giving a nod to Mr. Webb as she passed by the kitchen on the way to the study. James had not explicitly stated it, yet she knew he had not been with a woman since he had married. It renewed her determination to give him a wonderful holiday. He certainly deserved it. From what he had said, the man didn't do much of anything but work. On their first night together, all those days ago, he had told her his intention was to spend every waking moment at his office. She thought it an odd comment at the time, but now she knew why he preferred his office over his home.

Sometimes one must forsake one's own wishes for another.

He was a man who spent his life putting others before himself. Something she well understood, and something he had recently demonstrated yet again.

After a quiet dinner last night he had taken her to his bed and simply kissed her. Nothing else. Not even one heated touch that had hinted at a need for more. Even this morning he had held back. She did not doubt his desire for her—the erection that nudged her thigh when he had awoken her with a kiss had spoken for itself. But the moment her fingers had brushed the silken skin, just one glance, barely long enough to feel the heat of his body, he had pulled back. A kiss on her forehead and then he had swung his legs over the side of the bed with a cheerful declaration that breakfast would soon be waiting for them.

It was one of the many traits she adored about him—how he tempered his desires for her. After their ride yesterday afternoon, she had felt so exposed, so laid bare. A distinctly uncomfortable sensation. Confiding in James had not been easy. In fact, it had been the most difficult thing she had ever done. But she'd held tight to her trust in him, answered all his questions, placed her very self in his hands, and been rewarded with nothing less than compassion.

All right. So he hadn't merely held her hand and nodded his understanding. He had his own opinions about how she should handle Dash, and she wouldn't put it past him to strangle Lord Wheatly with his bare hands if ever given the opportunity. But rather than put her off, his responses now warmed her soul. It felt . . . good to know he cared enough to want to protect her, even if in Dash's case, his intent was to protect her from herself.

Last night James had sensed what she had needed and given

her exactly that. His strength and his patience. He had given her time to get comfortable with the notion that he knew her secrets. Time for that instinctive need to hide from his knowing eyes to fade to nothingness. He would continue to hold back, keep his own desires and needs tightly leashed, patiently waiting until he received a nudge from her that she once again welcomed his advances.

A nudge she fully intended to give him. And with the way his gaze had kept lingering on her chest throughout breakfast, she had a strong premonition he would be more than receptive.

Smiling, she raised her arm and rapped lightly on the oak door.

⁂

WITH a deliberate motion, James crossed out the name. The *Juliana* was due for a retrofit once she returned to port, and he wasn't of a mind to delay the lucrative voyage to the Far East. Closing his eyes, he mentally ticked through the ships in his line. Not the *Wilmington*. The *Prosperous* was still at Canning Dock undergoing repairs. At 350 tons, the *Katherine* was too small for the task. He wrote *Ambrose* in the margin. The ship should be back from Portugal by the time he returned to London. A couple of weeks to unload, ready the ship, and offer the crew a bit of leave. *Perfect.* He pulled a sheet of paper from his desk drawer to write a note to Decker to use the *Katherine* for the regular route to Portugal in place of the *Ambrose*.

At the knock on the door, he called, "Come in."

He looked up to see not Mrs. Webb but Rose standing in the doorway, a cream shawl about her shoulders. No more than ten minutes could have passed since she'd left him to his work. Not that he minded the interruption in the slightest, but still, given how fragile she had seemed since their discussion by the pond, he couldn't help but be a bit concerned by her unexpected appearance.

"Is there something you need?"

"Yes. The weather is being uncooperative today." She tipped her head toward the windows. "I was wondering if perhaps you'd care to take a short break."

All traces of her earlier reticence were gone. The smile that had once held a distinct echo of vulnerability was full of confidence. Where last night she had seemed as delicate as the ivory muslin gown she had worn to supper, now stood a woman secure in herself.

Taken aback by the abrupt change, he opened his mouth then shut it. The teasing glint in her light blue eyes indicated she had something specific in mind, yet he stopped himself from leaping to what could be the wrong conclusion. "What sort of break?" he asked, keeping his features schooled in an expression of mild curiosity.

Her answer was to shut the door. She reached behind her back. The click of the lock sliding home echoed in the study.

A bolt of anticipation shot through him. The pen in his hand clattered to the surface of his desk, the letter to Decker long forgotten. She let the cashmere shawl slip from her shoulders, fluttering to the floorboards. His pulse sped up as he watched her walk toward him, her hips swaying in a hypnotic rhythm that left no doubt as to her intention. Yet . . . they were in the study. "Here?"

She rounded the desk, trailing her fingertips along the edge. His cock jumped, recalling the ever so brief brush of those adept fingers the moment before he'd forced himself out of bed that morning.

"Yes. Here." She arched a delicate brow. "Unless there is a reason we shouldn't."

"No. No reason," he replied quickly. If she wanted to indulge here, he was more than willing and eager to accommodate her. Pushing back, he made to stand but stopped, hands braced on the arms of his chair. "Are you certain this is what you want?"

He held his breath, almost trembling with barely suppressed need. *Please, please, say yes, Rose.*

That smile turned positively sinful. "Yes. Quite certain." She stepped between his casually spread legs and cupped his jaw.

"Thank you for last night," she said, gravity briefly filling her gaze. "It meant more to me than you will ever know." Then her hand dropped down, fingertips coasting down his navy coat, as she leaned in to whisper hotly in his ear. "But I missed you."

He let out a low grunt as she palmed his hard cock through the placket of his trousers. His eyes drifted closed, savoring the way her fingers slid down his length to trace the needy head. "Damnation, Rose, I missed you, too."

"So, that break. Yes or no?"

He lifted his hips, pushing into her touch. "You're holding on to your answer."

"Indeed I am."

Her playful chuckle turned into a surprised squeak as he pulled her close, tumbling her onto his lap. Their mouths came together in an urgent kiss. Swift and fierce, the lust he'd kept locked up tight and hidden from view pounded through his veins as though it had been years and not just over twenty-four hours since he'd had the pleasure of her body.

In a flurry of movement, they bared only the essentials. The placket of his trousers yanked open, her skirt shoved to her waist. The wet tip of his cock bumped her inner thigh, the heat of her core so close yet so far away. A growl of frustration rumbled in his chest. Damn chair. The arms on either side kept her from being able to fully straddle his waist.

He twisted his head, breaking the kiss. "Hold on," he muttered gruffly. Gathering her in his arms, he stood. Her legs came around his waist, her arms about his neck, clinging to him. With his hands cradling her luscious backside, he lowered her onto his shaft.

"Oh, *James*." His name came out on a low groan, thick and slow as poured honey as he settled to the hilt.

A quick turn and he pressed her back up against the nearby wall and drove into her, snapping his hips. A part of him warned to slow down, to treat her with care, but the desperate moans hitching in her throat urged him onward. Hands gripping his shoulders, she thrust her hips against his, meeting each hard, relentless stroke.

The hot grip of her body, the way her breasts were pressed against his chest, the lightning-quick pants fanning his neck . . . Within no time at all, an orgasm was barreling toward him at breakneck speed. Too fast, too strong to be denied.

Turning, he set her on the edge of his desk. Dropped to his knees, shoved her skirt higher, spread her legs wider. And captured her clit between his lips. There was no teasing at all. No light flicks of his tongue. No lingering over the pure pleasure of giving her pleasure. He sucked hard, needing her to climax before he spilled all over the floorboards. His entire being was focused on her, waiting for the distinctive hitch in her breathy moans, the one that signaled success.

The moment he heard it, he bolted upright and took his cock, still wet from her body, in hand. One stroke and pearly white seed shot from the flushed crown, painting her inner thigh.

Grabbing hold of the edge of the desk, he hung his head and struggled to catch his breath. His knees trembled in the aftermath, barely able to support his weight. With effort, he lifted his head.

Sprawled on his desk, arms braced behind her and with her legs spread exposing the glistening wet folds of her sex, Rose looked absolutely ravished. The once tidy piles of papers were scattered about her. Her hair was a complete mess. The neat knot at her nape was partially undone, tendrils framing her flushed face with a long lock draping her shoulder, a silver pin clinging to the end.

Never had he done anything so impulsive as to take a woman against the wall, let alone on his desk. But damn, it felt good. Beyond good to just let go and fully give in to lust's demands. Hell, even though he could barely stand, he felt ready to take on anything and everything. He couldn't help but chuckle.

"You are wonderful, my dear."

A sated smile curving her lips, she let out a little purr and cupped the back of his neck, pulling him in for a kiss. "I take it you enjoyed the short break?"

"Most assuredly." If only every day could include such a decadent treat.

He reached down between her legs to pull a handkerchief from a desk drawer. After wiping up his seed, he tossed the soiled linen into the waste bin. Then he lifted her from the desk and buttoned his trousers before he gave in to the urge to have those lovely legs wrapped around his waist yet again.

She shook out her skirt. A few deft flicks of her wrist, and her hair was secured once again in its neat knot. "I'll leave you to your work, then."

"You don't need to leave. You could stay. It's still raining, so the back terrace is out of the question. I've got . . ." He pushed the papers on the desk aside, locating the newspaper he hadn't yet perused. "The *Times*. And books. Lots of those," he said, indicating the shelves on either side of the fireplace.

"Are you certain?" Her gaze strayed to his desk. "I do understand that you have responsibilities, James."

"And I can see to them with you here." He took hold of her hand and gave it a squeeze. "I just like having you near."

Her free hand fluttered, fingertips covering her mouth, as her chin tipped down.

"Rose?" Concern leached into his gut. What had he said wrong?

She peered up at him. Her eyes fairly brimming with tears yanked at his heart. "That is the nicest thing anyone has ever said to me," she whispered.

"Oh, sweetheart." He enveloped her in a hug, held her close.

After a long moment she eased back enough to meet his gaze. She gave him a little smile, the threat of tears now gone. "I like being near you, too."

He chuckled and dropped a kiss on her forehead. "We really are quite the pair, aren't we?"

"Yes, indeed."

⚜

A light mist clung to the windows of the study. The late-morning sky was still gray and dreary, offering the perfect weather to loiter near a warm fire. Rose was curled up on the comfortable leather couch with her shawl draped over her legs, covering her stocking-clad feet. Her slippers were on the floor, exactly where she had discarded them an hour ago. The logs in the hearth opposite her popped and crackled, the steady flames vanquishing the chill that threatened to seep into the room.

She flipped to the next page of the *Times*. She made it a point to try to keep up on current events. Blinking like a miss who didn't have a brain in her head when asked a question about the latest parliamentary debates never presented one in the best light. Though she would admit she found the advertisements much more interesting. Apparently a gentleman was seeking a lady in a purple hat that he had seen outside of Miller's bakery on Tuesday noon.

There was a soft scratch of a pen followed by the *swoosh* of paper. *James.* She had at first been reluctant to stay. Upon their arrival at the estate, he had said he needed a few hours each morning to see to correspondence from his office. It was the only concession he had asked for their holiday. She hadn't wanted to disturb him or distract him from his work. She had already pulled him from his desk once today. But the way he had asked, the hope in his eyes, as if just by staying she'd grant him his fondest wish . . .

She certainly could not have refused, nor had she wanted to. She could think of no better way to pass a rainy day than right here, near James.

Smiling to herself, she reached for the teacup on the end table and took a sip. A few minutes later a light tap on the door pulled her attention from the newspaper.

Mrs. Webb poked her gray head around the half-open door. "Mr. Archer, the post has arrived."

James flicked his fingers, motioning for her to enter. She set the stack on the corner of his desk and then refilled his cup from the coffeepot on the nearby cabinet.

"More tea, Miss Rose?"

With a smile of thanks, she declined the offer.

"Is there anything either of you would like in particular for supper this evening?"

Rose looked to James. At his inquiring expression, she gave him a little shrug. What was served mattered little as long as he was at the table with her.

"Chicken?" he asked.

She tipped her head. "Sounds delightful."

"Chicken it is, then." He turned to Mrs. Webb. "Perhaps Webb could roast it with rosemary, like he did on my last visit. That was quite good."

"Yes, it was," she said with a nod. "Consider it done." With that, the housekeeper left the room, shutting the door behind her.

Rose turned her attention back to the newspaper as James sorted through the post. The sounds of him working were oddly comforting. The flick of paper, the creaks of his chair as he shifted his weight. He let out a soft amused sound, just the barest beginnings of a chuckle. She glanced to him. A smile curved his mouth.

"Good news?"

He looked up from the letter in his hand. "It's from my sister, Rebecca. She is enjoying herself immensely in Town and the Season hasn't even started yet. I've never known a girl to be so taken with the idea of shopping and afternoon calls."

Rose remembered his sister from that day at Hyde Park. A beautiful and vivacious young woman. Though she had only met the girl once and hadn't spoken but a few words to her, she knew she was as sweet as James was kind.

"She also bade me to send you her well wishes."

"She did?" Rose asked, going still.

James tipped his head. "Apparently I was much too happy the morning of our departure, and you must have made an impression on her. She actually asked me if Miss Rose would be traveling to Honey House as well." Paper crinkled as he refolded the letter and put it in a desk drawer. "Suffice it to say, it wasn't the most comfortable conversation to have with one's young sister," he said, using a silver letter opener to break the seal on another letter from the stack.

"Understandable," she murmured, dropping her gaze to the newspaper on her lap, as the blissful feeling of content happiness drained out of her. Every last drop of it. Gone.

Dear Lord. How very improper it had been for him to have introduced his sister to her at the park. Gently bred young ladies were not even supposed to know women like her existed.

And she was at fault. She should not have smiled at him when she had first laid eyes on him standing there along the lane. Should have tipped her head in acknowledgment and turned, saving him the embarrassment. That moment crystallized with startling clarity in her mind—the way the smile in his eyes had dimmed for a brief second, the furrow flickering across his brow, before he had walked toward her. The pause before he had introduced his sister.

Ever the gentleman, he hadn't slighted her. He hadn't turned his back to her. Yet he had known, even though in her joy to see him she had forgotten, that such introductions were more than frowned upon by polite society.

All his kindness, all the compassion and care he showed her, didn't change the fact that she was not the type of woman a decent gentleman ever wanted to introduce to his sister. James would never want his beloved sister to be like her, and he would never, ever be proud to have her on his arm.

Pain stabbed into her chest. Lancing at her heart. Stealing her breath. And it hurt so very much because she knew, at that moment, that she had done the unthinkable. A truth she could no longer deny.

She had done what she had promised herself she would never do.

The hurt welled up inside, pricking the corners of her eyes, the pain nearly overwhelming her. She needed to get out of the study. *Now.*

Carefully folding the paper, she set it next to her hip and then slipped her feet into her slippers. She swallowed hard a couple of times before she felt confident enough to speak without a telling waver in her voice. "If you'll excuse me, the weather is so dreary I'm going to rest for a bit."

Looking up from the post, James gifted her with an indulgent smile, one so distinctly *him* that she hadn't a clue how she kept the polite mask fixed on her face. "All right, my dear. I shan't keep you, though I do thank you for keeping me company."

The house wasn't large by any means, but the walk upstairs seemed to stretch on indefinitely. Her carefully measured paces much too slow. Her knees so weak she wasn't at all sure she would be able to make it to the safety of her bedchamber.

As she turned down the short corridor, she resisted the urge to bolt that last remaining distance. When she finally reached her destination, she shut the door, her every movement so controlled her arm visibly trembled.

With her hand on the knob, she leaned her forehead against the cool wood.

"I love you," she whispered, needing to say it once, to give voice to the all-encompassing force filling her very soul.

She had fallen in love with James.

With a client.

A heart-wrenching moan erupted from her throat, one of purest desolation. She gripped the knob tightly, determined not to crumple to the floor in a heap. Once before she had indulged in that luxury, given in to the anguish, let it consume her, and had vowed never to do so again. Like a sole beacon on a never-ending sea, she clung to that vow. She had broken every other promise she had made to herself, but she would not break that one.

For she didn't know how long, the sounds of her stuttered breaths echoed in the room, seeming to surround her. Then summoning her strength, she took a deep breath. Let the air fill her lungs, let it out on a long exhale, and then forced her hand to unclench from the brass knob and turned from the door.

Just looking at the sunny yellow bedchamber made those tears well up anew. It suddenly felt wrong to be at his home, pretending as though she and James belonged together. A façade of domestic bliss with a whore.

Being with him was the very definition of dangerous, because it made her yearn for even more. For the husband she had dreamed of as a girl. Then there had only been vague notions, but this was what she had wanted. Dreamed of. A man who would look on her with kindness. Who would take her in his arms and hold her close, as though he never wanted to be parted from her.

And it could never be.

How she wished it could, though. Her soul begged for him, needed him. Needed to be able to just be near him.

But their time together could never go any further than this. Nights behind closed doors and a few stolen days far removed from prying eyes. She had known it since the moment she'd laid eyes on James, but she had made her choice all those years ago. Had chosen Dash, chosen her responsibilities, over the mere possibility of this, and she could not take it back now simply because her heart refused to heed all logic.

She should not have agreed to come to the country with him.

Should not have given herself a glimpse of what she could never have. Hell, she should have let him leave on their second night together. Let him walk out the door never to return, sparing her this agony that would be with her always.

But if nothing else, she had learned her lesson well and would be sure to never repeat her mistake again.

Her gaze focused on the clock on the bedside table. Noon had not come and gone yet. She knew what must be done, and she needed to do it now.

Seventeen

JAMES'S attention strayed once again from the report on his desk to the empty leather couch. Perhaps he would join Rose. The thought was tempting indeed. Just knowing she was in bed, alone, kept his mind from the latest delivery from Decker.

He tapped the end of his pen on the desk. He certainly wouldn't get much more accomplished sitting here. The idea of lazing away the afternoon in bed had taken root and refused to be pushed aside. Rose's soft bare skin pressed against his, lingering over every kiss, every touch. And he wouldn't make an arse of himself this time.

If she truly wanted to rest, if she hadn't simply been bored by keeping him company—and he wouldn't blame her, he'd be the first to admit he wasn't the height of excitement when he was tucked behind his desk—well, then he would keep his hands and his mouth to himself. As it was, they had already indulged once today. Right here, in fact. Her beautiful backside had been perched on the edge of the desk, legs spread wide enough to accommodate his shoulders. He swirled his tongue around his mouth, still able to taste her. Even the rich coffee hadn't been able to wipe away the memory of the distinctive sweetness of her body.

Thick and lush, arousal wound its way into his veins. He had her not two hours ago and already wanted more. Would he ever get enough of her?

Chuckling to himself, he shook his head.

No, he didn't believe he would ever have enough of Rose.

He slipped his pen in the silver pen holder beside the inkwell. The report be damned. It wasn't often the opportunity presented itself to spend an afternoon in bed with a woman. Surely no one would blame him for not letting it slip by. In any case, the small pile of papers on his right was proof he had succeeded in getting something accomplished that morning . . . something other than giving Rose an orgasm, that was.

Hands braced on the desk, he was just about to stand when a knock sounded on the door.

Rose?

No. She had gone upstairs not a half hour ago. His lips quirked at how quickly his mind had jumped to her and the accompanying little surge of excitement. Just the possibility of seeing her made him happy in a way he had never felt before. He was a man well and truly smitten, and he found the state quite suited him.

"Come in," he called.

The door opened to reveal Mrs. Webb. Her somber expression, the gravity in her hazel eyes, took him aback.

"Is something amiss?" he asked.

She nodded once, a slow reluctant bob of her gray head. "Mr. Archer, your guest is departing."

He could not have heard her correctly. "Pardon?"

"Miss Rose. She is departing."

As if to give credence to her words, the clop of hooves and the crunch of wheels on gravel passed by his study window, the unmistakable sound of his carriage being called to the front door.

His eyes flared as his stomach dropped. Mind flooded with shock, he bolted up from his desk. Mrs. Webb stepped aside just in time so he did not need to slacken his stride as he rushed through the doorway.

The sight of Rose in the small entrance hall brought him to an abrupt stop.

Dark cloak about her shoulders, she was tugging on her gloves. Mr. Webb picked up the trunk at her feet and took it outside.

The front door snapped shut, jarring him from the numbing blanket of shock.

"Where are you going?" The answer was obvious, but he couldn't bring himself to ask "Why are you leaving?"—it would make it too much of a reality.

She went still, one hand poised above the back of the other, fingertips gripping the edge of a black leather glove. Her profile revealed nothing. Eyes downcast, the fan of her lashes brushed her cheekbones. "I think it best I return to London." Her voice was low, the words measured and careful.

The prevailing question in his mind popped out. "Why?"

Her gaze darted about the entrance hall, pausing just over his shoulder before returning once again to her glove. One quick tug righted the glove and then she clasped her hands before her. "You said I could leave whenever I wished," she said, looking not at him but at the front door. "I wish to return to London now."

Confusion seized his brain. Had he done something wrong? They had had such a wonderful morning. He thought for certain she was enjoying herself. Three long strides brought him to her side. "Will you at least do me the courtesy of explaining why?"

She pierced him with the saddest of eyes. "I need to leave," she whispered, pleading with him, her voice cracking.

His first instinct was to reach out, take her in his arms, hold her close. But she was so damn brittle she appeared on the verge of breaking. As if one touch would shatter her.

Something had clearly upset her. What, though, he hadn't a clue and he knew he wouldn't get anything out of her while they were in the entrance hall with Mrs. Webb hovering down the corridor.

"All right," he said, even though every fiber of his being rebelled at the notion. Wanted to hold on tight to her and never let her go. But he had given her his word and couldn't very well refuse her request.

She flicked up the hood of her cloak. The hesitation before she placed her hand on his proffered arm cut to the quick. The team of four stood waiting just beyond the door. Their chestnut backs were already being to dampen, their leather harnesses glistening from the light misty rain. He helped her inside the carriage and then followed, taking a seat on the opposite bench. He rapped on the ceiling and with a jangle of harness, the carriage departed.

"Why do you need to leave?"

She shook her bowed head. It couldn't be much beyond noon, yet the gray skies cast the interior of the carriage in twilight darkness, leaving him unable to discern her features from within the dark shadow of her hood. He wanted to flip the darn thing back, not let her hide. But it felt like it would be too much of an invasion of privacy.

"Please, stay with me." It was the only thing he could think to say.

Her grip tightened on her clasped hands, so tight he was certain her knuckles had gone white under her gloves. "I can't."

"Why? Rose, I don't understand. Was it something I said? Something I did wrong? If it was, please tell me and it will never happen again. I assure you I did not mean to give you cause to leave. I want you to stay. I . . ." Resting his elbows on his knees, he leaned forward. "I've never been so happy in all of my life than when I am with you," he admitted. "This holiday, our time together, is very important to me. Please don't cut it short. Don't leave me now. I'm not prepared for it."

The carriage turned left onto the road that bordered his property, taking them farther away from Honey House and closer to London with each passing second. He did not even want to think about having to let her go. Ever. It wasn't as if he wasn't aware only two days remained of their holiday. He could damn well count and they had left London five days ago. Still, when he was with her, when they were together, the concept of it ending was not one that even nudged his mind.

Now she was making him face it. Head-on, with no opportunity to turn away and ignore it. The thought of not having her in his life hurt horribly. Returning to London, not being with her, not waking with her in his arms . . . he didn't know how he could return to his life. How could he face a woman who loathed the very notion of him after he had been with Rose?

A harsh wince crossed his face as he flinched against a sharp knife of pain. He wanted to drop to his knees, plead with Rose. Offer her everything he had if that was what it would take to gain her agreement to stay with him for two more days, to prolong the inevitable. But he had given his word to see her back to that house on Curzon Street whenever she wished. Pushing her too hard, forcing her hand, would be akin to a betrayal of her trust. Remaining silent, however, wasn't an option. He had to fight for her to stay.

"Please, Rose, just two more days."

From the corner of his eye, he caught the passing trees along the side of the road. The team of four was moving at a nice clip. With each rhythmic stride, a tiny bit of hope died. Each bit withering away, providing space for that once familiar hollow emptiness to fill his chest.

Rose remained silent and still. She was past the point of slipping through his fingers. She was gone. Had made the decision to leave him the moment she'd requested the carriage without informing him, thus refusing to even take him up on his original offer to see her back to London.

Desperation clogged his throat, but he somehow managed to voice one more "Please." He dared to reach out, to cover her hands with one of his. A tremble racked her body, the tremor radiating up his arm, squeezing his heart. Her breath caught, a faint little sound, but one he heard as if she had shouted.

And then she nodded.

He blinked. "You will stay?"

Another silent nod.

"Thank you," he said, as the purest, sweetest relief washed over him, sagging his shoulders. At his rap on the ceiling, the carriage slowed to a stop and he gave the driver the order to return to the house. Then he shifted to sit beside her. Hand shaking, he pulled back the hood.

Tears streamed down her pale cheeks. Her lashes were wet and spiky, glistening like black satin. He read the hurt in every tight line of her body. In the rigid set of her shoulders, in the compressed line of her lips, in her eyes clamped shut. And the sight nearly broke him.

Gathering her in his arms, he pulled her onto his lap, needing to offer whatever comfort he could. Chin tucked down, she looped her arms about his neck and rested her head against his shoulder.

"Rose, will you tell me why you wanted to leave?" he asked gently and with a fair amount of hesitation. He had gained her assent to stay and didn't want to risk losing it, yet he needed to know.

He felt her small hand curl into a fist against his nape. "I love you, but it hurts, James," she whispered against his chest. "Because I know I will never be a woman whom you can be proud of. That it makes you uncomfortable when your sister even mentions my name. I can't fault you for it, because it's what I am. Unfit for polite company. But that doesn't mean I don't wish it was otherwise."

The letter from Rebecca had pushed her to leave him? His mind refused to wrap itself around how that had led them to this point. He was aware she had explained it, but the jumps in logic were simply too large to—

His heart skipped a beat. "Did you say you love me?"

"Yes. I told myself I wouldn't. Promised myself. But how could I not love you?"

He squeezed his eyes shut, bowed his head over hers. "Say it again," he pleaded desperately, his heart and soul hanging on her next words.

He felt her shift within his arms. Soft lips brushed his jaw.

"I love you."

Clinging tightly to her, he struggled to regain his composure. Hell, he was the one who was supposed to be comforting her. But he had given up hope so long ago of ever hearing those words from a woman.

Rebecca loved him and told him as much often enough. But this was so *very* different.

"James?" Rose asked, concern clear in her voice.

"It's all right," he murmured hoarsely. He took a deep breath, swallowed hard to clear the constriction in his throat, and then opened his eyes. "It's just that it feels very good to be loved."

"Oh, James." Those beautiful light blue eyes welled anew with tears. With a light, comforting touch, she smoothed his hair back from his temples, the leather of her glove soft against his skin. She didn't say anything else, but he knew she understood.

He tipped his head down to brush his nose against hers. "You have my undying thanks for agreeing to stay. For coming here with me in the first place. Our time together truly does mean the world to me." Then he leaned back and looked deep into her eyes. She had said it hurt to love him. She had given him the most amazing gift, and the last thing he wanted was for it to cause her pain. He couldn't change the strictures of Society, but he could try to lessen their blow. "I must have you know that you have nothing but my respect and understanding for putting your family before yourself. Please don't believe I look down on you. Choices shape our lives, but they needn't define us."

Solemn and grave, she nodded. "You are a wonderful man, James." Then she cupped his jaw and brought his lips down to hers.

He resisted the urge to dive into her kiss and instead followed her lead and kept it light. Gentle. Savoring each smooth glide of her lips against his. To think this kiss almost was not . . .

With a little jolt, the carriage stopped. One more kiss and then he shifted her off his lap and onto the leather bench beside him. He exited the carriage, helped her out, and then hand in hand, they went back into Honey House.

Reluctant to part with her for even a moment, he waved aside Mrs. Webb's offer to unpack for Rose and saw to the task himself, with Rose's agreement, of course. Perched on the edge of the bed, a little smile flittering on her mouth, she pointed him toward the closet or the dresser as he pulled out each garment. Once the trunk was satisfyingly empty, he tumbled her back onto the bed and spent the afternoon reacquainting himself with every inch of her body. He only pulled himself out of her arms, and pulled his clothes back on, when the supper hour approached.

After a pleasant meal consisting of Webb's excellent rosemary chicken, they retired to the settee in the drawing room for tea and coffee. A part of him wanted to take her right back upstairs, to pick up where they had left off, with his lips tracing the delicate curve of her shoulder. But another part of him was reluctant to rush her to bed just yet.

Long after their cups were empty, they loitered on the settee, her tucked next to his side, talking about everything and nothing at all. With the night sky backing the windows, they went up to his bedchamber. And hours later, bodies sated and limbs tangled together, she fell asleep in his arms. For many moments, he simply lay there, her breaths gently fanning his chest, as he marveled at how wonderful it felt to be well and truly happy. To be loved. And he owed it all to Rose.

Tomorrow, he thought as sleep tugged at his mind. There was no way he could wait until their departure Wednesday, as previously planned. He hadn't realized it when he'd purchased the gift, but on some level he must have known even then she had captured his heart. And tomorrow, it would officially be hers.

✦

THE sun hung high in the clear blue sky, offering a tantalizing and welcome glimpse of summer, but the brisk breeze firmly reminded one it was spring. The muted green cashmere day dress covering her legs and the shawl about her shoulders warded off the breeze and allowed her to enjoy the sun's warmth. Rose rarely had time to relax when she was at Paxton Manor. With only one household servant, many tasks fell into her own hands. No matter the season, something either inside the house or about the grounds needed her attention.

Therefore she savored the opportunity to simply sit on the back terrace and read the newspaper while James saw to the day's correspondence in his study. But the newspaper lay idle next to her hip. It had not even been opened yet.

Their seven days were coming to a close. Only one more until they needed to return to the traveling carriage. She didn't regret her decision for a moment to return to the house with him. She knew it was odd to think thus, but in her mind the original holiday he had negotiated with her had ended yesterday, and with it every last trace of those pound notes that had once hung over her head. She had returned of her own free will, for no other reason than because she wanted to be with him and because he wanted to be with her.

But the hours she had left with him were rapidly dwindling. Soon there would be no more and their time together would be but a collection of memories. Each one precious. Each one treasured because it contained James.

No matter how much she wished it otherwise, no matter how much her heart begged and pleaded, she knew she could not see him once they left this house. He had found his way into her heart, imprinted himself on her soul. There wasn't a drop of regret, though. If ever a man deserved to be loved, it was James. As soon as she returned to London, however, she'd seek out Rubicon and inform the madam she would not welcome any further requests from him. Next month, if he presented himself at Rubicon's with the intent to spend another evening with her, his request would be denied.

Drastic measures indeed, but absolutely necessary.

The thought of seeing him there was more painful than never seeing him again. She would rather open her arms to a stranger than to him at that house. Being with him there would spoil her memories of their time together, and remind him anew of what she was. And the thought of accepting his hard-earned money . . . She winced. She simply could not do it again. Could not even put her hand in his knowing he'd had to pay for such a simple pleasure. No amount could make it right.

Letting out a sigh laden with the resignation of one about to go to the gallows, she adjusted the shawl about her shoulders. Why did tomorrow have to arrive? She wanted it to wait indefinitely, to stay suspended in the future forever. For it would hold the last day she would lay eyes on James. Feel his lips upon hers. Be the recipient of his adoring glances. The last day he would hold her close.

Her heart ached, a heavy weight in her chest that pulled at her very soul, demanding that she do whatever necessary, pay whatever the price, accept any and all conditions to be with him. But there was no way around it. No other solution to be found. She was becoming much too familiar with the feeling that she was his, whereas he was *not* hers.

And never would be.

The snap of a door shutting pulled her from her melancholy thoughts. Closing her eyes, she simply listened to the click of his footsteps on the flagstones, the sounds coming ever nearer. The long strides of his walk such a distinctive sound to her now, she knew without looking that it was James.

His shadow fell across her, blocking the warmth of the sun. "Aren't you enjoying yourself?"

She tipped her head back to meet his gaze and forced a smile. "Very much so."

Moving aside the copy of the *Times*, he settled next to her on the bench. "You cannot fool me, my dear." He brushed a fingertip over her bottom lip. "You've been exceedingly quiet today. Did not even once poke your pretty head into the study."

"I didn't want to disturb you."

"You could never disturb me. Tempt, yes. Disturb, no." He reached into his coat pocket and held out a small black box about the size of his palm. "Perhaps this will cheer you up."

Taken aback, she looked blankly at his offering.

"I was going to wait until tomorrow morning but . . ." He lifted one shoulder.

She gingerly took the box. Breath held, she slowly opened it, as if fearing what she would find. Resting on black velvet was a large, bloodred ruby set in delicate gold and affixed to a matching gold chain.

"If you don't like it, you can choose something else." There was a definite note of uncertainty in his voice.

With the lightest of touches, she traced the heart-shaped outline of the stone. Then she held up the necklace, letting it hang from her fingertips. The sun caught the facets, glinting off the surface. The setting was so delicate it made the ruby appear to float beneath the thin chain.

It was the height of elegance. Absolutely perfect. And it made her want to cringe.

Her hand shook the slightest bit as she put the necklace back in the box. "You do not need to give me this. It's not necessary."

A furrow marred his brow. "No gift ever should be."

But it wasn't a gift. Not a true gift. It was a pretty bauble a man gave a lover who pleased him. Just another form of compensation. A vail given for a job well done. A vail James was giving her.

And why did he have to give this to her today? Why not yesterday or the day prior? Why did he have to spoil their two days together with a firm reminder of just what she was to him?

He had to have purchased it the very day they left London. Had he believed it necessary? Expected? If that was the case, then she would correct him straightaway. Though at least he extended the courtesy of not presenting it to her just after he crawled out of her bed.

Closing the lid, she blocked out the temptation to claim the necklace as her own. To cherish it as a gift freely given, even if it truly was not.

She held it out to him. "You don't need to buy me gifts."

"No, I don't. But I wanted to. I selected it because I thought you would like it. Because I wanted . . ." He shook his head and looked out to the garden beyond the terrace, his mouth thinning. "I've never given a gift to a woman and received appreciation in response, much less a smile. I should at least be thankful you didn't chuck it across the garden." His hand hovered over the box and then he pulled back, leaving it in her outstretched palm. "I'm not taking it back. It's yours to do with it as you please. Sell it for all I care."

The pain on his face was unmistakable. It grabbed hold of her heart, a fierce wrench that squeezed so hard it pulled a gasp from her throat.

With another shake of his head, he got to his feet and made to leave. She reached out, grabbing his wrist. Given his greater strength, he could have easily pulled free. But he didn't. He merely stood there, his arm stretched behind him, her hand wrapped around his wrist, the line of his shoulders hard and stiff.

"Please, don't leave."

She heard the deep exhale, heard the pain in the way the air shuddered from his lungs. Then he slowly turned to face her, his face an expressionless mask. His gaze dropped to her hand, still wrapped tight about his wrist. She forced her fingers to release him. It was so very hard to let him go, yet she knew it would be nothing compared to tomorrow.

It took a moment to gather the words. "I'm . . . I'm sorry. I'm not well versed in receiving gifts. Gifts given for no other reason than the joy of giving. It's been . . . years since I have received such a gift." Long before her father passed away and she had made herself into a whore. "I should not have . . ." Unable to meet his hard eyes, she hung her head. "Thank you. It's perfect. Beyond beautiful."

A bird chirped in the distance. The breeze rustled the leaves on the low bushes beyond the stone balustrade lining the perimeter of the terrace. She chanced a glance up at him through her lashes, hoping beyond hope she had not just ruined their last full day together. How cold he must think her, and how cruel of her to treat his gift with such callous disregard. To assume he had felt obligated to give her such a thing. Time and time again he had proven he was not like every other man who had ever walked into her life. And yet again, she had met his efforts with distrust and suspicion. It was a marvel he had not thrown his hands up in defeat long ago. She truly did not deserve him.

"I am sorry, James. Please forgive me," she whispered.

He let out another sigh, but this one held the sound of acquiescence.

Her arm trembled as she held out the box again. "Will you do me the honor?"

His mouth tipped up at the edges the tiniest bit. "Of course," he said gruffly, taking the box.

Tugging her shawl down to bare her shoulders, she turned, presenting him with her back. The iron bench creaked faintly as he sat beside her. He reached around her. The stone was cool on her skin as it settled just above the valley of her breasts. Warm fingers brushed her nape, sending a delightful shiver down her spine as he did up the clasp.

Turning to face him, she feathered her fingertips over the stone. The most beautiful reminder of their time together, of the kind, noble man she would forever love.

"You have my heart, Rose."

She pressed her lips tight together, tears suddenly pricking the corners of her eyes. How was she ever going to let him go? "You do know I love you?"

He nodded.

She laid a hand over the ruby, holding tight to his heart. "Thank you. I will cherish it always," she said, doing her best to keep the tears from falling down her cheeks.

"Still no smile, though?" he asked, with a lopsided one of his own pulling his mouth.

A little chuckle bubbled from her chest. "Yes, you have my thanks and a smile." She threw her arms about him, burying her nose against the cravat covering his neck, taking a deep full breath of him. What had she ever done to deserve such a man as James? Then she pulled back enough to meet his gaze. "And you can have more, if you wish."

"More?" His arms came around her, large hands palming her backside.

She wiggled, rubbing her breasts against the hard wall of his chest, suddenly eager to be with him once again. "Can the stack of paperwork on your desk do without you for an hour?"

He gave her derrière a firm squeeze. "It can do without me for the rest of the day."

She let out a squeak of surprise when he abruptly got to his feet, taking her with him. His muscles bunched and flexed beneath his coat as he effortlessly shifted her, cradling her in his arms.

"When I saw the necklace at the shop, my first thought was of you wearing it and nothing else."

"Really?" She arched a brow. "Well, perhaps I can accommodate that request."

They could have passed both Mr. and Mrs. Webb in the corridor for all she noticed. She only had eyes for James. When they reached his bedchamber, he carefully set her on her feet beside the bed. The navy drapes were drawn back, allowing the rich, warm late-morning sunlight to flood the room.

Rather than tumble her onto the bed, he whispered, "Turn around."

She heeded his request. Quickened breaths fanned her nape as he unbuttoned her day dress. His fingers didn't move with confident ease down her back, rather he fumbled a bit, taking care with each small button. Clearly he wasn't accustomed to such a task and the knowledge warmed her heart.

Soon the cashmere dress was pooled around her feet. Then she felt him slip the pins from her hair. One by one, drawing each free until the length tumbled down her back. She heard a *swoosh* of fabric, and caught a flash of bottle green wool from the corner of her eye as he tossed his coat toward the chair. Turning, she made to unlace her stays but stopped when he raised a hand to stay her.

"May I?" he asked, with a shade of hesitation.

"Of course, James." She dropped her arms to her sides, offering herself to him.

He stepped so close the hem of her ivory chemise brushed his brown trousers. Lashes at half-mast, he slowly reached up toward her chest. His lips tipped up at the edges as he traced the ruby. "I'm glad you like it." The low words rumbled around her.

"I adore it because it's from you." She had received countless baubles over the years and promptly sold them all. Not a one held a bit of significance beyond their monetary value. This one, though, she would keep with her always, never to be parted with; his love worth more than any price.

His fingertip drifted down from the ruby, between the valley of her breasts to pull on one end of the narrow silk ribbon on her stays. The neat bow released. The tension around her ribs immediately eased. A deep full breath caused the laces to further loosen. A few quick tugs would finish the task, but instead he lingered. Pulling the ribbon through each eyelet, slowly unlacing her until with a barely audible wisp of sound, he pulled the ribbon free and let it flutter to the floor.

A push of the straps and her chemise and stays slipped off her shoulders, down her arms, falling to join the muted green cashmere.

He had never undressed her like this before. With the greatest of care, as if the act itself gave him as much pleasure as the result. He made her feel worshiped. Loved.

He dropped to his knees. Pressed a light kiss to her lower belly as his hands coasted from her waist down to her thighs. Intent on his task, he released the ribbons holding up her stockings. Both hands clasped around her leg, he gently coaxed the silk down one leg and then the other.

For a moment, he didn't move. Yet she felt the heat of his gaze as it roamed her bare body, leaving a flush of warmth in its wake. Then he looked up from his prone position. His heavily lidded eyes, burning with sexual promise, caused a bolt of anticipation to shoot through her, making her knees weak and her breath hitch in her chest. Large, callused hands swept up to the sensitive skin of her inner thighs. His touch no longer delicate and reverent but confident and sure. He brought one leg up to rest on his shoulder, the silk of his cream waistcoat slick beneath her calf.

Blindly reaching behind with one hand, she found the low footboard, gripped it tight. Using his thumbs, he parted her, baring her completely. Her head tilted back, eyes drifted shut, as his mouth descended onto her.

And she lost herself to everything but the pleasures of his tongue, his lips, his breath on her most intimate flesh. She threaded her fingers into his hair. Had to stop herself from gripping too tightly as he sucked hard then eased back to lap at her core. Low moans tumbled past her lips. He knew her body so well. Knew every fold, knew the most sensitive places. Knew how to ply her senses, to gather the climax, hold it right below the surface, allowing it to gather. To build. To coil tightly within.

Until it crashed over her. Her high-pitched cry echoed in her ears, mixed with the sharp pants of her breaths. His hands slid around to cup her backside, steadying her lest she crumple to her knees. Standing, he brought her with him, lifting her. Her legs instinctively wrapped around his waist.

He laid her gently onto the navy coverlet. His gaze didn't once leave her as he attacked the buttons on his waistcoat. The sunlight from the window behind him kissed the outline of his powerful body, his features slightly shrouded in shadows. Within a trice, his cravat, shirt, and trousers were on the floor.

The mattress shifted as he crawled onto the bed to lie on his side next to her. "Love you," he murmured, as he touched the heart resting over her own.

Then his hand drifted lower, fingers splaying. Gooseflesh rose across her skin, her breath catching. Cupping the back of his neck, she tugged, needing his kiss, needing the solid weight of his body to cover hers, needing him.

And the moment before his lips touched hers, she whispered, "Love you, forever."

Eighteen

THE afternoon sun streamed through the windows, providing a blanket of warmth he was most thankful for. Lighting the fire had been the last thing on his mind when he'd brought Rose up to his bedchamber. Nor would the Webbs have seen to it, as they had not expected him to have need of the room at such an hour. A day as fine as this one should be spent out of doors. He had even mentioned a walk to Mrs. Webb when the housekeeper had delivered coffee to his study earlier that morning.

Perhaps later, once Rose awakened, they could take a stroll about the grounds. For now, he was content to remain exactly where he was.

James brushed aside the dark length of her hair covering her back and traced the gold chain draping the delicate line of her neck. Rose was half sprawled over him, her cheek pressed to his chest. She had fallen asleep a good hour ago, but he hadn't followed her into a restful slumber.

How was he to part with her on the morrow? The answer was

simple. He couldn't. Couldn't possibly live without this, without her. He couldn't comprehend how he had managed for so long, the loneliness so all consuming. Day after endless day had numbed its effects. Numbed him. Now, though, after being with Rose . . .

But it left him caught between his obligations and his heart. Between the situation he had willingly placed himself in and what he needed most of all. He couldn't jeopardize Rebecca's future, yet he did not want to deposit Rose at that house. Couldn't fathom watching her walk through that back door and away from him. It went beyond petty jealousy, beyond his own selfish needs and desires. He knew she did not want to be there. Nor should she ever need to subject herself to that place again.

The problem tumbled about his mind as the direct rays of the sun began to ease back, creeping out of the room as the afternoon wore on.

Then he smiled.

The solution so simple he wanted to smack himself for not landing upon it sooner. And here he considered himself an astute businessman. But sometimes the obvious was the most difficult answer to find.

Gathering her close, he pressed a kiss to the top of her head. Of course, he still needed to gain her assent but a quick mental check turned up no cause at all for a refusal. If all went well tomorrow, then her trunk would remain satisfyingly empty.

She stirred, shifting up to peer at him with drowsy eyes, the ruby heart dangling from her neck.

"Good afternoon. Did you have a pleasant rest?" he asked.

"Very pleasant, thank you."

Stretching, she arched her back. Bare skin slid against bare skin, tempting him anew. But there was no need at all to rush toward indulgence. They had many more days ahead of them.

"The sun's still out. Would you care to take a stroll about the grounds?"

She let out a little lazy purr of pleasure. "That would be lovely."

❖

A sharp rap on the door roused Rose from sleep. Before she and James had retired last night, Rose had asked the housekeeper to wake them at dawn. The journey to London would take a full day. Therefore, a departure well before noon was required for a chance to arrive before midnight.

She kept her eyes closed tight as the ball of resistance welled up inside. But she fought it down. There was nothing to be done but accept it. She would leave James today. Bemoaning her fate would do nothing to change that fact. The best she could do was to continue to cherish their remaining time together.

Pushing up onto her elbows, she pressed a kiss to his lips. The next thing she knew she was being flipped onto her back. Crouched above her, James deepened the kiss. His hot tongue slipped into her mouth, stroking hers. A rumbling growl shook his chest. After a little nip to her bottom lip, he pulled back.

His hair stuck up at odd angles, his jaw darkened with a morning beard. The lingering haze of sleep softening his olive green eyes was beginning to give way to deep, heated desire. James in the morning. She soaked up the image, committing it to memory, determined never to forget it.

"Good morning," he said with a smile.

How could he be so happy? Their holiday was ending. "Good morning to you as well."

That smile turned wicked the instant before he dropped down again. Instinctively, she arched, tipping up her chin, giving him access to nuzzle her neck. Those soft lips drifted down, over the hollow of her throat. Sensation rippled through her, a potent temptation. Yet she resisted.

"James." She pushed on his rock-hard shoulders. "I need to pack."

"Why?" Playful and light, the word vibrated across her chest.

Must he make her say it out loud? "We need to return to London."

Still crouched over her, he pushed up onto straight arms. "*We* don't need to leave today. I must—the Season's to start tomorrow. But you don't need to leave." His gaze turned serious. "Stay."

She opened her mouth then shut it. Was he asking her to . . . No, he couldn't be asking that. But the tension seeping into her stomach whispered the former. "James, I don't understand."

"This house would be yours. I'll give you access to my accounts. You could use the money as you see fit. Replace everything your father gambled away, fund your brother's jaunts about town. It matters not to me what you do with it. I'll hire an estate manager so you needn't worry about keeping up the country house. You'll want for nothing, Rose, and you'll never need to return to Rubicon's again."

"You're asking me to be your mistress." It wasn't a question, but a statement.

He nodded. "Yes, that's what I'm asking. Will you stay with me?"

She briefly closed her eyes, fought to keep the wince from showing itself, and then pushed on his shoulders again. "James, please let me up."

As soon as he shifted aside, she threw her legs over the side of the bed and stood. Where had James thrown her wrapper last night? She looked to the wingback chair by the dresser, but it only held his coat and waistcoat, the haphazardly discarded garments barely clinging to one arm. "You want me to stay, but you are leaving today?"

"I want nothing more than to stay here with you, but I must return to London. As I've said, the Season starts tomorrow. Rebecca needs an escort for her coming-out."

Her gaze skipped about the room. Perhaps the foot of the bed. "And you must escort your wife as well."

A pause. "Yes." As she leaned down to grab the wrapper she

heard the ropes under the mattress creak. "I'll be back as soon as I can. It's not as if I intend to be gone for weeks at a time. I want to be here with you, not there."

"You have business interests in Town, James. You need to be there to tend to them," she countered as she slipped her arms into the silk sleeves, quite proud of how calm she was remaining. He was acting on impulse, without thought to the consequences. Once he realized that fact, this conversation would end and she would not have to actually voice a refusal.

"Many men conduct their business affairs from the country. Once the Season's over, I will still need to go to Town on occasion, but I intend to spend the majority of my days here, with you."

After tying the belt at her waist, she turned to face James, who now stood beside the bed, the gauzy dawn light caressing every inch of his bare skin, highlighting the strength and the power of his body. "You aren't allowed a mistress, James." She watched as a muscle ticked along his jaw. Saw the flash of hurt, but still she pressed onward. "You told me yourself. Your wife will refuse to sponsor your sister if she discovers I was here for a week. And you want me to remain for the foreseeable future?"

He scowled. "Not the foreseeable future. Indefinitely. Unless you grow tired of the place, and then we can sell it and find another." His controlled exhale filled the room. "She will never find out."

"Because you plan to hide me in the country." She couldn't do it. Absolutely refused. It didn't matter if it was a little town house on the edge of Mayfair or a country estate. She had promised herself years ago to never again become a man's possession. It wasn't that she didn't trust James implicitly. He would never physically harm her. The man wasn't capable of such action against a woman. But being kept on the side, hidden away, only allowed occasional glimpses of the man she loved . . . It would slowly destroy her.

His eyes softened, the mounting frustration replaced with compassion. He breached the distance between them, stopping to stand before her. "Rose, it is not because of you. I'm not ashamed of you. You do understand that, don't you? It's the best I can offer. The only solution. At least for now. If Rebecca marries well, then I can demand a separation. Until that time . . ." He sighed. "I want to be with you, Rose. Don't you want to be with me?"

Yes, she wanted to scream, but she somehow kept it inside. He was so close every breath held the clean, pure scent of him.

"I have been happier with you this past week than I have ever been," he said, filling the silence. "*We* are happy together. Do not try to deny it."

"I wouldn't dare," she whispered.

"It doesn't have to end, Rose."

He reached out, as if to take hold of her hand. Just before his fingers brushed hers, she stated quietly, "You have a wife, James." There it was. The one obstacle his love could not overcome.

He went still, hand hovering over hers.

"Even a separation won't change that. You will always belong to another." *And you can never be mine.*

Jaw clenched tight, he let out a short, low grunt, turning on his heel to grab his trousers from the floor. "She doesn't want me." he said, yanking them on. "Never has and never will. I wasn't her choice and she wasn't mine."

"You are still her husband. You belong to her."

"She does *not* want me!" A flick of his wrist and the placket was buttoned. "I have not shared my wife's bed for years, nor will I again."

"Don't you want children?"

"Yes. With you."

She wanted to clamp her hands over her ears, wished she had never heard those words from his lips. How could he be so cruel? "But they would be bastards."

"Hell, Rose." He dragged his hand through his hair, further disheveling the short strands. "That would matter not to me. I would love every child of ours."

"I know you would, James." And she did. He would make a wonderful father. A man a son would aspire to be like and a daughter would adore. "But love can't take away the stigma of being a bastard. You would sentence a child to that fate?"

He let out a growl of purest frustration. It rumbled through the room, the force of it pushing her back a step. Closing his eyes, he pressed his fingertips to his temples in a clear attempt to gather himself. "Then I will continue to ensure you do not get with child." He looked at her with an expectant glare, as if that concession alone should gain her assent.

"James, that isn't . . ." He obviously didn't understand. "You are still hers, and she has not given you up. Therefore, you cannot be mine. I won't take another woman's husband away from her. I left my first protector the moment I discovered he was a married man. At Rubicon's it is only one night. I suspected you were married after our first evening together, and I know I should not have—"

"Don't say it." His words snapped between them, so sharp they stung. "Do not turn me into a regret."

"Never. I wouldn't trade our time together for anything."

Jaw set, he stared at her for a long moment. "You understand the situation I am in?"

"Yes."

"And still you refuse me?"

"Yes," she whispered, turning her head toward the windows, unable to look at him for fear her resolve would crumble.

"You still have a brother to spoil. A family estate to shore up. I take it you intend to return to that house on Curzon Street."

Hugging herself tight, she nodded. Just the thought of another man touching her . . . Thick and viscous, disgust slid over her skin. She wanted to recoil, yet she kept the revulsion from her features, knowing James would jump at the chink in her armor. Poke and pry, until she admitted how very much she dreaded even stepping foot in that house.

"I offer you carte blanche, a home of your own, security, and that you refuse?" The confusion, the pain clear in his voice. "You would rather continue to work as a whore than live under my protection? I thought you loved me."

She kept her gaze fixed on the trees beyond the window, as a tremor began to seize her arms. "I do, James. With all my heart."

"Yet you would condemn me to . . . her," he spat the word, as if it left a foul taste in his mouth, "for the rest of my days."

Rose couldn't answer. Could not even nod. Couldn't acknowledge the heavy, aching truth in his accusation.

She loathes me. Can't stand the sight of me . . .

Her resolve teetered, precariously close to the edge.

His breaths quickened to harsh, rapid pants, the slightest of stutters behind each sharp inhale. The sound ramped the tension in the air, ratcheting it ever tighter.

"I love you!"

Startled at the outburst, her head snapped to him. His chest was heaving, biceps bulging, hands balled into fists at his sides. And then before her very eyes, the anger, the frustration, the fight drained out of him, leaving only the pain. His arms went limp. His breaths shallow yet deep, as if he were on the edge of exhaustion. He gave his head a slow, weary shake. "I love you, Rose," he whispered hoarsely.

She bit her bottom lip, hard enough to taste blood. Her soul screamed, pleaded for her to rush to him, throw her arms about him, promise him anything, do whatever it would take to ease his pain. But she made not a move.

The tranquil, happy life he had envisioned for them could not be, no matter how much his heart needed it.

He drew himself up straight, a blank mask falling over his features. "I'll call for Mrs. Webb to have your trunk packed. We best leave soon. If we change horses frequently, we can arrive in London tonight."

"We? You will see me back to London?" A lesser man would leave her to her own devices, push her out the door with only the clothes on her back. But not James.

He couldn't hide the hurt at her assumption. "I gave you my word, Rose," he said, as he pulled on a shirt.

"I did not mean to imply—"

He held up a hand to stay her. "Mrs. Webb will see to your packing shortly. Best change into something appropriate for the journey."

With that, he left the room, not even looking at her as he passed. The door snapped shut.

She buried her face in her hands. It took all of her effort to hold back the tears. She focused on each breath, focused on pushing the riotous mass down to a manageable level. A long day stretched ahead of her, and she knew she could not even begin to vent this horrendous agony tearing at her chest until she reached London.

⚓

THE rhythmic clop of the horses' hooves was the only sound that broke the silence as the carriage wound its way through the darkened streets of London. Rose had barely spoken more than two words to him since they had left Alton. Only the required politely murmured "thank you" when he had helped her from the carriage while the driver saw to a change of horses at the posting inns.

Part of him was still shocked she was sitting, silent and still, across from him. He should be alone, just about to stop at an inn for the night. He should have spent the morning lazing in bed with Rose. She should have kissed him good-bye around midafternoon. A bit melancholy at seeing him go, but happy and secure in the knowledge he would soon return to Honey House and to her.

Instead, they were blocks away from Madame Rubicon's. Had

departed Alton before nine, early enough to have no need to stop at an inn for the night along the way. And his offer had been met with a resounding refusal.

The woman had a resolve of steel. He had countered every one of her arguments, offered her free access to a fortune of rather ridiculous proportions, had given her his heart on a silver platter. The only thing he hadn't done was drop to his knees and beg, and he'd been damn near close to it.

But she had stood so firm he knew the effort would have been futile. She would not have relented, and he would have only humiliated himself. He had enough experience with humiliation. He'd rather not bear it from Rose's hand.

She wanted all of him. That was clear to him now. All or nothing. To stay with him, she needed his name. The one thing he could not give.

At her core, Rose was a daughter of a country gentleman. Those staunch, loyal values bred into her. It didn't matter that Amelia despised him, loathed him. He was married, and as Rose had so clearly told him, she would not take a woman's husband away from her.

Cursing Amelia to hell wouldn't resolve the situation. If not her, then it would be another. He had known since he was an adolescent that he would marry a lady. That he would do whatever necessary to hand Rebecca her fondest wish.

At the time, he could never have predicted his decision would have him depositing the woman he loved with all his heart at a goddamn brothel.

The carriage turned left onto Sloane Street, taking them ever nearer to that house, and he was powerless to do anything to stop it. He turned his attention from the view beyond the window. The passing streetlamps illuminated her profile, her gaze fixed on the neat rows of town houses. She was fooling no one, most of all him, with that indifferent mask.

The desolation was evident in the slightest of furrows marring her brow, in the shoulders that were no longer ramrod straight. She didn't want to return to that suite of rooms above Rubicon's office.

It was within his power to give her the means to walk away forever. She wouldn't accept him, but perhaps he could convince her to accept his aid nonetheless.

He cleared his throat. "I understand why you work at that house, Rose. No woman should ever feel forced into such a situation. But you needn't feel that way anymore. Allow me to give you fifty thousand pounds. I'll take you to your home in the country. We needn't even stop in that back courtyard. You never have to walk into that building again."

Looking down at her clasped hands and not him, she shook her head. Shadows now obscured the interior, cloaking the details of her beautiful features.

"It's a gift, Rose. I heard what you said this morning. I don't agree with it, I wish to God you didn't feel that way, but I respect your decision. I'll leave you at your front door. If you don't want me to see you home, allow me to secure you a private carriage to take you there safely. I have more money than I could spend in three lifetimes. Let me help you."

"Please don't ask me to take any more of your money, and please don't try to force it upon me. I'll simply return it."

"But Rose—"

"Thank you," she said, cutting him off, all abrupt politeness. "But please don't, James. I can't accept it."

The carriage slowed to a stop. With the slightest of hesitation, her hand fluttered up to her chest, fingertips tracing the outline of his heart then skimmed up, following the delicate chain to her neck.

Desperation grabbed hold of him. "Don't."

Hand stilling, she looked up.

"Don't even think of returning it," he said, low and determined. "I gave it to you because I wanted you to have it. That you will not stay with me, that you refuse my aid, does not change that fact."

"I would never think of returning it, unless you asked it of me," she murmured, pressing her palm to the stone.

"Good." He nodded once, short and curt, satisfied she understood.

Of its own accord, his gaze strayed to the window. The light streaming from the two windows illuminated the flagstone path leading to the door he had knocked on eight times. Seven for each night he had sought Rose, and once for the morning to finalize arrangements for the holiday that was at a close.

He had to let her go now.

He flexed his hands at his sides, pushing back the almost overpowering need to touch her one last time, to feel the warmth of her skin. Then shifting on the bench, he reached for the brass lever on the carriage door.

"No. Please stay here. I can see myself to the door."

Head tipped down, she gathered her cloak about her shoulders, flipped up the hood. Her skirt brushed his legs as she got out of the carriage.

"My heart is forever yours." Soft and light, yet heavy with regret, her parting words floated around him.

Broken heart in his throat, he lurched forward, reached out, needing her so desperately he could barely draw breath, and got nothing but a handful of air.

He waited until she was safely inside before giving the signal to his driver to move on. As soon as the carriage left the alley, he rapped again on the ceiling, this time to instruct his driver to take him to Hyde Park. He left the carriage behind at the gates, went to his favorite bench under the large oak tree, sat in the darkness alone where no one would hear him and no one would see him, and finally let out the anguish consuming his heart.

‡

"Thank you," she said to James's footman. "A servant will see it inside."

The footman set her trunk at her feet. His footsteps clicked on the flagstone path as he returned to the carriage.

Her arm shook as she lifted it to knock on the back door. She could feel the weight of James's gaze. Just knowing he was but a few paces behind her, that she would never lay eyes on him again . . .

"Please, open the door," she whispered, barely audible, barely able to get the words out.

It felt like an eternity as she waited for the door to open. When it finally did, she brushed past the maid with a hasty instruction to have the trunk delivered to her rooms.

She had the key in hand before she reached the narrow door at the top of the stairs. Not pausing to glance about the corridor to ensure it was empty, she rushed to her sitting room. It took a few tries to get the key into the lock. There was no sigh of relief when it finally slid home, only an all-encompassing need to get inside.

With a crack, she flung the door closed. She reached up to remove her cloak, but her fingers were shaking too hard to manage the clasp.

Then her arms dropped to her sides.

He was gone.

She had left him.

Her breath hitched sharply, caught in her chest. Her entire body trembled as she stood there in the dark room, the only light seeping from under the door.

A distinctive double knock echoed through the room. She opened her mouth to call for him to enter, but the words wouldn't come.

She heard the click of the knob turning, the very faint creak of the hinges.

"Rose? I have your trunk. Why are you standing in the dark?"

There was a *thump* behind her as Timothy set the trunk down, then light filled the room as he lit a candle.

"Rose?"

A gentle hand settled on her shoulder, turning her.

"Oh, Rose," he said, full of compassion, of sympathy, with a shadow of the pain that filled her entire being.

He wrapped his arms around her, held her close, and she couldn't hold it back a moment longer. The tears flowed down her cheeks, wetting his shirt, sobs racking her body.

She would never see James again.

Nineteen

ROSE pulled a sheet of paper from her desk drawer. The note that had been awaiting her a week ago when she returned to Paxton Manor lay open on the desk.

I was quite capable of taking care of my own responsibilities.

—*Dash*

One line followed by a short, terse signature. That was it.

He had correctly assumed who had settled his debts. She did not intend to keep it from him, but the day she left London she was in no condition to have a conversation with him. It still wasn't a conversation she particularly wanted to have. His note screamed his displeasure, but soon she would broach the subject with him, along with another more pressing matter.

Letting out a resigned sigh, she picked up her pen.

Dear Dash,

I hope this note finds you well. There is a matter of great importance I need to discuss with you. Please return to Paxton Manor at your earliest convenience.

—Love, Rose

After addressing the note and sealing it, she set down her pen. There wasn't a doubt in her mind he'd come home as soon as he read the letter. She had never asked him to come home before. The sheer uniqueness of her request would make it impossible for him to blithely brush aside.

Resting her elbows on the desk, she dropped her head into her hands.

How was she to tell him? She hadn't a clue, but she would only have a few days to find a way to do it.

She could not return to Rubicon's. She had thought she could do it, simply continue on, as long as James didn't walk through her door. She had done it countless times over the years. Had perfected the art of ignoring herself in favor of her clients. Rubicon's was her only source of income, after all. A requirement and not a choice she had the luxury of brushing aside.

But on the long ride to Bedfordshire, alone in the carriage with nothing but her aching heart, she realized she could not make the journey to London again. Being with another man would be a betrayal of the utmost proportions of the love she held in her heart for James. Her body, her soul, forever his.

By refusing his offer and refusing his aid, however, she had left herself with no means to support Dash or maintain the house or repair the coffers her father had drained. She had a bit left from the sum James had paid for her to accompany him to Honey House, but it would not last long. It wasn't even enough to cover Dash's quarterly allowance, let alone fund his extravagant lifestyle.

After a week at home, a week spent worrying and fretting and aching for James, a week during which she'd been so out of sorts her housekeeper had inquired after her health over a half dozen times, she had come to accept that what she had fought so hard to hide was now her only option.

The decision had not been an easy one. The underlying reason why she had continued to hide the truth from Dash was still an almost paralyzing worry. Beyond it, though, she was accustomed to managing everything herself, shouldering all of the burden. Asking for help was a foreign notion. But the time had come to ask for Dash's assistance and for her to stop sheltering him. He was eighteen years of age. A man. A spoiled young man, but she had to accept some of the blame for that. He was what she'd helped him to become. And as James had tried to explain, she was doing Dash a disservice by continuing to cater to his every whim. She had treated him like a thirteen-year-old boy for the past five years, and it was time he helped bear a bit of responsibility and have a say in his future. Together they would determine how to go on from here.

She had reconciled in her heart that James would not be in her future. She would always love him, her heart would ever ache for him, but nothing could come from wallowing in her sorrows. She must try to move on and make a life for herself in a manner where she could maintain a shred of self-respect.

With that thought fresh in her mind, she pulled out another sheet of paper and penned the necessary note to Rubicon. Then pushing back from the desk, she stood. Letters in hand, she left the drawing room and found her housekeeper, Sarah Thompson, on her knees cleaning the great expanse of white and black checkered marble covering the floor of the entrance hall.

If one walked through the front door, they would never guess the Marlowes no longer possessed a fortune. The main rooms of the sprawling country house were as grand as they had been a decade ago. Showplaces to impress, showcases to announce wealth. But if one looked beyond the doors kept closed tight, they'd find furniture draped in sheets. There was no reason to expend the effort to clean and dust rooms no longer in use. Between Sarah and herself, they had a hard enough time keeping the dust from collecting in the few rooms kept up in the event of an unexpected visit from Dash. It took an army of servants to maintain a house the size of Paxton Manor. An army she could not afford.

"Sarah, we need to air out Dash's bedchamber. He'll be visiting in a few days." The ceilings so high, the space so vast, her voice echoed.

Sarah dropped the sponge in the bucket and pushed back onto her knees. Forty years of age and widowed over a decade ago, she was her only companion in the house. Rose had never explicitly told Sarah why she left for one week out of every month, but after four years, the woman had to assume the true reason.

"How lovely," Sarah said, smiling. "It will be wonderful to have him in the house again. I'll be sure to stop at the butcher tomorrow to secure something suitable for suppers. Do you know how long he plans to visit?"

"At least a few days, perhaps more," she replied, uncertain how long Dash would remain at the house. She wasn't at all sure how he would react to her news. He might very well leave the day he arrived, never to return again.

But she had to hold faith in Dash. He may be rash and impetuous, but he cared for her. Loved her. He wouldn't turn his back on her once she explained how they had gotten by since their father's death. At least she hoped he wouldn't.

Her free hand fluttered up to brush lightly against the stone hidden beneath the demure bodice of her plain brown cambric day dress. Losing James had almost broken her. Losing her brother could very well see the deed done.

❧

WITH his arms crossed over his chest, James leaned against a column marking the perimeter of the dance floor. The drum of hundreds of voices competed with the music from the quintet in the corner, the sound filling his ears to the point where he couldn't make out one voice over another. The bright light from the chandeliers suspended from the high ceiling coupled with the press of so many bodies made the ballroom almost oppressively hot, the thick heat causing a trickle of sweat to form under his collar.

He shifted his weight and resisted the urge to tug at his cravat. The Forsythes' ball. The absolute last place he wanted to be. Around him ladies and gentlemen chatted merrily, yet he felt distinctly separate from them. As if he existed in his own numb void. And the fact that no one approached him seemed to confirm it.

He had been treated to Amelia's ire during the first few functions; the slash of her narrowed eyes, her hissed admonitions to stop glowering like an ill-mannered beast followed by a remark about how she wondered why she even expected better manners from the likes of him. He hadn't even heaved a sigh in response. Had merely stared back at her, wanting nothing more than for her to flitter off to join a group of her vaunted acquaintances. For her to just leave him alone.

His lack of any sort of response must have finally sunk into her shallow head, for he had been spared her ire last night and she had not approached him since they had parted ways at the bottom of the Forsythes' grand staircase.

Simply laying eyes on her should hurt—the woman was the most blatant reminder of why Rose had refused him—but oddly it didn't. He felt nothing. So hollow and empty inside only apathetic resignation could take root.

At least his evenings weren't a waste of his time. From what he could tell, Rebecca was a smashing success. A smile continually on her sweet face, gentlemen vying for her attention. By the end of the Season, she would have her choice of proposals, and hopefully one would be from a gentleman who suited her.

The music died down, leaving only the chatter of voices. He focused back on the gleaming parquet dance floor.

Clad in a white muslin gown, Rebecca curtsied to Lord Brackley as the man made his bow. Another gentleman came up to her to claim the next dance. Mr. Gregory Adams. A young buck and a known fortune hunter. James made a mental note to approach the man later, ensure Adams was aware he would never give his consent for him to even court Rebecca.

During prior years, he hadn't been bothered to make note of the various unmarried men of the ton, but now he had a vested interest in each and every one of them. The last thing he wanted was for Rebecca to be swayed by a handsome face and a pretty title. She deserved a man who would love her, cherish her to the end of her days, as he would have cherished Rose.

What felt like a dull, jagged blade pushed against his chest, demanding entry. He didn't fight at all as the blade sank deep, knowing the vast emptiness inside would soon swallow the ache.

"Good evening, Mr. Archer," came a cultured voice from his right.

He turned his head to find Brackley at his shoulder. Pushing from the column at his back, James stood up straight. With short blond hair and broad of shoulder, the man was almost as tall as himself, and therefore James did not need to look down to look him in the eye. "Evening, Lord Brackley."

"Your sister is a delight. A lovely young woman."

He tipped his head. "Indeed she is."

"Would you be available tomorrow morning? I wish to pay a call."

James had a fair idea why Brackley wished to have a conversation with him in private. Brackley was a pleasant fellow and in possession of an earl's title, but about as dull as James himself and at almost double Rebecca's age, he was too old for her. Definitely not someone who could snare her honest interest. Yes, James had noticed she had partnered him at prior functions, but as a respected member of Society, Brackley wasn't a man she would snub.

The man had clearly misinterpreted her kindness as a sign of interest.

"I'm afraid I cannot honor your request. I am tied up with appointments on the morrow." The appointments were nothing that couldn't be rescheduled, but perhaps he wasn't as numb as he thought if he was willing to postpone Brackley's disappointment.

A bit of the hope dimmed from Brackley's kind brown eyes. "Then perhaps the day after."

"If you must. I'll be at home Friday until ten in the morning."

"Thank you." An abbreviated bow and Brackley turned on his heel.

Letting out a sigh, James passed his gaze over the ballroom. Rebecca was still dancing with that fop. Definitely needed to seek him out later, discourage Adams before he latched too tightly to his sister and put off other suitors. Amelia—her blonde head adorned with a spray of white feathers—was nowhere to be found. A quick check showed Lord Albert was conspicuously absent as well.

There wasn't even a twinge of annoyance that Amelia had abandoned her chaperone duties, yet again, in favor of her lover. It was expected, and the reason why he remained in easy view of the evening's proceedings and did not hide himself off in a card room.

He pulled out his pocket watch. At least two more hours before Amelia and Rebecca would want to leave. He settled back against the column, resigned. Hell, resignation defined every minute of his day now. The resignation that came with the complete and utter absence of hope and happiness.

And so was his life now.

*

REBECCA turned from the vase of flowers and accepted the teacup from the maid. With a little curtsey, the girl left the drawing room.

It was midafternoon, and fortunately the weather was fair enough to accommodate a carriage ride about Hyde Park. Soon she would need to prepare for the five o'clock drive. Most everyone who held any sort of importance in Society would be out and about, providing ample opportunity to discuss the latest on-dits and perhaps for her to come across a certain gentleman. But first Amelia had wished to review the latest round of invitations.

A stack of pristine white parchment was on the low table in front of the settee on which Amelia sat. Given Rebecca's father's goal, he had certainly chosen well when he had selected a wife for James. The woman received invitations to most every affair and was accepted in the highest circles. By being Amelia's relation by marriage, Rebecca had also been accepted without hesitation, calming her initial worries that her lack of aristocratic blood would pose too great an obstacle to overcome.

She took the chair opposite from Amelia and brought her cup to her lips. But given James himself, her father had not chosen well. The past couple of weeks spent in such close company with Amelia confirmed Rebecca's belief that her brother and his wife fulfilled only the strictest requirement of a marriage. On paper and in name only, and nothing more. The two had absolutely nothing in common and seemed content to simply go their separate ways. James at his office absorbed by his work, as he was presently, and Amelia absorbed with herself. From what she could tell, they were only in the same room when it was for her benefit. Last night, for instance. Knowing James didn't much care for ton functions, she had tried to convince him his presence wasn't required. That it would be quite proper for her to attend with Amelia only. A married family relation was a suitable chaperone. But James had replied that he would serve as her escort all the same.

He really was the dearest of brothers. Willing to subject himself to what he clearly found to be miserable evenings, judging from his dampened mood of late, just for her.

"We shan't attend the Drakes' soirée," Amelia said, taking the invitation from the stack and setting it on her left. She picked up the next one, gave it a quick perusal, and then put it next to the Drakes' discarded note. "But the Cranbrooks' supper party should prove a pleasant affair."

Rebecca nodded, though her agreement wasn't a requirement. One's place in Society needed to be maintained, and she knew an important component was in the choice of invitations accepted. Mrs. Drake was a nice woman—Rebecca had made her acquaintance a week ago at an afternoon tea—but Mr. Cranbrook was a brother of an earl.

She continued to nod as Amelia went through the stack, planning their calendar for the next few weeks. More than once her attention strayed to the flowers on the console table, and on each occasion a little surge of happiness tingled through her.

"What is your opinion of Lord Caldwell?" Amelia asked, as the Dixons' note joined the stack of denied invitations.

She looked back to Amelia. "He has a pleasing countenance."

"I couldn't help but notice he asked you to dance at the Williamsons' affair. That is the third time he has partnered you. I do believe the interest is there. It but needs a bit of encouragement."

"Perhaps," Rebecca evaded. Caldwell was a handsome fellow. Sleek and refined, clearly a creature of Society. He also had a title and a passable fortune. Such a man should rise to the top, command her attention. Her father would certainly be nothing but pleased if she managed to become the Marchioness of Caldwell. But there was a strong possibility Lord Caldwell possessed a potential flaw she could not overlook.

"Perhaps?" A little scowl rippled across Amelia's face. "Do you doubt his interest?"

"No, but it is rumored he has a mistress. One he's quite fond of." She set down her empty teacup and crossed to the console table, wanting to touch the flowers yet again, to feel the velvet soft petals beneath her fingertips. "I know it's foolish, most married men keep mistresses, even James, but I'd rather not choose a husband who already has set that precedent."

"James does not have a mistress."

"Well, I'm not certain he would classify her as such, but she was with him when he recently went on holiday to the country," she said, adjusting the riot of red pansies in the vase. *He* sent her flowers, and not just any flowers, but her favorite variety.

It had been days ago when they had been standing near the refreshment table adorned with a couple of small sprays of pansies that she had casually mentioned her preference for them. Days ago, and he had remembered.

She couldn't help but smile. Lord Brackley . . . *Robert*—her lips silently formed the name—was a wonderful man. He preferred Town over the country, enjoyed the theatre, and most importantly, adored her. He was an earl, very well respected and in possession of a decent fortune, and to her knowledge, he was not in possession of a mistress nor did he seem the type to indulge in one. She had only been acquainted with him for three weeks, yet she knew in her bones he would make a very good husband.

In a way, Brackley reminded her a bit of James and not only in his appearance. He was tall with a substantial frame that brought to mind the grooms in her father's stable, just like James. But the similarities were more in their characters. Restrained, gentle, caring, and indulgent. He clearly needed someone to love.

And tomorrow he was going to speak to James. Had told her as much last night after he had danced with her a second time.

The little tingle of happiness flared throughout her body. There wasn't a doubt in her mind that James would have no cause to refuse Lord Brackley. By tomorrow afternoon she could be well on her way to becoming Lady Brackley.

It took more than a bit of effort to tamp down the grin, but she finally succeeded enough so she could turn from the flowers. She glanced to the low table before Amelia that now held only two stacks—the accepted and the discarded. "Have we finished with the invitations? If so, I should return to my bedchamber to change into something more appropriate for a drive about the park."

Rising from the settee, Amelia took the discarded stack and then flicked them into the hearth with a snap of her wrist. The flames flared then settled back to an even burn. "I shall meet you in the entrance hall."

Rebecca left the drawing room and went upstairs to her bedchamber, as she mentally ticked through her wardrobe. The deep green carriage dress perhaps? Lord Brackley had worn a green waistcoat the last time she'd seen him at the park, so she knew he didn't dislike the color. And the fit of the dress accentuated her figure.

Yes, the green dress would do quite nicely. As she passed a footman in the corridor, she requested that her maid join her in her bedchamber. If she was lucky, she would see Lord Brackley in just over an hour and be able to thank him personally for the beautiful flowers. And as she entered her bedchamber, she let the grin loose to spread across her mouth.

✳

"MAY I take your bag, Mr. Archer?" his butler asked as James walked through the front door of his town house.

"No, thank you, Markus. I can see to it myself."

He pulled out his pocket watch and checked the time. The women wouldn't look to leave for at least an hour. Rather than go straight to his bedchamber, he went to his study and shut the door. It wouldn't take him long to change, and he preferred to limit the time he was subjected to evening attire. Crisp, stiff cravats were never comfortable.

He had just settled behind his desk when a knock sounded on the door. At James's call, the door opened, revealing Hiller, one of the footmen.

"Good evening, Mr. Archer. Mrs. Archer and Miss Rebecca just finished supper. If you would like, I will alert the kitchen and have a place set at the table. My apologies for the short wait. We did not expect you so early else a place would be waiting for you."

"No need to look so concerned, Hiller. I take it the ladies have elected to stay at home this evening?" He had thought Rebecca had mentioned a supper party during the carriage ride home last night, but she must have been referring to another evening.

Hiller nodded. "Mrs. Archer has retired to her bedchamber and Miss Rebecca to the yellow sitting room."

If he had known Amelia had not accepted any invitations for the evening then he would have stayed at his office. Perhaps he should just return there? The thought was tempting indeed. He never did like being at the town house. If he expended the effort and simply kept abreast of his wife's social calendar, then he would have known he needn't leave his office early this evening. But that would include a discussion with Amelia. More than one actually, since calendars were apt to change at a moment's notice.

He glanced to the pile of papers on his desk. He had brought his bag home with him on the off chance the ladies had planned a late departure. Best to have something to occupy him while he waited—being left with nothing but his thoughts meant his mind would find a path to Rose, and that was definitely something he needed to avoid.

There really wasn't a *need* to make the long walk back to the docks. He could work there or here. Either way, a long, lonely night stretched ahead of him.

Ah well, he thought, barely able to summon the effort to care. At least it was something he was well acquainted with.

"No need to bother with the dining table," he told Hiller as the man saw to lighting the fire in the hearth. "I'll take supper here." For some reason, it felt less lonely to eat at his desk versus all by himself in the formal dining room. Servants stationed along the wall, each *clink* of his silverware echoing in the room. A cup of coffee at the long mahogany table before leaving the house in the morning never bothered him, but suppers were an entirely different situation. And after having shared a few with Rose . . .

The expected ache flared across his chest. Knowing there was nothing he could do to stop it, he simply let out a resigned sigh and waited for the ache to subside.

The fire lit, Hiller stood and tipped his head. "And Mrs. Archer requested to speak with you. She's in her bedchamber."

Brow furrowed, James opened his mouth, the word *why* on his tongue, and then snapped his jaw shut.

"Is there something you need, Mr. Archer?"

James shook his head. A servant would not have the answer. It wasn't as if Amelia would give an explanation to accompany her request. He couldn't recall the last time she had wanted to speak to him. If she needed him to serve as escort outside of the Season or if she planned to host a supper party, she sent him a note. As long as he wasn't home when she was apt to be up and about, then days upon days could pass without even laying eyes on her.

"Mrs. Archer seemed her usual self at supper."

He couldn't help but smile a bit at the footman's attempt to be helpful. His unease must be obvious, either that or Hiller knew Amelia's request went so far beyond the norm as to unsettle him. Pathetic, really, that his servants were aware of how much he loathed even the thought of speaking to his wife.

"Thank you, Hiller. I best not leave the lady of the house waiting," he said as he pushed from his desk.

No need to delay the inevitable. It would only prompt Amelia's ire. As he made his way upstairs it occurred to him that perhaps she simply wanted to discuss Rebecca. Perhaps she knew Brackley was due to call tomorrow and wanted to ensure he would handle the meeting appropriately, because, of course, a common merchant's son wouldn't be capable of managing such a task on his own.

He stopped before the door at the end of the corridor. Fist poised to knock, his stomach clenched into a hard knotted ball. A tight sensation spread up to engulf his chest, sending his pulse racing. He hadn't realized it until now, but the last time he had stood on this spot had been over two years ago and the outcome had been disastrous. Holding up his unbuttoned trousers with one hand, his shirt clutched in the other, he had fled through this door. Actually fled, like a dog with its tail between its legs.

One deep breath, and then another. Ignoring her request was a coward's option, and while he might sometimes show himself to be rather pathetic, he was no coward.

His sharp rap snapped along the corridor.

"Enter," came Amelia's muffled voice through the door.

Refusing to allow himself to think on it, he turned the knob and stepped inside, letting the door close behind him. Her bedchamber mirrored his own in size and shape. Large, with ample room for the necessary furniture along with a seating arrangement near the windows. Clad in a simple violet evening gown, Amelia sat on the ice blue brocade settee, a silver plate of tarts on the side table by her elbow.

He kept his gaze from straying to the large four-poster bed as he passed it, the plush rugs muffling his footsteps. He stopped a couple of paces from her and clasped his hands behind his back.

She didn't look up from her perusal of the book of fashion plates on her lap. "We are remaining at home tonight."

He waited for the explanation that was clearly not forthcoming, and then nodded once.

Without a care in the world, she turned the page. The silence stretched on. Too long. Did she expect him to leave? Was that all she wanted to tell him—that they were staying home tonight? Wouldn't a note have been sufficient?

He fought the urge to shift his weight. He was just about to ask if that would be all, when she spoke, her voice easy and unconcerned.

"Did you have a pleasant holiday in the country?"

"Yes." At least up until the last morning, but Amelia certainly did not need to hear such details.

Another flip of a page. "Did your guest enjoy herself as well?"

He swore his heart stopped. That tight sensation seized his chest. He could feel the color draining from his face.

She looked up and arched an inquiring brow. "Yes or no, James. Did your guest enjoy herself?"

Shock locked his mind, leaving him unable to determine the best response. A yes or a no would confirm Rose's presence, but it felt so very wrong to deny, to lie, to reply he hadn't had a guest, even though it could save Rebecca from her spite. It would be akin to denying the very existence of the woman he loved.

"I will take that as a yes. Or at least you believe she did," she said, not disguising her thoughts on the matter. Carefully coifed blonde head tipped down, she closed the book and set it at her hip, her movements graceful and elegant. Then she stood and pierced him with cold, hard light blue eyes. All vestige of politeness gone from her features. "Are you dim enough to believe the truth would never reach my ears?"

Who had told her? The Webbs would never pen Amelia a letter. No one at Rubicon's besides Rose knew his family name, let alone his address, and informing his wife about his time with Rose would lose the house a customer. Had one of his own servants overheard his conversation with Rebecca on the morning of his departure? The door to his study had been open. Had it been Amelia herself?

No, no. She would have caught him before he left the house, would not have waited a good week after his return to lay into him.

This was the reason why she had stayed home. He had not been mistaken. Rebecca had been referring to a supper party tonight. Whoever had told Amelia about Rose had done so today. There was no way she could have kept *this* contained for more than a few hours.

She took a step toward him. Before he was aware of it, he had taken a step back.

"Did you run from her bed as you did mine? Do you remember, James, how quickly you fled? Your limp cock dangling between your legs," she taunted, a cruel smile teasing her lips, taking the utmost pleasure from the opportunity to remind him of that night.

Rapid and harsh, his pulse slammed against his eardrums. He could practically feel her grab his ballocks, sharp claws sinking deep to rip them from his body. It was all he could do to not cringe, look away, to betray how much her taunts hurt. Hell, how he hated that she could reduce him to this with but a few words. Cut him down, until he felt like she was towering over him.

"You're nothing but a coarse, clumsy oaf. Inept." Disgust written all over her face, Amelia raked her gaze down his body. "I would hazard a guess she is with another man right at this moment, who can do for her what you cannot."

Rose would be with another man soon. Six days and she would lie with another, and then another, and another. He winced, breaths catching from the pain.

Small fists clenched at her sides, she advanced on him. His back hit the wall. She was so close her skirts brushed his legs. The sweet, cloying scent of her perfume made his stomach turn. Desperate to escape, desperate not to endure another word from her lips, he darted his gaze to the door, but he couldn't reach it without pushing her away. His arms locked at his sides, refusing to lay a hand on her. One touch and he had no doubt the gossip would be spread about the ton that he was an abuser of women.

"You are pathetic. A poor excuse for a man." Her sneer cut right through him. "Who was she, James? Certainly no acquaintance of mine. No such lady would even take a second look at you. But it matters not who." The gloating condescension slipped away, replaced with barely leashed rage, her slim body vibrating with the force of it.

She whirled away, stalked a few steps from him, her skirts swishing angrily about her legs. Just when he began to breathe easier, when he made to take a step from the wall, she turned on her heel and advanced on him again. His shoulder blade bumped the painting behind him, the gilt frame banging against the wall. By God, he was retreating from a little slip of a woman who barely reached his chest.

"What matters is that you did. You seem somewhat able to run a business," she said, clipped and short, jaw clenched. "Therefore I will assume your memory is not overly faulty and you do recall our conversation in regards to such arrangements." She stared up at him, nostrils flaring, a flush staining her cheeks crimson. "How dare you defy me?" she shouted, so loud the sound smacked his ears, left them ringing. "I am done with her. Done!"

Dread flooded him. "What?" he croaked.

"You cannot claim you were not well aware of the consequences, yet still you chose to humiliate me." Pure malice shone from Amelia's eyes. "I have had enough of pretending as though I care about that silly girl. Of associating my name with hers."

"No, Amelia. Please." Was he actually begging her? Was that his pitifully weak voice? But he could do nothing less. Had to try, though he knew it would not sway her one bit. She would take her wrath out on Rebecca, make his sweet sister pay. Rip Rebecca's happiness from her because he had been selfish enough to want but a glimpse of his own. "Please, Rebecca did nothing wrong."

"By tomorrow evening she will be ruined," she continued, deaf to his pleas. "No man will come near her, let alone allow his name to be sullied by her. She will be branded a harlot, a whore, shunned from polite society. No one will—"

It was as if something inside of him snapped. "Enough!" Shoulders back and standing tall, he took a step forward, stepping into her.

Startled, she backed up a step.

He kept advancing, pushing her without touching her to the center of the room. "You will do no such thing." He did not shout.

His voice was actually quite low. A low, threatening rumble that just hinted at the rage now thundering through his veins. "You will not say a word against Rebecca. I have tolerated your venom for years. Lived under your rules without protest. Said not a word as you took lover after lover. But this? You have pushed me too far. I expected you to withdraw your sponsorship, but you will *not* go so far as to ruin my sister out of spite. I will not tolerate it."

"You have no choice but to tolerate it, James," she shot back, clearly struggling to maintain her hold over him.

"Yes, I do have a choice. I should have exercised it long ago, should have known you would not see your promise through. I want you out of my house tonight. Go to your father's. I do not care what excuse you give your acquaintances or him, but I want you gone."

"I will do no such thing!"

"Yes, you will," he said with a determined calm he did not feel in the slightest. Never before had he been tempted to strike a woman. But at that moment, he had to force his arms to remain at his sides. Every cruel word she had ever slung at him roiled within, forming a noxious mass of pure, unadulterated loathing. "I do not want to lay eyes on you again. And if you dare to speak one word against my sister, you will find yourself not only ruined but left with only the clothes on your back. Do not forget, madam, under the law I own you. I am your husband." *But not for long.* He kept the last bit to himself, unwilling to show his hand just yet. In any case, it was much more satisfying to leave her in suspense. Let the worry build until it consumed her.

He turned on his heel, left her ashen faced, jaw hanging open. He shut the door behind him and then closed his eyes, his hand still on the knob. Damnation, he was shaking. Not from fear or dread over what was to come, but from anger. Rage. Not only at Amelia, but at himself. For allowing himself to have remained in this marriage for so long. For allowing that *woman* to ever hurt him. He could still taste the self-disgust, thick and heavy in his mouth. The absolute humiliation. But never again.

He felt not a drop of remorse for what he was about to do. The end result would see her reputation ruined beyond repair and would see him free.

He would be free. That last obstacle gone.

A smile curved his lips, hope filling him once again. So sweet, so pure. The very definition of bliss. And it made his eyes prick with the threat of tears.

She could be his. Forever.

He allowed himself a moment to bask in the happiness, and then with effort he reined himself in. Days stretched ahead of him before he could drop to one knee. Many tasks to attend to. Rebecca, his solicitor, his banker, a meeting with his servants to ensure they were aware Amelia was no longer welcome at the house—

A small hand settled on his forearm. "James?" came a low voice near his shoulder.

He opened his eyes. Rebecca stood beside him, remorse written all over her face.

"I'm so sorry," she said in a choked whisper. "I had no idea. If I had known, I would never have told her."

"It was you?"

"I didn't know. I swear it, James. We were in the drawing room this afternoon, discussing suitors, and I . . ."

"It's all right. Come with me." With a gentle hand, he led her to the yellow sitting room. The door was open. Only a small guest room separated it from Amelia's. No doubt Amelia's shouts had traveled easily through the walls.

The moment he shut the door, Rebecca picked up where he had cut her off. ". . . mentioned that I didn't want a husband who had a mistress. That I understood most married men, even you, kept them, but that I . . ."

"Rebecca. It's all right. Sit." He motioned toward the settee, which held her discarded embroidery hoop, the threaded needle dangling from the linen. "It is all right," he repeated again, as she stared up at him with wide, worried eyes. "It is not your fault."

"Yes, it—"

"No, it isn't. It is not your fault Amelia is the woman she is. In any case, it was bound to come to this point sooner or later." He moved the embroidery hoop to the side table and sat next to her, took her hand in his. "I'm sorry you had to hear our argument."

"She hates you," she said, shocked and astonished.

He tipped his head. "Now so more than ever. But do not fret over it. I certainly do not plan to. Amelia is leaving tonight, so you needn't even worry about having to speak to her. And I'll hire you a chaperone. Someone who can secure you the necessary invitations for the rest of the Season." There had to be some older matron who would be willing to take on Rebecca. The girl had already started to establish herself, so it wasn't as if he'd be asking someone to take on an unknown entity. "It may take me a couple of days to see the task done, but I will do my best not to have this matter with Amelia disturb your stay in London for any length of time. I want you to have every opportunity to find a husband who suits you."

"Oh, James." She gave him a teary smile and then threw her arms around him. "I cannot believe what you have done for me. You did not have to do it, you know that? You did not have to marry that foul woman."

"I didn't have to, but I wanted to see you happy," he said, rubbing her back. "And I hope you can still find someone who will make you happy." Someone who could make her as happy as just the thought of Rose made him.

"You are the dearest of brothers," she said against his chest, her arms gripping him tight. Then she sat back and wiped her eyes. "I believe I already have found someone."

"Really?"

"Do you not have an appointment with Lord Brackley tomorrow morning?"

"Brackley? Isn't he a bit old for you?" And dull, but he kept that to himself.

"No. Not at all."

"He's older than I am."

"For a man, you're not very old, James."

He certainly felt old.

"Lord Brackley is only three and thirty. The perfect age for a man to marry. He is settled, established, ready to take a wife. And he meets your requirement."

"And what is that?"

"That he adore me." Tipping her chin to her chest, she giggled. "And he does." She peered up at him, imploring. "Please say you will accept him if he asks for my hand? He will make me happy."

"Are you certain?" He wouldn't at all have thought to match the two up, but Brackley was a good man. Decent and kind. Rebecca could choose far worse. And as an earl, he was respected enough to be able to shield her from any of Amelia's spite, in the event the woman was dim enough to still make an attempt to ruin her.

"Yes, I am certain."

"Then if he asks, he is yours." He gave her hand a pat. "Now I want you to retire to your room for the rest of the evening. Get some rest. I need to go have a word with the servants, make sure Amelia's trunks are packed. If you hear her shouting again, just ignore her." He highly doubted she'd leave peacefully, but he didn't want her antics to upset Rebecca. "And never fear, I will be in my study tomorrow at ten, awaiting Brackley's call."

With that, he pressed a kiss to her forehead. He saw her safely to her room, had the necessary conversation with the staff (which resulted in more than one sigh of relief), sent off a quick note to his solicitor requesting the man's immediate presence, and then stood by the front door, arms crossed over his chest. To her credit, Amelia didn't dally nor did she rail or scream. Clearly trying to retain as much dignity as she could, she came down the stairs, her maid and three footmen in tow lugging her trunks. She looked right through him, as though he wasn't even there, and sailed out the front door and into the waiting carriage.

She wouldn't be able to ignore him for long.

Thirty minutes later found him in his study, assuring his shocked solicitor that he did know exactly what he was about.

"Yes, I need you to have criminal conversation charges brought against Lord Albert Langholm, and I want the process expedited as much as money will allow. He is the son of a peer, not a peer himself, so there is no need to wait until Parliament retires in the summer. I do not want him to have the opportunity to flee to the Continent. I want him charged, found guilty. At the same time, I need you to start the process so that I can obtain a legal separation from Amelia on the grounds of her adultery."

Seated in the leather chair opposite his desk, Milton pursed his lips and then shrugged. Highly competent and trustworthy, the man had served James well since he had hired him a few years ago, and he didn't doubt Milton would see to the tasks with his usual efficient attention to detail. "As you wish. Is there an amount you are looking for in damages from Lord Albert?"

"It matters not to me. I don't need or want his money. Whatever sum you settle on is acceptable. I just need him to be found guilty so I can petition Parliament for a divorce."

"You will have to give testimony. Provide details that could prove to be . . . uncomfortable."

"I am aware of that." Certainly not something he was looking forward to, but a necessary step.

It took another hour to answer all of Milton's questions, providing the necessary information for the man to start what was sure to be just the beginning of stacks of paperwork. He didn't envy the man the task, but he paid him quite well, so it shouldn't be much of a hardship.

With a tip of his head and his assurances the charges against Lord Albert would be filed tomorrow, Milton gathered his leather bag and left James alone in the study.

James tipped his head back against his chair. The desolation that had once settled about him like a damn suffocating cloak whenever he was in this house was now gone. For many long moments he merely stared at the ceiling, smiling, simply reveling in the feeling of . . . lightness.

He had just started what would be a long, arduous, and costly process, but the end result would be more than worth it. He wanted to tell Rose now. This moment. Needed to be able to take her in his arms, whisper in her ear that they could always be together, pledge his heart and his name to her forever.

But he had to wait. She would not return to town for six more days. It would be better this way, though. Better that he could present her with concrete proof of his intentions to free himself from Amelia to wipe away any doubts that may form.

On that sixth day, however, he fully intended to present himself in Rubicon's office at promptly eight o'clock. Perhaps he could coax Rose into taking another walk with him about the park. He could tell her there, along the bank of the Serpentine, on the same spot where she had first given herself to him.

The plan fixed in his mind, he pushed from his desk, suddenly hungry. He found a servant in the corridor and requested supper. After a bite to eat, he retired to his bedchamber. And as he lay down he found that even though he was alone, even though Rose was not beside him, his bed didn't feel as lonely as it once did.

Twenty

"WHY couldn't I find a groom in the stables?"

Empty plates in hand, Rose turned toward the kitchen door. Dash stood in the doorway, saddlebag in hand. The dark waves of his hair appeared windblown and his black coat held a bit of dust from the road. Judging from the lethargic slouch of his shoulders, he had ridden straight from London, which accounted for why he had arrived a day earlier than she expected.

"Good evening, Dash. Welcome home." She was genuinely happy to see him, but she couldn't deny the trepidation seeping into her stomach.

Sarah took the plates Rose had been clearing from the plain wooden table in the corner of the kitchen. They had just finished supper. "I'll finish up here," she said in an undertone, and then added, with a smile directed at Dash, "It is good to have you home, Mr. Marlowe."

Dash stiffened. "Thank you, Mrs. Thompson." He declined Sarah's offer to cook him something for supper, claiming he'd stopped at an inn along the way.

"Come along, Dash," Rose said, leaving the kitchen. "I'll show you to your room so you can clean up after the long journey."

"I remember where my room is located. You needn't show me," he said, trailing a couple of steps behind her. "Rose, why couldn't I find a groom in the stables? I had to unsaddle the horse myself."

"Because he had already gone for the night. I don't have a need for a stable full of horses, and therefore the groom does not need to reside on the property. He comes up from the village in the mornings and departs well before supper."

She rounded the banister and started to go up the stairs but stopped when she realized his footsteps were not following her. She turned.

He stood at the foot of the stairs. "I told you, you don't need to show me to my bedchamber." A pause. "So what is this matter of great importance? You appear in good health, so I'm assuming it does not relate to that."

"I am fine, Dash." As fine as could be, given the circumstances. "Let us go into the drawing room."

Dash followed her inside, dropping his saddlebag near the door. She had been in the room before supper, reviewing the estate's ledger and bemoaning the meager number under the latest entry, but the fire had since burned down to embers. Dropping to her knees, she added a couple of logs to the grate and then prodded the fire back to life.

"Where are the servants? And where is Gregory?" he asked, referring to the man who had once served as butler.

"I let them go, all except for Sarah." She took a deep breath, laid a palm over the stone hidden beneath her bodice, the gesture now so innate the stone was pressing against her chest before she was even aware she had lifted her arm. Then dropping her hand to her side, she stood to face him. "Have a seat," she said, flicking her fingers to the settee and chairs.

"Why did you let them go?" Reluctant suspicion laced his tone. "Rose?" he queried when she didn't immediately answer.

"Well, I am going to have a seat." There was no way she could stand through the conversation. Her knees already felt weak. She settled on the settee, taking much longer than necessary to adjust her skirt about her legs.

She had worked so hard to keep the truth from him, but she found success wasn't always pleasant. She would have much rather preferred for him to have figured a bit of it out for himself.

"I let the staff go because I could not afford to keep them." She smoothed a palm over her knee in a failed attempt to press out a wrinkle in the drab green dress.

He let out a little sound of exasperation. She could well imagine the roll of his eyes that would have accompanied such a sound.

"It isn't necessary to be such a miser, Rose. Servants aren't that large of an expense."

She looked up, held his gaze. She could still see the boy he had once been. The boy who had tried so hard not to cry when she'd told him of their father's death. His mouth stiff, his lean frame drawn tight, unable to stop that first tear from rolling down his cheek.

It was so very tempting to take the excuse he had just handed her. To claim she had merely been trying to be a prudent guardian of the estate. To turn the conversation to his gambling habit and give that as the source of her note. "Servants are a large expense when you have nothing."

"Don't be ridiculous, Rose. We have plenty of money. Father left it to us. I read the will." He ignored her arched brow. When had he read it? She had kept it locked in the safe behind Mother's portrait in the study. In fact, it was still there. "Except for a bit for the staff, he left it all to us. This house, the property, and his accounts."

"He had sold all of the property that generated income. All we have is what you can see outside the window." Hands clasped tight, she swallowed hard. "He left us this house, and he left us debts, Dash. That is all."

She could well understand the confusion flickering across his face. She had never given him reason before to believe they did not have more than enough, and certainly enough for him to squander on whatever caught his fancy.

"That can't be correct." He dropped down into the chair opposite her. "You paid for Eton, Oxford, my apartments, my d——" He broke off, then quickly added, "My allowances."

"I did, and yes, I paid your recent gambling debts as well." He had the good sense to avert his eyes. "But the funds did not come from Father."

"Then where did the money come from?"

Her resolve teetered, her mind frantically searching for a plausible explanation. Anything but the truth. She had thought herself prepared for this moment. Had lain awake in bed for the last two nights, replaying the conversation in her head. But she felt not a drop of the calm, objective detachment she had planned to call upon when the time came to answer the question she knew he would ask.

"Where, Rose?"

Resignation and shame swept over her. Closing her eyes, she dropped her head. "It came from me."

The logs in the hearth shifted, crackled. Then silence. She strained to hear, unable to even detect the sounds of his breaths. Head still bowed, she peeked up.

His face had gone stark white, all the blood drained from his features, his eyes wide. "No. You didn't."

Suddenly weary beyond measure, all she could do was lift a shoulder in a poor attempt at a shrug.

"No," he said again, this time stronger, the word soaked in desperation.

"How else was I to come up with the money?"

He shot to his feet. "No!"

She let out a sigh. "What does it matter, Dash? I'm done with it in any case."

"That's why you've been in London. You were—"

His wince cut right through her. Yet she refused to crumble.

"Why did you never tell me?" he demanded.

"I couldn't tell you after Father had passed away. You were heartbroken." Dash adored the man, had put him on a pedestal long ago and never taken him down. Still looked on their father's memory through the eyes of a boy. But not anymore. She had just tarnished that precious, perfect image Dash held of him. "And I didn't want you to suffer because he had gambled away everything."

"So you decided to sell yourself?"

She nodded. "It was the only solution. Father didn't just leave us penniless, he left us with a mountain of debt that needed immediate attention."

"And you never saw fit to inform me of any of this?"

"You were thirteen at the time. A boy."

"I have not been thirteen for five years."

She tipped her head. "As I have been informed of late, yes, you are no longer a boy. I admit, I should have been more open with you, but you're my younger brother. I can't help but want to protect you and provide for you. I don't want to argue with you about that, though. That chapter of my life is now closed. I am done with it, and that is why I called you home." The tight knot in her stomach began to unwind. He now knew the worst of it and had not stormed out of the house, disgusted and appalled at how low she had sunk. Had not, so far of yet, turned his back on her. "The debts have been settled, but the coffers are still nigh to dry. I cannot afford to keep up the house or fund your allowance, not to mention your other expenses. I need your help, Dash, to determine how we should go on from here."

He stared at her for a long moment. A wince wrinkled his brow and then his gaze, heavy with regret, slipped over her shoulder to the window behind her. "If I had known, I would never have let you do it."

"I know," she stated quietly.

A short nod and he dropped back into the chair, leaning forward to rest his elbows on his knees, the despair now gone. "Why haven't you sold the house?"

"It's yours. Your birthright."

"Rosie, when was the last time I was here?" Her heart clenched at the endearment. She had not lost him. Her faith had not been misplaced. "I've never cared for the country and . . . this was *his* house. It reminds me too much of him. I could never live here again. It's not entailed, therefore unless you have an objection, I propose we sell it."

She had called Paxton Manor home all her life. It would be hard to part with it, but it truly had become more of a burden than anything. "All right."

"The apartments in London are paid for, correct?" At her nod, he continued in a remarkably steady and businesslike fashion, "Then we can use some of the proceeds from the sale of the house to see you settled. Where would you like to live?"

"I don't know. I haven't given it any thought." The only place she wanted to be was with James, but that was never to be.

"Well, think on it. You have a bit of time." He reached across the distance separating them to give her a reassuring pat on the knee. "Perhaps a nice cottage in the country, though I do worry about you living alone. I would much prefer to see you settled with a husband."

"That will never happen, so best to give up hope now."

"Why ever not? You're a beautiful woman. It wouldn't take much effort at all for you to find a husband."

"You forget, Dash, what I have been. No decent man would want to take a whore to wife, not even a retired one." The blunt words hurt, but they were necessary. The only way for Dash to see the truth.

But rather than put him off the subject, it only brought her compassion. "Oh, Rosie." He shifted to sit beside her, took her hand in his. "I'm certain that's not true. If he loved you, it wouldn't matter."

"Yet I could never love him back," she whispered. "My heart belongs to another, but he can never be mine."

"Who?" he asked gently.

"It matters not. It is over and done with." Unwilling to speak another word of James, she pulled her hand from his. Dwelling on him would do no good. Nothing could come from it but more heartache. "I would like to see you return to school. You need to complete your education."

For that statement, she got a roll of his eyes. "Oxford again?" But he didn't bristle with affront, rather he stood and gave his coat a tug to straighten it. "I do intend to return, but not at the moment. I need to see you settled and the house sold." Then his gaze turned serious. "I won't let you down again."

In the span of a few minutes, he had grown up before her eyes. His stance stronger, more confident. Determined. Not that of a boy, but of a man.

He held out his hand. "Come along, we should retire for the night. And I find myself in need of a guide to my bedchamber. I seem to have forgotten where it is," he said, with a hint of his impish charm.

"Of course," she said, placing her hand in his and letting him help her to her feet. "It's up in the nursery. I'd be more than happy to lead the way."

With a look of mock affront, he nudged her with his elbow. If he had indeed still been a reckless young boy, he would have nudged her hard enough to land her on her backside. As it was, her stride didn't even falter as they left the drawing room.

"My apologies. I couldn't resist," she said, the chuckle lingering in her voice.

She could never have James, but she had not lost her brother.

Her future would likely include a small little cottage, someplace in the country far removed from Town. Not much, but it would allow her to hold her head high, something she had not been able to do in years.

❧

"Unfortunately she is not available," Rubicon said, the usual gracious smile completely absent.

With sheer force of will, James kept himself from leaping to the first conclusion that popped into his mind. "What do you mean?"

She held up a hand. "Let's not have a repeat of one of our prior meetings, shall we?" Her blunt words, laced with heavy sarcasm, took him aback. "Rose is not here. She did not return this month."

His mind seized with shock. Then he dropped into the scarlet leather chair, gripped the arms of the chair tightly. He hated the thought of her being at Rubicon's, but he *needed* her there tonight. It had never crossed his mind that she wouldn't be there.

How was he to find her? He realized she had never told him where she resided. Likely done deliberately. Why hadn't he ever asked where she lived? Vague references to the country were of little help when most of England could be classified as "the country." He could understand her keeping her personal life hidden from clients, but he wasn't just one of her clients. He was the man who loved her. And why in God's name had he never specifically asked her for her family name? He knew so much about her, yet also so little. Frustration welled up inside. Frustration at himself, not at her.

Her brother, perhaps? He resided in town. But tracking down an eighteen-year-old buck when all he had was the name "Dash" would be an effort in futility. If he did find him, what would he tell him? "I need to speak to your sister?" As if the young man would just point him in the right direction. No man with a modicum of sense would willingly offer up his sister to a stranger, and it wasn't as if James could give an explanation for how he had met Rose. She never wanted her brother to know of her time spent at Madame Rubicon's.

It was all he could do to keep his expression blank, to hide the tumult of emotion within. The hope that had been building from the moment when he'd made the decision to seek out his solicitor drained out of him in a great rush, leaving him beyond numb.

He had lost her.

"I understand your disappointment," Rubicon said, though she spoke without a trace of compassion. "Rose is a woman without compare, but there are many beautiful women in this house. Perhaps you could be tempted by a lovely blonde tonight?"

He barely heard the madam, just shook his head. Then he went still, that day at the park crystallizing in his mind with startling clarity.

Perhaps he could speak to someone who knew Rose's whereabouts.

"Or maybe a striking redhead? I can summon a few for you to select from if you so desire."

"Not necessary. I would like to see Mr. Timothy Ashton."

In all his dealings with the madam, he had never witnessed shock. She had certainly not expected that request from him. But it only took a moment for her to snap her slack jaw shut, to gather her composure, though the question was still clear as day in her eyes. He did not care one whit what she thought of him. Let her think him a goddamn sodomite, if it would put him on a path that led to Rose.

"Is he available this evening?" he asked, impatient to have the matter settled. If not, he'd wait right here until the man made himself available.

"Yes. You are in luck." She paused. "Are you acquainted with Mr. Ashton?"

"I wish to spend some time with him this evening." He pulled the fold of pound notes from his pocket and slapped them on her desk. "The usual rate?" Rubicon had made it clear to him on previous occasions that Rose was the brothel's most prized possession. He highly doubted Ashton fetched such a price, but he was in no mood to negotiate.

As he hoped, her eyes glinted with a distinct note of greed. "Yes." She took the pound notes, tucking them in her desk drawer. Then she reached behind to tug on a velvet rope, not the one she had used in the past. Within a moment, a servant entered the office and stopped next to her desk. She scrawled out a note and handed it to the servant, who departed as quickly and quietly as he had entered.

In a rustle of scarlet silk, she stood and rounded the desk. "If you will come with me."

He bolted up from the chair and followed so close on her heels the tips of his shoes brushed her skirt. She didn't lead him toward the hidden door, but to the main door of the office. Hand on the brass knob, she glanced over her shoulder, a superior, mocking look in her eyes. Then the door swung open, revealing another servant at the ready.

"One of the staff will show you the way."

He followed the servant down the corridor, in the opposite direction of the muted voices coming from the right. The servant didn't once glance at him or speak one word, as she led James through the servants' area of the house and down the stairs he had traversed many times. When they reached the small entrance space, she opened the door opposite the kitchen, taking him down yet another flight of stairs. A bit of dampness seeped from the stone walls on either side. She stopped at the door at the end of the stairs and rapped once on it. A pause. Then the click of the latch echoed off the stone walls as she opened the door.

The instant he stepped over the threshold, the door shut behind him with a heavy thud.

Holy Hell.

He would never have guessed a room like this existed. It certainly didn't match any of the other areas of the house. A massive bed with a wrought iron frame dominated one wall. The sight of the leather straps tied to the four posts, the ends laid out on the scarlet silk sheets, made his skin crawl. A mahogany cabinet dominated another wall—he didn't even want to know what it contained. A single chain about a foot in length was suspended from the ceiling a few paces from the foot of the bed. And beneath it was a man, on his knees and clad in black breeches and nothing else, his dark blond head bowed in submission.

"Ashton?"

His head snapped up. Absolute shock and then his gaze hardened for one brief instant before he dropped his chin to his chest. "I am yours to do with as you please." The words were stilted, weighed down with the obvious effort required to mask the pure malice James had glimpsed.

"For Christ's sake, get up."

With a wary glance, Timothy Ashton got to his feet in a single graceful movement.

"You are Rose's friend, are you not?" He didn't wait for Ashton's nod as he already knew the answer. Rose had referred to him as *the dearest of friends*. "Then you are aware she did not return to Town. I need to speak with her. Do you know the location of her country house?"

"Why?"

"It is of no concern of yours."

"I'm afraid it is, Mr. Archer," he replied, all politeness yet backed with steel. He seemed completely unaffected by the surroundings. They could very well be at White's, debating the latest bill before Parliament. "Rose is my friend."

"I respect that, and I would not ask if it were not imperative. I need to speak with her."

"She won't accept your money."

"I am well aware of that."

"Then why do you need to speak to her?" Ashton crossed his

arms over his bare chest, resolute, refusing to offer up any information unless James answered his question to his satisfaction.

"I intend to ask for her hand," he admitted.

Ashton lifted a suspicious brow. "You are already married."

"Not for long."

"You are divorcing your wife?"

He tipped his head.

Ashton didn't question him further. The man only said three words, a smile tugging on his lips. "Bedfordshire. Paxton Manor."

It took a moment for James to realize the significance of what Ashton had said. Then his entire being leapt eagerly onto those three words. "You have my utmost thanks." He was at the door, knob in hand, when he turned back.

Ashton still stood beneath that length of chain. He was the same man he had met at the park, yet it was difficult to reconcile the image of that polished young gentleman with the man who stood in this room. He couldn't shake the impression that the man didn't belong here. In an odd sort of way, Ashton reminded him of Rose.

"Why do you work down here?" The question popped out of his mouth before it even formed in his head.

The smile tipping his lips turned melancholy. "Those who pass through that door do not fool themselves or attempt to fool me with their reasons for being here. They are brutally honest in their pursuit of pleasure. No whispered words, no polite games, no illusion of intimacy. It may seem harsh, even cruel, but to me it is the safest room in the house." He looked to his bare feet. A wince crossed his brow. "You broke her heart," he whispered.

"It was not my intention."

"But you did so nonetheless."

"It will not happen again," he vowed. He would never again do anything to cause her even the slightest bit of pain. She had already borne enough in her life.

Perhaps Ashton held another answer Rose had refused to provide.

"Rose had a protector before she came to this house. Do you happen to know his name?"

"Lord Wheatly. Why do you ask?"

James kept the satisfied smile from his lips. "She was with him for a year, correct?"

"Yes."

"The second protector, not the lord who was married, correct?" He needed to be certain he had the right name. She had provided the identity of her first protector, but for the life of him, he couldn't recall the gentleman's name.

"Yes."

"Thank you." He opened the door.

"Archer," Ashton said, calling him back. "Why do you need his name?"

James turned, hand on the knob. "That man hurt her," he growled.

A couple of hours later found James waiting in the midnight shadows outside of a nondescript town house on the edge of Mayfair. A few discreet inquiries had garnered him the address of the man's current mistress.

He knew of Wheatly. Had seen him at various functions recently, though fortunately he had never shown an interest in Rebecca. He had an edge about him that led James to believe his polite manners didn't go beyond the surface. And now he knew his assessment of Wheatly's character had been correct.

The front door opened and Wheatly emerged, tugging on his gloves. The rage that had been simmering boiled to the surface. Without a word, James stepped from the shadows, right fist clenched and ready at his side.

The crunch of the man's nose breaking beneath his fist was one of the most satisfying sounds James had ever heard.

⚜

Rose rubbed the rag harder in an effort to get the tarnish out of the intricate engraving on the large silver platter. It was a beautiful piece. All of it was. She cast her gaze over the table covered with dishes and platters, vases and candlesticks, silverware and goblets. She could still remember how the dining table had once looked, set and ready for guests. The long mahogany table gleaming with a fresh coat of polish, the heavy crystal stemware catching the light from the chandelier above.

But it was an image she hadn't seen for well over five years, and one she would never see again.

When the platter finally gleamed to her satisfaction, she set it down and picked up a candlestick. Sarah was seated a little ways down the table, her head bowed over a punch bowl, the sleeves of her brown dress shoved to her elbows. Polishing the silver was a task neither of them looked upon with relish, but it was a necessary one. She couldn't very well leave the potential new owners of Paxton Manor with a cupboard of dirty silver.

She wouldn't deny she would miss the house, but she certainly would not miss the work that went along with it. Dash had left just that morning to return to London to hire someone to manage the sale of the house for them.

To her surprise, he had stayed a few days and promised to return shortly. While they had spent a fair number of hours devoted to discussing the estate, it had been nice to have him home. It had been so long since she had spent an extended amount of time with him. Since he had gone to school, it had only been short visits, an hour here and there. That had been all.

The lure of the gambling tables and late nights devoted to who knew what sort of debauchery with his acquaintances had caused her to worry about him going to London alone, but he had assured her the worries were for naught. *I won't let you down again*, he had repeated. Though she would admit to a bit of lingering worry at the way he evaded her question when she asked if there were any debts she wasn't aware of. She had a niggling suspicion he had made use of his repaired credit, but she didn't press him.

The candlestick now gleaming like new, she put it down and picked up a serving spoon. It felt odd to be in the house today. The ingrained habit of four years made her a tiny bit restless at having denied it.

Had James gone to Rubicon's last night? Simply the barest shadow of the possibility, even if so very remote given their parting, it pulled at her heart. She could well imagine the hurt that would cross his face when Rubicon denied his request. She knew she could never return to that house, never see him there again, yet . . .

With a firm shake of her head, she dismissed the thought and concentrated on the stubborn tarnish clinging to the handle of the spoon.

Late afternoon turned into early evening, the sunlight streaming through the windows now a rich golden amber. Half of the mahogany surface of the table was now visible, physical proof of her and Sarah's labors. Dropping her rag, she gathered the pieces they had just finished cleaning. She'd take them to the silver cupboard and then go help Sarah with supper. Arms laden with candlesticks and candelabras, she turned from the table, but stopped short.

There it was again. A knock at the door.

She put down her burden and went out into the entrance hall, footsteps ringing on the marble floor. She wiped her hands on her apron that was no longer white but marred with thick, iron gray smudges, tucked a stray hair behind her ear, and then opened the door.

She blinked.

Yes, that was James standing on her doorstep wearing the broadest of grins.

Her heart leapt. Every bit of the emotion she had tried to tamp down for the past fortnight flooded her senses.

"Good evening, Rose."

She gave her head a little shake. His lips were moving. He must be speaking to her.

"Rose? Are you all right?" That broad grin had dimmed.

"Yes, quite well," she heard herself reply.

"Good. You had me concerned there for a moment."

"I did not expect to find you on my doorstep."

"You did make it rather difficult to find you, but here I am."

"But, James, why are you here?" He had returned to Rubicon's last night. She knew it without a doubt. A quick glance around his broad shoulder revealed the familiar traveling carriage stationed just beyond the foot of the stone stairs. "I hope you did not make the journey to Bedfordshire under the false assumption that I was not sincere in my intentions. I will not accept your money again," she said with a conviction she did not feel in the slightest.

To have him standing before her once again. So close, if she but reached out, she could press her hand to his chest, feel the heat of his body seeping through the navy coat, the strong beats of his heart against her palm.

"That's not why I'm here. I respect your decision and understand why you stood so firm against my protests." He pulled a folded sheet of paper from his coat pocket. "I have done what I should have done long ago," he said gravely.

She took the proffered note warily. The paper crinkled as she unfolded it. A page from the *Times*? Why would he give this to her? It was dated April twenty-seventh. Two days ago. If she had the time to spare to peruse the news, she could have read this yesterday. The post only caused a day's delay.

Her gaze skimmed down the page, coming to an abrupt halt at the last article.

Crim.Con.—Sheriff's Court, London

An action was brought forth by Mr. James Archer against Lord
Albert Langholm . . . for criminal conversation with the Plaintiff's wife, Mrs. Amelia Archer . . . verdict for the Plaintiff. One
thousand pounds in damages awarded.

The rapid beats of her pulse echoed in her ears. "James?" She
looked up at him with pleading eyes, so very afraid to hope.

"I am divorcing her." He couldn't disguise the pleasure it clearly
brought him to say those words.

"Why, though?"

"I could no longer tolerate her venom, and she was foolish enough
to threaten the loss of Rebecca's reputation."

"But what about Rebecca? Won't you lose your wife's
sponsorship?"

"Yes, but it's no longer needed. Within a few months' time, Rebecca will become the Countess of Brackley. She wants a grand
wedding at St. George's," he lifted a shoulder, as if to say nothing
less would have been expected, "and I'm certain my father will give
it to her. I, however, do not have such a fondness for grand affairs.
I prefer the country, something simple and quiet in a small church
with only a handful of family members."

He paused. Held her gaze. That grin flittered, just teasing the
edges of his mouth, his eyes soft and warm and filled with an anticipation she was afraid to name.

"I love you, Rose."

I love you, too. But the words were stuck in her throat. She had
convinced herself she would never be able to speak them again, and
now that the opportunity was remarkably, unbelievably presented
to her again, they refused to lodge free.

"May I have your hand, my dear?" he asked, holding his out,
palm up.

In a daze, she tucked the newspaper into her apron pocket.

The moment her hand slipped into his, sensation shot up her arm, wrapped around her heart. His grip strong yet gentle. The calluses on his palm and on the tips of his fingers an exact fit to her memories.

His gaze never left hers as he dropped to one knee. "Will you do me the great honor of becoming my wife?"

Her other hand flew up to cover her mouth, fingers trembling against her lips. "Yes," she whispered, and then stronger, infusing the word with all the love she held for him in her heart, "Yes!"

The next thing she knew, she was in his arms, her fingers gripping his shoulders, and he was giving her the kiss she never believed she'd ever have again. The kiss continued on and on. His lips gliding over hers, sweet and silken, soft yet firm. Determined yet gentle. *James.*

With a little teasing nip to her bottom lip, he pulled back enough to break the kiss.

"Thank you. You have made me the happiest of men." Then a bit of gravity seeped into his gaze. "It will be at least another month or two before I am fully free. I'm pushing my solicitor as fast as he can go, but these matters take time. You do understand?"

"Of course." The wait mattered not. What mattered was that someday the man she loved would be hers and she would be his.

"Thank you," he murmured. Those olive green eyes drifted down, paused on her lips, and then lower. He unwound one arm from her waist and reached up, fingertips brushing her neck, sending a delightful shiver down her spine. With a little tug, he pulled the stone from beneath her bodice, held it in his palm. "You're wearing it."

At the awe, the trace of disbelief in his voice, she said, "It is the most precious gift I have ever received. I could never part with it."

To do so would be akin to giving up his love, something she could and would never do. His love gave her hope, and his love gave her strength. Enough strength to leave her old life behind, and now she could start anew. With him. Have the husband, the family, that had filled a young girl's dreams.

Looking deep into his eyes, she covered his hand with hers, the stone pressed between their palms, and pledged her heart, her very self to him. "I am forever yours, James."